POPULAR PUBLICATIONS · FACSIMILE EDITIONS

Fantastic Novels Magazine #1
(July 1940)

The companion magazine to *Famous Fantastic Mysteries, Fantastic Novels Magazine* initially reprinted longer stories from the Frank A. Munsey library of classic fantasy & science fiction pulps, including stories from magazines such as *Argosy, The All-Story, The Scrap Book* and *The Cavalier.* The first issue contains classic stories by Austin Hall & Homer Eon Flint, and Perley Poore Sheehan, and artwork by Virgil Finlay.

Authors:

Austin Hall, Homer Eon Flint, Perley Poore Sheehan

Illustrators:

Virgil Finlay

Fantastic Novels

Vol. I   JULY, 1940   No. I

Complete Book-Length Novel

The September Fantastic Novels Will Be On Sale July 10
Featuring "The People of the Golden Atom"   By Ray Cummings
A Complete Novel

THE FRANK A. MUNSEY COMPANY, Publisher, 280 Broadway, New York, N. Y.
WILLIAM T. DEWART, *President & Treasurer;* WILLIAM T. DEWART, JR., *Secretary*

THE CONTINENTAL PUBLISHERS & DISTRIBUTORS, LTD.
3 La Belle Sauvage, Ludgate Hill, London, E.C., 4
Paris: HACHETTE & CIE, 111 Rue Reaumur

The Rhamda's strength was not human. He was working us toward the Blind Spot. . .
. . . A great volume of sound! The whir of a thousand vibrations! I fell. . . .

Virgil Finlay

The Blind Spot

By AUSTIN HALL and HOMER EON FLINT

A Complete Fantastic Novel

PROLOGUE

PERHAPS it were just as well to start at the beginning. A mere matter of news.

All the world at the time knew the story; but for the benefit of those who have forgotten I shall repeat it. I am merely giving it as I have taken it from the papers with no elaboration and no opinion—a mere statement of facts. It was a celebrated case at the time and stirred the world to wonder. Indeed, it still is celebrated, though to the layman it is forgotten.

It has been labeled and indexed and filed away in the archives of the profession. To those who wish to look it up it will be spoken of as one of the great unsolved mysteries of the century. A crime that leads two ways, one into murder—sordid, cold, and calculating; and the other into the nebulous screen that thwarts us from the occult.

Perhaps it is the character of Dr. Holcomb that gives the latter. He was a great man and a splendid thinker. That he should have been led into a maze of cheap necromancy is, on the face, improbable. He had a wonderful mind. For years he had been battering down the skepticism that had bulwarked itself in the material.

He was a psychologist, and up to the day the greatest, perhaps, that we have known. He had a way of going out before his fellows—it is the way of genius—and he had gone far, indeed, before them. If we would trust Dr. Holcomb we have much to live for; our religion is not all hearsay and there is a great deal in science still unthought of. It is an un-fortunate case; but there is much to be learned in the circumstance that led the great doctor into the Blind Spot.

CHAPTER I

RHAMDA AVEC

ON A certain foggy morning in September, 1905, a tall man wearing a black overcoat and bearing in one hand a small satchel of dark-reddish leather, descended from a Geary Street car at the foot of Market Street, San Francisco. It was a damp morning; a mist was brooding over the city blurring all distinctness, and even from the center of the loop the buildings facing East Street blurred in a dim, uncertain line.

The man glanced about him; a tall man of certain trim lines and distinctness and a quick, decided step and bearing. In the shuffle of descending passengers he was outstanding, a certain inborn grace that without the blood will never come from training. Men noticed and women out of instinct cast curious furtive glances and then turned away; which was natural, inasmuch as the man was plainly old. But for all that many ventured a second glance—and wondered.

An old man with the poise of twenty, a strange face of remarkable features, swarthy, of an Eastern cast; perhaps Indian; whatever the certainty of the man's age there was still a lingering suggestion of splendid youth. If one persisted in a third or fourth look this suggestion took almost a certain tone, the man's age dwindled, years dropped from him, and the quizzical smile that played on the lips seemed almost foreboding of boyish laughter.

We say foreboding because in this case it is not mistaken diction. Foreboding suggests coming evil; the laughter of boys is whole-hearted. It was merely that things were not exactly as they should be; it was not natural that age should be so youthful. The fates were playing, and in this case for once in the world's history their play was cross-wise.

It is a remarkable case from the beginning and we are stating from facts. The man crossed to the window of the Key Route and purchased a ticket for Berkeley, after which, with the throng, he passed the turnstile and on to the boat that was waiting. He took the lower deck, not from choice, apparently, but more because the majority of his fellow passengers, being men, were bound in his direction. The same chance brought him to the cigar-stand. The men about him purchased cigars and cigarettes, and, as is the habit of all smokers, strolled off with delighted relish. The man watched them. Had any one noticed his eyes he would have noted a peculiar color and a light of surprise. With the prim step that made him so distinctive he advanced to the news-stand.

"Pardon me; but I would like to purchase one of those." Though he spoke perfect English it was in a strange manner, after the fashion of one who has found something that he has just learned how to use. At the same time he made a suggestion with his tapered fingers indicating the tobacco in the case and that already lighted by his companions. The clerk looked up.

"A cigar, sir? Yes, sir. What will it be?"

"A cigar?" Again the strange articulation. "Ah, yes, that is it. Now I remember. And it has a little sister, the cigarette. I think I shall take a cigarette, if—if—if you will show me how to use it."

It was a strange request. The clerk was accustomed to all manner of men and their brands of humor; he was about to answer in kind when he looked up and into the man's eyes. He started.

"You mean," he asked, "that you have never before seen a cigar or cigarette; that you do not know how to use them? A man as old as you are."

The stranger laughed. It was rather resentful, but for all of that of a hearty taint of humor.

"So old? Would you say that I am as old as that; if you will look again—"

The young man did and what he beheld is something that he could not quite account for: the strange conviction of this remarkable man; of age melting into youth, of an uncertain freshness, the

smile, not of sixty, but of twenty. The young man was not one to argue, whatever his wonder; he was first of all a lad of business; he could merely acquiesce.

"The first time! This is the first time you have ever seen a cigar or cigarette?"

The stranger nodded.

"The first time. I have never beheld one of them before this morning. If you will allow me?" He indicated a package. "I think I shall take one of these."

THE clerk took up the package, opened the end, and shook out a single cigarette. The man rolled it in his hand after the manner of the others; then he lighted it and, as the smoke poured out of his mouth, held the cigarette tentatively in his fingers.

"Like it?" It was the clerk who asked.

The other did not answer, his whole face was the expression of having just discovered one of the senses. He was a splendid man and, if the word may be employed of the sterner sex, one of beauty. His features were even: that is to be noted, his nose chiseled straight and to perfection, the eyes of a peculiar somberness and luster almost burning, of a black of such intensity as to verge into red and to be devoid of pupils, and yet, for all of that, of a glow and softness. After a moment he turned to the clerk.

"You are young, my lad."

"Twenty-one, sir."

"You are fortunate. You live in a wonderful age. It is as wonderful as your tobacco. And you still have many great things before you."

"Yes, sir."

The man walked on to the forward part of the boat; leaving the lad, who had been in a sort of daze, watching. But it was not for long. The whole thing had been strange and to the lad almost inexplicable. The man was not insane, he was certain; and he was just as sure that he had not been joking. From the start he had been taken by the man's refinement; he was one of intellect and education; he was positive that he had been sincere. Yet—

The ferry detective happened at that moment to be passing. The clerk made an indication with his thumb.

"That man yonder," he spoke, "the one in black. Watch him." Then he told his story. Whereat the detective laughed and walked forward.

It is a most fortunate incident. It was a strange case. That mere act of the cigar clerk placed the police on the track and gave to the world the only clue that it holds of the Blind Spot.

The detective had laughed at the lad's

recital—most any one had a patent for being queer—and if this gentleman had a whim for a certain brand of humor that was his business. Nevertheless, he would stroll forward.

The man was not hard to distinguish; he was standing on the forward deck facing the wind and peering through the mist at the gray, heavy heave of the water. Alongside of them the dim shadow of a sister ferry screamed its way through the fogbank. That he was a landsman was evidenced by his way of standing; he was uncertain; at every heave of the boat he would shift sidewise. An unusually heavy roll caught him slightly off-balance and jostled him against the detective. The latter held up his hand and caught him by the arm.

"A bad morning," spoke the officer. "B-r-r-r! Did you notice the Yerba Buenna yonder? She just grazed us. A bad morning."

The stranger turned. As the detective caught the splendid face, the glowing eyes and the youthful smile, he started much as had done the cigar clerk. The same effect of age melting into youth and—the officer being much more accustomed to reading men—a queer sense of latent and potent vision. The eyes were soft and receptive, but for all that of the delicate strength and color that comes from abnormal intellect. He noted the pupils, black, glowing, of great size, almost filling the iris and the whole melting into intensity that verged into red. Either the man had been long without sleep or he was one of unusual intelligence and vitality.

"A nasty morning," repeated the officer.

"Ah! Er, yes—did you say it was a nasty morning? Indeed, I do not know, sir. However, it is very interesting."

"Stranger in San Francisco?"

"Well, yes. At least, I have never seen it."

"H-m!" The detective was a bit nonplussed by the man's evident evasion. "Well, if you are a stranger I suppose it is up to me to come to the defense of my city. This is one of Frisco's fogs. We have them occasionally. Sometimes they last for days. This one is a low one. It will lift presently. Then you will see the sun. Have you ever seen Frisco's sun?"

"My dear sir"—this same slow articulation—"I have never seen your sun nor any other."

"Hum!"

It was an answer altogether unexpected. Again the officer found himself gazing into the strange, refined face and wonderful eyes. The man was not blind, of that he was certain. Neither was his voice harsh nor testy. Rather was it soft and polite, of one merely stating a fact. Yet how could it be? He remembered the cigar clerk. Neither cigar nor sun! Of what manner of land could the man come from? A detective has a certain gift of intuition. Though on the face of it, outside of the man's personality, there could be nothing to it but a joke, he chose to act upon the impulse. He pulled back the door which had been closed behind them and reentered the boat. When he returned the boat arrived at the pier.

"You are going to Oakland?"

It was a chance question.

"No, to Berkeley. I take a train here, I understand. Do all the trains go to Berkeley?"

"By no means. I am going to Berkeley myself. We can ride together. My name is Jerome. Albert Jerome."

"Thanks. Mine is Avec. Rhamda Avec. I am much obliged. Your company may be instructive."

H E DID not say more; but watched with unrestrained interest their maneuver into the slip. A moment later they were marching with the others through the ways to the trains that were waiting. Just as they were seated and the electric was pulling out of the pier the sun breaking through the mist blazed with splendid light through the cloud rifts. The stranger was next to the window where he could look out over the water and beyond at the citied shoreline, whose sea of housetops extended and serried to the peaks of the first foot-hills. The sun was just coming over the mountains.

The detective watched. There was sincerity in the man's actions. It was not acting. When the light first broke he turned his eyes full into the radiance. It was the act of a child and, so it struck the officer, of the same trust and simplicity—and likewise the same effect. He drew away quickly; for a moment blinded.

"Ah!" he said. "It is so. This is the sun. Your sun is wonderful!"

"Indeed it is," returned the other. "But rather common. We see it every day. It's the whole works, but we get used to it. For myself I cannot see anything strange in the 'sun's still shining.' You have been blind, Mr. Avec? Pardon the question. But I must naturally infer. You say you have never seen the sun. I suppose—"

He stopped because of the other's smile; somehow it seemed a very superior one, as if predicting a wealth of wisdom.

"My dear Mr. Jerome," he spoke, "I have never been blind in my life. I say it is wonderful! It is glorious and past describing. So is it all, your water, your boats, your ocean. But I see there is one thing even stranger still. It is yourselves. With all your greatness you are only part of your surroundings. Do you know what is your sun?"

"Search me," returned the officer. "I'm no astronomer. I understand they don't know themselves. Fire, I suppose, and a hell of a hot one! But there is one thing that I can tell."

"And this—"

"Is the truth."

If he meant it for insinuation it was ineffective. The other smiled kindly. In the fine effect of the delicate features, and most of all in the eyes was sincerity. In that face was the mark of genius—he felt it—and of a potent superior intelligence. Most of all did he note the beauty and the soft, silky superluster of the eyes.

We have the whole thing from Jerome, at least this part of it; and our interest being retrospect is multiplied far above that of the detective. The stranger had a certain call of character and of appearance, not to say magnetism. The officer felt himself almost believing and yet restraining himself into caution of unbelief. It was a remark preposterous on the face of it. What puzzled Jerome was the purpose; he could think of nothing that would necessitate such statements and acting. He was certain that the man was sane.

In the light of what came after great stress has been laid by a certain class upon this incident. We may say that we lean neither way. We have merely given it in some detail because of that importance. We have yet no proof of the mystic and, until it is proved, we must lean, like Jerome, upon the cold material. We have the mystery, but, even at that, we have not the certainty of murder.

Understand, it was intuition that led Jerome into that memorable trip to Berkeley; he happened to be going off duty and was drawn to the man by a chance incident and the fact of his personality. At this minute, however, he thought no more of him than as an eccentric, as some refined, strange, wonderful gentleman with a whim for his own brand of humor. Only that could explain it. The man had an evident curiosity for everything about him, the buildings, the street, the cars, and the people. Frequently he would mutter: "Wonderful, wonderful, and all the time we have never known it. Wonderful!"

As they drew into Lorin the officer ventured a question.

"You have friends in Berkeley. I see you are a stranger. If I may presume, perhaps I may be of assistance?"

"Well, yes, if—if—do you know of a Dr. Holcomb?"

"You mean the professor. He lives on Dwight Way. At this time of the day you would be more apt to find him at the university. Is he expecting you?"

It was a blunt question and of course none of his business. Yet, just what another does not want him to know is ever the pursuit of a detective. At the same time the subconscious flashing and wondering at the name Rhamda Avec—surely neither Teutonic nor Sanscrit nor anything between.

"Expecting me? Ah, yes. Pardon me if I speak slowly. I am not quite used to speech—yet. I see you are interested. After I see Dr. Holcomb I may tell you. However, it is very urgent that I see the doctor. He—well, I may say that we have known each other a long time."

"Then you know him?"

"Yes, in a way; though we have never met. He must be a great man. We have much in common, your doctor and I; and we have a great deal to give to your world. However, I would not recognize him should I see him. Would you by any chance—"

"You mean would I be your guide? With pleasure. It just occurs that I am on friendly terms with your friend Dr. Holcomb."

CHAPTER II

THE PROFESSOR OF PHILOSOPHY

AND now to start in on another angle. There is hardly any necessity for introducing Dr. Holcomb. All of us, at least, those who read, and, most of all, those of us who are interested in any manner of speculation, knew him quite well. He was the professor of philosophy at the University of California: a great man and a good one, one of those fine academic souls who, not only by their wisdom, but by their character, have a way of stamping themselves upon generations; a speaker of the upstanding class, walking on his own feet and utterly fearless when it came to dashing out on some startling philosophy that had not been borne up by his forebears.

He was original. He believed that the philosophies of the ages are but stepping stones, that the wisdoms of the earth looked but to the future, and that the study of the classics, however essential, are but the ground work for combining and working out the problems of the future. He was epigrammatic, terse, and gifted with a quaint humor with which he was apt, even when in the driest philosophy, to drive in and clinch his argument.

Best of all, he was able to clothe the most abstract thoughts in language so simple and concrete that he brought the deepest of all subjects down to the scope of the commonest thinker. It is needless to say that he was copy. The papers about the bay were ever and anon running some startling story of the professor.

Had they stuck to the text it would all have been well; but a reporter is a reporter; in spite of the editors there were numerous little elaborations to pervert the context. A great man must be careful of his speech. Dr. Holcomb was often busy refuting; he could not understand the need of these little twistings of wisdom. It kept him in controversy; the brothers of his profession often took him to task for these little distorted scraps of philosophy. He did not like journalism. He had a way of consigning all writers and editors to the devil.

Which was vastly amusing to the reporters. Once they had him going they poised their pens in glee and began splashing their venomous ink. It was tragic; the great professor standing at bay to his tormentors. One and all they loved him and one and all they took delight in his torture. It was a hard task for a reporter to get in at a lecture; and yet it was often the lot of the professor to find himself and his words featured in his breakfast paper.

On the very day before this the doctor had come out with one of his terse startling statements. He had a way of inserting parenthetically some of his scraps of wisdom. It was in Ethics 2b. We quote his words as near as possible:

"Man, let me tell you, is egotistic. All our philosophy is based on ego. We live threescore years and we balance it with all eternity. We are it. Did you ever stop and think of eternity? It is a rather long time. What right have we to say that life, which we assume to be everlasting, immediately becomes retrospect once it passes out of the conscious individuality which it is allotted upon this earth? The trouble is ourselves. We are five-sensed. We weigh everything with our senses. Everything! We so measure eternity. Until we step out into other senses, which undoubtedly exist, we shall never arrive at the conception of infinity. Now I am going to make a rather startling announcement.

"The past few years have promised a culmination which has been guessed at and yearned for since the beginning of time. It is within, and still without, the scope of metaphysics. Those of you who have attended my lectures have heard me call myself the material idealist. I am a mystic sensationalist. I believe that we can derive nothing from pure contemplation. There is mystery and wonder in the veil of the occult. The earth, our life, is merely a vestibule of the universe. Contemplation alone will hold us all as inapt and as impotent as the old Monks of Athos. We have mountains of literature behind us, all contemplative, and whatever its wisdom, it has given us not one thing outside of the abstract. From Plato down to the present our philosophy has given us not one tangible proof, not one concrete fact which we can place our hands on. We are virtually where we were originally; and we can talk, talk, talk from now until the clap of doomsday.

"What then?

"My friends, philosophy must take a step sidewise. In this modern age young science, practical science, has grown up and far surpassed us. We must go back to the beginning, forget our subjective musings and enter the concrete. We are five-sensed, and in the nature of things we must bring the proof down into the concrete where we can understand it. Can we pierce the nebulous screen that shuts us out of the occult? We have doubted, laughed at ourselves and been laughed at; but the fact remains that always we have persisted in the believing.

"I have said that we shall never, never understand infinity while within the limitations of our five senses. I repeat it. But that does not infer that we shall never solve some of the mystery of life. The occult is not only a supposition, but a fact. We have peopled it with terror, because, like our forebears before Columbus, we have peopled it with imagination.

"And now to my statement.

"I have called myself the Material Idealist. I have adopted an entirely new trend of philosophy. During the past years, unknown to you and unknown to my friends, I have allied myself with practical science. I desired something concrete. While my colleagues and others were pounding out tomes of wonderful sophistry I have been pounding away at the screen of the occult. This is a proud moment. I have succeeded. Tomorrow I shall bring to you the fact and the substance. I have lifted up the curtain and flooded it with the light of day.

7

You shall have the fact for your senses. Tomorrow I shall explain it all. I shall deliver my greatest lecture; in which my whole life has come to a focus. It is not spiritualism nor sophistry. It is concrete fact and common sense. The subject of my lecture tomorrow will be: 'The Blind Spot.' "

HERE begins the second part of the mystery.

We know now that the great lecture was never delivered. Immediately the news was scattered out of the class-room upon the campus. It became common property. It was spread over the country and was featured in all the great metropolitan dailies. In the lecture-room next morning seats were at a premium; students, professors, instructors and all the prominent people who could gain admission crowded into the hall; even the irrepressible reporters had stolen in to take down this greatest scoop of the century. The place was jammed until even standing room was unthought of. The crowd, dense and packed and physically uncomfortable, waited.

The minutes dragged by. It was a long, long wait. But at last the bell rang that ticked the hour. Every one was expectant. And then fifteen minutes passed by, twenty—the crowd settled down to waiting. At length one of the colleagues stepped into the doctor's office and telephoned to his home. His daughter answered.

"Papa? Why he left over two hours ago for the campus."

"About what time?"

"Why, it was about seven-thirty. You know he was to deliver his lecture today on the Blind Spot. I wanted to hear it, but he told me I could have it at home. He said he was to have a wonderful guest and I must make ready to receive him. Isn't papa there?"

"Not yet. Who was this guest? Did he say?"

"Oh, yes! In a way. A most wonderful man. And he gave him a wonderful name, Rhamda Avec. I remember because it is so funny. I asked papa if he was Sanscrit; and he said he was much older than that. Just imagine!"

"Did your father have his lecture with him?"

"Oh, yes. He glanced over it at breakfast. He told me he was going to startle the world as it had never been since the day of Columbus."

"Indeed."

"Yes. And he was terribly impatient. He said he had to be at the college before eight to receive the great man. He was to deliver his lecture at ten. And afterward he would have lunch at noon and he would give me the whole story. I am all impatience."

"Thank you."

Then he came back and made the announcement that there was a little delay; but that Dr. Holcomb would be there shortly. But he was not. At twelve o'clock there were still some people waiting. At one o'clock the last man had slipped out of the room—and wondered. In all the country there was but one person who knew. That one was an obscure man who had yielded to a detective's intuition and had fallen inadvertently upon one of the greatest mysteries of modern times.

CHAPTER III

"NOW THERE ARE TWO"

THE rest of the story is unfortunately all too easily told. We go back to Jerome and his strange companion.

At Center Street station they alighted and walked up to the campus. Under the Le Conte oaks they met the professor. He was trim and happy, his short, well-built figure clothed in black, his snow-white whiskers trimmed to the usual square crop and his pink skin glowing with splendid health. The fog had by this time lifted and the sun was just beginning to overcome the chilliness of the air; on the elevation beyond them the buildings of the great university; and back of it all the huge C upon the face of Charter Hill. There was no necessity for an introduction.

The two men apparently recognized each other at once. So we have it from the detective. There was sincerity in the delight of their hand-clasp. A strange pair, both of them with the distinction and poise that come from refinement and intellectual training; though in physique they were almost opposite, there was still a strange, almost mutual, bond between them. The professor was short, well-set, and venerable; his white hairs matched well the dignity of his wisdom. The other was tall, lithe, graceful, and of that illusive poise that blended into youthfulness. His hair was black; his features well cut, and of the slightly swarthy tinge that suggested an Eastern extraction. Unlike the professor, his face was smooth; he had no trace of beard and very little evidence that he could grow one. Dr. Holcomb was beaming.

"At last!" he greeted. "At last! I was sure we could not fail. This, my dear Dr. Avec, is the greatest day since Columbus."

The other took the hand.

"So this is the great Dr. Holcomb. Yes, indeed, it is a great day; though I know nothing about your Columbus. So far it has been simply wonderful. I can scarcely credit my senses. So near and yet so far. How can it be? A dream? Are you sure, Dr. Holcomb?"

"My dear Rhamda, I am sure that I am the happiest man that ever lived. It is the culmination. I was certain we could not fail; though, of course, to me also it is an almost impossible climax of fact. I should never have succeeded without your assistance."

The other smiled.

"That was of small account, my dear doctor. To yourself must go the credit; to me the pleasure. Take your sun, for instance, I—but I have not the language to tell you."

But the doctor had gone to abstraction.

"A great day," he was beaming. "A great day! What will the world say? It is proved." Then suddenly: "You have eaten?"

"Not yet. You must allow me a bit of time. I thought of it; but I had not quite the courage to venture."

"Then we shall eat," said the other man. "Afterward we shall go up to the lecture-room. Today I shall deliver my lecture on the Blind Spot. And when I am through you shall deliver the words that will astonish the world."

But here it seems there was a hitch. The other shook his head kindly. It was evident that while the doctor was the leader the other was a co-worker who must be considered.

"I am afraid, professor, that you have promised a bit too much. I am not entirely free yet, you know. Two hours is the most that I can give you; and not entirely that. There are some details that may not be neglected. It is a far venture and now that we have succeeded this far there is surely no reason why we cannot go on. However, it is necessary that I return to the house on Chatterton Place. I have but slightly over an hour left."

The doctor was plainly disappointed.

"But the lecture?"

"It means my life, professor, and the subsequent success of our experiment. A few details, a few minutes. Perhaps if we hurry we can get back in time."

The doctor glanced at his watch. "Twenty minutes for the train, twenty for the boat, ten minutes; that's an hour, two hours. These details? Have you any idea how long, Rhamda?"

"Perhaps not more than fifteen minutes."

"We have still two hours. Fifteen minutes; perhaps a little bit late. Tell you what. I shall go with you. You can eat upon the boat."

We have said that the detective had intuition. He had it still. Yet he had no rational reason for suspecting either the professor or his strange companion. Furthermore he had never heard of the Blind Spot in any way whatsoever; nor did he know a single thing of philosophy or anything else in Holcomb's teaching. He knew the doctor as a man of eminent standing and respectability. It was hardly natural that he should suspect anything sinister to grow out of this meeting of two refined scholars. He attached no great importance to the trend of their conversation. It was strange to be sure; but he felt, no doubt, that living in their own world they had a way and a language of their own. He was no scholar.

Still, he could think. The man Rhamda had made an assertion that he could not quite uncover. It puzzled him. As we say, he had intuition. Something told him that for the safety of his old friend it might be well for him to shadow the strange pair to the city.

When the next train pulled out for the pier the two scholars were seated in the forward part of the car. In the last seat was a man deeply immersed in a morning paper.

It is rather unfortunate. In the natural delicacy of the situation Jerome could not crowd too closely. He had no certainty of trouble; no proof whatever; he was known to the professor. The best he could do was to keep aloof and follow their movements. At the ferry building they hailed a taxi and started up Market Street. Jerome watched them. In another moment he had another driver and was winding behind in their wheel tracks. The cab made straight for Chatterton Place. In front of a substantial two-story house it drew up. The two old men alighted. Jerome's taxi passed them.

They were then at the head of the steps; a woman of slender beauty with a wonderful loose fold of black hair was talking. It seemed to the detective that her voice was fearful, of a pregnant warning, that she was protesting Nevertheless, the old men entered and the door slammed behind them. Jerome slipped from the taxi and spoke a few words to the chauffeur. A moment later the two men were holding the house under surveillance.

They did not have long to wait. The man called Rhamda had asked for fifteen minutes. At the stroke of the second the front door reopened. Some one was laughing; a melodious enchanting laugh and feminine. A woman was speaking. And then two forms in the doorway. A man and a woman. The man was Rhamda Avec, tall, immaculate, black clad and distinguished. The woman, Jerome was not certain that she was the same who opened the door or not; she was even more beautiful. She was laughing. Like her companion she was clad in black, a beautiful shimmering material which sparkled in the sun like the rarest silk. The man glanced carelessly up and down the street for a moment. Then he assisted the lady down the steps and into the taxi. The door slammed; and before the detective could gather his scattered wits they were lost in the city.

Jerome was expecting the professor. Naturally when the door opened he looked for the old gentleman and his companion. It was the doctor he was watching, not the other. Though he had no rational reason for expecting trouble he had still his hunch and his intuition. The man and woman aroused suspicion; and likewise upset his calculation. He could not follow them and stay with the professor. It was a moment for quick decision. He wondered. Where was Dr. Holcomb? This was the day he was to deliver his lecture on the Blind Spot. He had read the announcement in the paper coming over on the boat, together with certain comments by the editor. In the lecture itself there was mystery. This strange one, Rhamda, was mixed in the Blind Spot. Undoubtedly he was the essential fact and substance. Until now he had not scented tragedy. Why had Rhamda and the woman come out together? Where was the professor? Where indeed?

A T THE end of a half-hour Jerome ventured across the street. He noted the number 288. Then he ascended the steps and clanged at the knocker. From the sounds that came from inside, the place was but partly furnished. Hollow steps sounded down the hallway, shuffling, like weary bones dragging slippers. The door opened and an old woman, very old, peered out of the crack. She coughed. Though it was not a loud cough it seemed to the detective that it would be her last one; there was so little of her.

"Pardon me, but is Dr. Holcomb here?"

The old lady looked up at him. The eyes were of a blank expressionless blue; she was in her dotage.

"You mean—oh, yes, I think so, the pretty man with the white whiskers. He was here a few minutes ago, with that other. But he just went out, sir, he just went out."

"No, I don't think so. There was a man went out and a woman. But not Dr. Holcomb."

"A woman? There was no woman."

"Oh, yes, there was a woman—a very beautiful one."

The old lady dropped her hand. It was trembling.

"Oh, dear," she was saying. "This makes two. This morning it was a man and now it is a woman, that makes two."

It seemed to the man as he looked down in her eyes that he was looking into great fear; she was so slight and frail and helpless and so old; such a fragile thing to bear burden and trouble. Her voice was cracked and just above a shrill whisper, almost uncanny. She kept repeating:

"Now there are two. Now there are two. That makes two. This morning there was one. Now there are two."

Jerome could not understand. He pitied the old lady.

"Did you say that Dr. Holcomb is here?"

Again she looked up: the same blank expression, she was evidently trying to gather her wits.

"Two. A woman. Dr. Holcomb. Oh, yes, Dr. Holcomb. Won't you come in?"

She opened the door.

Jerome entered and took off his hat. Judicially he repeated the doctor's name to keep it in her mind. She closed the door carefully and touched his arm. It seemed to him that she was terribly weak and tottering; her old eyes, however expressionless, were full of pitiful pleading. She was scarcely more than a shadow.

"You are his son?"

Jerome lied; but he did it for a reason. "Yes."

"Then come."

She took him by the sleeve and led him to a room, then across it to a door in the side wall. Her step was slow and tottering; twice she stopped to sing the dirge of her wonder. "First a man and then a woman. Now there is one. You are his son." And twice she stopped and listened. "Do you hear anything? A bell? I love to hear it: and then afterward I am afraid. Did you ever notice a bell? It always makes you think of church and the things that are holy. This is a beautiful bell—first—"

Either the woman was without her reason or very nearly so: she was very weak and tottering.

"Come, mother, I know, first a bell, but Dr. Holcomb?"

The name brought her back again. For a moment she was blank trying to recall her senses. And then she remembered. She pointed to the door.

"In there—Dr. Holcomb. That's where they come. That's where they go. Dr. Holcomb. The little old man with the beautiful whiskers. This morning it was a man; now it is a woman. Now there are two. Oh, dear; perhaps we shall hear the bell."

Jerome began to scent a tragedy. Certainly the old lady was uncanny; the house was bare and hollow; the scant furniture was threadbare with age and mildew; each sound was exaggerated and fearful, even their breathing. He placed his hand on the knob and opened the door.

"Now there are two. Now there are two."

The room was empty. Not a bit of furniture; a blank, bare apartment with an old-fashioned high ceiling. Nothing else. Whatever the weirdness and adventure Jerome was getting nowhere. The old lady was still clinging to his arm and still droning:

"Now there are two. Now there are two. This morning a man; now a woman. Now there are two."

"Come, mother, come. This will not do. Perhaps—"

But just then the old lady's lean fingers clinched into his arm; her eyes grew bright; her mouth opened and she stopped in the middle of her drone. Jerome grew rigid. And no wonder. From the middle of the room not ten feet away came the tone of a bell, a great silvery voluminous sound—and music. A church bell. Just one stroke, full toned, filling all the air till the whole room was choked with music. Then as suddenly it died out and runed into nothing. At the same time he felt the fingers on his arm relax; and a heap at his feet. He reached over. The life and intelligence that was so near the line was just crossing over the border. The poor old lady! Here was a tragedy he could not understand. He stooped over to assist her. He was trembling. As he did so he heard the drone of her soul as it wafted to the shadow:

"Now there are two."

CHAPTER IV

GONE

JEROME was a strong man, of iron nerve, and well set against emotion; in the run of his experience he had been plumped into many startling situations;

but none like this. The croon of the old lady thrummed in his ears with endless repetition. He picked her up tenderly and bore her to another room and placed her on a ragged sofa. There were still marks on her face of former beauty. He wondered who she was and what had been her life to come to such an ending.

"Now there are two," the words were withering with oppression. Subconsciously he felt the load that crushed her spirit. It was as if the burden had been shifted; he sensed the weight of an unaccountable disaster.

The place was musty and ill-lighted. He looked about him, the dank, close air was unwashed by daylight. A stray ray of sunshine filtering through the broken shutter slanted across the room and sought vainly to dispel the shadow. He thought of Dr. Holcomb. Dr. Holcomb and the old lady. "Now there are two." Was it a double tragedy? First of all he must investigate.

The place was of eleven rooms, six downstairs and five on the upper story. With the exception of one broken chair there was no furniture upstairs; four of the rooms on the lower floor were partly furnished, two not at all. A rear room had evidently been to the old lady the whole of her habitation, serving as kitchen, bedroom, and living-room combined. Except in this room there were no carpets whatever. His steps sounded hollow and ghostly; the boards creaked and each time he opened a door he was oppressed by the same gloom of darkness and stagnation. There was no trace of Dr. Holcomb.

He remembered the bell and sought vainly on both floors for anything that would give him a clue to the sound. There was nothing. The only thing he heard was the echoing of his own creaking footsteps and the unceasing blur that thrummed in his spirit, "Now there are two."

At last he came to the door and looked out into the street. The sun was shining and the life and pulse was rising from the city. It was daylight; plain, healthy day. It was good to look at. On the threshold of the door he felt himself standing on the border of two worlds. What had become of the doctor and who was the old lady; and lastly and just as important who was the Rhamda and his beautiful companion?

Jerome telephoned to headquarters.

It is a strange case.

At the precise minute when his would-be auditors were beginning to fidget over his absence the police of San Francisco had started the search for the great doc-

11

tor. Jerome had followed his intuition. It had led him into a tragedy and he was ready to swear almost on his soul that it was twofold. The prominence of the professor, together with his startling announcement of the day previous and the world-wide comment that it had aroused, elevated the case to a national interest.

Dr. Holcomb had promised to tear away the veil of the occult. He was not a man to talk idly. The world had long regarded him as one of its greatest thinkers. It was a mystery that had shrouded over the ages. Since man first blubbered out of apehood he had fought with this great riddle of infinity. And now, in the lecture on the Blind Spot, was promised the great solution; and not only the solution, but the fact, and substance to back it.

What was the Blind Spot? The world conjectured, and, like the world has been since beginning, it scoffed and derided. Some there were, however, men well up in the latest discoveries of science, who did not laugh. They counseled forbearance; they would wait for the doctor and his lecture.

There was no lecture. In the teeth of our expectation came the startling word that the doctor had disappeared. Apparently when on the very verge of announcing his discovery he had been swallowed by the very force that he had loosened. There was nothing in known science, outside of optics, that could in any way be blended with the Blind Spot. There were but two solutions; either the professor had been a victim of a clever rogue, or he had been overcome by the rashness of his own wisdom. At any rate, it was known from that minute on as "THE BLIND SPOT."

PERHAPS it is just as well to take up the findings of the police. The police of course eluded from the beginning any suggestion of the occult. They are material; and were convinced from the start that the case had its origin in downright villainy. Man is complex; but being so, is oft overbalanced by evil. Some genius had made a fool of the doctor.

In the first place a thorough search was made for the professor. The place at No. 288 Chatterton Place was ransacked from cellar to attic. The records were gone over and it was found that the property had for some time been vacant; that the real ownership was vested in a number of heirs scattered about the country.

The old lady had apparently been living on the place simply through sufferance. No one could find out who she was.

A few tradesmen in the vicinity had sold her some scant supplies and that was all. The stress that Jerome placed upon her actions and words was given due account of. There were undoubtedly two villains; but also there were two victims. That the old lady was such as well as the professor no one has doubted. The whole secret lay in the strange gentleman with the Eastern cast and complexion. Who was Rhamda Avec?

And now comes the strangest part of the story. Ever, when we recount the tale there is something to overturn the theories of the police. It has become a sort of legend in San Francisco; one to be taken with a grain of salt, to be sure, but for all that, one at which we may well wonder. Here the supporters of the professor's philosophy hold their strongest point—if it is true. Of course we can venture no private opinion, never having witnessed. It is this:

Rhamda Avec is with us and in our city. His description and drawn likeness has been published many times. There are those who aver that they have seen him in the reality of the flesh walking through the crowds of Market Street.

He is easily distinguished, tall and distinctive, refined to an ultra degree, and with the poise and alertness of a gentleman of reliance and character. Women look twice and wonder; he is neither old nor young; when he smiles it is like youth breaking in laughter. And with him often is his beautiful companion.

Men vouch for her beauty and swear that it is of the super kind that drives to distraction. She is fire and flesh and carnal—she is superbeauty. There is allurement about her body; sylphlike, sinuous; the olive tint of her complexion, the wonderful glory of her hair and the glowing night-black of her eyes. Men pause; she is of the superlative kind that rob the reason, a supreme glory of passion and life and beauty, at whose feet fools and wise men would slavishly frolic and folly. She seldom speaks, but those who have heard her say that it is like rippling water, of gentleness and softness and of the mellow flow that comes from love and passion and from beauty.

Of course there is nothing out of the ordinary in their walking down the streets. Anybody might do that. The wonder comes in the manner in which they elude the police. They come and go in the broad, bright daylight. Hundreds have seen them. They make no effort at concealment, nor disguise. And yet no fantoms were ever more unreal than they to those who seek them. Who are they? The officers have been summoned on many occasions; but each and every time in some manner or way they have contrived to elude them. There are some who have consigned them to the limbo of illusion. But we do not entirely agree.

In a case like this it is well to take into consideration the respectability and character of those who have witnessed. Fantoms are not corporeal; these two are flesh and blood. There is mystery about them; but they are substance, the same as we are. All the secrets of the universe have not been unriddled by any means. We believe in Dr. Holcomb; and whether it was murder or mystery, we do not think we shall solve it until we have discovered the laws and the clues that led the great doctor up to the Blind Spot.

And lastly:

If you will take the Key Route ferry some foggy morning you may see something to convince you. It must be foggy and the air must be gray and drab and somber. Take the lower deck. Perhaps you shall see nothing. If not try again; for they say you shall be rewarded. Watch the forward part of the boat; but do not leave the inner deck. The great Rhamda watching the gray swirl of the water!

He stands alone, in his hands the case of reddish leather, his feet slightly apart and his face full of a great hungry wonder. Watch his features: they are strong and aglow with a great and wondrous wisdom; mark if you see evil. And, remember. Though he is like you he is something vastly different. He is flesh and blood; but perhaps the master of one of the greatest laws that man can attain to. He is the fact and the substance that was promised, but was not delivered by the professor.

This account has been taken from one of the Sunday editions of our papers. I do not agree with it entirely. Nevertheless, it will serve as an excellent foundation for my own adventures; and what is best of all, save labor.

CHAPTER V

PALS

MY NAME is Harry Wendel.

I am an attorney and until recently boasted of a splendid practice and an excellent prospect for the future. I am still a young man; I have a good education and still have friends and admirers. Such being the case, you no doubt wonder why I give a past inference to my practice and what the future might hold for me. Listen:

I might as well start 'way back. I shall do it completely and go back to the fast-receding time that glowed with childhood.

The first that I can remember is a wriggling ornery mess of curls and temper; for be it known, I have from the beginning been of that passionate vindictive stamp that surcharges the hot emotions of life into high moments.

It is a recollection of childish disaster —I go 'way back. I had been making strenuous efforts to pull the tail out of the cat that I might use it for a feather duster. My desire was supreme logic. I could not understand objection; the cat resisted for certain utilitarian reasons of its own and my mother through humane sympathy. I had been scratched and spanked in addition: it was the first storm center that I remember. I had been punished but not subdued. At the first opportunity I stole out of the house and onto the lawn that stretched out to the sidewalk.

I remember the day. The sun was shining, the sky was clear, and everything was green with springtime. For a minute I stood still and blinked in the sunlight. It was beautiful and soft and balmy; the world at full exuberance; the buds upon the trees, the flowers, and the songbirds singing. I could not understand it. It was so beautiful and soft. My heart was still beating fiercely, still black with perversity and stricken rancor. The world had no right to be so. I hated with the full rush of childish anger.

And then I saw.

Across the street coming over to meet me was a child of my age. He was fat and chubby, a mass of yellow curls and laughter; when he walked he held his feet out at angles as is the manner of fat boys and his arms away from his body; he had on his first pair of pants and a white blouse like I wore on Sunday. I slid off the porch quietly. Here was something that could suffer for the cat and my mother. At my rush he stopped in wonder. I remember his smiling face and my anger. In an instant I had him by the hair and was biting with all the fury of vindictiveness.

At first he set up a great bawl for assistance. He was fat and passive, a beautiful, good-natured child. He could not understand; he screamed and held his hands aloft to keep them out of my reach. Then he tried to run away. But I had learned from the cat that had scratched me. I clung on, biting, tearing. It was good to rend him, to rip off his blouse and collar; the shrill of his scream was music: it was conflict, sweet and delicious; it was strife, swift as instinct.

At last I stopped him; he ceased trying to get away and began to struggle. It was better still; it was resistance. But he was stronger than I; though I was quicker he managed to get me by the shoulders, to force me back, and finally to upset me. Then in the stolid way, and after the manner of fat boys, he sat upon my chest. When our startled mothers came upon the scene they so found us—I upon my back, clinching my teeth and threatening all the dire fates of childhood, and he waiting either for assistance or until my ire should retire sufficiently to allow him to release me in safety.

"Who did it? Who started it?"

That I remember plainly.

"Hobart, did you do this?" The fat boy backed off quietly and clung to his mother; but he did not answer.

"Hobart, did you start this?"

Still no answer.

"Harry, this was you; you started it. Didn't you try to hurt Hobart?"

I nodded.

My mother took me by the hand and drew me away.

"He is a rascal, Mrs. Fenton, and has a temper like sin; but he will tell the truth, thank goodness."

I am telling this not for the mere relation, but by the way of introduction. It was my first meeting with Hobart Fenton. It is necessary that you know us both and our characters. Our lives are so entwined and so related that without it you could not get the gist of the story. In the afternoon I came across the street to play with Hobart. He met me smiling. It was not in his healthy little soul to hold resentment. I was either all smiles or anger. I forgot as quickly as I battled. That night there were two happy youngsters tucked into the bed and covers.

SO WE grew up; one with the other. We played as children do and fought as boys have done from the beginning. I shall say right now that the fights were mostly my fault. I started them one and all; and if every battle had the same beginning it likewise had the same ending. That first fight was but the forerunner of all the others. Though we have always been chums we have always been willing to battle. The boys would place a chip upon his shoulder to see me start it. He has always outweighed me. I have knocked off a thousand chips and have taken a thousand beatings. I have still one more coming. I would knock a chip off Hobart Fenton's shoulder if he weighed a ton.

Please do not think hard of Hobart.

He is the kindest soul in the world; there never was a truer lad nor a kinder heart. He loved me from the beginning. He was strong, healthy, fat, and, like fat boys, forever laughing. He followed me into trouble and when I was retreating he valiantly defended the rear. Stronger, sturdier, and slower, he has been a sort of protector from the beginning. I have called him the Rear Guard; and he does not resent it.

I have always been in mischief, restless, and eager for anything that would bring quick action; and when I got into deep water Hobart would come along, pluck me out and pull me to shore and safety. Did you ever see a great mastiff and a fox terrier running together? It is a homely illustration; but an apt one.

We were boys together, with our delights and troubles, joys and sorrows. I thought so much of Hobart that I did not shirk stooping to help him take care of his baby sister. That is about the supreme sacrifice of a boy's devotion. In after years, of course, he has laughed at me and swears I did it on purpose. I do not know, but I am willing to admit that I think a whole lot of that sister.

Side by side we grew up and into manhood. We went to school and into college. In our prep days we began playing football. Even in the beginning he was sturdy, strong and surtopped all the fellows. I was wiry, alert, full of action and small. We were kept together, he at center, and I at quarter. There was a force between us that was higher than all training, an intuition, a strength and confidence that reached out of the cradle.

I knew his actions, every move and quiver; when I took the ball there was no danger of the play being blocked. He was in front of me fighting to shield me and to give me a chance for action. Together, at least, so spoke the critics, we were a great pair. We were never separated but once. That was in college; it was the only time I had doubts of my ability as a player. Robbing me of that broad back was like stealing my instinct. We had grown double. For all of my training and experience I could not function; my football wits were foggy, I lost all the snap of action. It was so with Hobart. He was slow and bewildered; he lost all the zest and force that made him a great center. The coaches perceived it immediately. Thereafter we were never used in a game unless they could keep us together.

And now just a bit more. Even as we were at odds in our physical builds and our dispositions, so were we in our studies. From the beginning Hobart has had a mania for screws, bolts, nuts, and

14

pistons. He is practical: he likes mathematics; he can talk you from the binomial theorem up into Calculus; he is never so happy as when the air is buzzing with a conversation charged with induction coils, alternating currents, or atomic energy. The whole swing and force of popular science is his kingdom. I will say for Hobart that he is just about in line to be king of it all. Today he is in South America, one of our greatest engineers. He is bringing the water down from the Andes; and it is just about like those strong shoulders and that good head to restore the land of the Incas.

About myself? I went into the law. I enjoy an atmosphere of strife and contention. I might have made a good soldier; but as there was no prospect of immediate war I was content with strife forensic. I liked books and discussion and I thought that I would like the law. On the advice of my elders I took up an A. B. course and then entered the law college, and in due time was admitted to practice. It was while pursuing this letters course that I first ran into philosophy. I was a lad to enjoy quick, pithy, epigrammatic statements. I have always favored a man who hits from the shoulder. Professor Holcomb was of terse, heavy thinking; he spoke what he thought and he did not quibble. He favored no one.

FRANKLY speaking, I will say that the old white-haired professor left his stamp upon me. He was one of the kind whose characters influence generations. I loved him like all the rest; though I was not above playing a trick on the old fellow occasionally. Still he had a wit of his own and seldom came out second best, and when he lost out he could laugh like the next one. I was deeply impressed by the doctor. As I took course after course under him I was convinced that for all of his dry philosophy the old fellow had a trick up his sleeve; he had a way of expounding that was rather startling; likewise, he had a scarcely concealed contempt for some of the demigods of our old philosophy.

What this trick was I could never uncover. I hung on and dug into great tomes of wisdom. I became interested and gradually took up with his speculation; for all of my love of action I found that I had a strong subcurrent for the philosophical.

Now I roomed with Hobart. When I would come home with some dry tome and would lose myself in it by the hour he could not understand it. I was preparing for the law. He could see no advantage to be derived from this digging into speculation. He was practical and unless he could drive a nail into a thing or at least dig into its chemical elements it was hard to get him interested.

"Of what use is it, Harry? Why waste your brains? These old fogies have been pounding on the question for three thousand years. What have they got? You could read all their literature from the pyramids down to the present skyscrapers and you wouldn't get enough practical wisdom to drive a dump-cart."

"That's just it," I answered. "I'm not hankering for a dump-cart. You have an idea that all the wisdom in the world is locked up in the concrete; unless a thing has wheels, pistons, some sort of combustion, or a chemical action you are not interested. What gives you the control over your machinery? Brains! But what makes the mind go?"

Hobart blinked.

"Fine," he answered. "Go on."

"Well," I answered, "that's what I am after."

He laughed.

"Great. Well, keep at it. It's your funeral, Harry. When you have found it let me know and I'll beat you to the patent."

With that he turned to his desk and dug into one of his everlasting formulas. Just the same, next day when I entered Holcomb's lecture-room I was in for a surprise. My husky roommate was in the seat beside me.

"What's the big idea?" I asked.

"Big idea is right, Harry," he grinned. "Just thought I would beat you to it. Had a dickens of a time with Dan Clark, of the engineering department. Told him I wanted to study philosophy. The old boy put up a beautiful holler. Couldn't understand what an engineer would want with psychology or Ethics 2b. Neither could I until I got to thinking last night when I went to roost. Because a thing has never been done is no reason why it never will be; is it, Harry?"

"Certainly not. I don't know just what you are driving at. Perhaps you intend to take your notes over to the machine shop and hammer out the Secret of the Absolute."

He grinned.

"Pretty wise head at that, Harry. What did you call it? The Secret of the Absolute. Will remember that. I'm not much on phrases; but I am sure of the strong boy with the hammer. You don't object to my sitting here beside you; so that I, too, may drink in the little drops of wisdom.

15

It was in this way that Hobart entered into the study of philosophy. When the class was over and we were going down the steps he patted me on the shoulder.

"Not so bad, Harry. Not so bad. The old doctor is there; he's got them going. Likewise little Hobart has got a big idea."

Now it happened that this was just about six weeks before Dr. Holcomb announced his great lecture on the Blind Spot. It was not more than a week after registration. In the time ensuing Fenton became just as great an enthusiast as myself. His idea, of course, was chimerical and a blind; his main purpose was to get in with me where he could argue me out of my folly.

He wound up by being a convert of the professor.

Then came the great day. The night of the announcement we had a long discussion. It was a deep question. For all of my faith in the professor I was hardly prepared for a thing like this. Strange to say I was the skeptic; and stranger still, it was Hobart who took the side of the doctor.

"Why not?" he said. "It merely comes down to this: you grant that a thing is possible and then you deny the possibility of a proof—outside of your abstract. That's good paradox, Harry; but almighty poor logic. If it is so it certainly can be proven. There's not one reason in the world why we can't have something concrete. The professor is right. I am with him. He's the only professor in all the ages."

Well, it turned out as it did. It was a terrible blow to us all. Most of the world took it as a great murder or an equally great case of abduction. There were but few, even on the campus, who embraced the side of the doctor. It was a case of villainy, of a couple of remarkably clever rogues and a trusting scholar.

But there was one whose faith was not diminished. He had been one of the last to come under the influence of the doctor. He was practical and concrete, and not at all attuned to philosophy; he had not the training for deep dry thinking. He would not recede one whit. One day I caught him sitting down with his head between his hands. I touched him on the shoulder.

"What's the deep study, pal?" I asked him.

He looked up. By his eyes I could see that his thoughts had been far away.

"What's the deep study?" I repeated.

"I was just thinking, Harry; just thinking."

"What?"

"I was just thinking, Harry, that I would like to have about one hundred thousand dollars and about ten years' leisure."

"That's a nice thought," I answered; "I could think that myself. What would you do with it?"

"Do? Why, there is just one thing that I would do if I had that much money. I would solve the Blind Spot."

THIS happened years ago while we were still in college. Many things have occurred since then. I am writing this on the verge of disaster. How little do we know! What was the idea that buzzed in the head of Hobart Fenton? He is concrete, physical, fearless. He is in South America. I have cabled to him and expect him as fast as steam can bring him. The great idea and discovery of the professor is a fact, not fiction. What is it? That I cannot answer. I have found it and I am a witness to its potency.

Some law that has been missed through the ages; phenomena that should not have been discovered. It is inexorable and insidious; it is concrete. Out of the unknown comes terror. Through the love for the great professor I have pitted myself against it. From the beginning it has been almost hopeless. I remember that last digression in ethics. "The mystery of the occult may be solved. We are five-sensed. When we bring the thing down to the concrete we may understand."

Sometimes I wonder at the Rhamda. Is he a man or a fantom? Does he control the Blind Spot? Is he the substance and the proof that was promised by Dr. Holcomb? Through what process and what laws did the professor acquire even his partial control over the phenomena? Where did the Rhamda and his beautiful companion come from? Who are they? And lastly — what was the idea that buzzed in the head of Hobart Fenton?

When I look back now I wonder. I have never believed in fate. I do not believe in it now. Man is the master of his own destiny. We are cowards else. I lay my all on honor. Whatever is to be known we should know it. One's duty is ever to one's fellows. Heads up and onward. I am not a brave man, perhaps, under close analysis; but once I have given my word I shall keep it. I have done my bit; my simple duty. Perhaps I have failed. In holding myself against the Blind Spot I have done no more than would have been done by a million others. I have only one regret. Failure is seldom rewarded. I had hoped that my life would be the last; I have a dim hope still. If I fail in the end, there must be still one more to follow.

Understand. I do not expect to die. It is

the unknown that I am afraid of. I who thought that we knew so much have found it still so little. There are so many laws in the weave of Cosmos that are still unguessed. What is this death that we are afraid of? What is life? Can we solve it? Is it permissible? What is the Blind Spot? If Hobart Fenton is right it has nothing to do with death. If so, what is it?

My pen is weak. I am weary. I am waiting for Hobart. Perhaps I shall not last. When he comes I want him to know my story. What he knows already will not hurt repeating. It is well that man shall have it; it may be that we shall both fail—there is no telling; but if we do the world can profit by our blunders and guide itself—perhaps to the mastery of the phenomenon that controls the Blind Spot.

I ask you to bear with me. If I make a few mistakes or I am a bit loose, remember the stress under which I am writing. I shall try to be plain so that all may follow.

CHAPTER VI

CHICK WATSON

NOW to go back.

In due time we were both of us graduated from college. I went into the law and Hobart into engineering. We were both successful. There was not a thing to foreshadow that either of us was to be jerked from his profession. There was no adventure, but lots of work and the plentiful reward of proportion.

Perhaps I was a bit more fortunate. I was a lover and Hobart was still a confirmed bachelor. It was a subject over which he was never done joshing. It was not my fault. I was innocent. If the blame ran anywhere it would have to be placed upon that baby sister. We had wheeled her on the sidewalks; watched her toddle in her first footsteps; and to keep her from crying had missed many a game of marbles. Seriously, at the time I do not think I had any thought of the future. When she had grown into an awkward bundle of arms and legs and pigtails I would have run away at the suggestion. That is just it.

It happened as it has happened since God first made the maiden. One fall Hobart and I started off for college. We left Charlotte at the gate a girl of fifteen years and ten times as many angles. I pulled one of her pigtails, kissed her, and told her I wanted her to get pretty. When we came home next summer I went over to pull the other pigtail. I did not pull it. I was met by the fairest little lady I had ever looked on. And I could not kiss her. Seriously, was I to blame?

Now to the incident.

It was a night in September. Hobart had completed the details of his affairs and had booked passage to South America. He was to sail next morning. We had dinner that day with his family, and then came up to San Francisco for a last and farewell bachelor night. We could take in the opera together, have supper at our favorite café, and then turn in. It was a long hark back to our childhood; but for all that we were still boys together.

I remember that night. It was our favorite opera—"Faust." It was the one piece that we could agree on. Looking back since, I have wondered at the coincidence. The old myth age to youth and the subcurrent sin with its stalking, laughing, subtle *Mephistopheles*. Even the introductory Faust — the octogenarian, scholar — the *Mephisto*, the element of the supernatural—all have woven into color. It is strange that we should have taken in this one opera on this one evening. I recall our coming out of the building; our minds thrilling to the music and the subtle weirdness of a master.

A fog had fallen—one of those thick, heavy, gray mists that sometimes come upon us in September. Into its somber depths the crowd disappeared like shadows. The lights upon the streets blurred yellow. At the cold sheer contact we hesitated upon the sidewalk.

I had on a light overcoat. Hobart, bound for the tropics, had no such protection. It was cold and miserable, a chill wind stirring from the north was unusually cutting. Hobart raised his collar and dug his hands into his pockets.

"Brr," he muttered; "brr, some coffee or some wine! Something."

The sidewalks were wet and slippery, the mists settling under the lights had the effect of drizzle. I touched Hobart's arm and we started across the street.

"Brr is right," I answered, "and some wine. Brr. Notice the shadows, like ghosts."

We were half across the street before he answered; then he stopped.

"Ghosts! Did you say ghosts, Harry?" I noted a strange inflection in his voice. He stood still and peered into the fog bank. His stop was sudden and suggestive. Just then a passing taxicab almost caught us and we were compelled to dodge quickly. Hobart ducked out of the way and I side-stepped in another direction. We came up together on the sidewalk. Again he peered into the shadow.

"Confound that cab," he was saying,

"now we have gone and missed him."

He took off his hat and then put it back on his head. It was his favorite trick when bewildered. I looked up and down the street.

"Didn't you see him? Harry! Didn't you see him? It was Rhamda Avec!"

I had seen no one; that is to notice; I did not know the Rhamda. Neither did he.

"The Rhamda? You don't know him." Hobart was puzzled.

"No," he said; "I do not; but it was he, just as sure as I am a fat man."

I whistled. I recalled the tale that was now a legend. The man had an affinity for the fog mist. To come out of "Faust" and to run into the Rhamda! What was the connection? For a moment we both stood still and waited.

"I wonder—" said Hobart. "I was just thinking about that fellow to-night. Strange! Well, let's get something hot—some coffee."

But it had given us something for discussion. Certainly it was unusual. During the past few days I had been thinking of Dr. Holcomb; and for the last few hours the tale had clung with reiterating persistence. Perhaps it was the weirdness and the tremulous intoxication of the music. I was one of the vast majority who disbelieved it. Was it possible that it was, after all, other than the film of fancy? There are times when we are receptive; at that moment I could have believed it.

WE ENTERED the café and chose a table slightly to the rear. It was a contrast to the cold outside; the lights so bright, the glasses clinking, laughter and music. A few young people were dancing. I sat down; in a moment the lightness and jollity had stirred my blood. Hobart took a chair opposite. The place was full of beauty. With the thrill of youth I noted the marvelous array of girls and women. In the back of my mind blurred the image of the Rhamda. I had never seen him; but I had read the description. I wondered absently at the persistence. I recall Hobart's reiteration.

"On my honor as a fat man."

I have said that I do not believe in fate. I repeat it. Man should control his own destiny. A great man does. Perhaps that is it. I am not great. Certainly it was circumstance.

In the back part of the room at one of the tables was a young man sitting alone. Something caught my attention. Perhaps it was his listlessness or the dreamy unconcern with which he watched the dancers; or it may have been the utter forlornness of his expression. I noted his unusual pallor and his cast of dissipation, also the continual working of his long, lean fingers. There are certain set fixtures in the night life of any city. But this was not one. He was not an habitué. From the first I sensed it. There was a certain greatness to his loneliness and his isolation. I wondered.

Just then he looked up. By a mere coincidence our eyes met. He smiled, a weak smile and a forlorn one, and it seemed to me rather pitiful. Then as suddenly his glance wandered to the door behind me. Perhaps there was something in my expression that caught Hobart's attention. He turned about.

"Say, Harry, who is that fellow? I know that face, I'm certain."

"Come to think, I have seen him myself. I wonder—"

The young man looked up again. The same weary smile. He nodded. And again he glanced over my shoulder toward the door. His face suddenly hardened.

"He knows us at any rate," I ventured.

Now Hobart was sitting with his face toward the entrance. He could see any one coming or going. Following the young man's glance he looked over my shoulder. He suddenly reached over and took me by the forearm.

"Don't look around," he warned; "take it easy. As I said—on my honor as a fat man."

The very words foretold. I could not but risk a glance. Across the room a man was coming down the aisle—a tall man, dark, and of a very decided manner. I had read his description many times; I had seen his likeness as drawn by certain sketch artists of the city. They did not do him justice. He had a wonderful way and presence—you might say, magnetism. I noticed the furtive wandering glances that were cast, especially by the women. He was a handsome man beyond denying, about the handsomest I had ever seen. The same elusiveness.

At first I would have sworn him to be of sixty; the next minute I was just as certain of his youth. There was something about him that could not be put to paper, be it strength, force or vitality; he was subtle. His step was prim and distinctive, light as shadow, in one hand he carried the red case that was so often mentioned. I breathed an exclamation.

Hobart nodded.

"Am I a fat man? The famous Rhamda! What say? Ah, ha! he has business with our wan friend yonder. See! I would give just about three pfennigs to get the trend of their discourse."

And it was so. He took a chair opposite

the wan one. The young man straightened. His face was even more familiar, but I could not place him. His lips were set; in their grim line—determination; whatever his exhaustion there was still a will. Somehow one had a respect for this weak one; he was not a mere weakling. Yet I was not so sure that he was not afraid of the Rhamda. He spoke to the waiter. The Rhamda began talking. I noted the poise in his manner; it was not evil, rather was it calm—and calculating. He made an indication. The young man drew back. He smiled; it was feeble and weary, but for all that disdainful. Though one had a pity for his forlornness, there was still an admiration.

The waiter brought glasses.

The young man swallowed his vintage at a gulp, the other picked his up and sipped it. Again he made the indication. The youth dropped his hand upon the table, a pale blue light followed the movement of his fingers. The older man pointed. So that was their contention? A jewel? After all our fantom was material enough to desire possession; his solicitude was calmness; but for all that aggression. I could sense a battle; but the young man turned the jewel to the palm side of his fingers; he shook his head.

The Rhamda drew up. For a moment he waited. Was it for surrender? Once he started to speak, but was cut short by the other. For all of his weakness there was spirit to the young man. He even laughed. The Rhamda drew out a watch. He held up two fingers. I heard Hobart mumble.

"Two minutes. Well, I'm betting on the young one. Too much soul. He's not dead; just weary."

H E WAS right. At exactly one hundred and twenty seconds the Rhamda closed his watch. He spoke something. Again the young man laughed. He lit a cigarette; from the flicker and jerk of the flame he was trembling. But he was still emphatic. The other arose from the table, walked down the aisle and out of the building. The youth spread out both arms and dropped his head upon the table.

It was a little drama enacted almost in silence. Hobart and I exchanged glances. The mere glimpse of the Rhamda had brought us both back to the Blind Spot. Was there any connection? Who was the young man with life sapped out? I had a flitting recollection of a face strangely familiar. Hobart interrupted my thoughts.

"I'd give just about one leg for the gist of that conversation. That was the Rhamda; but who is the other ghost?"

"Do you think it has to do with the Blind Spot?"

"I don't think," averred Hobart. "I know. Wonder what's the time." He glanced at his watch. "Eleven thirty."

Just here the young man at the table raised up his head. The cigarette was still between his fingers; he puffed lamely for a minute, taking a dull note of his surroundings. In the well of gaiety and laughter coming from all parts of the room his actions were out of place. He seemed dazed; unable to pull himself together. Suddenly he looked at us. He started.

"He certainly knows us," I said. "I wonder—by George, he's coming over."

Even his step was feeble. There was exertion about every move of his body, the wanness and effort of gone vitality; he balanced himself carefully. Slowly, slowly, line by line his features became familiar, the underlines of another, the ghost of one departed. At first I could not place him. He held himself up for breath. Who was he? Then it suddenly came to me—back to the old days at college—an athlete, one of the best of fellows, one of the sturdiest of men! He had come to this!

Hobart was before me.

"By all the things that are holy!" he exclaimed. "Chick Watson! Here, have a seat. In the name of Heavens, Chick! What!"

The other dropped feebly into the chair. The body that had once been so powerful was a skeleton. His coat was a disguise of padding.

"Hello, Hobe; hello, Harry," he spoke in a whisper. "Not much like the old Chick, am I? First thing, I'll take some brandy."

It was almost tragic. I glanced at Hobart and nodded to the waiter. Could it be Chick Watson? He had been an athlete; had tipped two hundred pounds and had been a letter man on the varsity. I had seen him a year before, hale, healthy, prosperous. And here he was— a wreck!

"No," he muttered, "I'm not sick—not sick. Lord, boys, it's good to meet you. I just thought I would come out for this one last night, hear some music, see a pretty face, perhaps meet a friend. But I am afraid, afraid—" He dropped off like one suddenly drifting into slumber.

"Hustle that waiter," I said to Hobart. "Hurry that brandy."

The stimulant seemed to revive him. He lifted up suddenly. There was fear in his eyes; then on seeing himself among friends—relief. He turned to me

"Think I'm sick, don't you?" he asked.

"You certainly are," I answered.

"Well, I'm not."

For a moment silence. I glanced at Hobart. Hobart nodded.

"You're just about in line for a doctor, Chick, old boy," I said. "I am going to see that you have one. Bed for you, and the care of mother—"

He started; he seemed to jerk himself together.

"That's it, Harry; that's what I wanted. It's so hard for me to think. Mother, mother! That's why I came down-town. I wanted a friend. I have something for you to give to mother."

"Rats," I said. "I'll take you to her. What are you talking about?"

But he shook his head.

"I wish that you were telling the truth, Harry. But it's no use—not after to-night. All the doctors in the world could not save me. I'm not sick, boys, far from it."

Hobart spoke up.

"What is it, Chick I have a suspicion. Am I right?"

Chick looked up; he closed his eyes.

"All right, Hobe, what's your suspicion?"

Fenton leaned over. It seemed to me that he was peering into the other's soul. He touched his forearm.

"Chick, old boy, I think I know. But tell me. Am I right? It's the Blind Spot."

At the words Watson opened his eyes; they were full of hope and wonder, for a moment, and then, as suddenly of a great despair. His body went to a heap. His voice was feeble.

"Yes," he answered, "I am dying—of the Blind Spot."

CHAPTER VII

THE RING

IT WAS a terrible thing; death stalking out of the Blind Spot. We had almost forgotten. It had been a story hitherto —a wonderful one to be sure, and one to arouse conjecture. I had never thought that we were to be brought to its shivering contact. It was out of the occult; it had been so pronounced by the professor; a great secret of life holding out a guerdon of death to its votaries. Witness Chick Watson, the type of healthy, fighting manhood—come to this. He opened his eyes feebly; one could see the light; the old spirit was there—fighting for life. What was this struggle of soul and flesh? Why had the soul hung on? He made another effort.

"More drink," he asked; "more drink. Anything to hold me together. I must tell you. You must take my place and—and

—fight the Blind Spot! Promise that—"

"Order the drinks," I told Hobart. "I see Dr. Hansen yonder. Even if we can not save him we must hold him until we get his story."

How well do I remember. What a meaning has that moment! The restaurant was full of people. In the midst of the flow of repartee, while youth danced and music welled, Death was keeping us company. We must arouse no attention. We must save him if possible; but most of all hold him until he had given us what he knew. We would avenge him. What was this Rhamda and his Blind Spot?

The doctor came over.

"A strange case," he murmured. "Pulse normal; not a trace of fever. Not sick, you say—" Hobart pointed to his head. "Ah, I see! Mr. Wendel, I would suggest home and a bed."

Just here Watson opened his eyes again. They rested first upon the doctor, then upon myself, and finally upon the brandy. He took it up and drank it with eagerness. It was his third one; it gave him a bit more life.

"Didn't I tell you, boys, that there is not a doctor on earth that can save me? Excuse me, doc. I am not sick. I told them. I am far past physic; I have gone beyond medicine. All I ask is stimulant and life enough to tell my story."

"My boy," asked the dcotor kindly, "what ails you?"

Watson smiled. He touched himself on the forehead.

"Up here, doc. There are things in the world with which we may not tamper. I tried it. Somebody had to do it and somebody has to do it yet. You remember Dr. Holcomb; he was a great man; he was after the secret of life. He began it."

Dr. Hansen started.

"Lord!" he exclaimed, looking at us all; "you don't mean this man is mixed up in the Blind Spot?"

We nodded. Watson smiled; again he dropped back into inertia; the speech he had made was his longest yet; the brandy was coming into effect.

"Give him brandy," the doctor said; "it is as good as anything. It will hold him together and give him life for a while. Here." He reached into his pocket and flicked something into the glass. "That will help him. Gentlemen, do you know what it means? I had always thought! I knew Dr. Holcomb! Crossing over the border! It may not be done! The secret of life is impossible. Yet—"

Watson opened his eyes again; his spirit seemed to suddenly flicker into defiance.

"Who said it is impossible? Who said

it? Gentlemen, it is, too, possible. Dr. Holcomb—pardon me. I do not wish to appear as a sot; but this brandy is about the only thing to hold me together. I have only a few hours left."

He took the glass, and at one gulp downed the contents. I do not know what the doctor had dropped into it. Chick revived suddenly; a strange light blazed up in his eyes, like life rekindled.

"Ah, now I am better. So?"

He turned to us all; then to the doctor.

"So you say the secret of life is impossible?"

"I—"

Chick smiled wanly. "May I ask you: what is it that has just flared up within me? I am weak, anemic, fallen to pieces; my muscles have lost the power to function, my blood runs cold, I have been more than two feet over the border. And yet—a few drinks of brandy, of stimulants, and you have drawn me back, my heart beats strongly, for an hour. By means of drugs you have infused a new life—which of course is the old—and driven the material components of my body into correlation. It is the function of medicine to so dish out and doctor to our bodies; to keep life in us. You are successful for a time; so long as nature is with you; but all the while you are held aghast by the knowledge that the least flaw, the least disarrangement, and you are beaten.

"It is your business to hold this life or what you may. When it has gone your structures, your anatomy, your wonderful human machine is worthless. Where has it come from? Where has it gone? I have drunk four glasses of brandy; I have a lease of four short hours. Ordinarily it would bring reaction; it is poison, to be sure; but it is driving back my spirit, giving me life and strength enough to tell my story—in the morning I shall be no more. By sequence I am a dead man already. Four glasses of brandy; they are speaking. Whence comes this affinity of substance and of shadow?"

We all of us listened, the doctor most of all. "Go on," said the doctor.

"Can't you see?" repeated Watson. "There is affinity between substance and shadow; and therefore your spirit or shadow or what you will is concrete, is in itself a substance. It is material just as much as you are. Because you do not see it is no proof that it is not substance. That pot palm yonder does not see you; it is not blessed with eyes."

THE doctor looked at Watson; he spoke gently.

"This is very old stuff, my boy, out of our abstract philosophy. No man knows the secret of life. Not even yourself.'

The light in Watson's eyes grew brighter, he straightened; he began slipping the ring from his finger.

"No," he answered. "I do not. I have tried and it was like playing with the lightning. I sought for life and it is giving me death. But there is one man living who has found it."

"And this man?"

"Is Dr. Holcomb!"

We all of us started. We had every one given the doctor up as dead. The very presence of Watson was tragedy. We did not doubt that he had been through some terrible experience. There are things in the world that may not be unriddled. Some power, some sinister thing was reaching for his vitality. What did he know about the professor? Dr. Holcomb had been a long time dead.

"Gentlemen. You must hear my story; I have not long to tell it. However before I start here is a proof for a beginning."

He tossed the ring upon the table.

It was Hobart who picked it up. A beautiful stone, like a sapphire; blue but uncut and of a strange pellucid transparency—a jewel undoubtedly; but of a kind we had never seen. We all of us examined it, and were all, I am afraid, a bit disappointed. It was a stone and nothing else.

Watson watched us. The waiter had brought more brandy, and he was sipping it, not because he liked it, he said, but just to keep himself at the proper lift.

"You do not understand it, eh? You see nothing? Hobart, have you a match? There, that's it; now give me the ring. See—" He struck the match and held the flame against the jewel. "Gentlemen, there is no need for me to speak. The stone will give you a volume. It's not trickery, I assure you, but fact. There, now, perfect. Doctor, you are the skeptic. Take a look at the stone."

The doctor picked it up casually and held it up before his eyes. At first he frowned; then a look of incredulity; his chin dropped and he rose in his chair.

"My God," he exclaimed, "the man's living! It—he—"

But Hobart and I had crowded over. The doctor held the ring so we could see it. Inside the stone was Dr. Holcomb!

It was a strenuous moment, and the most incredible. We all of us knew the doctor. It was not a photograph, nor a likeness; but the man himself. It was beyond all reason that he could be in the jewel; indeed there was only the head visible; one could catch the expression of life, the movements of the eyelids. It was natural and life. Yet how could it be? What was it? It was Hobart who spoke first.

"Chick," he asked, "what's the meaning? Were it not for my own eyes I would call it impossible. It is absurd on the face. The doctor! Yet I can see him—living. Where is he?"

Chick nodded.

"That's the whole question. Where is he? I know and yet I know nothing. You are now looking into the Blind Spot. The doctor sought the secret of life—and found it. He was trapped by his own wisdom!"

CHAPTER VIII

THE NERVINA

FOR a moment we were silent. The jewel reposed upon the table. What was the secret of its phenomena? I could think of nothing in science that would explain it. It was a kind I had never seen. How had Watson come into its possession? What was the tale he had to tell? The lean, long figure that clutched for brandy! What force was this that had driven him to such a verge? He was resigned; though he was defiant he had already conceded his surrender. I had known him a year before, hale, happy, joyous, and successful. The whole thing was hidden. Was it Rhamda Avec? Dr. Hansen spoke.

"Watson," he asked, "what do you know about the Blind Spot?"

"Nothing."

We all turned to Chick. Hobart ordered more brandy. The doctor's eyes went to slits. I could not but wonder. The man had told us but a moment before that he was dying of the Blind Spot. Yet he knew nothing! I had to speak.

"Chick," I asked, "who is Rhamda Avec?"

Watson turned.

"You saw him a few minutes ago? You saw him with me? Let me ask you."

"Yes," I answered, "I saw him. Most everybody did. Is he invisible? Is he really the fantom they say?"

Somehow the mention of the name made him nervous; he looked cautiously about the room.

"That I don't know, Harry. It— If I can only get my wits together. Is he a fantom? Yes, I think so. I can't understand him. At least, he has the powers we attribute to an apparition. He is strange and unaccountable. Sometimes you see him, sometimes you don't. He was mixed up, you remember, with Professor Holcomb. The first known of him was on the day the doctor was to deliver his lecture on the Blind Spot. He was tracked, you know, to the very act. Then came in the Nervina."

"And who is the Nervina?"

Watson looked at me blankly.

"The Nervina?" he asked. "The Nervina—what do you know about the Nervina?"

"Nothing. You just now mentioned her."

His mind seemed to ramble. He looked about the room rather fearfully. Perhaps he was afraid.

"Did I mention her? I don't know, Harry, my wits are muddled. The Nervina? She is a goddess. Never was and never will be woman. She loves; she never hates, and still again she does not love. She is beautiful; too beautiful for man. I have quit trying."

"Is she Rhamda's wife?"

His eyes lit fire.

"No!"

"Do you love her?"

He went blank again; but at last he spoke slowly.

"No, I do not love her. What's the use? She is not for me. I did; but I learned better. I was after the professor—and the Blind Spot. She—"

Again that look of haunted pursuit. He glanced about the room. Whatever had been his experience, it was plain that he had not given up. He held something and he held it still. What was it?

"You say you didn't find the Blind Spot?"

"No, I did not find it."

"Have you any idea?"

"My dear Harry," he answered, "I am full of ideas. That's the trouble. I am near it. It is the cause of my present condition. I don't know just what it is nor where. A condition, or a combination of phenomena. You remember the lecture that was never delivered? Had the doctor spoken that morning the world would have had a great fact. He had made a great discovery. It is a terrible thing." He turned the ring so we could all see it—beyond all doubt it was the doctor. "There he is—the professor. If he could only speak. The secret of the ages. Just think what it means. Where is he? I have taken that jewel to the greatest lapidaries and they have one and all been startled. Then they all come to the same conclusion—trickery—Chinese or Hindu work, they say; most of them want to cut."

"Have you taken it to the police?"

"No."

"Why?"

"I would simply be laughed at."

"Have you ever reported this Rhamda?"

"A score of times. They have come and sought; but every time he has gone out —like a shadow. It's got to be an old story now. If you call them up and tell them they laugh."

"How do you account for it?"

"I don't. I—I—I'm just dying."

"And not one member of the force—surely?"

"Oh, yes. There's one. You have heard of Jerome. He was the ferry detective. Perhaps you have read of it in the supplements. It's a bit melodramatic; but still follows the facts fairly well. Jerome followed the professor and the Rhamda to the house of the Blind Spot, as he calls it. He's not a man to fool. He had eyes and he saw it. He will not leave it till he's dead."

"But he did not see the Blind Spot, did he? How about trickery? Did it ever occur to you that the professor might have been murdered?"

WATSON reached over and turned up the jewel.

"Take a look at that, Harry. Does that look like murder? When you see the man living?"

Here Hobart came in.

"Just a minute, Chick. My wise friend here is an attorney. He's always the first into everything, especially conversation. It's been my job pulling Harry out of trouble. Just one question."

"All right."

"Didn't you—er—keep company, as they say, with Bertha Holcomb while at college?"

A kind look came into the man's eyes; he nodded; his whole face was soft and saddened.

"I see. That naturally brought you to the Blind Spot. You are after her father. Am I correct?"

"Exactly."

"All right. Perhaps Bertha has taken you into some of her father's secrets. He undoubtedly had data on this Blind Spot. Have you ever been able to locate it?"

"No!"

"I see. This Rhamda? Has he ever sought that data?"

"Many, many times."

"Does he know you haven't it?"

"No."

"So. I understand. You hold the whip hand through your ignorance. Rhamda is your villain—and perhaps this Nervina? Who is she?"

"A goddess."

Hobart smiled.

"Oh, yes!" He laughed. "A goddess. Naturally! They all are. There are about forty in this room at the present mo-ment, my dear boy. Watch them dance!"

Now I had picked up the ring. It just fitted the natural finger. I tried it on and looked into the jewel. The professor was growing dimmer. The marvelous blue was returning, a hue of fascination, not the hot flash of the diamond; but the frozen light of the iceberg. It was frigid, cold, terrible, blue, alluring. To me at the moment it seemed alive and pulselike. I could not account for it. I felt the lust for possession. Perhaps there was something in my face. Watson leaned over and touched me on the arm.

"Harry," he asked, "do you think you can stand up under the burden? Will you take my place?"

I looked into his eyes; in their black depths was almost entreaty. How haunting they were, and beseeching.

"Will you take my place?" he begged. "Are you willing to give up all that God gives to the fortunate? Will you give up your practice? Will you hold out to the end? Never surrender? Will—"

"You mean will I take this ring?"

He nodded.

"Exactly. But you must know beforehand. It would be murder to give it to you without the warning. Either your death or that of Dr. Holcomb. It is not a simple jewel. It defies description. It takes a man to wear it. It is subtle and of destruction; it eats like a canker; it destroys the body; it frightens the soul—"

"An ominous piece of finery," I spoke. "Wherein—"

But Watson interrupted. There was appeal in his eyes.

"Harry," he went on, "I am asking. Somebody has got to wear this ring. He must be a man. He must be fearless; he must taunt the devil. It is hard work, I assure you. I cannot last much longer. You loved the old doctor. If we get at this law we have done more for mankind than either of us may do with his profession. We must save the old professor. He is living and he is waiting. There are perils and forces that we do not know of. The doctor went at it alone and fearless; he succumbed to his own wisdom. I have followed after, and I have been crushed down—perhaps by my ignorance. I am not afraid. But I do not want my work to die. Somebody has got to take it and you are the man."

They were all of them looking at me. I studied the wonderful blue and its light. The image of the great professor had dimmed almost completely. It was a sudden task and a great one. Here was a law; one of the great secrets of Cosmos. What was it? Somehow the lure caught into my vitals. I was not afraid; perhaps because I had too much health. I could not picture myself ever coming to the extremity of my companion. Besides, it was a duty. I owed it to the old doctor. It seemed somehow that he was speaking. Though Watson did the talking I could feel him calling. Would I be afraid? Besides, there was the jewel. It was calling; already I could feel it burning into my spirit. I looked up.

"Do you take it, Harry?"

I nodded.

"I do. God knows I am worthless enough. I'll take it up. It may perchance give me a chance to tangle with this famous Rhamda."

"Be careful of this Rhamda, Harry. And above all do not let him have the ring."

"Why?"

"Because. Now listen. I am not saying this absolutely, understand. Nevertheless the facts all point in one direction. Hold the ring. Somewhere in that great luster lies a great secret; it controls the Blind Spot. The Rhamda himself may not take it off your finger. You are immune from violence. Only the ring itself may kill you."

He coughed.

"God knows," he spoke, "it has killed me."

It was rather ominous. The mere fact of that cough and his weakness was enough. One would come to this. He had warned me, and he had sought me with the same voice as the warning.

"But what is the Blind Spot?"

"Then you take the ring? What is the time? Twelve. Gentlemen—"

Now here comes in one of the strange parts of my story—one that I cannot account for. Over the shoulder of Dr. Hansen I could watch the door. Whether it was the ring or not I do not know. At the time I did not reason. I acted upon impulse. It was an act beyond good breeding. I had never done such a thing before. I had never even seen the woman. The woman? Why do I say it? She was never a woman—she was a girl—far, far transcendent. It was the first time I had ever seen her—standing there before the door. I had never beheld such beauty, such profile, poise—the witching, laughing, night black of her eyes; the perfectly bridged nose and the red, red lips that smiled, it seemed to me, in sadness. She hesitated, and as if puzzled, lifted a jeweled hand to her raven mass of hair. To this minute I cannot account for my action, unless, perchance, it was the ring. Perhaps it was. Anyway, I had risen.

How well do I remember.

It seemed to me that I had known her a long, long time. There was something about her that was not seduction; but far, far above it. Some place I had seen her, had known her. She was looking and she was waiting for me. There was something about her that was super feminine. I thought it then, and I say it now.

Just then her glance came my way. She smiled, and nodded; there was a note of sadness in her voice.

"Harry Wendel!"

There is no accounting for my action, nor my wonder; she knew me. Then it was true! I was not mistaken! Some place I had seen her. I felt a vague and dim rush of dreamy recollections. Ah, that was the answer! She was a girl of dreams and fantoms. Illusive as beauty; as tender as love and with the freshness of a fairy. Even then I knew it; she was not a woman; not as we conceive her; she was some materialization out of Heaven. Why do I talk so? This strange beauty that is woman! From the very first she held me in a thrall that has no explanation.

"Do we dance?" she asked simply.

THE NEXT moment I had her in my arms and we were out among the dancers. That my actions were queer and entirely out of reason never came to me. There was a call about her beautiful body and in her eyes that I could not answer. There was a fact between us, some strange bond that was beyond even passion. She was lithe as a fairy, like the air; she was subtle. I danced, and in an extreme emotion of happiness. A girl out of the dreams and the ether—a sprig of life woven out of the moonbeams!

"Do you know me?" she asked as we danced.

"Yes," I answered, "and no. I have seen you; but I do not remember; you come from the sunshine."

She laughed prettily.

"Do you always talk like this?"

"When I dance with the fairies."

"Perhaps I am not a fairy."

"You are out of my dreams," I answered: "it is sufficient. But who are you?"

She held back her pretty head and looked at me; her lips drooped slightly at the corners, a sad smile, and tender, in the soft wonderful depths of her eyes —a pity.

"Harry," she asked, "are you going to wear this ring?"

So that was it. The ring and the maiden. What was the bond? There was weirdness in its color, almost cabalistic —a call out of the occult. The strange beauty of the girl, her remarkable presence, and her concern. Whoever and whatever she was her anxiety was not personal. In some way she was woven up with this ring and poor Watson.

"I think I shall," I answered.

Again the strange querulous pity, and hesitation; her eyes grew darker, almost pleading.

"You won't give it to me?"

How near I came to doing it I shall not tell. It would be hard to say it. I knew vaguely that she was playing; that I was the plaything. It is hard for a man to think of himself as being toyed with. From the very first she was a thing of spirit, clothed in the flesh and alluring. She was certain; she was confident of my weakness. It was resentment, perhaps, and pride of self that gave the answer.

"I think I shall keep it."

"Do you know the danger, Harry? It is death to wear it. A thousand perils—"

"Then I shall keep it. I like peril. You wish the ring. If I keep it I may have you. This is the first time I have danced with the girl out of the moonbeams."

Her eyes snapped, and she stopped dancing. I do not think my words displeased her. She was still a woman.

"Is this final? You are a fine young man, Mr. Wendel. I know you. I stepped in to save you. You are playing with something stranger than the moonbeams. No man may wear that ring and hold to life. Again, Harry, I ask you; for your own sake."

At this moment we passed Watson. He was watching; as our eyes glanced he shook his head. Who was this girl? She was as beautiful as sin and as tender as a virgin. What interest had she in myself?

"That's just the reason," I laughed. "You are too interested. You are too beautiful to wear it. I am a man; I revel in trouble; you are a girl. It would not be honorable to allow you to take it. I shall keep it."

She had overreached herself, and she knew it. She bit her lip. But she took it gracefully; so much so, in fact, that I thought she meant it.

"I am sorry," she answered slowly. "I had hopes. It is terrible to look at Watson and then to think of you. It is, really"— a faint tremor ran through her body; her hand trembled—"it is terrible. You young men are so unafraid. It is too bad."

Just then the door was opened; outside I could see the bank of fog; someone passed. She turned a bit pale.

"Excuse me. I must be going. Oh, Harry, don't you see I'm sorry—"

She held out her hand—the same sad little smile. On the impulse of the moment, unmindful of place, I drew it to my lips and kissed it. She was gone.

I returned to the table. The three men were watching me: Watson analytically, the doctor with wonder, and Hobart with plain disgust. Hobart spoke first.

"Nice for sister Charlotte, eh, Harry? This is our last bachelor night, all right!"

His contemptuous eyes took measure from tip to tip of my body.

I had not a word to say. In the full rush of the moment I knew that he was right. It was all out of reason. I had no excuse outside of sheer insanity—and dishonor. The doctor said nothing. It was only in Watson's face that there was a bit of understanding.

"Hobart," he said, "I have told you. It is not Harry's fault. It is the Nervina. No man may resist her. She is beauty incarnate; she weaves with the hearts of men, and she loves no one. It is the ring. She, the Rhamda, the Blind Spot, and the ring. I have never been able to unravel them. Please do not blame Harry. He went to her even as I. She has but to beckon. But he kept the ring. I watched them. This is but the beginning."

But Hobart muttered: "She's a beauty all right—a beauty. That's the rub. I know Harry—I know him as a brother, and I want him so in fact. But I'd hate to trust that woman."

Watson smiled.

"Never fear, Hobart, your sister is safe enough. The Nervina is not a woman. She is not of the flesh."

"Brrr," said the doctor, "you give me the creeps."

Watson reached for the brandy; he nodded to the doctor.

"Just a bit more of that stuff if you please. It is stimulating, it gives me life. Whatever it is, on the last night one has no fear of habit. There— Now, gentlemen, if you will come with me, I shall take you to the house of the Blind Spot."

CHAPTER IX

"NOW THERE ARE THREE"

I SHALL never forget that night. When we stepped to the sidewalk the whole world was shrouded. The heavy fog clung like depression; life was gone out—a foreboding of gloom and disaster. It was cold, dank, miserable; one shuddered instinctively and battered against the wall with steaming columns of breath. Just outside the door we were detained.

"Dr. Hansen?"

Some one stepped beside us.

"Dr. Hansen?"

"Yes, sir."

"A message, sir."

The doctor made a gesture of impatience.

"Bother!" he spoke. "Bother! A message. Nothing in the world would stop me! I cannot leave."

Nevertheless he stepped back into the light.

"Just a minute, gentlemen."

He tore open the envelope. Then he looked up at the messenger and then at us. His face was startled—almost frightened.

"Gentlemen," he said, "I am sorry. Not a thing in the world would detain me but this. I would go with you, but I may not. My duty as a physician. I had hopes." He came over to me and spoke softly. "I am going to send you one of the greatest specialists in the city in my stead. This young man should have attention. It were a crime else. Have you the address?"

"288 Chatterton," I answered.

"Very well, I am sorry, very much disappointed. However, it is my daughter, and I cannot do otherwise. Continue the brandy for a while—and this." He slipped an envelope into my hand. "By that time Dr. Higgins will be with you."

"You think there is hope?" I asked.

"There is always hope," replied the doctor.

I returned to my companions. They were walking slowly. It was work for poor Watson. He dragged on, leaning on Hobart's arm. But at last he gave up.

"Boys," he spoke, "I can't make it. I'm too far gone. I had thought— Oh, what a lapse it has been! I am eighty years of age; one year ago I was a boy. If I only had some more brandy. I have some at the house. We must make that. I must show you; there I can give you the details."

"Hail a cab," I said. "Here's one now."

A few minutes later we were before the House of the Blind Spot. It was a two-story drab affair, much like a thousand others, old-fashioned, and might have been built in the early nineties. It had been outside of the fire limits of 1906, and so had survived the great disaster. Chatterton is a short street running lengthwise along the summit of the hill. A flight of stone steps descended to the sidewalk.

Watson straightened up with an effort.

"This is the house," he spoke. "I came here a year ago. I go away tonight. I had hoped to find it. I promised Bertha. I came alone. I had reasons to believe I had solved it. I found the Rhamda and the Nervina. I had iron will and courage—also strength. The Rhamda was never able to control me. My life is gone but not my will. Now I have left him another. Do not surrender, Harry. It is a gruesome task; but hold on to the end. Help me up the steps. There now. Just wait a minute till I procure a stimulant."

He did not ring for a servant. That I noticed. Instead he groped about for a key, unlocked the door and stumbled into a room. He fumbled for a minute among some glasses.

"Will you switch on a light?" he asked.

Hobart struck a match; when he found it he pressed the button.

"There now," said Watson. "Boys, I can hope you don't think evil of me, but I cannot help it. I never drank, you know. It is the only thing that will hold me—this liquor. I must explain what I can—then. Well, one of you must take my place."

I was thankful for the liquor. Without it he would revert to the stupor. Life was at a low ebb. He was striving to condense enough of it to tell the story. I thought of the envelope that Dr. Hansen had given me and passed it over. At the same time I breathed a prayer for the specialist.

THE room in which we were standing was a large one, fairly well furnished, and lined on two sides with book-shelves; in the center was an oak table cluttered about with papers, a couple of chairs, and on one of them a long pipe, which, somehow, I did not think of as Watson's. He noticed my look.

"Jerome's," he explained. "We live here —Jerome the detective, and myself. He has been here since the day of the doctor's disappearance. I came a year ago. He is in Nevada at present. That leaves me alone. You will notice the books. Mostly occult: partly mine, partly the detective's. We have gone at it systematically from the beginning. We have learned almost everything but what would help us. Mostly sophistry—and guesswork. Beats all how much ink has been wasted to say nothing. We were after the Blind Spot."

"But what is it? Is it in this house?"

"I can answer one part of your question," he answered, "but not the other. It is here somewhere, some place. Jerome is positive of that. You remember the old lady? The one who died? Her actions were rather positive even if feeble. She led Jerome to this next room." He turned and pointed; the door was opened. I could see a sofa and a few chairs; that was all.

"It was in there. The bell. Jerome never gets tired of telling. A church bell. In the center of the room. At first I did not believe; but now I accept it all. I know, but what I know is by intuition."

"Sort of sixth sense?"

"Yes. Or foresight."

"You never saw this bell nor found it? Never were able to arrive at an explanation?"

"No."

"How about the Rhamda? The Nervina? Do they come to this house?"

"Not often."

"How do they come in? Through the window?"

He smiled rather sadly. "I do not know. At least they come. You shall see them yourself. The Rhamda has something to do with Dr. Holcomb. Somehow his very concern tells me the doctor is safe. Undoubtedly the professor made a great discovery. But he was not alone. He had a co-worker—the Rhamda. For reasons of his own the Rhamda wishes to control the Blind Spot."

"Then the professor is in this Blind Spot."

"We think so. At least it is our conjecture. We do not know."

"Then you do not think it trickery?"

"No, hardly. Harry, you know better than that. Can you imagine the great doctor the dupe of a mere trickster? The professor was a man of great science and was blessed with an almighty sound head. But he had one weakness."

Hobart spoke up.

"What is it, Chick? I think I know what you mean. The old boy was honest?"

"Exactly. He had been a scholar all his life. He taught ethics. He believed in right. He practiced his creed. When he came to the crucial experiment he found himself dealing with a rogue. The Rhamda helped him just so far; but once he had the professor in his power it was not his purpose to release him until he was secure of the Blind Spot."

"I see," I spoke. "The man is a villain. I think we can handle him."

But Watson shook his head.

"That's just it, Harry! The man! If he were a man I could have handled him in short order. That's what I thought at first. Do not make any mistake. Do not try violence. That's the whole crux of the difficulty. If he were only a man! Unfortunately, he is not."

"Not a man!" I exclaimed. "What do you mean? Pray, then, what is he?"

"He is a fantom."

I glanced at Hobart and caught his eye. Hobart believed him! The poor pallid face of Watson, the athlete; there was nothing left to him but his soul! I shall not forget Watson as he sat there, his lean, long fingers grasping the brandy glass, his eyes burning and his life holding back from the pit through sheer will and courage. Would I come to this?

Would I have the strength to measure up to his standard?

Hobart broke the tension.

"Chick is right. There is something in it, Harry. Not all of the secrets of the universe have been unlocked by any means. By the way, shake me out one of those coffin-nails. I never smoked one in my life, but I have heard they are good for the nerves. There. Light it. Now, Chick, about details. Have you any data —any notes?"

Watson rose. I could see he was grateful.

"You believe me, don't you, Hobart? It is good. I had hoped to find someone, and I found you two. Harry, remember what I have told you. Hold the ring. You take my place. Whatever happens, stick out to the end. You have Hobart to help you. Now just a minute. The library is here; you can look over my books. I shall return in a moment."

HE STEPPED out into the hall; we could hear his weary feet dragging down the hallway—a hollow sound and a bit uncanny. Somehow my mind rambled back to that account I had read in the supplement—Jerome's story—"Like weary bones dragging slippers." And the old lady. Who was she? Why was every one in this house pulled down so exhaustion—the words of the old lady, I could almost hear them; the dank air murmuring their recollection. "Now there are two. Now there are two!"

I shook it off and endeavored to amuse myself by watching the pathetic contest that was going on between Hobart's fat fingers and the cigarette. You didn't shake Hobart very often. He had taken to tobacco. I was nervous. Came the insistent shivering croon out of the stillness. "Now there are two. Now there are two!"

"What's the matter, Harry?"

Perhaps I was frightened. I do not know. I looked around. The sound of Watson's footsteps had died away; there was a light in the back of the building coming towards us.

"Nothing! Only—damn this place, Hobart. Don't you notice it? It's enough to eat your heart out."

"Rather interesting," said Hobart. Just the same he burned himself and the smoke got into his eyes. It was too interesting for me. I stepped over to the shelves and looked at the titles. Sanscrit and Greek; German and French—the Vedas, Sir Oliver Lodge, Besant, Spinoza, a conglomeration of all ages and tongues; a range of metaphysics that was as wide as Babel, and about as enlightening. As Babel? Over my shoulders came the strangest sound of all, weak, piping, tremulous, fearful—"Now there are two. Now there are two." My heart gave a fearful leap. "Soon there will be three! Soon—"

I turned suddenly about. I had a fearful thought. I looked at Hobart. A strange, insidious fear clutched up at me. Was the thought intrinsic? If not, where had it come from? Three! I strained my ears to hear Watson's footsteps. He was in the back part of the building. I must have some air.

"I am going to open the door, Hobart," I spoke. "The front door, and look out into the street."

"Don't blame you much. Feel a bit that way myself. About time for Dr. Higgins. Here comes Chick again. Take a look outside and see if the doc is coming."

I opened the door and looked out into the dripping fog bank. What a pair of fools we were! We both knew it, and we were both seeking an excuse. We looked at each other. In the next room through the curtains I could see the weak form of Watson; he was bearing a light.

Suddenly the light went out.

I was at high tension; the mere fact of the light was nothing, but it meant a world at that moment—a strange sound —a struggle—then the words of Watson —Chick Watson's:

"Harry! Harry! Hobart! Harry! Come here! It is the Blind Spot!"

It was in the next room. The despair of that call is unforgettable, like that of one suddenly falling into space. Then the light dropped to the floor. I could see the outlines of his figure and a weird, single string of incandescence. Hobart turned and I leaped. It was a blur, the form of the man melting into nothing. I sprang into the room, tearing down the curtains. Hobart was on top of me. But we were too late. I could feel the vibrancy of something uncanny as I rushed across the room intervening. Through my mind the staccatoed thrill of terror. It had come suddenly, and in climax. It was over before it had commenced. We landed full force into the room. The light had gone out. Only by the gleam from the other room could we make out each other's faces. The air was vibrant, magnetic. There was no Watson. But we could hear his voice. Dim and fearful, coming down the corridors of time.

"Hold that ring, Harry! Hold that ·ing!" Then the faint despair out of the ·weary distance, faint, but a whole volume:

"The Blind Spot!"

It was over just that quickly. The whole thing climaxed into an instant. It is difficult to describe. One cannot always analyze sensations. Mine, I am afraid, were muddled. A thousand insistent thoughts clashed through my brain. Horror, wonder, doubt! I have only one persistent and predominating recollection. The old lady! I could almost feel her coming out of the shadows. There was sadness and pity; out of the stillness and the corners. What had been the dirge of her sorrow?

"Now there are three!"

CHAPTER X

MAN OR FANTOM?

IT WAS Hobart who came to first. His voice was good to hear. It was natural; it was sweet and human, but it was pregnant with disappointment: "We are fools, Harry; we are fools!"

I could only stare. I remember saying: "The Blind Spot?"

"Yes," returned Hobart, "the Blind Spot. But what is it? We saw him go. Did you see it?"

"It gets me," I answered. "He just vanished into space. It—" Frankly I was afraid.

"It tallies well with the supplements. The old lady and Jerome. Remember?"

"And the bell?" I looked about the room.

"Exactly. Phenomena! Watson was right. I just wonder—but the bell? Remember the doctor? 'The greatest day since Columbus.' No, don't cross the room, Harry, I am a bit leary. A great discovery! I should say it was. How do you account for it?"

"Supernatural."

Fenton shook his head.

"By no means! It is the gateway to the universe—into Cosmos." His eyes sparkled. "My Lord, Harry! Don't you see! Once we control it. The Blind Spot! What is beyond? We saw Chick Watson go. Before our eyes. Where did he go to? It beats death itself."

I started across the room, but Hobart caught me with both arms: "No, no, no, Harry. My Lord! I don't want to lose you. No! You foolhardy little cuss—stand back!"

He threw me violently against the wall. The impact quite took my breath.

On the instant the old rush of temper surged up in me. From boyhood we had these moments. Hobart settled himself and awaited the rush that he knew was coming. In his great, calm, brute strength there was still a greatness of love.

"Harry," he was saying, "for the love of

Heaven, listen to reason! Have we got to have a knock-down and drag-out on this of all nights? Have I got to lick you again? Do you want to roll into the Blind Spot?"

Why did God curse me with such a temper? On such moments as this I could feel something within me snapping. It was fury and unreason. How I loved him! And yet we had fought a thousand times over just such provocation. Over his shoulders I could see the still open door that led into the street; the heavy form was hanging through the opening; out of the corner of my eye I caught the lines of the form stepping out of the shadows—it crossed the room and stood beside Hobart Fenton. It was Rhamda Avec!

I leaped. The fury of a thousand conflicts—and the exultation. For the glory of such moments it is well worth dying. One minute flying through the air—the old catapult tackle—and the next a crashing of bone and sinew. We rolled over, head on, and across the floor. Curses and execrations; the deep base voice of Hobart:

"Hold him, Harry! Hold him! That's the way! Hold him! Hold him!"

We went crashing about the room. He was the slipperiest thing I had ever laid hold of. But he was bone—bone and sinew; he was a man! I remember the wild thrill of exultation at the discovery. It was battle! And death! The table went over, we went spinning against the wall, a crash of falling bookcases, books and broken glass, a scurry and a flying heap of legs and arms. He was wonderfully strong and active, like a panther. Each time I held him he would twist out like a cat, straighten, and throw me out of hold. I clung on, fighting, striving for a grip, working for the throat. He was a man—a man! I remembered that he must never get away. He must account for Watson.

In the first rush I was a mad man. The mere force of my onslaught had borne him down. But in a moment he had recovered and was fighting systematically. As much as he could he kept over on one side of me, always forcing me toward the inner room where Watson had disappeared. In spite of my fury he eluded every effort that I made for a vital part. We rolled, fought, struck and struggled.

I could hear Hobart's bass thundering: "Over! Over! Under! Look out! Now you've got him! Harry! Harry! Look out! Hold him, for the love of Heaven! I see his trick. That's his trick. The Blind Spot!"

It was like Hobart tearing through the center in the days of old. We were rolled clear over, picked, heaved, shoved against the front wall. There were three! The great heaving bulk of Fenton; the fighting tiger between us; and myself! Surely such strength was not human; we could not pin him; his quickness was uncanny; he would uncoil, twist himself and throw us loose. Gradually he worked us away from the front wall and into the center of the room.

WE KNEW his game now, both of us. He was working us toward the inner room and his cursed Blind Spot. He would throw us into the abyss. We were all in rags and tatters. I was torn and bleeding. The tense face of Hobart, his veins standing out, his muscles bulged, all as flitting as vision. The Rhamda twisted. We went whirling around, the three of us rolling over—through the door.

Could any mere man fight so? Hobart was as good as a ton; I was as much for action. Slowly, slowly in spite of our efforts, he was working us toward the Blind Spot. Confident of success, he was over, around, and in and under. In a spin of a second he went into the aggressive. He fairly bore us off our feet. We were on the last inch of our line; the stake was—

What was it? We all went down. A great volume of sound! We were inside a bell! My whole head buzzed to music and a roar; the whir of a thousand vibrations; the inside of sound. I fell face downward; the room went black.

What was it? How long I lay there I do not know. A dim light was burning. I was in a room. The ceiling overhead was worked in a grotesque pattern; I could not make it out. My clothes were in tatters and my hand was covered with blood. Something warm was trickling down my face. What was it? The air was still and sodden. Who was this man beside me? And what was this smell of roses?

I lay still for a minute, thinking. Ah, yes! It came back. Watson—Chick Watson! The Blind Spot! The Rhamda and the bell! Surely it was a dream. How could all this be in one short night? It was like a nightmare and impossible. What was this smell of roses? I raised up on my elbow and looked at the form beside me. It was Hobart Fenton. He was unconscious.

For a moment my mind was whirring; I was too weak and unsteady. I dropped back and wondered absently at the odor of roses. Roses meant perfume, and perfume meant a woman. What could—Something touched my face—something soft; it plucked tenderly at my tangled hair and drew it away from my forehead. It was the hand of a woman!

29

"You poor, foolish boy! You foolish boy!"

Some place I had heard that voice; it had a touch of sadness; it was familiar; it was soft and silken like music that might have been woven out of the moonbeams. Who was it that always made me think of the moonbeams? I lay still, thinking.

"He dared; he dared; he dared!" she was saying. "As if there were not two! He shall pay for this! Am I to be a plaything? You poor boy!"

Then I remembered. I looked up. It was the Nervina. She was stooping over with my head against her. How beautiful her eyes were! In their depths was a pathos and a tenderness that was past a woman's, the same slight droop at the corners of the mouth, and the wistfulness; her features were relaxed like a mother's—a wondrous sweetness and pity.

"Harry," she asked, "where is Watson? Did he go?"

I nodded.

"Into the Blind Spot?"

"Yes. What is the Blind Spot?"

She ignored the question.

"I am sorry," she answered. "So sorry. I would have saved him. And the Rhamda; was he here, too?"

I nodded. Her eyes flashed wickedly.

"And—and you— Tell me, did you fight with the Rhamda? You—"

"It was Watson," I interrupted. "This Rhamda is back of it all. He is the villain. I would hold him. He can fight like a tiger; whoever he is, he can fight."

She frowned slightly; she shook her head.

More than ever now I noticed the sadness and wistfulness; her beauty was unlike any other; her eyes, so black, were for all that soft; in their depths lurked pity and tenderness—a great longing. I wondered vaguely what it was; who was she?

"You young men," she said. "You young men! You are all alike! Why must it be? I am so sorry. And you fought with the Rhamda? You could not overcome him, of course. But tell me, how could you resist him? What did you do?"

What did she mean? I had felt his flesh and muscle. He was a man. Why could he not be conquered—not be resisted?

"I do not understand," I answered. "He is a man. I fought him. He was here. Let him account for Watson. We fought alone at first, until he tried to throw me into this Thing. Then Hobart stepped in. Once I thought we had him, but he was too slippery. He came near putting us both in. I don't know. Something happened—a bell."

HER hand was on my arm, she clutched it tightly, she swallowed hard; in her eyes flashed the fire that I had noticed once before, the softness died out, and their glint was almost terrible.

"He! The bell saved you? He would dare to throw you into the Blind Spot!"

I lay back. I was terribly weak and uncertain. This beautiful woman! What was her interest in myself?

"Harry," she spoke, "let me ask you. I am your friend. If you only knew! I would save you. It must not be. Will you give me the ring? If I could only tell you! You must not have it. It is death—yes, worse than death. No man may wear it."

So that was it. Again and so soon I was to be tempted. Was her concern feigned or real? Why did she call me Harry? Why did I not resent it? She was wonderful; she was beautiful; she was pure. Was it merely a subtle play for the Rhamda? I could still hear Watson's voice ringing out of the Blind Spot; "Hold the ring! Hold the ring!" I could not be false to my friend.

"Tell me first," I asked. "Who is this Rhamda? What is he? Is he a man?"

"No."

Not a man! I remembered Watson's words: "A fantom!" How could it be? At least I would find out what I could.

"Then tell me, what is he?"

She smiled faintly; again the elusive tenderness lingered about her lips, the wistful droop at the corners.

"That I may not tell you, Harry. You could not understand. Would that I could."

Certainly I could not understand her evasion. I studied and watched her—her wondrous hair, the perfection of her throat, the curve of her bosom.

"Then he is supernatural."

"No, not that, Harry. That would explain everything. One can not go above Nature. He is living just as you are."

I studied a moment.

"Are you a woman?" I asked suddenly.

Perhaps I should not have asked it; she was so sad and beautiful, somehow I could not doubt her sincerity. There was a burden back of her sadness, some great yearning unsatisfied, unattainable. She dropped her head. The hand upon my arm quivered and clutched spasmodically; I caught the least sound of a sob. When I looked up her eyes were wet and sparkling.

"Oh," she said. "Harry, why do you ask it? You are the only man who has ever guessed. A woman! Harry, a woman! To live and love and to be loved. What must it be? There is so much of life that is sweet and pure. I love it—I love it! I can

30

have everything but the most exalted thing of all. I can live, see, enjoy, think, but I can not have love. Your humblest maiden is a queen beside me. You knew it from the first. How did you know it? Would that I were woman. Your life is beautiful. How did you know? You said— Ah, it is true! I am out of the moonbeams." She controlled herself suddenly. "Excuse me," she said simply. "But you can never understand. May I have the ring?"

It was like a dream—her beauty, her voice, everything. But I could still hear Watson. I was to be tempted, cajoled, flattered. What was this story out of the moonbeams? Certainly she was the most beautiful girl I had ever seen. Why had I asked such a question?

"I shall keep the ring," I answered.

She sighed. A strange weakness came over me; I was drowsy; I lapsed again into unconsciousness; just as I was fading away I heard her speaking: "I am so sorry!"

CHAPTER XI

BAFFLED

WAS it a dream? The next I knew somebody was dousing water down my neck. It was Hobart Fenton. "Lord," he was saying, "I thought you were never coming to. What hit us? You are pretty well cut up. That was some fight. This Rhamda, who is he? Can you figure him out? Did you hear that bell? What was it?"

I sat up. Hobart was bathing my face. We were both in tatters. Hobart had washed my hands.

"Where is the Nervina?" I asked.

"The who?" He was bewildered. "Oh, I guess she's down at the café. Thought you had forgotten her. Wasn't her mate enough? It might be healthy to forget his Nervina."

He was a pretty sight; his clothes were ribbons; his plump figure was breaking out the seams. He regarded me critically.

"What do you think of the Blind Spot?" he asked. "Who is the Rhamda? He put us out pretty easily."

"But the girl?" I interrupted. "The girl? Confound it, the girl?"

It was some time before I could make him understand; even then he refused to believe me.

"It was all a dream," he said; "all a dream."

But I was certain.

Fenton began prodding about the room. I do not believe any apartment was ever so thoroughly ransacked. We even tore up the carpet. When we were through he sat in the midst of the débris and wiped his forehead.

"It's no use, Harry—no use. We might know better. It can't be done. Yet you say you saw a string of incandescence."

"A single string; the form of Watson; a blur—then nothing," I answered.

He thought. He quoted the professor: "'Out of the occult. I shall bring you proof and the substance. It will be concrete—within the reach of your senses.' Is that not what the doctor said?"

"Then you believe Professor Holcomb?"

"Why not? Did we not see it? I know a deal of material science; but nothing like this. I always had faith in Dr. Holcomb. After all, it is not impossible. First we must go over the house thoroughly."

We did. Most of all, we were interested in that bell. We did not think, either of us, that so much noise could come out of nothing. It was too material. The other we could credit to the occult; but not the sound. It had drowned our consciousness; perhaps it had saved us from the Rhamda. But we found nothing. We went over the house systematically. It was much as it had been previously described, only now a bit more furnished. The same dark, musty smell and the same suggestive silence. We returned to the lower floor and the library. It was a sorry sight. We straightened up the shelves and returned the books to their places.

It was getting along in the morning. Hobart sailed at nine o'clock. We must have new clothing and some coffee; likewise we must collect our wits. I had the ring, and had given my pledge to Watson. I was muddled. We must get down to sane action. First of all we must return to our rooms.

The fog had grown thicker; one could almost taste it. I could not suppress a shudder. It was cold, dank, repressive. Neither of us spoke a word on our way down-town. Hobart opened the door to our apartment; he turned on the lights. We had always kept a small outfit with which to warm up a light lunch. We both of us did a deal of night work and often made hot coffee as the morning approached.

In a few moments we had our hot, steaming cups. Still we did not speak. Hobart sat in his chair, his elbows on the table and his head between his hands. My thoughts ran back to that day in college when he had said: "I was just thinking, Harry, if I had one hundred thousand dollars, I would solve the Blind Spot."

That was long ago. We had neither of us thought that we would come to the fact.

"Well," I spoke, "have you got that

hundred thousand dollars? You had an idea once."

He looked up.

"I've got it yet. I am not certain. It is merely a theory. But it's not impossible."

He had a pretty solid head on his fat body. He had no use for sophistry; he was too material, too wedded to bolts and pistons. I was interested.

"Well, what is it?"

HE TOOK another drink of coffee and settled back in his chair.

"It is energy, Harry—force. Nothing but energy—and Nature."

"Then it is not occult?" I asked.

"Certainly it is. I did not say that. It is what the professor promised. Something concrete for our senses. If the occult is, it can certainly be proven. The professor was right. It is energy, force, vibration. It has a law. The old doctor was caught somehow. We must watch our step and see that we are not swallowed up also. Perhaps we shall go the way of Watson."

I shuddered.

"I hope not. But explain. You speak in volumes. Come back to earth."

"That's easy, Harry. I can give you my theory in a few short words. You have studied physiology, haven't you? Well, that's where you can get your proof—or rather let me say my theory. What is the Blind Spot?"

"In optics?"

"We'll forego that," he answered. "I refer to this one."

I thought a moment.

"Well," I said, "I don't know. It was something I could not see. Watson went out before our eyes. He was lost."

"Exactly. Do you get the point?"

"No."

"It is this. What you see is merely energy. Your eye is merely a machine. It catches certain colors. Which in turn are merely ratios of vibration. There is nothing to matter but force, Harry; if we could get down deep enough and knew a few laws, we could transmute it."

"What has it to do with the occult?"

"Merely a fact. The eye machine catches only certain ratios of energy. There are undoubtedly any number of ratios; the eye cannot see them."

"Then this would account for the Blind Spot?"

"Exactly. A localized spot, a condition, a combination of phenomena, anything entering it becomes invisible."

"Where does it go to?"

"That's it. Where? It's one of the things that man has been guessing at for the ages. The professor is the first phi-losopher with sound sense. He went after it. 'Tis a pity he was trapped."

"By the Rhamda?"

"Undoubtedly."

"Who is he?"

Hobart smiled.

"How do I know? Where did he come from? If we knew his story, we would know everything. 'A fantom,' so Watson says. If so, it only strengthens our theory. It would make man and matter only a part of creation. Certainly it would clear up a lot of doubts."

"And the ring?"

"It controls the Blind Spot."

"In what way?"

"That's for us to find out."

"And Watson? He is in this land of doubt?"

"At least he is in the Blind Spot. Let me try the ring."

He struck a match.

It was much as it had been in the restaurant, only a bit more startling; the blue faded, the color went out, and it became transparent. For a moment. There was an effect of space and distance that I had not noted before, almost marvelous. If I would describe it at all, I would say a crystal corridor of a vastness that can scarcely be imagined. It made one dizzy, even in that bit of jewel: one lost proportion, it was height, distance, space immeasurable. For an instant. Then the whole thing blurred and clouded. Something passed across the face; the transparency turned to opaqueness, and then —two men. It was as sudden as a flash— the materialization. There was no question. They were alive. Watson was with the professor.

It was a strange moment. Only an hour before one of them had been with us. It was Watson, beyond a doubt. He was alive; one could almost believe him in the jewel. We had heard his story: "The screen of the occult; the curtain of shadow." We had seen him go. There was an element of horror in the thing, and of fascination. The great professor! The faithful Watson! Where had they gone?

It was not until the color had come back and the blue had regained its luster that either of us looked up. Could such a thing be unraveled? Fenton turned the stone over thoughtfully. He shook his head.

"In that jewel, Harry, lies the secret. I wish I knew a bit more about physics, light, force, energy, vibration. We have got to know."

"Your theory?"

"It still holds good."

I thought.

"Let me get it clear, Hobart. You say

that we catch only certain vibrations."

"That's it. Our eyes are instruments, nothing else. We can see light, but we cannot hear it. We hear sound, but we cannot see it. Of course they are not exactly parallel. But it serves the point. Let us go a bit further. The eye picks up certain ratios. Light is nothing but energy vibrating at a tremendous speed. It has to be just so high for the eye to pick it up. A great deal we do not get. For instance, we can only catch one-twelfth of the solar spectrum. We have been too much from Missouri. We believed only what we could see. Science has pulled us out of the rut. It may pull us through the Blind Spot."

"And beyond."

Hobart held up his hands.

"It is almost too much to believe. We have made a discovery. We must watch our step. We must not lose. The work of Dr. Holcomb shall not go for nothing."

"And the ring?"

He consulted his watch.

"We have only a short time left. We must map our action. We have three things to work on—the ring, the house, Bertha Holcomb. It's all up to you, Harry. Find out all that is possible; but go slow. I shall be in the offing. Trace down that ring; find out everything that you can. Go see Bertha Holcomb. Perhaps she can give you some data. Watson said no; but perhaps you may uncover it. Take the ring to a lapidary; but do not let him cut it. Last of all, and most important, buy the house of the Blind Spot. Draw on me. Let me pay half, anyway."

"I shall move into it," I answered.

He hesitated a bit.

"I am afraid of that," he answered. "Well, if you wish. Only be careful. Remember I shall return just as soon as I can get loose. If you feel yourself slipping or anything happens, cable."

The hours passed all too quickly. When day came we had our breakfast and hurried down to the pier. It was hard to have him go. His last words were like Hobart Fenton. He repeated the warning.

"Watch your step, Harry; watch your step. Take things easy; be cautious. Get the house. Trace down the ring. Be sure of yourself. Keep me informed. If you need me, cable. I'll come if I have to swim."

His last words; and not a year ago. It seems now like a lifetime. As I stood upon the pier and watched the ship slipping into the water, I felt it coming upon me. It had grown steadily, a gloom and oppression not to be thwarted; it is silent and subtle and past defining—like shadow. The gray, heavy heave of the water;

the great hull of the steamer backing into the bay; the gloom of the fog bank. A few uncertain lines, the shrill of the siren, the mist settling; I was alone. It was isolation.

I had been warned by Watson. But I had not guessed. At the moment I sensed it. It was the beginning. Out of my heart I could feel it—solitude.

In the great and populous city I was to be alone, in all its teeming life I was to be a stranger. It has been a year—a year! It has been a lifetime. A breaking down of life!

I have waited and fought and sought to conquer. One cannot fight against shadow. It is merciless and inexorable. There are secrets that may be locked forever. It was my duty, my pledge to Watson, what I owed to the Professor. I have hung on grimly; what the end will be I do not know. I have cabled for Fenton.

CHAPTER XII

A DEAL IN REALTY

BUT to return. There was work that I should do—much work if I was going after the solution. In the first place, there was the house. I turned my back to the waterfront and entered the city. The streets were packed, the commerce of man jostled and threaded along the highways; there was life and action, hope, ambition. It was what I had loved so well. Yet now it was different.

I realized it vaguely, and wondered. This feeling of aloofness? It was intrinsic, coming from within, like the withering of one's marrow. I laughed at my foreboding; it was not natural; I tried to shake myself together.

I had no difficulty with the records. In less than an hour I traced out the owners, "an estate," and had located the agent. It just so happened that he was a man with whom I had some acquaintance. We were not long in coming to business.

"The house at No. 288 Chatterton?"

I noticed that he was startled; there was a bit of wonder in his look—a quizzical alertness. He motioned me to a chair and closed the door.

"Sit down, Mr. Wendel; sit down. H-m! The house at No. 288 Chatterton? Did I hear you right?"

Again I noted the wonder; his manner was cautious and curious. I nodded.

"Want to buy it or just lease it? Pardon me, but you are sort of a friend. I would not like to lose your friendship for the sake of a mere sale. What is your—"

"Just for a residence," I assisted. "A place to live in."

"I see. Know anything about this place?"

"Do you?"

He fumbled with some papers. For an agent he did not strike me as being very solicitous for a commission.

"Well," he said, "in a way, yes. A whole lot more than I'd like to. It all depends. One gets much from hearsay. What I know is mostly rumor." He began marking with a pencil. "Of course I don't believe it. Nevertheless I would hardly recommend it to a friend as a residence."

"And these rumors?"

He looked up; for a moment he studied; then:

"Ever hear of the Blind Spot? Perhaps you remember Dr. Holcomb—in 1905, before the quake. It was a murder. The papers were full of it at the time; since then it has been occasionally featured in the supplements. I do not believe in the story; but I can trust to facts. The last seen of Dr. Holcomb was in this house. It is called the Blind Spot."

"Then you believe in the story?" I asked.

He looked at me.

"Oh, you know it, eh? No, I do not. It's all buncomb; reporters' work and exaggeration. If you like that kind of stuff, it is weird and interesting. But it hurts property. The man was undoubtedly murdered. The tale hangs over the house. It is impossible to dispose of the place."

"Then why not sell it to me?"

He dropped his pencil; he was a bit nervous.

"A fair question, Mr. Wendel—a very fair question. Well, now, why don't I? Perhaps I shall. There's no telling. But I'd rather not. Do you know, a year ago I would have jumped at an offer. Fact is, I did lease it—the lease ran out yesterday —to a man named Watson. I don't believe a thing in this nonsense; but what I have seen during the past year has tested my nerve considerably."

"What about Watson?"

"Watson? A year ago he came to see me in regard to this Chatterton property. Wanted to lease it. Was interested in the case of Dr. Holcomb; asked for a year's rental and the privilege of renewal. I don't know. I gave it to him; but when he drops in again I am going to fight almighty hard against letting him hold it longer."

"Why?"

"Why? Why, because I don't believe in murder. A year ago he came to me the healthiest and happiest man I ever saw; today he is a shadow. I watched that boy go down. Understand, I don't believe a damn word I'm saying; but I have seen it. It's that cursed house. I say no, when I reason; but it keeps on my nerves; it's on my conscience. It is insidious. Every month when he came here I could see disintegration. One year ago he was an athlete; today he is a shadow. There is nothing left of the boy but a soul. It is pitiful to see a young man stripped of life like that; forlorn, hopeless, gone. He has never told me what it is; but I have wondered. A battle; some conflict with—there I go again. It's on my nerves, I tell you, on my nerves. If this keeps up I'll burn it."

IT WAS a bit foreboding. Already I could feel the tugging at my heart that had done for Watson. This man had watched my friend slipping into the shadow; I had come to take his place.

"Watson has gone," I said simply; "that's why I am here."

He straightened up.

"You know him then. He was not—"

"He went last night; he has left the country. He was in very poor health. That's why I am here. I knew very well the cloud that hangs over the property; it is my sole reason for purchasing."

"You don't believe in this nonsense?"

I smiled. Certainly the man was perverse in his agnosticism; he was stubborn in disbelief. It was on his nerves; on his conscience; he was afraid.

"I believe nothing," I answered; "neither do I disbelieve. I know all the story that has been told or written. I am a friend of Watson. You need not scruple in making me out a bill of sale. It's my own funeral. I abide by the consequences."

He gave a sigh of relief. After all, he was human. He had honor; but it was after the brand of Pontius Pilate. He wished nothing on his conscience.

Armed with the keys and the legal title, I took possession. In the daylight it was much as it had been the night before. Once across its threshold, one was in dank and furtive suppression; the air was heavy; a mold of age had streaked the walls and gloomed the shadows. I put up all the curtains to let in the rush of sunlight, likewise I opened the windows. If there is anything to beat down sin, it is the open measure of broad daylight.

The house was well situated; from the front windows one could look down the street and out at the blue bay beyond the city. The fog had lifted and the sun was shining upon the water. I could make out the ferryboats, the islands, and the long piers that lead to Oakland, and still farther beyond the hills of Berkeley. It was a long time since those days in college. Under the shadow of those hills

I had first met the old doctor. I was only a boy then.

I could not but think of that day in Ethics 2b. I had doubted then, and had been a bit of a skeptic. With the clutch at my heart-strings I could now sense the truth that had weighted the wisdom of Dr. Holcomb. It was foreboding; there is not a thing on earth as terrible as loneliness and isolation. I turned into the building. Even the sound of my footsteps was foreign; the whole place was pregnant with stillness and shadow; life was gone out. It was fearful; I felt the terror clutching upon me, a grimness that may not be spoken; there was something breaking within me. I had pledged myself for a year. Frankly I was afraid.

But I had given my word. I returned to my apartments and began that very day the closing out of my practice. In a fortnight I had completed everything and had moved my things to the room of Chick Watson.

CHAPTER XIII

ALBERT JEROME

JUST as soon as possible I hurried over to Berkeley. I went straight to the bungalow on Dwight Way; I inquired for Miss Holcomb. She was a young woman, now in her twenties, decidedly pretty, a blonde, and of the intelligent bearing that one would expect in the daughter of the professor.

Coming on such an errand, I was at a loss just how to approach her. I noted the little lines about the corners of her eyes, the sad droop of her pretty mouth. Plainly she was worried. As I was removing my hat she caught sight of the ring upon my finger.

"Oh," she said; "then you come from Mr. Watson. How is Chick?"

"Mr. Watson"—I did not like lying, but I could not but feel for her; she had already lost her father—"Mr. Watson has gone on a trip up-country—with Jerome. He was not feeling well. He has left this ring with me. I have come for a bit of information."

She bit her lips; her mouth quivered.

"Could you not get this from Mr. Watson? He knows about the stone. Did he not tell you? How came it into your possession? What has happened?"

Her voice was querulous and suspicious. I had endeavored to deceive her for her own sake; she had suffered enough already. I could not but wince at the pain in her beautiful blue eyes. She stood up.

"Please, Mr. Wendel; do not be clumsy. Do not regard me as a mere baby. Tell me what has happened to Chick. Please—"

She stopped in a flow of emotion. Tears came to her eyes; but she held control. She sat down.

"Tell me all, Mr. Wendel. It is what I expected." She blinked to hold back her tears. "It is my fault. You would not have the ring had nothing happened. Tell me. I shall be brave."

And brave she was—splendid. With the tug at my own heart I could understand her. What an uncertainty and dread she must have been under! I had been in it but a few days; already I could feel the weight. At no time could I surmount the isolation; there was something going from me minute by minute. With the girl there could be no evasion; it were better that she have the truth. I made a clean breast of the whole affair.

"And he told you no more about the ring?"

"That is all," I answered. "He would have told us much more, undoubtedly, had he not—"

She gulped back her sorrow; she was under a brave control.

"You saw him go—you saw this thing?"

"That is just it, Miss Holcomb. We saw nothing. One minute we were looking at Chick, and the next at nothing. Hobart understood it better than I. At least he forbade my crossing the room. There is a danger point, a spot that may not be crossed. He threw me back. It was then that the Rhamda came upon the scene."

She frowned slightly.

"This Rhamda. He is the great man papa was to have for luncheon. I am afraid; sometimes I fear that papa was the victim of plain villainy. But I would not say so. Most of the time I think that he made a great discovery; this Rhamda, he holds the secret; perhaps for our own good. Somehow I am afraid of the occult. Do you blame the Rhamda?"

"To a certain extent," I answered. "He is certainly a prime factor; whether his presence that night had aught to do with the miracle or was just accidental, I cannot say. But I do know that both he and the Nervina are concerned over the ring."

She arched her eyebrows.

"Tell me about the Nervina. When Chick spoke of her, I could always feel jealous. Is she beautiful?"

"Most beautiful, the most wonderful girl I have ever seen, though I would hardly class her as one to be jealous of. She is above that. She is vital and super-beauty; but she is not evil. If I would take her at her word, she is the maiden of the moonbeams; but I am not sure that I was not dreaming. Above all she wants the ring. I have promised Watson, and of course I shall keep it. But I would like its history."

"I think I can give you some information there," she answered. "The ring, or rather the jewel, was given to papa about twenty years ago by a Mr. Kennedy. He had been a scholar of papa's back in Chillicothe, Ohio, when papa taught district school. He came here often in those days to talk over old times. Papa had the jewel set in a ring; but he never wore it."

"Why?"

"I do not know."

"How did Watson come to link it up with the Blind Spot?"

"That, I think, was an accident. He was in college, you know, at the time of father's disappearance. In fact, he was in Ethics 2b. I was attending high school. Our love was just in its inception. He came here often, and during one of his visits I showed him the ring. That was several years ago."

"I see."

"Well, about a year ago he was here again, and asked to see the jewel. We were to be married, you understand; but I had always put it off because of father. Somehow I felt that he would return. It was in the late summer, about September; it was in the evening; it was getting dark. I gave Chick the ring, and stepped into the garden to cut some flowers. I know it was in the evening because I had such difficulty in selecting the blossoms. I remember that Chick struck a match in the parlor. When I came back he seemed to be excited."

"Did he ask you for the ring?"

"Yes. He wanted to wear it. And he suddenly began to talk of papa. It was that night that he took it upon himself to find him."

"I see. Not before that night? Did he take the ring then?"

"Yes. We went to the opera. I remember it well, because that night was the first time I ever knew Chick to be gloomy."

"Ah!"

"Yes. You know how jolly he always was. When we returned that night he would scarcely say a word. I thought he was sick; but he said he was not; said he just felt that way."

"I understand. And he kept getting glummer? Did you suspect the jewel? Did he ever tell you anything?"

She shook her head.

"No. He told me nothing, except that he would find papa. Of course, I became excited and wanted to know. But he insisted that I could not help; that he had a clue, and that it might take time. From that night I saw very little of him. He leased the house on Chatterton Place. He seemed to lose interest in myself; when he did come over he would act queerly. He talked incoherently, and would often make rambling mention of a beautiful girl called Nervina. You say it is the ring? Tell me, Mr. Wendel, what is it? Has it really anything to do with papa?"

I nodded.

"I think it has, Miss Holcomb. And I can understand poor Chick. He is a very brave man. It is a strange jewel and of terrible potence; that much I know. It devitalizes; it destroys. I can feel it already. It covers life with the fog of decay. The same solitude has come upon myself. Nevertheless I am certain it has much to do with the Blind Spot. It is a key of some sort. The very interest of the Rhamda and the Nervina tells us that. I think it was through this stone that your father made his discovery."

She thought a moment.

"Had you not better return it? It is really terrible, Mr. Wendel. You are a strong man. While you still have health? If you keep it, it will be only one more."

"You forget, Miss Holcomb, my promise to Chick. I loved your father, and I loved Watson. It is a great secret, and, if the professor is right, one which man has sought through the ages. I would be a coward to forego my duty. If I fail I have another to take my place."

"Oh," she said, "it is horrible. First papa; then Chick; now it is you; and afterward it will be Mr. Fenton."

"It is our duty," I returned. "One by one. Though we fail, each one of us may pass a bit more on to his successor. In the end we win. It is the way of man."

I HAD my way. She turned over all the data and notes that had been left by the professor; but I had never found a thing in them that could be construed to an advantage. My real quest was to trace down the jewel. The man Kennedy's full name was, I learned, Wudge Kennedy. He had lived in Oakland. It was late in the afternoon when I parted with Miss Holcomb and started for the city.

I remember it well because of a little incident that occurred immediately after our parting. I was just going down the steps when I looked up one of the side streets. It was flanked by fraternity houses. A few students were loitering here and there. But there was one who was not a student. I recognized him instantly, and I wondered. It was the Rhamda. This was enough to make me suspicious. But there was one thing more. Farther up the street was another figure.

When I came down the steps the Rhamda moved, and his move was somehow duplicated by the other. In itself this was enough to clear up some of my doubts concerning the fantom. His actions were too simple for an apparition. Only a man could act like that, and a crude one. I did not know then the nerve of the Rhamda. There was no doubt that I was being shadowed.

To make certain, I took the by-streets and meandered by a devious route to the station. There was no question; one and two they followed. I knew the Rhamda; but who was the other?

At the station we purchased tickets, and when the train pulled in I boarded the smoker. The other two took another coach—the stranger was a thick-set individual with a stubby, gray mustache. On the boat I did not see them; but at the ferry building I made a test to see that I was followed. I hailed a taxi and gave specific instructions to the driver.

"Drive slowly," I told him "I think we shall be followed."

And I was right; in a few minutes there were two cars dogging our wheel-tracks. I had no doubt concerning the Rhamda; but I could not understand the other. At No. 288 Chatterton we stopped, and I alighted. The Rhamda's car passed, then the other. Neither stopped. Both disappeared about the corner. I took the numbers; then I went into the house. In about a half hour a car drew up at the curb. I stepped to the window. It was the car that had tracked the Rhamda's. The stubby individual stepped out; without ceremony he ran up the steps and opened the door. It was a bit disconcerting, I think, for both. He was plain and blunt—and honest.

"Well," he said, "where's Watson? Who are you? What do you want?"

"That," I answered, "is a question for both of us. Who are you, and what do you want? Where is Watson?"

Just then his eyes dropped and his glance fell on the ring. His jaw fell and his eyes widened.

"My name is Jerome," he said simply. "Has something happened to Watson? Who are you?"

We were standing in the library; I made an indication toward the other room. "In there," I said. "My name is Wendel."

He took off his hat and ran the back of his hand across his forehead.

"So that pair got him, too! I was afraid of them all the while. And I had to be away. Do you know how they did it? What's the working of their game? It's almighty devilish and certainly clever. They played that boy for a year; they knew they would get him in the end. So did I.

"He was a fine lad, a fine lad. I knew this morning when I came down from Nevada that they had him. Found your duds. A stranger. House looked queer. But I had hopes that he may have gone over to see his girl. Just thought I'd wander over to Berkeley. Found that bird Rhamda under a palm tree watching the Holcomb bungalow. It was the first time I'd seen him since that day that things went amiss with the professor. In about ten minutes you came out. I stayed with him while he tracked you back here. I followed him back down-town and lost him. Tell me about Watson."

HE SAT down; during my recital he spoke not a word. He consumed one cigar after another; when I stopped for a moment he merely nodded his head and waited until I continued. He was sturdy and frank, of an iron way and vast common sense. I liked him. When I had finished he remained silent; his grief was of a solid kind; he had liked poor Watson.

"I see," he said. "It is as I thought. He told you more than he ever told me."

"He never told you?"

"Not much. He was a strange lad—about the loneliest one I have ever seen. There was something about him from the very first that was not natural; I could not make him out. You say it is the ring. He always wore it. I laid it to this Rhamda. He was always meeting him. I could never understand it. Try as I would, I could not get a trace of the fantom."

"The fantom?"

"Most assuredly. Would you call him human?" His gray eyes were flecked with light. "Come now, Mr. Wendel, would you?"

"Well," I answered, "I don't know. Not after what I have seen. But for all that, I have proof of his sinews. I am inclined to blend the two. There is a law somewhere, a very natural one. The Blind Spot is undoubtedly a combination of phenomena; it has a control. We do not know what it is, or where it leads to; neither do we know the motive of the Rhamda. Who is he? If we knew that, we would know everything."

"And this ring?"

"I shall wear it."

"Then God help you. I watched Watson. It's plain poison. You have a year; but you had better count on six months. We must look up this Wudge Kennedy. He gave the jewel to the professor. But the doctor did not wear it. Not so you could notice. You had better count on half a year; the first six months are not so bad; but the last—it takes a man! Wendel, it takes a man! Already you are eating your heart out. Oh, I know— you have opened the windows; you want sunshine and air. In six months I shall have to fight to get one open. It gets into the soul; it is stagnation; you die by inches. Better give me the ring."

"This Wudge Kennedy," I evaded, "we must find him. We have time. One clue may lead us on. Tell me what you know of the Blind Spot."

"Very easy," he answered; "you have it all. I have been here a number of years. You will remember I fell into the case through intuition. I have never had any definite proof, outside the professor's disappearance, the old lady, and that bell; unless perhaps it is the Rhamda. But from the beginning I have been positive.

"Taking that lecture in ethics as a starter, I built up my theory. There is a Blind Spot. We have that from the professor. All the clues lead to this building. It is something that I cannot understand. It is out of the occult. It is a bit too much for me. I moved into the place and waited. I have never forgotten that bell, nor the old lady. You and Fenton are the only ones who have seen the Blind Spot."

I had a sudden thought.

"The Rhamda! I have read that he has the manner of inherent goodness. Is it true? You have conversed with him. I have not had the pleasure."

"He has. He did not strike me as a villain. He is intrinsic, noble, out of self. I have often wondered."

I smiled. "Perhaps we are thinking the same thing. Is this it? The Blind Spot is a secret that man may not attain to. It is unknowable and akin to death. The Rhamda knows it. He could not head off the professor. It is something that must be held from mankind. He has simply employed Dr. Holcomb's wisdom to trap him; now that he has him secure, he intends to hold him. It is for our own good."

"Exactly. Yet—"

"Yet?"

"He was very anxious to put you and Fenton into this very Spot."

"That is so. But may it not be that we, too, knew a bit too much?"

He could not answer that.

Nevertheless, we were both of us convinced concerning the Rhamda. It was merely a digression of thought, a conjecture. He might be good; but we were both positive of his villainy. It was his motive, of course, that weighed up his character; could we find that, we would uncover everything.

CHAPTER XIV

A NEW ELEMENT

WUDGE KENNEDY was not so easily found. There were many Kennedys. About two-thirds of Ireland had apparently migrated to San Francisco under that name and had lodged in the directory. Of course Wudge was an uncommon name. We went through the lists on both sides of the bay, but found nothing; the old directories had mostly been destroyed by fire or had been thrown away as worthless; but at last we unearthed one. In it we found the name of Wudge Kennedy.

He had two sons—Patrick and Henry. One of these, Hank, we ran down in the Mission. He was a great, red-headed, broad-shouldered Irishman. He was just eating supper when we called; there were splotches of white plaster on his trousers.

I came right to the point: "Do you know anything about this?" I held out the ring.

He took it in his fingers; his eyes popped. "What, that! Well, I guess I do! Where'd you get it?" He called out to the kitchen: "Say, Mollie, come here. Here's the old man's jool!" He looked at me a bit fearfully. "You are not wearing it?"

"Why not?" I asked.

"Why? Well, I don't know exactly. I wouldn't wear it for a million dollars. It ain't a jool; it's a piece of the divil. The old man gave it to Dr. Holcomb—or sold it, I don't know which. He carried it in his pocket once, and he came near dying."

"Unlucky?" I asked.

"No, it ain't unlucky; it just rips your heart out. It would make you hate your grandmother. Lonesome! Lonesome! I've often heard the old man talking."

"He sold it to Dr. Holcomb? Do you know why?"

"Well, yes. 'Twas that the old doc had some scientific work. Dad told him about his jool. One day he took it over to Berkeley. It was some kind of thing that the professor just wanted. He kept it. Dad made him promise not to wear it."

"I see. Did your father ever tell you where he got it?"

"Oh, yes. He often spoke about that. The old man wasn't a plasterer, you know—just a laborer. He was digging a basement. I was only a kid then. It was a funny basement—a sort of blind cellar. There was a stone wall right across the middle, and then there was a door of wood to look like stone. You can go down into the back cellar, but not into the front. If you don't know about the door, you will never find it. Dad often spoke about that. He was working in the back cellar when he found this. 'Twas sticking in some blue clay."

"Where was this place? Do you remember?"

"Sure. 'Twas up on Chatterton Place. Pat and I was kids then; we took the old man's dinner."

"Do you know the number?"

"It didn't have no number; but I know the place. 'Tis a two-story house, and was built in 'ninety-one."

I nodded. "And afterward you moved to Oakland?"

"Yes."

"Did your father ever speak of the reason for this partition?"

"He never knew of one. It was none of his business. He was merely a laborer, and did what he was paid for."

"Do you know who built it?"

"Some old guy. He was a cranky cuss with side-burns. He used to wear a stove-pipe hat. I think he was a chemist. Whenever he showed up he would run us kids out of the building. I think he was a bachelor."

This was all the information he could give, but it was a great deal. Certainly it was more than I had hoped for. The house had been built by a chemist; even in the construction there was mystery. I had never thought of a second cellar; when I had explored the building I had taken the stone wall for granted. It was so with Jerome. It was the first definite clue that really brought us down to earth. What had this chemist to do with the phenomena?

After all, back of everything was lurking the mind of man.

We hastened back to the house and into the cellar. By merely sounding along the wall we discovered the door; it was cleverly constructed and for a time defied our efforts; but Jerome cut it open by means of a jimmy and a pick. The outside was a clever piece of sham work shaped like stone and smeared over with cement. In the dim light we had missed it. We had high expectations.

But we were disappointed. The apartment contained nothing; it was smeared with cobwebs and hairy mold; but outside of a few empty bottles and the gloomy darkness there was nothing. We tapped the walls and floor and ceiling. Beyond all the doubt the place once held a secret; if it held it still, it was cleverly hidden. After an hour or two of search we returned to the upper part of the building.

JEROME was not discouraged.

"We are on the right track, Mr. Wendel; if we can only get started. I have an idea. This chemist—it was in 'ninety-one—that's more than twenty years."

"What is your idea?"

"The Rhamda. What is the first thing that strikes you? His age. With every one that sees him it is the same. First a certainty of years, then a flitting notion of youth. He is elusive. At first you take him for an old man; if you study him long enough, you are positive that he is in his twenties. May he not be this chemist?"

"What becomes of the doctor and his Blind Spot?"

"The Blind Spot," answered Jerome, "is merely a part of the chemistry."

I whistled. The thing was getting devilish.

Next day I hunted up a jeweler. I was careful to choose one with whom I was acquainted. I asked for a private consultation. When we were alone I took the ring from my finger.

"Just an opinion," I asked. "You know gems. Can you tell me anything about this one?"

He picked it up casually, and turned it over; his mouth puckered. For a minute he studied.

"That? Well, now." He held it up. "Humph. Wait a minute."

"Is it a gem?"

"I think it is. At first I thought I knew it right off; but now—wait a minute."

He reached in the drawer for his glass. He held the stone up for some minutes. His face was a study; queer little wrinkles twisting from the corners of his eyes told his wonder. He did not speak; merely turned the stone round and round. At last he removed his glass and held up the ring. He was quizzical.

"Where did you get this?" he asked.

"That is something I do not care to answer. I wish to know what it is. Is it a gem? If so, what kind?"

He thought a moment and shook his head.

"I had thought I knew every gem on

39

earth. But I don't know. This is a new one. It is beautiful—just a moment." He stepped to the door. In a moment another man stepped in. The jeweler motioned toward the ring. The man picked it up and again the examination. At last he laid the glass and the ring both upon the table.

"What do you make of it, Henry?" asked the jeweler.

"Not me," answered the second one. "Never saw one like it."

It was as Watson had said. No man had ever identified the jewel. The two men were puzzled; they were interested. The jeweler turned to me.

"Would you care to leave it with us for a bit; you have no objection to us taking it out of the ring?"

I had not thought of that. I had business down the street. I consulted my watch.

"In half an hour I shall be back. Will that time be sufficient?"

"I think so."

It was an hour before I returned. The assistant was standing at the door of the office. He spoke something to the one inside and then made an indication to myself. He seemed excited; when I came closer I noted that his face was full of wonder.

"We have been waiting," said he, "for almost an hour; we did not examine the stone; it was not necessary. It is truly wonderful." He was a short, squat man with a massive forehead. "Just step inside."

Inside the office the jeweler was sitting beside a table; he was leaning back in his chair; he had his hands clasped over his stomach. He was gazing toward the ceiling; his face was a bit of a study, full of wonder and speculation.

"Well?" I asked.

For answer he merely elevated his finger; he pointed toward the ceiling.

"Up there," he spoke. "Your jewel or whatever it is. 'Tis a good thing we were not in the open air. 'Twould be going yet."

I looked up. Sure enough. Against the ceiling was the gem. It was a bit disconcerting; though I will confess that in the first moment I did not catch the full significance.

The jeweler closed one eye and studied first myself and then the beautiful thing against the ceiling.

"What do you make of it?" he asked.

Really, I had not made anything; it was a bit of a shock; I had not grasped the full impossibility. I did not answer.

"Don't you see, Mr. Wendel? Impossible! Contrary to nature! Lighter than air. We took it out of the ring and it popped out like a bullet. Thought I'd dropped it. Began looking on the floor. Could not find it; looked up and saw Reynolds, here, with his eyes popping out like marbles. He was looking at the ceiling."

" 'There's your jewel up there,' he says, 'on the ceiling.' "

I thought a moment.

"Then it is not a gem?"

He shrugged his shoulders. "Not if I am a jeweler. Who ever heard of a stone without weight? It has no gravity, that is, apparently. I doubt whether it is a substance. I don't know what it is."

It was puzzling. I would have given a good deal just then for a few words with Dr. Holcomb. The man, Kennedy, had kept it in his pocket? How had he held it prisoner? The professor had had use for it in some scientific work! No wonder! Certainly it was not a jewel. What could it be? It was solid. It was lighter than air. Could it be a substance? If not; what was it?

"What would you advise?"

In answer the jeweler reached for the telephone. He gave a number.

"Hello. Say, is Ed there? This is Phil. Tell him to step to the phone. Hello! Say, Ed, I want you to come over on the jump. Something to show you. Too busy? No, you're not. Not for this. I'm going to teach you some chemistry. No; this is serious. What is it? I don't know. What's lighter than air? Lots of things? Oh, I know. But what solid? That's why I'm asking. Come over. All right. At once."

He hung up the receiver.

"My brother," he spoke. "It has passed beyond my province and into his. He is a chemist. As an expert he may give you a real opinion."

Surely we needed one. It was against reason. It had taken me completely off my feet. I took a chair and joined the others in the contemplation of that blue dot upon the ceiling. We could speculate and conjecture; but there was not one of us deep enough to even start a theory. Plainly it was what should not be. We had been taught physics and science; we had been drilled to fundamentals. This went back of our beginnings. If this thing could be, then the foundations upon which we stood were shattered. But one little law! Back in my mind was buzzing the enigma of the Blind Spot. They were woven together. Some law that had eluded the ken of mankind.

THE chemist was a tall man with a hook nose and black eyes that clinched like rivets. He was a bit impatient. He looked keenly at his brother. "Well, Phil, what is it?" He pulled out a watch. "I haven't much time."

There was a contrast between them. The jeweler was fat and complacent. He merely sat in his chair, his hand on his waistband and a stubby finger elevated toward the jewel. He seemed to enjoy it.

"You're a chemist, Ed. Here's a test for your wisdom. Can you explain that? No, over here. Above your head. That jewel?"

The other looked up.

"What's the idea? New notion for decoration? Or"—a bit testily—"is this a joke?" He was a serious man; his black eyes and the nose spoke his character.

The jeweler laughed gently.

"Listen, Ed—" Then he went into explanation; when he was through the chemist was twitching with excitement.

"Get me a ladder. Here, let me get upon the table; perhaps I can reach it. Sounds impossible, but if it's so, it's so; it must have an explanation."

Without ado and in spite of the protests of his brother he stepped upon the polished surface of the table. He was a tall man; he could just barely reach it with the tip of his finger. He could move it; but each time it clung as to a magnet. After a minute of effort he gave it up. When he looked down he was a different man; his black eyes glowed with wonder.

"Can't make it," he said. "Get a stepladder. Strange!"

With the ladder it was easy. He plucked it off the ceiling. We pressed about the table. The chemist turned it about with his fingers.

"I wonder," he was saying. "It's a gem. Apparently. You say it has no gravity. It can't be. Whoop!" He had let it slip out of his fingers. Again it popped on its way to the ceiling. He caught it with a deft movement of his hand. "The devil! Did you ever see! And a solid! Who owns this?"

That brought it back to me. I explained what I could of the manner of my possession.

"I see. It is very interesting. Something I have never seen—and—frankly—something strictly against what I've been taught. Nevertheless, it is not impossible. We are witnesses at least. There are many things that we do not know. Would you care if I take this over to the laboratory?"

It was a new complication. If it were not a jewel there was a chance of its being damaged. I was as anxious as he; but I had been warned as to its possession.

"I shall not harm it. I shall see to that. I have suspicions and I'd like to verify them. A chemist does not blunder across such a thing every day. I am a chemist." His eyes glistened.

"Your suspicions?" I asked.

"A new element."

This gem. A new element. Perhaps that would explain the Blind Spot. It was not exactly of earth. Everything had confirmed it.

"You— A new element? How do you account for it? It defies your laws. Most of your elements are evolved through tedious process. This is picked up by chance."

"That is so. But there are still a thousand ways. A meteor, perhaps; a bit of cosmic dust—there are many shattered comets. Our chemistry is earthly. There are undoubtedly new elements that we do not know of. Perhaps in enormous proportion."

I let him have it. It was the only night I had been away from the ring. I may say that it is the only time I have ever been free from its isolation.

WHEN I called at his office next day I found that he had merely confirmed his suspicions. It defied analysis; there was no reaction. Under all tests it was a stranger. The whole science that had been built up to explain everything had here explained nothing. However there was one thing that he had uncovered—heat. Perhaps I should say magnetism. It was cold to man. I have spoken about the icy blue of its color. It was cold even to look at. The chemist placed it in my hand.

"Is it not so?"

It was. The minute it touched my palm I could sense the weird horror of the isolation; the stone was cold. Like a piece of ice.

This was the first time I had ever had it in direct contact with the flesh. Set in the ring its impulse had always been secondary.

"You notice it? It is so with me. Now then. Just a minute."

He pressed a button. A young lady answered his ring; she glanced first at myself and then at the chemist.

"Miss Mills, this is Mr. Wendel He is the owner of the gem. Would you take it in your hand?

"And please tell Mr. Wendel how it feels—"

She laughed; she was a bit perplexed.

"I do not understand"—she turned to me—"we had the same dispute yesterday. See, Mr. White, says that it is cold; but it is not. It is warm; almost burning.

All the other girls think just as I do."

"And all the men as I do," averred the chemist, "even Mr. Wendel."

"Is it cold to you?" she asked. "Really—"

It was a turn I had not looked for. It was akin to life—this relation to sex. Could it account for the strange isolation and the weariness? I was a witness to its potence. Watson! I could feel myself dragging under. I had just one question:

"Tell me, Miss Mills. Can you sense anything else; I mean beyond its temperature?"

She smiled a bit. "I don't know what you mean exactly. It is a beautiful stone. I would like to have it."

"You think its possession would make you happy?"

Her eyes sparkled.

"Oh," she exclaimed, "I know it would! I can feel it!"

It was so. Whatever there was in the bit of sapphirine blue, it had life. What was it? It had relation to sex. In the strict line of fact it was impossible.

When we were alone again I turned to the chemist.

"Is there anything more that you uncovered? Did you see anything in the stone?"

He frowned. "No. Nothing else. This magnetism is the only thing. Is there anything more?"

Now I had not said anything about its one great quality. He had not stumbled across the image of the two men. I could not understand it. I did not tell him. Perhaps I was wrong. Down inside me I sensed a subtle reason for secrecy. It is hard to explain. It was not perverseness; it was a finer distinction; perhaps it was the influence of the gem. I took it back to the jeweler again and had it reset.

CHAPTER XV

AGAIN THE NERVINA

IT WAS at this point that I began taking notes. There is something psychological to the Blind Spot, weird and touching on to the spirit. I know not what it is; but I can feel it. It impinges on to life. I can sense the ecstasy of horror. I am not afraid. Whatever it is that is dragging me down, it is not evil. My sensations are not normal.

For the benefit of my successor, if there is to be one, I have made an elaborate detail of notes and comments. After all, the whole thing, when brought down to the end, must fall to the function of science. When Hobart arrives, whatever my fate, he will find a complete and comprehensive record of my sensations. I shall keep it up to the end. Such notes being dry and sometimes confusing I have purposely omitted them from this narrative. But there are some things that must be given to the world. I shall pick out the salient parts and give them chronologically.

Jerome stayed with me. Rather I should say he spent the nights with me. Most of the time he was on the elusive trail of the Rhamda. From the minute of our conversation with Kennedy he held to one conviction. He was positive of that chemist back in the nineties. He was certain of the Rhamda. Whatever the weirdness of his theory it would certainly bear investigation. To myself it is too much of Ponce de Leon. Perhaps I might say—of the devil. But Jerome stayed with it. When he was not on the trail over the city he was at work in the cellar. Here we worked together.

We dug up the concrete floor and did a bit of mining. I was interested in the formation.

From the words of Wudge Kennedy the bit of jewel had been discovered at the original excavation. We found the blue clay that he spoke of, but nothing else. Jerome dissected every bit of earth carefully. We have spent many hours in that cellar.

But most of the time I was alone. When not too worn with the loneliness and weariness I worked at my notes. It has been a hard task from the beginning. Inertia, lack of energy! How much of our life is impulse! What is the secret that backs volition? It has been will—willpower from the beginning. I must thank my ancestors. Without the strength and character built up through generations, I would have succumbed utterly.

Even as it is I sometimes think I am wrong in following the dictate of Watson. If I was only sure. I have pledged my word and my honor. What did he know? I need all the reserve of character to hold up against the Nervina. From the beginning she has been my opponent. What is her interest in the Blind Spot, and myself? Who is she? I cannot think of her as evil. She is too beautiful, too tender; her concern is so real. Sometimes I think of her as my protector, that it is she, and she alone, who holds back the power which would engulf me. Once she made a personal appeal.

Jerome had gone. I was alone. I had dragged myself to the desk and my notes and data. It was along toward spring and in the first shadows of the early evening. I had turned on the lights. It was the first labor I had done for several days. I had a great deal of work before me. I had begun some time before to take down my temperature. I was careful of everything now, as much as I could be under the depression. So far I had discerned nothing that could be classed as pathologic.

There is something subtle about the Nervina. She is much like the Rhamda. Perhaps they are the same. I heard no sound. I have no notion of a door or entrance. Watson had said of the Rhamda, "Sometimes you see him, sometimes you don't." It is so with the Nervina. I remember only my working at the data and the sudden movement of a hand upon my desk—a girl's hand. It was bewildering. I looked up.

I had not seen her since that night. It was now eight months—did I not know, I would have recorded them as years. Her expression was a bit more sad—and beautiful. The same wonderful glow of her eyes, night-black, and tender; the softness that comes from passion, and love, and virtue. The same wistful droop of the perfect mouth. What a wondrous mass of hair she had! From the first I had been struck with her beauty—the lines of her face and figure—the longing that could not be suppressed—something elusive and ethereal. I dropped my pen. She took my hand. I could sense the thrill of contact; cool and magnetic.

"Harry!"

She said no more; I did not answer; I was too taken by surprise and wonder. She was far above all women; there was such a tenderness in her eyes and such a pity. She was as the Rhamda; she was different. I could feel her concern as I would a mother's. What was her interest in myself? The contact of her hand sent a strange pulse through my vitals; she was so beautiful. Could it be? Watson had said he loved her. Could I blame him?

"Harry," she asked, "how long is it to continue?"

SO THAT was it. Merely an envoy to accept surrender. I was worn utterly, weary of the world, lonely. But I had not given up. I had strength still, and will enough to hold out to the end. Perhaps I was wrong. If I gave her the ring—what then?

"I am afraid," I answered, "that it must go on. I have given my word. It has been much harder than I had expected. This jewel? What has it to do with the Blind Spot?"

"It controls it."

"Does the Rhamda desire it?"

"He does."

"Why does he not call for it person-ally? Why does he not make a clean breast of it? It would be much easier. He knows and you know that I am after Dr. Holcomb and Watson. I might even forego the secret. Would he release the doctor?"

"No, Harry, he would not."

"I see. If I gave up the ring it would be merely for my personal safety. I am a coward—"

"Oh," she said, "do not say that. You must give the ring to me—not to the Rhamda. It must not control the Blind Spot."

"What is the Blind Spot? Tell me."

"Harry," she spoke, "I cannot. It is not for you or any other mortal. It is a secret that should never have been uncovered. It might be the end. In the hands of the Rhamda it would certainly be the end of mankind."

"Who is the Rhamda? Who are you? You are too beautiful to be merely woman. Are you a spirit?"

She pressed my hand ever so slightly. "Do I feel like a spirit? I am material as much as you are. We live, see—everything."

"But you are not of this world?"

Her eyes grew sadder; a soft longing.

"Not exactly, Harry, not exactly. It is a long story and a very strange one. I may not tell you. It is for your own good. I am your friend"—her eyes were moist —"I—don't you see? Boy, I would save you!"

I did not doubt it. Somehow she was like a girl of dreams, pure as an angel; her wistfulness only deepened her beauty. It came like a shock at the moment. I could love this woman. She was —what was I thinking? My guilty mind ran back to Charlotte. I had loved her since boyhood. I would be a coward— then a wild fear. Perhaps of jealousy.

"The Rhamda? Is he your husband? You are the same—"

"Oh," she answered, "why do you say it?" Her eyes snapped and she grew rigid. "The Rhamda! My husband! If you only knew. I hate him! We are enemies. It was he who opened the Blind Spot. I am here because he is evil. To watch him. I love your world, I love it all. I would save it. I love—"

She dropped her head. Whatever she was, she was not above sobbing. What was the history of this beautiful girl? Who was she?

I touched her hair; it was of the softest texture I have ever seen; the luster was like all the beauty of night woven into silk. She loved, loved; I could love— I was on the point of surrender.

"Tell me," I asked, "just one thing

43

more. If I give you this ring would you save the doctor and Chick Watson?"

She raised her head; her eyes glistened; but she did not answer.

"Would you?"

She shook her head. "I cannot," she answered. "That cannot be. I can only save you for—for—Charlotte."

Was it vanity in myself? I do not know. It seemed to me that it was hard for her to say it. Frankly, I loved her. I knew it. I loved Charlotte. I loved them both. But I held to my purpose.

"Are the professor and Watson living?"

"They are."

"Are they conscious?"

She nodded. "Harry," she said, "I can tell you that. They are living and conscious. You have seen them. They have only one enemy—the Rhamda. But they must never come out of the Blind Spot. I am their friend and yours."

A sudden courage came upon me. I remembered my word to Watson. I had loved the old professor. I would save them. If necessary I would follow to the end. Either myself or Fenton. One of us would solve it!

"I shall keep the ring," I said. "I shall avenge them. Somehow, somewhere, I feel that I shall do it. Even if I must follow—"

She straightened at that. Her eyes were frightened.

"Oh," she said, "why do you say it? It must not be! You would perish! You shall not do it! I must save you. You must not go alone. Three—it may not be. If you go, I go with you. Pardon my excitement; but I know. Perhaps—oh, Harry!"

She dropped her head again; her body shook with her sobbing; plainly she was a girl. No real man is ever himself in the presence of a woman's tears. I was again on the point of surrender. Suddenly she looked up.

"Harry," she spoke sadly, "I have just one thing to ask. You must see Charlotte. You must forget me; we can never— You love Charlotte. I have seen her; she is a beautiful girl. You have not written. She is worried. Remember your love that has grown out of childhood. It is beautiful and holy. I wish to save you. Remember what you mean to her happiness. Will you go?"

That I could promise.

"Yes, I shall see Charlotte."

"Thanks."

She rose from her chair. I held her hand. Again, as in the restaurant, I lifted it to my lips. She flushed and drew it away. She bit her lip. Her beauty was a kind I could not understand.

"You must see Charlotte," she said, "and you must do as she says."

With that she was gone. There was a car waiting; the last I saw was its winking tail-light dimming into the darkness.

What did this girl mean to me?

CHAPTER XVI

CHARLOTTE

LEFT alone, I began thinking of Charlotte. I loved her; of that I was certain. I could not compare her with the Nervina. She was like myself, human, possible. I had known her since boyhood. The other was out of the ether; my love for her was something different; she was of dreams and moonbeams; there was a film about her beauty, illusion; she was of spirit.

I wrote a note to the detective and left it upon my desk. After that I packed a suitcase and hurried to the depot. If I was going I would do it at once. I could not trust myself too far. This visit had been like a breath of air; for the moment I was away from the isolation. The loneliness and the weariness! How I dreaded it! I was only free from it for a few moments. On the train it came back upon me and in a manner that was startling.

I had purchased my ticket. When the conductor came through he passed me. He gathered tickets all about me; but he did not notice me. At first I paid no attention; but when he had gone through the car several times I held up my ticket. He did not stop. It was not until I had touched him that he gave me a bit of attention.

"Where have you been sitting?" he asked.

I pointed to the seat. He frowned slightly.

"There?" he asked. "Why? Did you say you were sitting in that seat? Where did you get on?"

"At Townsend."

"Queer," he answered; he punched the ticket and stuck a stub in my hat-band. "Queer. I passed that seat several times. It was empty!"

Empty! It was almost a shock. Could it be that my isolation was becoming physical as well as mental? What was this gulf that was widening between myself and my fellows?

It was the beginning of another phase. I have noticed it many times; on the street, in public places; everywhere. I thread in and out among men. Sometimes they see me, sometimes they don't. It is strange. The oppression of the thing is terrifying—the isolation. I feel at times as though I might be vanishing out of the world!

It was late when I reached my old home; but the lights were still burning. My favorite dog, Queen, was on the veranda. As I came up the steps she growled slightly, but upon recognition went into a series of circles about the porch. My father opened the door. I stepped inside. He touched me on the shoulder, his jaw dropped.

"Harry!" he exclaimed.

Was it as bad as that? How much meaning may be placed in a single intonation! I was weary to the point of exhaustion. The ride upon the train had been too much. I was not sick. Yet I knew what must be my appearance.

My mother came in. For some moments I was busy protesting my health. But it was useless; it was not until I had partaken of a few of the old nostrums that I could placate her.

"Work, work, work, my boy," said my father, "nothing but work. It will not do. You are a shadow. You must take a vacation. Go to the mountains; forget your practice for a short time."

I did not tell them. Why should I? I promised vaguely that I would not labor hard. I decided right then that it was my own battle. It was enough for me without casting the worry upon others. Yet I could not see Charlotte without calling on my parents.

A S SOON as possible I crossed the street to the Fentons'. Someone had seen me in town. Charlotte was waiting. She was the same beautiful girl I had known so long; the blue eyes, the blond, wavy mass of hair, the laughing mouth and the gladness. But she was not glad now. It was almost a repetition of what had happened at home, only here a bit more personal. She clung to me almost in terror. I did not realize that I had gone down so much. I knew my weariness; but I had not thought my appearance so dejected. I remembered Watson. He had been wan, pale, forlorn. After what brief explanation I could give, I proposed a stroll in the moonlight.

It was a full moon; a wonderful night; we walked down the avenue under the elm trees. Charlotte was beautiful, and worried; she clung to my arm with the eagerness of possession. I could not but compare her with the Nervina. There was a contrast; Charlotte was fresh, tender, clinging, the maiden of my boyhood. I had known her all my life; there was no doubt of our love.

Who was the other? She was something higher, out of mystery, out of life

—almost—out of the moonbeams. I stopped and looked up. The great full orb was shining. I did not know that I spoke.

"Harry," asked Charlotte, "who is the Nervina?"

Had I spoken?

"What do you know about the Nervina?" I asked.

"She has been to see me. She told me. She said you would be here tonight. I was waiting. She is very beautiful. I never saw anyone like her. She is wonderful!"

"What did she say?"

"She! Oh, Harry. Tell me. I have waited. Something has happened. Tell me. You have told me nothing. You are not like the old Harry."

"Tell me about the Nervina. What did she say? Come, Charlotte, tell me everything. Am I so much different from the old Harry?"

She clutched my arm fearfully; she looked into my eyes.

"Oh," she said, "how can you say it? You haven't laughed once. You are melancholy; you are pale, drawn, haggard. You keep muttering. You are not the old Harry. Is it this Miss Nervina? She was so interested. At first I thought she loved you; but she does not. She wanted to know all about you, about our love. She was so interested. What is this danger?"

I did not answer.

"You must tell me. This ring? She said that you must give it to me. What is it?" she insisted.

"Did she ask that? She told you to take the ring? My dear," I asked, "if it were the ring and it were so sinister would I be a man to give it to my loved one?"

"It would not hurt me?"

But I would not. Something warned me. It was anything to get it out of my possession. The whole thing was haunting, weird, ghostly. Always I could hear Watson. I had a small quota of courage and will-power. I clung steadfastly to my purpose.

It was a sad three hours. Poor Charlotte! I shall never forget it. It is the hardest task on earth to deny one's loved one.

She had grown into my heart and into its possession. She clung to me tenderly, tearfully. I could not tell her. Her feminine instinct sensed disaster. In spite of her tears I insisted. It had been my last word to Watson. Come what may I would stay with duty. When I kissed her good night she did not speak. But she looked up at me through her tears. It was the hardest thing of all for me to bear.

CHAPTER XVII

THE SHEPHERD

WHEN I returned to the city next morning I took my dog. It was a strange whim; but one which was to lead to a remarkable development. I have ever been a lover of dogs. I was lonely. There is a bond between a dog and his master. It goes beyond definition; it roots down into nature. I was to learn much.

She was an Australian shepherd. She had been presented to me by a rugby player from New Zealand. The Australian dog is about at the head of dogdom, the result of countless generations of elimination. When man chooses for utility he is inexorable in selection. She was of a tawny black and bob-tailed from birth.

What is the power that lies behind instinct? How far does it go? I had a notion that the dog would be outside the sinister clutch that was dragging me under.

Happily Jerome was fond of dogs. He was reading. When I entered with Queen tugging at the chain he looked up. The dog recognized the heart of the man; when he stooped to pet her she moved her stub tail in an effusion of affectionate acceptance. Jerome had been reading Le Bon's peculiar theory on the evolution of force. His researches after the mystery had led him into the depths of speculation; he had become quite a scholar. After our first greetings I unhooked the chain and let Queen have the freedom of the house. I related what had happened. The detective closed the book and sat down. The dog waited a bit for further petting; but missing that she began sniffing about the room. There was nothing strange about it of course. I myself paid not the slightest attention. But the detective was watching. While I was telling my story he was following every movement of the shepherd. Suddenly he held up one finger. I turned.

It was Queen. A low growl, guttural and suspicious. She was standing about a foot from the portières that separated the library from the other room—where we had lost Watson, and where Jerome had had his experience with the old lady. Tense and rigid, one forepaw held up stealthily, her stub tail erect and the hair along her back bristled. Again the low growl. I caught Jerome's eyes. It was queer.

"What is it, Queen?" I spoke.

At the sound of my voice she wagged her tail and looked about; then stepped between the curtains. Just her head. She drew back; her lips drawn from her teeth; snarling. She was rigid, alert, vitalized. Somehow it made me cold. She was a brave dog; she feared nothing. The detective stepped forward and pulled the curtains apart. The room was empty. We looked into each other's faces. What is there to instinct? What is its range? We could see nothing.

But not so the dog. Her eyes glowed. Hate, fear, terror, her whole body rigid.

"I wonder," I spoke. I stepped into the room. But I had not counted on the dog. Her intelligence was out of instinct. With a yelp she was upon me, had me by the calf of the leg and was drawing me back. She stepped in front of me; a low, guttural growl of warning. But there was nothing in that room; of that we were certain.

"Beats me," said the detective. "How does she know? Wonder if she would stop me?" He stepped forward. It was merely a repetition. She caught him by the trouser-leg and drew him back. She crowded us away from the curtain. It was almost magnetic. Now we could not hear a sound. We were both positive; and we were both uncertain. From the very beginning there had been mystery in that apartment. We could see nothing, neither could we feel; was it possible that the dog could see beyond us? The detective spoke first:

"Take her out of the room. Put her in the hall; tie her up."

"What's the idea?"

"Merely this; I am going to examine the room. No, I am not afraid. I'll be almighty glad if it does catch me. Anything so long as I get results."

But it did us no good. We examined the room many times that night; both of us. In the end there was nothing, only the weirdness and uncertainty and the magnetic undercurrent which we could feel, but could not fathom. When we called in the dog she stepped to the portières and commenced her vigil. She crouched slightly back of the curtains, alert, ready, waiting. It was a strange thing from the beginning. Her post of honor. From that moment she never left the spot except under compulsion. We could hear her at all times of the night; the low growl, the snarl, the defiance. She was restless; it was instinct; out of her nature she could sense the strange insidious pregnancy.

But there was a great deal more that we were to learn from the dog. It was Jerome who first called my attention. A small fact at the beginning; but of a strange sequence. This time it was the ring. Queen had the habit that is common to most dogs; she would lap my hand to show her affection. It was nothing in itself; but for one fact—she always chose the left hand. It was the detective who first noticed it. Always and at every opportunity she would lap the jewel. We made little tests to try her. I would remove the ring from one hand to the other; then hold it behind me. She would follow.

It was a strange fact; but of course not inexplicable. A scent or the attraction of taste might account for it. However, these little tests led to a rather remarkable discovery. Were it not that I was a witness and have repeated it many times I would not relate it. What is the line between intelligence and instinct?

One night we had called the dog from her vigil. As usual she came to the jewel; by a mere chance I pressed the gem against her head. It was a mere trifle; yet it was of consequence. A few minutes before I had dropped a handkerchief on the opposite side of the room; I was just then thinking about picking it up. It was only a small thing, yet it put us on the track of the gem's strangest potence. The dog walked to the handkerchief. She brought it back in her mouth. At first I took it for a mere coincidence. I repeated the experiment with a book. The same result. I looked up at Jerome.

"What's the matter?" Then when I explained: "The dickens! Try it again."

Over and over again we repeated it, using different articles, pieces of which I was certain she did not know the name. There was a strange bond between the gem and the intelligence, some strange force emanating from its luster. On myself it was depressing; on the dog it was life itself. At last Jerome had an inspiration.

"Try the Rhamda," he said; "think of him. Perhaps—"

It was most surprising. Certainly it was remarkable. It was too much like intelligence; a bit too uncanny. At the instant of the thought the dog leaped backward.

Such a strange transformation; she was naturally gentle. In one instant she had gone mad. Mad? Not in the literal interpretation; but figuratively. She sprang back; snapping; her teeth bared, her hair bristled. Her nostrils drawn. With one bound she leaped between the curtains.

Jerome jumped up. With an exclamation he drew the portières. I was behind him. The dog was standing at the edge of the room. She was bristling; defiance; hate, vigilance.

The room was empty. What did she see? What!

ONE thing was certain. Though we were sure of nothing else we were certain of the Rhamda. We could trust the canine's instinct. Every previous experiment that we had essayed had been crowned with success. We had here a fact, but no explanation. If we could only put things together and draw out the law.

I thought of Fenton. If we had only his good, sound head. He was an accumulation of data; from boyhood he had genius for coaxing the concrete out of facts and abstractions. It was not work for a lawyer or a detective, but for a man of science. It is hard to forget the dog and that moment. She was vicious, her whole body bristled with vibrancy and defiance. It was instinct; the subtle force that goes beyond the five senses. I was positive that she could not see; but she knew. Was it the Rhamda?

It was merely a confirmation From the first we had been certain. The beginning had been coincident with his appearance at the ferry. I had been waiting, and not without dread, for him to strike. He had interfered with Watson. I recalled that night in the restaurant. Why had he not struck at myself? Was it the Nervina? A happy thought came to me at the moment. I would try the Nervina.

With a bit of persuasion we coaxed Queen back into the library. I would again test the strange potency of the gem. I spoke to Jerome.

It was as I suspected.

Instead of madness the dog went into an effusion of delight. It is a fact almost too remarkable to relate. What was this quality that lurked in the jewel? What was the jewel? I had taken it to chemists; not a one could tell me. The Nervina—a friend. It was true. I had always half believed; but I had still doubted. Now I was sure. It was certainly an assurance for Jerome and myself. We had a bit to go on. Perhaps we could patch up the facts and weave some sort of discovery.

It was late when we retired. I could not sleep. The restlessness of the dog held back my slumber. She would growl sullenly, then stir about for a new position; she was never quite still. I could picture her there in the library, behind the curtains, crouched, half resting, half slumbering, always watching. I would waken in the night and listen; a low guttural warning, a sullen whine—then stillness. It was the same with my companion. We could never quite understand it. Perhaps we were a bit afraid.

But one can become accustomed to

most anything. It went on for many nights without anything happening, until one night.

It was a dark night; exceedingly dark, with neither moon nor starlight; one of those nights of inky intenseness. It was about one o'clock. I had been awakened about half an hour before. By the light of a match I had looked at my watch. It was twelve thirty-five. I remember that distinctly. I cannot say just exactly what woke me. The house was strangely silent and still; the air seemed stretched and laden. It was summer. Perhaps it was the heat. I only knew that I awoke suddenly and blinked in the darkness.

In the next room with the door open I could hear the heavy breathing of the detective. That is all that there was to break the stillness, a heavy feeling lay against my heart. I had grown accustomed to dread and isolation; but this was different. Perhaps it was premonition. I do not know. And yet I was terribly sleepy; I remember that.

I struck a match and looked at my watch on the bureau—twelve thirty-five. No sound—not even Queen—not even a rumble from the streets. I lay back and dropped into slumber. Just as I drifted off into sleep I had a blurring fancy of sound, guttural, whining, fearful—then suddenly drifting into incoherent rumbling fantasms—a dream. I awoke suddenly. Some one was speaking. It was Jerome.

"Harry!"

I was frightened. It was like something clutching out of the darkness. I sat up. I did not answer. It was not necessary. The incoherence of my dream had been external. The library was just below me. I could hear the dog pacing to and fro, and her snarling. Snarling? It was just that. It was something to arouse terror.

She had never growled like that—it was positive, I could hear her suddenly leap back from the curtains. She barked. Never before had she come to that. Then a sudden lunge into the other room—a vicious series of snapping, barks, yelps—pandemonium—I could picture her leaping—at what! Then suddenly I leaped out of bed. The barks grew faint, faint, fainter—into the distance.

IN THE darkness I could not find the switch. I bumped into Jerome. Our contact in the middle of the room upset us. We were lost in our confusion. It was a moment before we could find either a match or a button to turn on the lights. But at last—I shall not forget that moment; nor Jerome. He was rigid; one arm held aloft, his eyes bulged out. The whole house was full of sound—full-toned—vibrant—magnetic. It was the bell.

I jumped for the stairway. But I was not so quick as Jerome. With three bounds we were in the library with the lights turned on. The sound was running down to silence. We tore down the curtains and rushed into the room. It was empty!

There was not even the dog. Queen had gone! In a vain rush of grief I began calling and whistling. It was a flooded moment. The poor, brave shepherd. She had seen it and rushed full into its face.

It was the last night that I was to have Jerome. We sat up until daylight. For the thousandth time we went over the house in detail, but there was nothing. Only the ring. At the suggestion of the detective I touched the match to the sapphire. It was the same. The color diminishing, and the translucent corridors deepening into the distance; then the blur and the coming of shadows—the men, Watson and the professor—and my dog.

Of the men, only the heads showed; but the dog was full figure; she was sitting, apparently on a pedestal, her tongue was lolling out of her mouth and her face full of that gentle intelligence which only the Australian shepherd is heir to. That is all—no more—nothing. If we had hoped to discover anything through her medium we were disappointed. Instead of clearing up, the whole thing had grown deeper.

I have said that it was the last night that I was to have Jerome. I did not know it then. Jerome went out early in the morning. I went to bed. I was not afraid in the daylight. I was certain now that the danger was localized. As long as I kept out of that apartment I had nothing to fear. Nevertheless, the thing was magnetic. A subtle weirdness pervaded the building. I did not sleep soundly. I was lonely; the isolation was crowding in on me. In the afternoon I stepped out on the streets.

I have spoken of my experience with the conductor. On this day I had the certainty of my isolation; it was startling. In the face of what I was and what I had seen it was almost terrifying. It was the first time I thought of sending for Hobart. I had thought I could hold out. The complete suddenness of the thing set me to thinking. I thought of Watson. It was the last phase, the feebleness, the wanness, the inertia! He had gone down through exhaustion. He had been a far stronger man than I in the beginning. I had will-power, strength of mind to hold me if it would continue.

I must cable Fenton. While I had still an ego in the presence of men, I must reach out for help. It was a strange thing and inexplicable. I was not invisible. Don't think that. I simply did not individualize. Men did not notice me—till I spoke. As if I were imperceptibly losing the essence of self. I still had some hold to the world. While it remained I must get word to Hobart. I did not delay. Straight to the office I went and paid for the cable.

CANNOT HOLD OUT MUCH LONGER. COME AT ONCE.   —HARRY.

I was a bit ashamed. I had hoped I had counted upon myself. I had trusted in the full strength of my individuality. I had been healthy—strong—full blooded. On the fulness of vitality one would live forever. There is no tomorrow. It was not a year ago. I was eighty. It had been so with Watson. What was this subtle thing that ate into one's marrow? I had read of banshees, lemures and leprechauns; they were the ghosts and the fairies of ignorance; but they were not like this. It was impersonal, hidden, inexorable. It was mystery. And I believed that it was Nature.

I knew it now. Even as I write I can sense the potence of the force about me. It has overcome the professor. It has crushed down Watson. Some law, some principle, some force that science has not uncovered. The last words of the doctor: "I shall bring the occult into the concrete; for your senses. You shall have the proof and the substance."

What is that law that shall bridge the chaos between the mystic and the substantial? I am standing on the bridge; and I cannot see it. What is the great law that was discovered by Dr. Holcomb? Who is the Rhamda? Who is the Nervina?

Jerome has not returned. I cannot understand it. It has been a week. I am living on brandy—not much of anything else—I am waiting for Fenton. I have taken all my elaborations and notes and put them together. Perhaps I—

This is the last of the strange document left by Harry Wendel. The following memorandum is written by Charlotte Fenton.

CHAPTER XVIII

CHARLOTTE'S STORY

I DO not know. It is so hard to write after what has happened. I am but a girl; and I cannot think as men do;

much less analyze. I do not understand.

Hobart says that it is why I am to write it. It is to be a plain narrative. Besides, he is very busy and cannot do it himself. It was Harry's intention and is that of Hobart that the world shall know of the Blind Spot. There must be some record. I shall do my best and hold out of my writing as much as I can of my emotion. I shall start in with the Nervina.

It was the first I knew; the first warning. Looking back I cannot but wonder. No person I think who has ever seen the Nervina can do much else; she is so beautiful! Beautiful? Why do I say it? I should be jealous and I should hate her; it is the way of woman. Yet I do not. Why is it?

It was about eight months after Hobart had left for South America. I remember those eight months as the longest of my life; because of Harry. I am a girl and I like attention; all girls do. Ordinarily he would come over every fortnight at least. After Hobart had gone he came once only. Instead of calling personally, he wrote letters. We were to be married, and of course I resented the inattention.

It seemed to me that no business could be of enough importance if he really loved me. Even his letters were few and far between. What he wrote were slow and weary and of an undertone that I could not fathom. I had all of the girl's wild fears and fancies. I—loved Harry. I could not understand it. I had a thousand fearful thoughts and jealousies; but they were feminine and in no way approximated even the beginning of the truth. Inattention was not like Harry. It was not until the coming of the Nervina that I was afraid.

Afraid? I will not say that—exactly. It was rather a suspicion, a queer undercurrent of wonder and doubt. The beauty of the girl, her interest in Harry and myself, her concern over this ring, put me a bit on guard. I wondered what this ring had to do with Harry Wendel.

She did not tell me in exact words or in literal explanation; but she managed to convey all too well a lurking impression of its sinister potence. It was something baleful, something the very essence of which would break down the life of the one who wore it. Harry had come into its possession by accident and she would save him. She had failed through direct appeal. Now she had come to me.

She was very beautiful, the most wonderful girl I had ever seen, and the most magnetic. If I may follow Harry's words, she was superfeminine. Certainly she was that. A bit too wistful and of spirit to make one jealous. She did not say a word of the Blind Spot. All I knew was her wonderful beauty, and the tender delicacy of her manner.

And the next day came Harry. It was really a shock. Though I had been warned by the girl I was not half afraid until I saw him. He was not Harry at all, but another. His eyes were dim and they had lost their luster; when they did show light at all, it was of a kind that was a bit fearful. He was wan, worn, and gone to a shadow, as if he had gone through a long illness.

He said that he had not been sick. He maintained that he was quite well physically. I was afraid. And on his finger was this ring of which the girl had spoken. Its value must have been incalculable. Wherever he moved his hand its blue flame cut a path through the darkness. But he said nothing about it. I waited and wondered and was afraid. It was not until our walk under the elmtrees that it was mentioned.

It was a full moon; a wonderful, mellow moon of summer. He stopped suddenly and gazed up at the orb above us. It seemed to me that his mind was wandering, he held me closely—tenderly. He was not at all like Harry. There was a missing of self, of individuality; he spoke in abstractions.

"The maiden of the moonbeams?" he spoke. "What can it mean?"

And then I asked him. He has already told of our conversation. It was the ring of which the Nervina had told me. It had to do with the Blind Spot—the great secret that had taken Dr. Holcomb. It was his duty that he had sworn to another. In the ring lurked the power of disintegration. He would not give it to me. I worked hard, for even then I was not afraid of it. Something told me—I must do it to save him. It was weird, and something I could not understand—but I must do it for Harry.

I failed. Though he was broken in every visible way there was one thing as strong as ever—his honor. He had ever that. It had always been the strong part of Harry; when he had given his word naught could break it. He would neither lie nor quibble; he was not afraid; he had been the same in his boyhood. When we parted that night he kissed me. I shall never forget how long he looked into my eyes, nor his sadness. That is all. The next morning he left for San Francisco.

And then came the end. A message; abrupt and sudden. It was some time after and it put a period to my increasing stress and worry. It read:

CITY OF PERU DOCKS TONIGHT AT EIGHT FORTY-TWO. MEET ME AT THE PIER. HOBART COMING. —HARRY.

It was a short message and a bit twisted. Under ordinary circumstances he would have motored down and brought me back to greet Hobart. It was a bit strange that I should meet him at the pier. However, I had bare time to get to the city if I hurried.

I shall never forget that night.

It was dark when I reached San Francisco. I went up by way of Oakland and Niles and took the ferry across the bay. I was a full twenty minutes early at the pier. A few people were waiting. I looked about for Harry. He was to meet me and I was certain that I would find him. But he was not there. Of course there was still time. He was sure to be on hand to greet Hobart.

Nevertheless, I had a vague mistrust. Since that strange visit I had not been sure. Harry was not well. There was something to this mystery that he had not told me. I am a girl, of course, and it was possible that I could not understand it. Yet I would that I knew. Why had he asked me to meet him at the pier? Why did he not come? When the boat docked and he was still missing I was doubly worried.

HOBART came down the gangplank. He was great, strong, healthy, and it seemed to me in a terrible hurry. He scanned the faces hurriedly and ran over to me.

"Where's Harry?" He kissed me and in the same breath repeated, "Where's Harry?"

"Oh, Hobart!" I exclaimed. "What is the matter with Harry? Tell me. It is something terrible! I do not know."

He was afraid. Plainly I could see that! There were lines of anxiety about his eyes. He clutched me by the arm and drew me away.

"He was to meet me here," I said. "He did not come. He was to meet me here! Oh, Hobart, I saw him a short time ago. He was—it was not Harry at all! Do you know anything about it? He said he would meet me at the pier. Why did he not come? What is it?"

For a minute he stood still, looking at me. I had never seen Hobart frightened; but at that moment there was that in his eyes which I could not understand. He caught me by the arm and started out almost on a run. There were many people and we dodged in and out and among them. Hobart carried a suitcase. He hailed a taxi.

I do not know how I got into the car. It is a blur. I was frightened. The whole thing was unusual. Some terrible thing had occurred, and Hobart knew it. I remember a few words spoken to the driver. "Speed, speed, no limit; never mind the law—and Chatterton!" After that the convulsive jerking over the cobbled streets, a climbing over hills and twisted corners. And Hobart at my side. "Faster—faster," he was saying; "faster! My Lord, was there ever a car so slow! Harry! Harry!" I could hear him breathing a prayer. "Oh, for a minute." Another hill; the car turned and came suddenly to a stop! Hobart leaped out.

A somber two-story house; a light burning in one of the windows, a dim light, almost subdued and uncanny. I had never seen anything so lonely as that light; it was gray, uncertain, scarcely a flicker. Perhaps it was my nerves. I had scarcely strength to climb the steps that led up from the sidewalk. Hobart grasped the knob and thrust open the door; I can never forget it. The dim light, the room, the desk and the man! Harry!

It is hard to write. The whole thing! The room; the walls lined with books; the dim, pale light, the faded green carpet, and the man. Pale, worn, shadowed almost a semblance. Was it Harry Wendel? He had aged forty years. He was stooped, withered, exhausted. A bottle of brandy on the desk before him. In his weak, thin hand an empty wine-glass. The gem upon his finger glowed with a flame that was almost wicked; it was blue, burning, giving out sparkles of light—like a color out of hell. The path of its light was unholy—it was too much alive.

We both sprang forward. Hobart seized him by the shoulders.

"Harry, old boy; Harry! Don't you know us? It is Hobart and Charlotte."

It was terrible. He did not seem to know. He looked right at us. But he spoke in abstractions.

"Two," he said. And he listened. "Two! Don't you hear it?" He caught Hobart by the arm. "Now, listen. Two! No, it's three. Did I say three? Can't you hear? 'Tis the old lady. She speaks out of the shadows. There! There! Now, listen. She has been counting to me. Always she says three! Soon 'twill be four."

What did he mean? What was it about? Who was the old lady? I looked around. I saw no one. Hobart stooped over. I began crying. He began slowly to recognize us. It was as if his mind had wandered and was coming back from a far place. He spoke slowly; his words were incoherent and rambling.

"Hobart," he said; "you know her. She is the maiden out of the moonbeams. The Rhamda, he is our enemy. Hobart, Charlotte. I know so much. I cannot tell you. You are two hours late. It is a strange thing. I have found it and I think I know. It came suddenly. The discovery of the great professor. Why did you not come two hours earlier? We might have conquered."

He dropped his head upon his arms; then as suddenly he raised up. He drew the ring from his finger.

"Give it to Charlotte," he said. "It will not hurt her. Do not touch it yourself. Had I only known. Watson did not know—"

He straightened; he was tense, rigid, listening.

"Do you hear anything? Listen! Can you hear? 'Tis the old lady. There—"

But there was not a sound; only the rumble of the streets, the ticking of the clock, and our heart-beats. Again he went through the counting.

"Hobart!"

"Yes, Harry."

"And Charlotte! The ring—ah, yes, it was there. Keep it. Give it to no one. Two hours ago we might have conquered. But I had to keep the ring. It was too much, too powerful; a man may not wear it. Charlotte"—he took my hand and ran the ring upon my finger. "Poor Charlotte, you have loved me, girl, all your life. I have loved you. Here is the ring. The most wonderful—"

Again he dropped over. He was weak—there was something going from him minute by minute.

"Water," he asked. "Water? Hobart, some water."

It was too pitiful. Harry. Our Harry—come to a strait like this! Hobart rushed to another room with the tumbler. I could hear him fumbling. I stooped over Harry. But he held up his hand.

"No, Charlotte, no. You must not. If—"

He stopped. Again the strange attention, as if he were listening to something far off in the distance; the pupils of his hollow, worn, lusterless eyes were pinpoints. He stood on his feet rigid, quivering; then he held up his hand. "Listen!"

But there was nothing. It was as it was before; merely the murmuring of the city night, and the clock ticking.

"It is the dog! Do you hear her? And the old lady. Now listen, 'Two! Now there are two! Three! Three! Now there are three!' There—now." He turned to me. "Can you hear it, Charlotte? No?

It is strange. Perhaps—" He pointed to the corner of the room. "That paper. Will you—"

I shall always go over that moment. I have thought over it many times and have wondered at the sequence. Had I not stepped across the library, what would have happened?

What was it?

I had stooped to pluck up the piece of paper. A queer, crackling, snapping sound, almost audible. I have a strange recollection of Harry standing up by the side of the desk—a flitting vision. An intuition of some terrible force. It was out of nothing—nowhere—approaching. I turned about. And I saw it—the dot of blue.

Blue! That is what it was at first. Blue and burning, like the flame of a million jewels centered into a needlepoint. On the ceiling directly above Harry's head. It was scintillating, coruscating, opalescent; but it was blue most of all. It was the color of life and of death; it was burning, throbbing, concentrated. I tried to scream. But I was frozen with horror. The dot changed color and went to a dead-blue. It seemed to grow larger and to open. Then it turned to white and dropped like a string of incandescence, touching Harry on the head.

What was it? It was all so sudden. A door flung open and a swish of rushing silk. A woman! A woman! A beautiful girl! The front door opened. And the Nervina! It was she!

Never have I seen anyone like her. She was so beautiful. In her face all the compassion a woman is heir to. For scarcely a second she stopped.

"Charlotte," she called. "Charlotte—oh, why did you not save him! He loves you!" Then she turned to Harry. "It shall not be. He shall not go alone. I shall save him, even beyond—"

With that she rushed upon Harry. It was all in an instant. Her arms were outstretched. The dimming form of Harry and the incandescence. The splendid impassioned girl. Their forms intermingled. A blur of her beautiful body and Harry's wan, weary face. A flash of light, a thread of incandescence, a quiver—and they were gone.

The next I knew was the strong arms of my brother Hobart. He gave me the water that he had fetched for Harry. He was terribly upset, but very calm. He held the glass up to my lips. He was speaking.

"Don't worry, sis. Don't worry. I know now. I think I know. I was just in time to see them go. I heard the bell. Harry is safe. It is the Nervina. I shall get Harry. We'll solve the Blind Spot."

CHAPTER XIX

HOBART FENTON TAKES UP THE TALE

RIGHT here at the outset, I had better make a clean breast of something which the reader will very soon suspect, anyhow: I am a plain, unpoetic, blunt-speaking man, trained as a civil engineer, and in most respects totally dissimilar from the man who wrote the first account of the Blind Spot.

Harry had already touched upon this. He came of an artistic, esthetic family; the Wendels were all culture. I think Harry must have taken up law in the hope that the old saying would prove true: "The only certain thing about law is its uncertainty." For he dearly loved the mysterious, the unknowable; he liked uncertainty for its excitement; and it is a mighty good thing that he was honest, for he would have made a highly dangerous crook.

Observe that I use the past tense in referring to my old friend. I do this in the interests of strict, scientific accuracy, to satisfy those who would contend that, having utterly vanished from sight and sound of man, Harry Wendel is no more.

But in my own heart is the firm conviction that he is still very much alive.

Within an hour of his astounding disappearance, my sister, Charlotte, and I made our way to a hotel; and despite the terrible nature of what had happened, we managed to get a few hours' rest. The following morning Charlotte declared herself quite strong enough to discuss the situation. We lost no time.

It will be remembered that I had spent nearly the whole of the preceding year in South America, putting through an irrigation scheme. Thus, I knew little of what had occurred in that interval. On the other hand, Harry and I had never seen fit to take Charlotte into our confidence as, I now see, we should have done.

So we fairly pounced upon the manuscript which Harry had left behind. This manuscript is now in the hands of the publishers, together with a sort of postscript, written by Charlotte, describing the final events of that tragic night in the house at 288 Chatterton Place, when Harry so mysteriously vanished.

Of course the disappearance of Dr. Holcomb—the initial victim of the Blind Spot—has always been public property. Not so the second vanishing—that of Albert Watson, known to us as Chick. His connection with the mystery has heretofore been kept from the world. And the same is true of Harry's going.

Hence the reader will readily imagine

"Give me the ring," she said. "It is worse than death for any man who wears it . . .
I am your friend—"
But what was the Rhamda to her? Was it not for him that she wanted the ring?

the intense interest with which Charlotte and I traced Harry's account. And by the time we had finished reading it, I for one, had reached one solid conclusion.

"I'm convinced, sis, that the stranger—Rhamda Avec—is an out-and-out villain. Despite his agreeable ways, and all, I think he was solely and deliberately to blame for Professor Holcomb's disappearance. Consequently, this Rhamda is, in himself, a very valuable clue as to Harry's present predicament."

And I related some additional details of the struggle which took place between us two football players and the wonderfully strong and agile Rhamda. I showed the scar of a certain memorable scratch on my neck.

"Proof that he's a pretty substantial sort of a fantom," I said. (It will be recalled that Jerome, the detective, who was the first man to see the Rhamda, considered Avec to be supernatural.) "Fantoms don't generally possess fingernails!"

Referring to Harry's notes, I pointed out something which bore on this same point. This was the fact that, although Avec had often been seen on the streets of San Francisco, yet the police had never been able to lay hands on him. This seemed to indicate that the man might possess the power of actually making himself visible or invisible, at will.

"Only"—I was careful to add—"understand, I don't rank him as a magician, or sorcerer; nothing like that. I'd rather think that he's merely in possession of a scientific secret, no more wonderful in itself than, say, wireless. He's merely got hold of it in advance of the others, that's all."

"Then you think that the woman, too, is human?"

"The Nervina?" I hesitated. "Perhaps you know more of this part of the thing than I do, sis."

"I only know"—slowly—"that she came and told me that Harry was soon to call. And somehow, I never felt jealous of her, Hobart." Then she added: "At the same time, I can understand that Harry might —might have fallen in love with her. She —she was very beautiful."

Charlotte is a brave girl. There were tears in her eyes, as she spoke of her lover, but she kept her voice as steady as my own.

We next discussed the disappearance of Chick Watson. These details are already familiar to the reader of Harry's story; likewise what happened to Queen, his Australian shepherd. Like the other vanishings, it was followed by a single stroke on that prodigious, invisible bell —what Harry calls "the Bell of the Blind Spot." And he has already mentioned my opinion, that this phenomenon signifies the closing of the portal of the unknown —the end of the special conditions which produce the bluish spot on the ceiling, the incandescent streak of light, and the vanishing of whoever falls into the affected region. The mere fact that no trace of the bell ever was found has not shaken that opinion.

And thus we reached the final disappearance, that which took away Harry. Charlotte contrived to keep her voice as resolute as before, as she said:

"He and the Nervina vanished together. I turned around just as she rushed in, crying out, 'I can't let you go alone! I'll save you, even beyond.' That's all she said, before—it happened."

"You saw nothing of the Rhamda then, sis?"

"No."

And we had neither seen nor heard of him since. Until we got in touch with him, one important clue as to Harry's fate was out of our reach. There remained to us just one thread of hope— the ring, which Charlotte was now wearing on her finger.

Harry has already described this jewel, but it will not hurt to repeat the details. The ring is remarkable solely for the gem, a large, uncut stone more or less like a sapphire, except that it is a very pale blue indeed. I hardly know how to describe that tint; there is something elusive about it, depending largely upon the conditions of the light, together with some other variable quality—I realize that this seems impossible—a quality which lies in the stone itself, always changing, almost alive. Nevertheless, the stone is not scintillating; it is uncut. It emits a light which is not a gleam, much less a flame; it is a dull glow, if you can imagine a pale blue stone emitting so weird a quality.

I LIT a match and held it to the face of the gem. As happened many times before, the stone exhibited its most astounding quality. As soon as faintly heated, the surface at first clouded, then cleared in a curious fashion, revealing a startlingly distinct, miniature likeness of the four who had vanished into the Blind Spot.

I make no attempt to explain this. Somehow or other, that stone possesses a telescopic quality which brings to a focus, right in front of the beholder's eyes, a tiny "close-up" of our departed friends. Also, the gem magnifies what it reveals, so that there is not the slightest doubt that Dr. Holcomb, Chick Watson, Queen and Harry Wendel are actually reproduced—I shall not say, contained—in that gem. Neither shall I say that they are reflected; they are simply reproduced there.

Also, it should be understood that their images are living. Only the heads and shoulders of the men are to be seen; but there is animation of the features, such as cannot be mistaken. Granted that these four vanished in the Blind Spot—whatever that is—and granted that this ring is some inexplicable window or vestibule between that locality and this commonplace world of ours, then, manifestly, it would seem that all four are still alive.

"I am sure of it!" declared Charlotte, managing to smile, wistfully, at the living reproduction of her sweetheart. "And I think Harry did perfectly right, in handing it to me to keep."

"Why?"

"Well, if for no other reason than because it behaves so differently with me, than it did with him."

She referred, of course, to the very odd relationship of temperature to sex, which the stone reveals. When I, a man, place my skin in contact with the gem, there is an unmistakably cold feeling. But when any woman touches the stone, the feeling is just as distinctly *warm*.

"Hobart, I am inclined to think that this fact is very significant. If Chick had only known of it, he wouldn't have insisted that Harry should wear it; and then—"

"Can't be helped," I interrupted quickly. "Chick didn't know; he was only certain that some one—*some one*—must wear the ring; that it must not pass out of the possession of humans. Moreover, much as Rhamda Avec may desire it—and the Nervina, too—neither can secure it through the use of force. Nobody knows why."

Charlotte shivered. "I'm afraid there's something spooky about it, after all."

"Nothing of the sort," with a conviction that has never left me. "This ring is a perfectly sound fact, as indisputable as the submarine. There's nothing supernatural about it; for that matter, I personally doubt if there's *anything* supernatural. Every phenomenon which seems, at first, so wonderful, becomes commonplace enough as soon as explained. Isn't it true that you yourself are already getting used to that ring?"

"Ye-es," reluctantly. "That is, partly. If only it was some one other than Harry!"

"Of course," I hurried to say, "I only wanted to make it clear that we haven't any witchcraft to deal with. This whole mystery will become plain as day, and that darned soon!"

"You've got a theory?"—hopefully.

"Several; that's the trouble!" I had to admit. "I don't know which is best to follow out.

"It may be a spiritualistic thing after all. Or it may fall under the head of 'abnormal psychology.' Nothing but hallucinations, in other words."

"Oh, that won't do!"—evidently distressed. "I know what I saw! I'd doubt my reason if I thought I'd only fancied it!"

"So would I. Well, laying aside the spiritualistic theory, there remains the possibility of some hitherto undiscovered scientific secret. And if the Rhamda is in possession of it, then the matter simmers down to a plain case of villainy."

"But how does he do it?"

"That's the whole question. However, I'm sure of this"—I was fingering the ring as I spoke. The reproduction of our friends had faded, now, leaving that dully glowing pale blue light once more. "This ring is absolutely real; it's no hallucination. It performs as well in broad daylight as in the night; no special conditions needed. It's neither a fraud nor an illusion.

"In short, sis, this ring is merely a phenomenon which science has not yet explained! That it can and will be explained is strictly up to us!"

I referred again to Harry's notes. In them he tells of having taken the ring to a jeweler, also to a chemist; and of having discovered still another singular thing. This, as the reader will recall, is the gem's anomalous property of combining perfect solidity with extreme lightness. Although as hard and as rigid as any stone, it is so extraordinarily light that it is buoyant in air. A solid, lighter than air.

"Sis," I felt like prophesying, "this stone will prove the key to the whole mystery! Remember how desperately anxious the Rhamda has been to get hold of it?

"Once we understand these peculiar properties, we can mighty soon rescue Harry!"

"And Mr. Watson," reminded Charlotte. She had never met Bertha Holcomb, to whom Chick had been engaged; but she sympathized very deeply with the heartbroken daughter of the old professor. It was she who had given Chick the ring. "It has taken away both her father and her sweetheart!"

And it was just then, as I started to make reply, that a most extraordinary thing occurred. It happened so very unexpectedly, so utterly without warning, that it makes me shaky to this day whenever I recall the thing.

From the gem on Charlotte's finger—or rather, from the air surrounding the ring—came an unmistakable sound. We saw nothing whatever; we only heard. And it was as clear, as loud and as startling as though it had occurred right in the room where we were discussing the situation.

It was the sharp, joyous bark of a dog.

CHAPTER XX

THE HOUSE OF MIRACLES

LOOKING back over what has just been written, I am sensible of a profound gratitude. I am grateful, both because I have been given the privilege of relating these events, and because I shall not have to leave this wilderness of facts for someone else to explain.

Really, if I did not know that I shall have the pleasure of piecing together these phenomena and of setting my finger upon the comparatively simple explanation; if I had to go away and leave this account unfinished, a mere collection of curiosity-provoking mysteries, I should not speak at all. I should leave the whole affair for another to finish, as it ought to be finished.

All of which, it will soon appear, I am setting forth largely in order to brace and strengthen myself against what I must now relate.

Before resuming, however, I should mention one detail which Harry was too modest to mention. He was—or is—unusually good-looking. I don't mean to claim that he possessed any Greek-god beauty; such wouldn't gibe with a height of five foot seven. No; his good looks was due to the simple outward expression, through his features, of a certain noble inward quality which would have made the homeliest face attractive. Selfishness will spoil the handsomest features; unselfishness will glorify.

Moreover, simply because he had given his word to Chick Watson, that he would wear the ring, Harry took upon himself the most dangerous task that any man could assume, and he had lost. But had he known in advance exactly what was going to happen to him, he would have stuck to his word, anyhow. And since there was a sporting risk attached to it, since the thing was not perfectly sure to end tragically, he probably enjoyed the greater part of his experience.

But I'm not like that. Frankly, I'm an opportunist; essentially, a practical sort of fellow. I have a great admiration for idealists, but a much greater admiration for results. For instance, I have seldom given my word, even though the matter is unimportant; for I will cheerfully break my word if, later on, it should develop that the keeping of my word would do more harm than good.

I realize perfectly well that this is dangerous ground to tread upon; yet I must refer the reader to what I have accomplished in this world, as proof that my philosophy is not as bad as it looks.

I beg nobody's pardon for talking about myself so much at the outset. This account will be utterly incomprehensible if I am not understood. My method of solving the Blind Spot mystery is, when analyzed, merely the expression of my personality. My sole idea has been to get *results*.

As Harry has put it, a proposition must be reduced to concrete form before I will have anything to do with it. If the Blind Spot had been a totally occult affair, demanding that the investigation be conducted under cover of darkness, surrounded by black velvet, crystal spheres and incense; demanding the aid of a clairvoyant or other "medium" I should never have gone near it. But as soon as the mystery began to manifest itself in terms that I could understand, appreciate and measure, then I took interest.

That is why old Professor Holcomb appealed to me; he had proposed that we prove the occult by physical means. "Reduce it to the scope of our five senses," he had said, in effect. From that moment on I was his disciple.

I have told of hearing that sharp, welcoming bark, emitted either from the gem or from the air surrounding it. This event took place on the front porch of the house at 288 Chatterton, as Charlotte and I sat there talking it all over. We had taken a suite at the hotel, but had come to the house of the Blind Spot in order to decide upon a course of action. And, in a way, that mysterious barking decided it for us.

We returned to the hotel, and gave notice that we would leave the next day. Next, we began to make preparations for moving at once into the Chatterton Place dwelling.

That afternoon, while in the midst of giving orders for furnishings and the like, there at the hotel, I was called to the telephone. It was from a point outside the building.

"Mr. Fenton?"—in a man's voice. And when I had assured him; "You have no reason to recognize my voice. I am—Rhamda Avec."

"The Rhamda! What do you want?"

"To speak with your sister, Mr. Fenton." Odd how very agreeable the man's tones! "Will you kindly call her to the telephone?"

I saw no objection. However, when Charlotte came to my side I whispered for her to keep the man waiting while I darted out into the corridor and slipped downstairs, where the girl at the switchboard put an instrument into the circuit for me. Money talks. However—

"MY DEAR child," the voice of Avec was saying, "you do me an injustice. I have nothing but your welfare at heart. I assure you, that if anything should happen to you and your brother while at 288 Chatterton, it will be through no fault of mine.

"At the same time, I can positively assure you that, if you stay away from there, no harm will come to either of you; absolutely none! I can guarantee that. Don't ask me why; but, if you value your safety, stay where you are, or go elsewhere, anywhere other than to the house in Chatterton Place."

"I can hardly agree with you, Mr. Avec." Plainly Charlotte was deeply impressed with the man's sincerity and earnestness. "My brother's judgment is so much better than mine, that I—" and she paused regretfully.

"I only wish," with his remarkable gracefulness, "that your intuition were as strong as your loyalty to your brother. If it were, you would know that I speak the truth when I say that I have only your welfare at heart."

"I—I am sorry, Mr. Avec."

"Fortunately, there is one alternative," even more agreeable than before. "If you prefer not to take my advice, but cling to your brother's decision, you can still avoid the consequences of his determination to live in that house. As I say, I cannot prevent harm from befalling you, under present conditions; but these conditions can be completely altered if you will make a single concession, Miss Fenton."

"What is it?" eagerly.

"That you give me that ring!"

He paused for a very terse second. I wished I could see his peculiar, young-old face—the face with the inscrutable eyes; with their expression of youth combined with the wisdom of the ages; the face that urged, rather than inspired, both curiosity and confidence. Then he added:

"I know why you wear it; I realize that the trinket carries some very tender associations. And I would never ask such a concession did I not know, were your beloved here at this moment, he would endorse every word that I say; and—"

"Harry!" cried Charlotte, her voice shaking. "He would tell me to give it to you?"

"I am sure of it! It is as though he, through me, were urging you to do this!"

For some moments there was silence. Charlotte must have been tremendously impressed. It certainly was amazing the degree of confidence that Avec's voice induced. I wouldn't have been greatly surprised had my sister—

It occurred to me that, if the man wanted the gem so badly, it was queer that he had not attempted to get it by forceful means. Remember how weak Chick Watson was that night in the café, and how easily the Rhamda could have taken the ring away from him.

Moreover, he had never attempted to force Harry to part with it; in that struggle of ours his only aim had been to throw Harry and me into that fatal room, before the closing of the Spot. Only the ringing of the bell saved us. Why didn't he employ violence to get the ring? Was it possible that we were misjudging him, after all; and that, instead of being the scoundrel that we thought him to be—

"Mr. Avec," came Charlotte's voice, hesitatingly, almost sorrowfully. "I — I would like to believe you; but—but Harry himself gave me the ring, and I feel—oh, I'm sure that my brother would never agree to it!"

"I understand." Somehow the fellow managed to conceal any disappointment he may have felt. He contrived to show only a deep sympathy for Charlotte, as he finished: "If I find it possible to protect you, I shall, Miss Fenton."

After it was all over, and I returned to the rooms, Charlotte and I concluded that it might have been better had we made some sort of compromise. If we had made a partial concession, he might have told us something of the mystery. We ought to have bargained. We decided that if he made any attempt to carry out what I felt sure was merely a thinly veiled threat to punish us for keeping the gem, we must not only be ready for whatever he might do, but try to trap and keep him as well.

That same day found us back at 288 Chatterton. Harry has already mentioned the place in detail. And I can't blame him for feeling more or less uneasiness when, at various times, he approached the house. Very likely it was because the house needed painting. Any once-handsome residence, when allowed to fall into disrepair, will readily suggest all sorts of spooky things.

Inside, there was altogether too much evidence that the place had been bachelors' quarters. It will be recalled that both Harry and Jerome, the detective, lived there for a year after Chick's previous residence.

The first step was to clean up. We hired lots of help, and made a quick, thorough job of both floors. The basement we left untouched. And the next day we put a force of painters and decorators to work; whereby hangs the tale.

"Mr. Fenton," called the boss painter, as he varnished the "trim" in the parlor, "I wish you'd come and see what to make of this."

I stepped into the front room. He was pointing to the long piece of finish which spanned the doorway leading into the dining-room. And he indicated a spot almost in the exact middle, a spot covering a space about five inches broad and as high as the width of the wood. In outline it was roughly octagonal.

"I've been trying my best," stated Johnson, "to varnish that spot for the past five minutes. But I'll be darned if I can do it!"

And he showed what he meant. Every other part of the door-frame glistened with freshly applied varnish; but the octagonal region remained dull, as though no liquid had ever touched it. Johnson dipped his brush into the can, and applied a liberal smear of the fluid to the place. Instantly the stuff disappeared. "Blamed porous piece of wood," eyeing me queerly. "Or—do you think it's merely porous, Mr. Fenton?"

For answer I took a brush and repeatedly daubed the place. It was like dropping ink on a blotter. The wood sucked up the varnish as a desert might suck up water.

"There's about a quart of varnish in the wood already," observed Johnson, as I stared and pondered. "Suppose we take it down and weigh it?"

INSIDE of a minute we had that piece of trim down from its place. First, I carefully examined the timber framework behind, expecting to see traces of the varnish where, presumably, it had seeped through. There was no sign. Then I inspected the reverse side of the finish, just back of the peculiar spot. I thought I might see a region of wide open pores in the grain of the pine. But the back looked exactly the same as the front, with no difference in the grain at any place.

Placing the finish right side up, I proceeded to daub the spot some more. There was no change in the results. At last I took the can, and without stopping, poured a quart and a half of the fluid into that paradoxical little area.

"Well, I'll be darned!"—very loudly from Johnson. But when I looked up I saw that his face was white, and his lips shaking.

His nerves were all a-jangle. To give his mind a rest, I sent him for a hatchet. When he came back his face had regained its color. I directed him to hold the pine upright, while I, with a single stroke, sank the tool into the end of the wood.

It split part way. A jerk, and the wood fell in two halves.

"Well?" from Johnson, blankly.

"Perfectly normal wood, apparently." I had to admit that it was impossible to distinguish the material which constituted that peculiar spot, from that which surrounded it.

I sent Johnson after more varnish. Also, I secured several other fluids, including water, milk, ink, and machine-oil. And when the painter returned we proceeded with a very thorough test indeed.

Presently it became clear that we were dealing with a phenomenon of the Blind Spot. All told, we poured about nine pints of liquids into an area of about twenty square inches; all on the outer surface, for the split side would absorb nothing. And to all appearances we might have continued to pour indefinitely.

Ten minutes later I went down into the basement to dispose of some rubbish. (Charlotte didn't know of this defection in our housekeeping.) It was bright sunlight outside. Thanks to the basement windows, I needed no artificial luminant. And when my gaze rested upon the ground directly under the parlor, I saw something there that I most certainly had never noticed before.

The fact is, the basement at 288 Chatterton never did possess anything worthy of special notice. Except for the partition which, it will be remembered, Harry Wendel and Jerome, the detective, were the first in years to penetrate—except for that secret doorway, there was nothing down there to attract attention. To be sure, there was a quantity of up-turned earth, the result of Jerome's vigorous efforts to see whether or not there was any connection between the Blind Spot phenomena which he had witnessed and the cellar. He had secured nothing but an appetite for all his digging.

However, it was still too dark for me to identify what I saw at once. I stood for a few moments, accustoming my eyes to the light. Except that the thing gleamed oddly like a piece of glass, and that it possessed a nearly circular outline about two feet across, I could not tell much about it.

Then I stooped and examined it closely. At once I became conscious of an odor which, somehow, I had hitherto not noticed. Small wonder; it was as indescribable a smell as one could imagine. It seemed to be a combination of several that are not generally combined.

Next instant it flashed upon me that the predominating odor was a familiar one. I had been smelling it, in fact, all morning.

But this did not prevent me from feeling very queer, indeed, as I realized what lay before me. A curious chill passed around my shoulders, and I scarcely breathed.

At my feet lay a pool, composed of all the various liquids that had been poured, up-stairs, into that baffling spot in the wood.

CHAPTER XXI

OUT OF THIN AIR

EXCEPT for the incident just related, when several pints of very real fluids were somehow "materialized" at a spot ten feet below where they had vanished, nothing worth recording occurred during the first seven days of our stay at 288 Chatterton.

Seemingly nothing was to come of the Rhamda's warning.

On the other hand we succeeded, during that week, in working a complete transformation of the old house. It became one of the brightest spots in San Francisco. It cost a good deal of money, all told, but I could well afford it, having recently received my fee for the work in the Andes. I possessed the hundred thousand with which, I had promised myself and Harry, I should solve the Blind Spot. That was what the money was for.

On the seventh day after the night of Harry's going, our household was increased to three members. For it was then that Jerome, who was the last person to see Dr. Holcomb before his disappearance, and who stayed in that house with Chick Watson and also with Harry —returned from Nevada, whence he had gone two weeks before on a case.

"Not at all surprised," commented he, when I told him of Harry's disappearance. "Sorry I wasn't here.

"That crook, Rhamda Avec, in at the end?"

He gnawed stolidly at his cigar as I told him the story. He said nothing until he had heard the whole story; then, after briefly approving what I had done to brighten the house, he announced:

"Tell you what. I've got a little money out of that Nevada case; I'm going to take another vacation and see this thing through."

We shook hands on this, and he moved right into his old room. I felt, in fact, mighty glad to have Jerome with us. Although he lacked a regular academic training, he was fifteen years my senior, and because of contact with a wide variety of people in his work, both well-informed and reserved in his judgment. He could not be stampeded; he had courage; and, above everything else, he had the burning curiosity of which Harry has written.

I was up-stairs when he unpacked. And I noted among his belongings a large, rather heavy automatic pistol. He nodded when I asked if he was willing to use it in this case.

"Although"—unbuttoning his vest—"I don't pin as much faith to pistols as I used to.

"The Rhamda is, I'm convinced, the very cleverest proposition that ever lived. He has means to handle practically anything in the way of resistance." Jerome knew how the fellow had worsted Harry and me. "I shouldn't wonder if he can read the mind to some extent; he might be able to foresee that I was going to draw a gun, and beat me to it, with some new weapon of his own."

Having unbuttoned his vest, Jerome then carefully displayed a curious contrivance mounted upon his breast. It consisted of a broad metal plate, strapped across his shirt, and affixed to this plate was a flat-springed arrangement for firing, simultaneously, the contents of a revolver cylinder. To show how it worked, Jerome removed the five cartridges and then faced me.

"Tell me to throw up my hands," directed he. I did so; his palms flew into the air; and with a steely snap the mechanism was released.

Had there been cartridges in it, I should have been riddled, for I stood right in front. And I shuddered as I noted the small straps around Jerome's wrists, running up his sleeves, so disposed that the act of surrendering meant instant death to him who might demand.

"May not be ethical, Fenton"—quietly —"but it certainly is good sense to shoot first and explain later—when you're handling a chap like Avec. Better make preparations, too."

I objected. I pointed out what I have already mentioned; that, together with the ring, the Rhamda offered our only clues to the Blind Spot. Destroy the man, and we would destroy one of our two hopes of rescuing our friends from the unthinkable fate that had overtaken them.

"No"—decisively. "We don't want to kill; we want to *keep* him. Bullets won't do. I see no reason, however, why you shouldn't load that thing with cartridges containing chemicals which would have an effect similar to that of a gas bomb. Once you can make him helpless, so that you can put those steel bracelets on him, we'll see how dangerous he is, with his hands behind him!"

"I get you"—thoughtfully. "I know a chemist who will make up 'Paralysis' gas for me, in the form of gelatin capsules. Shoot 'em at the Rhamda; burst upon striking. Safe enough for me, and yet put him out of the business long enough to fit him with the jewelry."

"That's the idea."

B UT I had other notions about handling the Rhamda. Being satisfied that mere strength and agility were valueless against him, I concluded that he, likewise realizing this, would be on the lookout for any possible trap.

Consequently, if I hoped to keep the man, and force him to tell us what we wanted to know, then I must make use of something other than physical means. Moreover, I gave him credit for an exceptional amount of insight. Call it a super-instinct, or what you will, the fellow's intellect was transcendental.

I could not hope for success unless I equalled his intellect, or surpassed it.

Once decided that it must be a battle of wits I took a step which may seem, at first, a little peculiar.

I called upon a certain lady to whom I shall give the name of Clarke, since that is not the correct one. I took her fully and frankly into my confidence. It is the only way, when dealing with a practitioner. And since, like most of my fellow citizens, she had heard something of the come and go, elusive habits of our men, together with the Holcomb affair, it was easy for her to understand just what I wanted.

"I see," she mused. "You wish to be surrounded by an influence that will not so much protect you, as vitalize and strengthen you whenever you come in contact with Avec. It will be a simple matter. How far do you wish to go?" And thus it was arranged, the plan calling for the cooperation of some twenty of her colleagues.

My fellow engineers may sneer, if they like. I know the usual notion: that the "power of mind over matter" is all in the brain of the patient. That the efforts of the practitioner are merely inductive, and so on.

But I think that the most skeptical will agree that I did quite right in seeking whatever support I could get before crossing swords with a man as keen as Avec.

Nevertheless, before an opportunity arrived to make use of the intellectual machinery which my money had started into operation, something occurred which almost threw the whole thing out of gear.

It was the evening after I had returned from Miss Clarke's office; the same day Jerome returned, the fifth after the Spot had closed upon Harry. Both Charlotte and I had a premonition, after supper, that things were going to happen. We all went into the parlor, sat down, and waited.

Presently we started the victrola. Jerome sat nearest the instrument, where he could, without rising, lean over and change the records. And all three of us recall that the selection being played at the moment was "I Am Climbing Mountains," a sentimental little melody sung by a popular tenor. Certainly the piece was far from being melancholy, mysterious, or otherwise likely to attract the occult.

I remember that we played it twice, and it was just as the singer reached the beginning of the final chorus that Charlotte, who sat nearest the door, made a quick move and shivered, as though with cold.

From where I sat, near the dining-room door, I could see through into the hall. Charlotte's action made me think that the door might have become unlatched, allowing a draft to come through. Afterward she said that she had felt something rather like a breeze pass her chair.

In the middle of the room stood a long, massive table, of conventional library type. Overhead was a heavy, burnished copper fixture, from which a cluster of electric bulbs threw their brilliance upward, so that the room was evenly lighted with the diffused rays as reflected from the ceiling. Thus, there were no shadows to confuse the problem.

The chorus of the song was almost through when I heard, from the direction of the table, a faint sound, as though someone had drawn fingers lightly across the polished oak. I listened; the sound was not repeated, at least not loud enough for me to catch it above the music. Next moment, however, the record came to an end; Jerome leaned forward to put on another, and Charlotte opened her mouth as though to suggest what the new selection might be. But she never said the words.

It began with a scintillating iridescence, up on the ceiling, not eight feet from where I sat. As I looked the spot grew, and spread, and flared out. It was blue, like the elusive blue of the gem; only, it was more like flame—the flame of electrical apparata.

Then, down from that blinding radiance there crept, rather than dropped, a single thread of incandescence, vivid, with a tinge of the color from which it had surged. Down it crept to the floor; it was like an irregular streak of lightning, hanging motionless between ceiling and floor, just for the fraction of a second. All in total silence.

And then the radiance vanished, disappeared, snuffed out as one might snuff out a candle. And in its stead—

There appeared a fourth person in the room.

CHAPTER XXII

THE ROUSING OF A MIND

IT WAS a girl; not the Nervina, that woman who had so mysteriously entered Harry Wendel's life, and who had vanished from this earth at the same time as he. No; this girl was quite another person.

Even now I find it curiously hard to describe her. For me to say that she was the picture of innocence, of purity, and of dainty yet vigorous youth, is still to leave unsaid the secret of her loveliness.

For this stranger, coming out of the thin air into our midst, held me with a glorious fascination. From the first I felt no misgivings, such as Harry confesses that he experienced when he fell under the Nervina's charm. I knew as I watched the stranger's wondering, puzzled features, that I had never before seen any one so lovely, so attractive, and so utterly beyond suspicion.

It was only later that I noted her amazingly delicate complexion, fair as her hair was golden; her deep blue eyes, round face, and girlish, supple figure; or her robe-like garments of soft, white material. For she began almost instantly to talk.

But we understood only with the greatest of difficulty. She spoke as might one who, if living in perfect solitude for a score of years, might suddenly be called upon to use language. And I remembered that Rhamda Avec had told Jerome that he had only *begun* the use of language.

"Who are you?" was her first remark, in the sweetest voice conceivable. But there was both fear and anxiety in her manner. "How—did I —get—here?"

"You came out of the Blind Spot!" I spoke, jerking out the words nervously, and, as I saw, too rapidly. I repeated them more slowly. But she did not comprehend.

"The — Blind — Spot," she pondered. "What—is that?"

Next instant, before I could think to warn her, the room trembled with the terrific clang of the Blind Spot bell. Just one overwhelming peal; no more. At the same time there came a revival of the luminous spot in the ceiling. But, with the last tones of the bell, the spot faded to nothing.

The girl was pitifully frightened. I sprang to my feet and steadied her with one hand—something that I had not dared to do as long as the Spot remained open. The touch of my fingers, as she swayed, had the effect of bringing her to herself. She listened intelligently to what I said.

"The Blind Spot"—speaking with the utmost care—"is the name we have given to a certain mystery. It is always marked by the sound you have just heard; that bell always rings when the phenomenon is at an end."

"And—the—phenomenon," uttering the word with difficulty, "what is that?"

"You," I returned. "Up till now three human beings have disappeared into what we call the Blind Spot. You are the first to be seen coming out of it."

"Hobart," interrupted Charlotte, coming to my side. "Let me."

I stepped back, and Charlotte quietly passed an arm around the girl's waist. Together they stepped over to Charlotte's chair; and I noted the odd way in which the newcomer walked, unsteadily, uncertainly, like a child taking its first steps. I glanced at Jerome, wondering if this tallied with what he recalled of the Rhamda; and he gave a short nod.

"Don't be frightened," said Charlotte softly, "we are your friends. In a way we have been expecting you, and we shall see to it that no harm comes to you.

"Which would you prefer—to ask questions, or to answer them?"

"I" — the girl hesitated — "I — hardly —know. Perhaps—you had—better—ask something first."

"Good. Do you remember where you came from? Can you recall the events just prior to your arrival here?"

THE girl looked helplessly from the one to the other of us. She seemed to be searching for some clue. Finally she shook her head in a hopeless, despairing fashion.

"I can't remember," speaking with a shade less difficulty. "The—last thing—I recall is—seeing—you three—staring—at me."

This was a poser. To think, a person who, before our very eyes, had materialized out of the Blind Spot, was unable to tell us anything about it!

Still this lack of memory might be only a temporary condition, brought on by the special conditions under which she had emerged; an after-effect, as it were, of the semi-electrical phenomena. And it turned out that I was right.

"Then," suggested Charlotte, "suppose you ask us something."

The girl's eyes stopped roving and rested definitely, steadily, upon my own. And she spoke; still a little hesitantly:

"Who are you? What is your name?"

"Name?" taken wholly by surprise. "Ah—it is Hobart Fenton. And"—automatically—"this is my sister Charlotte. The gentleman yonder is Mr. Jerome."

"I am glad to know you, Hobart," with perfect simplicity and apparent pleasure; "and you, Charlotte," passing an arm around my sister's neck; "and you—mister." Evidently she thought the title of "mister" to be Jerome's first name!

Then she went on to say, her eyes coming back to mine:

"Why do you look at me that way, Hobart?"

Just like that! I felt my cheeks go hot and cold by turns. For a moment I was helpless; then I made up my mind to be just as frank and candid as she.

"Because you're so good to look at!" I blurted out. "I never appreciated my eyesight as I do right now!"

"I am glad," she returned, simply and absolutely without a trace of confusion or resentment. "I know that I rather like to look at you—too."

Another stunned silence. And this time I didn't notice any change in the temperature of my face; I was too busily engaged in searching the depths of those warm blue eyes.

She did not blush, or even drop her eyes. She smiled, however, a gentle, tremulous smile that showed some deep feeling behind her unwavering gaze. And her breast heaved slightly.

I recovered myself with a start. Was I to take advantage of her ignorance? As things stood, the girl was as innocent and impressionable as an infant. I drew my chair up in front of her and took both her hands firmly in mine. Whereupon my resolution nearly deserted me. How warm, and soft, and altogether adorable

they were. I drew a long breath and began:

"My dear miss—ah— By the way, what is your name?"

"I"—regretfully, after a moment's thought—"I don't know, Hobart."

"Quite so," as though the fact was commonplace. "We will have to provide you a name. Any suggestions, sis?"

Charlotte hesitated only a second. "Let's call her Ariadne; it was Harry's mother's name."

"That's so; fine! Do you like the name —Ariadne?"

"Yes," both pleased and relieved. At the same time she looked oddly puzzled, and I could see her lips moving silently as she repeated the name to herself.

Not for an instant did I let go of those wonderful fingers. "What I want you to know, Ariadne, is that you have come into a world that is, perhaps, more or less like the one that you have just left. For all I know it is one and the same world, only, in some fashion not yet understood, you may have transported yourself to this place. Perhaps not.

"Now, we call this a room, a part of a house. Outside is a street. That street is one of hundreds in a vast city, which consists of a multitude of such houses, together with other and vastly larger structures. And these structures all rest upon a solid material, which we call the ground, or earth.

"The fact that you understand our language indicates that either you have fallen heir to a body and a brain which are thoroughly in tune with ours, or else —and please understand that we know very, very little of this mystery—or else your own body has somehow become translated into a condition which answers the same purpose.

"At any rate, you ought to comprehend what I mean by the term 'earth.' Do you?"

"Oh, yes," brightly. "I seem to understand everything you say, Hobart."

"Then there is a corresponding picture in your mind to each thought I have given you?"

"I think so," not so positively.

"Well," hoping that I could make it clear, "this earth is formed in a huge globe, part of which is covered by another material, which we term water. And the portions which are not so covered, and are capable of supporting the structures which constitute the city, we call by still another name. Can you supply that name?"

"Continents," without hesitation.

"Fine!" This was a starter anyhow. "We'll soon have your memory working!

"However, what I really began to say is this; each of these continents—and they are several in number—is inhabited by people more or less like ourselves. There is a vast number, all told. Each is either male or female, like ourselves—you seem to take this for granted, however—and you will find them all exceedingly interesting.

"Now, in all fairness," letting go her hands at last, "you must understand that there are, among the people whom you have yet to see, great numbers who are far more—well, attractive, than I am.

"And you must know," even taking my gaze away, "that not all persons are as friendly as we. You will find some who are antagonistic to you, and likely to take advantage of—well, your unsophisticated viewpoint. In short"—desperately—"you must learn right away not to accept people without question; you must form the habit of reserving judgment, of waiting until you have more facts, before reaching an opinion of others.

"You must do this as a matter of self-protection, and in the interests of your greatest welfare." And I stopped.

SHE seemed to be thinking over what I had said. In the end she observed:

"This seems reasonable. I feel sure that wherever I came from such advice would have fit.

"However"—smiling at me in a manner to which I can give no name other than affectionate—"I have no doubts about you, Hobart. I know you are absolutely all right."

And before I could recover from the bliss into which her statement threw me, she turned to Charlotte with, "You too, Charlotte; I know I can trust you."

But when she looked at Jerome she commented: "I can trust you, mister, too; almost as much, but not quite. If you didn't suspect me, I could trust you completely."

Jerome went white. He spoke for the first time since the girl's coming.

"How—how did you know that I suspect you?"

"I can't explain; I don't know myself." Then, wistfully: "I wish you would quit suspecting me, mister. I have nothing to conceal from you."

"I know it!" Jerome burst out, excitedly, apologetically. "I know it now! You're all right, little girl; I'm satisfied of that from now on!"

She sighed in pure pleasure. And she offered one hand to Jerome. He took it as though it were a humming-bird's egg, and turned almost purple. At the same time the honest, fervid manliness which backed the detective's professional nature shone through for the first time in my knowledge of him. From that moment his devotion to the girl was as absolute as that of the fondest father who ever lived.

Well, no need to detail all that was said during the next hour. Bit by bit we added to the girl's knowledge of the world into which she had emerged, and bit by bit there unfolded in her mind a corresponding image of the world from which she had come. With increasing readiness she supplied unexpressed thoughts. And when, for an experiment, we took her out on the front porch and showed her the stars, we were fairly amazed at the thoughts they aroused.

"Oh!" she cried, in sheer rapture. "I know what those are!" By now she was speaking fairly well. "They are stars!" Then: "They don't look the same. They're not outlined the same as what I know. But they can't be anything else!"

Not outlined the same. I took this to be a very significant fact. What did it mean?

"Look"—showing her the constellation Leo, on the ecliptic, and therefore visible to both the northern and southern hemispheres—"do you recognize that?"

"Yes," decisively. "That is, the arrangement; but not the appearance of the separate stars."

And we found this to be true of the entire sky. Nothing was entirely familiar to her; yet, she assured us, the stars could be nothing else. Her previous knowledge told her this, without explaining why, and without a hint as to the reason for the dissimilarity.

"Is it possible," said I, speaking half to myself, "that she has come from another planet?"

For we know that the sky, as seen from any of the eight planets in this solar system, would present practically the same appearance; but if viewed from a planet belonging to any other star-sun, the constellations would be more or less altered in their arrangement, because of the vast distances involved. As for the difference in the appearance of the individual stars, that might be accounted for by a dissimilarity in the chemical make-up of the atmosphere.

"Ariadne, it may be you've come from another world!"

"No," seemingly quite conscious that she was contradicting me. For that matter there wasn't anything offensive about her kind of frankness. "No, Hobart. I feel too much at home to have come from any other world than this one."

Temporarily I was floored. How could she, so ignorant of other matters, feel so sure of this? There was no explaining it.

We went back into the house. As it happened, my eye struck first the victrola. And it seemed a good idea to test her knowledge with this device.

"Is this apparatus familiar to you?"

"No. What is it for?"

"Do you understand what is meant by the term 'music'?"

"Yes," with instant pleasure. "This is music." She proceeded, without the slightest self-consciousness, to sing in a sweet clear soprano, and treated us to the chorus of "I Am Climbing Mountains"!

"Good Heavens!" gasped Charlotte. "What can it mean?"

For a moment the explanation evaded me. Then I reasoned: "She must have a sub-conscious memory of what was being played just before she materialized."

And to prove this, I picked out an instrumental piece which we had not played all evening. It was the finale of the overture to "Faust"; a selection, by the way, which was a great favorite of Harry's, and is one of mine. Ariadne listened in silence to the end.

"I seem to have heard something like it before," she decided slowly. "The melody, not the—the instrumentation."

"But it reminds me of something that I like very much." Whereupon she began to sing for us. But this time her voice was stronger and more dramatic; and as for the composition—all I can say is it had a wild, fierce ring to it, like "Men of Harlech"; only the notes did not correspond to the chromatic scale. *She sang in an entirely new musical system.*

"By George!" when she had done. "Now we *have* got something! For the first time, folks, we've heard some genuine, unadulterated Blind Spot stuff!"

"You mean," from Charlotte, excitedly, "that she has finally recovered her memory?"

It was the girl herself who answered. She shot to her feet, and her face became transfigured with a wonderful joy. At the same time she blinked hurriedly, as though to shut off a sight that staggered her.

"Oh, I remember! I"—she almost sobbed in her delight—"it is all plain to me, now! I know who I am!"

CHAPTER XXIII

THE RHAMDA AGAIN

I COULD have yelled for joy. We were about to learn something of the Blind Spot—something that might help us to save Harry, and Chick, and the professor!

Ariadne seemed to know that a great deal depended upon what she was about to tell us. She deliberately sat down, and rested her chin upon her hand, as though determining upon the best way of telling something very difficult to express.

As for Charlotte, Jerry, and myself, we managed somehow to restrain our curiosity enough to keep silence. But we could not help glancing more or less wonderingly at our visitor. Presently I realized this, and got up and walked quietly about, as though intent upon a problem of my own.

Which was true enough. I had come to a very startling conclusion—I, Hobart Fenton, had fallen in love!

What was more, this affection of the heart had come to me, a very strong man, just as an affection of the lungs is said to strike such men—all of a sudden and hard. One moment I had been a sturdy, independent soul, intent upon a scientific investigation, the only symptoms of sentimental potentialities being my perfectly normal love for my sister and for my old friend. Then, before my very eyes, I had been smitten thus!

And the worst part of it was, I found myself *enjoying* the sensation. It made not the slightest difference to me that I had fallen in love with a girl who was only a step removed from a wraith. Mysteriously she had come to me; as mysteriously she might depart. I had even to know from what sort of country she had come!

But that made no difference. She was *here*, in the same house with me; I had held her hands; and I knew her to be very, very real indeed just then. And when I considered the possibility of her disappearing just as inexplicably as she had come—well, my face went cold, I admit. But at the same time I felt sure of this much—I should never love any other woman.

The thought left me sober. I paused in my pacing and looked at her. As though in answer to my gaze she glanced up and smiled so affectionately that it was all I could do to keep from leaping forward and taking her right into my arms.

I turned hastily, and to cover my confusion I began to hum a strain from the part of "Faust" to which I have referred. I hummed it through, and was beginning again, when I was startled to hear this from the girl: "Oh, then you are Hobart!"

I wheeled, to see her face filled with a wonderful light.

"Hobart," she repeated, as one might repeat the name of a very dear one. "That—that music you were humming! Why, I heard Harry Wendel humming that yesterday!"

I suppose we looked very stupid, the

three of us, so dumfounded that we could do nothing but gape incredulously at that extraordinary creature and her equally extraordinary utterance. She immediately did her best to atone for her sensation.

"I'm not sure that I can make it clear," she said, smiling dubiously, "but if you will use your imaginations and try to fill in the gaps in what I say you may get a fair idea of the place I have come from, and where Harry is."

We leaned forward, intensely alert. I shall never forget the pitiful eagerness in poor Charlotte's face. It meant more to her, perhaps, than to any one else.

At that precise instant I heard a sound, off in the breakfast room. It seemed to be a subdued knocking, or rather a pounding at the door.

Frowning at the interruption, I stepped through the dining-room into the breakfast room, where the sounds came from. And I was not a little puzzled to note that the door to the basement was receiving the blows.

Now, I had been the last to visit the basement, and had locked the door—from force of habit, I suppose—leaving the key in the lock. It was still there. And there is but one way to enter that basement: through this one door, and no other.

"Who is it?" I called out peremptorily. No answer; only a repetition of the pounds.

"What do you want?"—louder.

"Open this door, quick!" came a muffled reply.

The voice was unrecognizable. I stood and thought quickly; then shouted:

"Wait a minute, until I get a key!"

I motioned to Charlotte. She tiptoed to my side. I whispered something in her ear; and she slipped off into the kitchen, there to phone Miss Clarke and warn her to notify her colleagues at once. And so, as I unlocked the door, I was fortified by the knowledge that I would be assisted by the combined mind-force of a score of highly developed intellects.

I was a little surprised, a second later, to see that the intruder was Rhamda Avec. What reason to expect any one else?

"How did you get down there?" I demanded. "Don't you realize that you are liable to arrest for trespass?"

I said it merely to start conversation But it served only to bring a slight smile to the face of this professed friend of ours, for whom we felt nothing but distrust and fear.

"Let us not waste time in trivialities, Fenton," he rejoined gently. He brushed a fleck of cobweb from his coat. "By this time you ought to know that you cannot

deal with me in any ordinary fashion."

I made no comment as, without asking my leave or awaiting an invitation, he stepped through into the dining-room and thence into the parlor. I followed, half tempted to strike him down from behind, but restrained more by the fact that I must spare him than from any compunctions. Seemingly he knew this as well as I; he was serenely at ease.

And thus he stood before Jerome and Ariadne. The detective made a single sharp exclamation; and furtively shifted his coat sleeves. He was getting that infernal breast gun into action. As for Ariadne, she stared at the new arrival as though astonished, at first.

WHEN Charlotte returned, a moment later, she showed only mild surprise. She quietly took her chair and as quietly moved her hand so that the gem shone in full view of our visitor.

But he gave her and the stone only a single glance, and then rested his eyes upon our new friend. To my anxiety, Ariadne was gazing fixedly at him now, her expression combining both agitation and a vague fear.

It could not have been due entirely to his unusual appearance; for there was no denying that this gray-haired yet youth-faced man with the distinguished courteous bearing, looked even younger that night than ever before. No; the girl's concern was deeper, more acute. I felt an unaccountable alarm.

From Ariadne to me the Rhamda glanced, then back again; and a quick, satisfied smile came to his mouth. He gave an almost imperceptible nod. And, keeping his gazed fixed upon her eyes, he remarked carelessly:

"Which of these chairs shall I sit in, Fenton?"

"This one," I replied instantly, pointing to the one I had just quit.

Smiling, he selected a Roman chair a few feet away.

Whereupon I congratulated myself. The man feared me, then; yet he ranked my mentality no higher than that! In other words, remarkably clever though he might be, and as yet unthwarted, he could by no means be called omnipotent. He was limited; hence he was human, or something likewise imperfect, and likewise understandable if only my own mind might become—

"For your benefit, Mr. Jerome, let me say that I phoned Miss Fenton and her brother a few days ago, and urged them to give up their notion of occupying this house or of attempting to solve the mystery that you are already acquainted with. And I prophesied, Mr. Jerome, that their refusal to accept my advice would be followed by events that would justify me.

"They refused, as you know; and I am here to-night to make a final plea, so that they may escape the consequences of their wilfulness."

"You're a crook! And the more I see of you, Avec, the more easily I can understand why they turned you down!"

"So you, too, are prejudiced against me," regretted the man in the Roman chair. "I cannot understand this. My motives are quite above question, I assure you."

"Really!" I observed sarcastically. I stole a glance at Ariadne; her eyes were still riveted, in a rapt yet half-fearful abstraction, upon the face of the Rhamda. It was time I took her attention away.

I called her name. She did not move her head, or reply. I said it louder: "Ariadne!"

"What is it, Hobart?"—very softly.

"Ariadne, this gentleman possesses a great deal of knowledge of the locality from which you came. We are interested in him, because we feel sure that, if he chose to, he could tell us something about our friends who—about Harry Wendel." Why not lay the cards plainly on the table? The Rhamda must be aware of it all, anyhow. "And as this man has said, he has tried to prevent us from solving the mystery. It occurs to me, Ariadne, that you might recognize this man. But apparently—"

She shook her head just perceptibly. I proceeded:

"He is pleased to call his warning a prophecy; but we feel that a threat is a threat. What he really wants is that ring."

Ariadne had already, earlier in the hour, given the gem several curious glances. Now she stirred and sighed, and was about to turn her eyes from the Rhamda to the ring when he spoke again; this time in a voice as sharp as a steel blade:

"I do not enjoy being misunderstood, much less being misrepresented, Mr. Fenton. At the same time, since you have seen fit to brand me in such uncomplimentary terms, suppose I state what I have to say very bluntly, so that there may be no mistake about it. If you do not either quit this house, or give up the ring—*now*—you will surely regret it the rest of your lives!"

FROM the corner of my eye I saw Jerome moving slowly in his chair, so that he could face directly toward the Rhamda. His hands were ready for the swift, upward jerk which, I knew, would stifle our caller.

As for my sister, she merely turned the ring so that the gem no longer faced the Rhamda; and with the other hand she reached out and grasped Ariadne's firmly.

Avec sat with his two hands clasping the arms of that chair. His fingers drummed nervously but lightly on the wood. And then, suddenly, they stopped their motion.

"Your answer, Fenton," in his usual gentle voice. "I can give you no more time."

I did not need to consult Charlotte or Jerome. I knew what they would have said.

"You are welcome to my answer. It is —no!"

As I spoke the last word my gaze was fixed on the Rhamda's eyes. He, on the other hand, was looking toward Ariadne. And at that very instant an expression, as of alarm and sorrow, swept into the man's face.

My glance jumped to Ariadne. Her eyes were closed, her face suffused; she seemed to be suffocating. She gave a queer little sound, half gasp and half cry.

Simultaneously Jerome's hands shot into the air. The room shivered with the stunning report of his breast gun. And every pellet struck the Rhamda and burst.

A look of intense astonishment came into his face. He gave Jerome a fleeting glance, almost of admiration; then his nostrils contracted with pain as the deadly gas attacked his lungs.

Another second, and each of us was reeling with the fumes. Jerome started toward the window, to raise it, then sank back into his chair. And when he turned around—

He and I and Charlotte saw an extraordinary thing. Instead of succumbing to the gas, Rhamda Avec somehow recovered himself. And while the rest of us remained still too numb to move or speak, he found power to do both.

"I warned you plainly, Fenton," as though nothing in particular had happened. "And now see what you have brought upon the poor child!"

I could only roll my head stupidly, to stare at Ariadne's now senseless form.

"As usual, Fenton, you will blame me for it. I cannot help that. But it may still be possible for you to repent of your folly and escape your fate. You are playing with terrible forces. If you do repent, just follow these instructions"—laying a card on the table—"and I will see what I can do for you. I wish you all good night."

And with that, pausing only to make a courtly bow to Charlotte, Rhamda Avec turned and walked deliberately, dignifiedly from the room, while two men and a woman stared helplessly after him and allowed him to go in peace.

CHAPTER XXIV

THE LIVING DEATH

AS SOON as the fresh air had revived us somewhat, we first of all examined Ariadne. She still lay unconscious, very pale, and alarmingly limp. I picked her up and carried her into the next room, where there was a sofa, while Jerome went for water and Charlotte brought smelling-salts.

Neither of these had any effect. Ariadne seemed to be scarcely breathing; her heart beat only faintly, and there was no response to such other methods as friction, slapping, or pinching of fingernails.

"We had better call a doctor," decided Charlotte promptly, and went to the phone.

I picked up the card which the Rhamda had left. It contained simply his name, together with one other word—the name of a morning newspaper. Evidently he meant for us to insert an advertisement as soon as we were ready to capitulate.

"Not yet!" the three of us decided, after talking it over. And we waited as patiently as we could during the fifteen minutes that elapsed before the telephoning got results.

It brought Dr. Hansen, who, it may be remembered, was closely identified with the Chick Watson disappearance. He made a rapid but very careful examination.

"It has all the appearance of a mild electrical shock. What caused it, Fenton?"

I told him. His eyes narrowed when I mentioned Avec, then widened in astonishment and incredulity as I related the man's inexplicable effect upon the girl, and his strange immunity to the poison gas. But the doctor asked nothing further about our situation, proceeding at once to apply several restoratives. All were without result. As a final resort, he even rigged up an electrical connection, making use of some coils which I had upstairs, and endeavored to arouse the girl in that fashion. Still without result.

"Good Lord, Hansen!" I finally burst out, when he stood back, apparently baffled. "She's simply *got* to be revived! We can't allow her to succumb to that scoundrel's power, whatever it is!"

"Why not a blood transfusion?" eagerly, as an idea came to me. "I'm in perfect condition. What about it? Go to it, doc!"

He slowly shook his head. And beyond a single searching glance into my eyes, wherein he must have read something more than I had said, he regretfully replied:

"This is a case for a specialist, Fenton. Everything considered, I should say that she is suffering from a purely mental condition; but whether it had a physical or a psychic origin, I can't say."

In short, he did not feel safe about going ahead with any really heroic measures until a brain specialist was called in.

I had a good deal of confidence in Hansen. And what he said sounded reasonable. So we agreed to his calling in a Dr. Higgins—the same man, in fact, who was too late in reaching the house to save Chick on that memorable night a year before.

His examination was swift and convincingly competent. He went over the same ground that Hansen had covered, took the blood pressure and other instrumental data, and asked us several questions regarding Ariadne's mentality as we knew it. Scarcely stopping to think it over, Higgins decided:

"The young woman is suffering from a temporary dissociation of brain centers. Her cerebrum does not co-act with her cerebellum. In other words, her conscious mind, for lack of means to express itself, is for the time being dormant as in sleep.

"But it is not like ordinary sleep. Such is induced by fatigue of the nerve channels. This young woman's condition is produced by shock; and since there was no physical violence, we must conclude that the shock was psychic.

"In that case, the condition will last until one of two things occurs; either she must be similarly shocked back into sensibility—and I can't see how this can happen, Fenton, unless you can secure the cooperation of the man to whom you attribute the matter—or she must lie that way indefinitely."

"Indefinitely!" I exclaimed, sensing something ominous. "You mean—"

"That there is no known method of reviving a patient in such a condition. It might be called psychic catalepsy. To speak plainly, Fenton, unless this man revives her, she will remain unconscious until her death."

I shuddered. What horrible thing had come into our lives to afflict us with so dreadful a prospect?

"Is—is there no hope, Dr. Higgins?"

"Very little"—gently but decisively. "All I can assure you is that she will not die immediately. From the general state of her health, she will live at least forty-eight hours. After that—brace yourself, man!—you must be prepared for the worst at any moment."

I turned away quickly, so that he could not see my face. What an awful situation! Poor little girl, stricken in this fashion through my own stubbornness—how, I didn't know—but stricken like that! Unless we could somehow lay hands on the Rhamda—

I hunted up Jerome. I said:

"Jerry, the thing is plainly up to you and me. Higgins gives us two days. Day after tomorrow morning, if we haven't got results by that time, we've got to give in and put that ad in the paper. But I don't mean to give in, Jerry! Not until I've exhausted every other possibility!"

"What're you going to do?"—thoughtfully.

"Work on that ring. I was a fool not to get busy sooner. That gem can probably tell me a part of the truth. As for the rest, that's up to you! You've got to get yourself on the Rhamda's trail as soon as you can, and camp there! The first chance you get, ransack his room and belongings, and bring me every bit of data you find. Between him and the ring, the truth ought to come out."

"All right. But don't forget that—" pointing to the unexplained spot on the wood of the doorway. "You've got a mighty important clue there, waiting for you to analyze it."

And he went and got his hat, and left the house. His final remark was that we wouldn't see him back until he had something to report about our man.

FIVE O'CLOCK the next morning found my sister and me out of our beds and desperately busy. She spent a good deal of time, of course, in caring for Ariadne. The poor girl showed no improvement at all; and we got scant encouragement from the fact that she looked no worse. But she lay there, the fairylike thing that she was, making me wonder if nature had ever intended such a treasure to become ill.

Not a sound escaped her lips; her eyes remained closed; she gave no sign of life, save her barely perceptible breathing and her other automatic functions. It made me sick at heart just to look at her; so near, and yet so fearfully far away.

But when Charlotte could spare any time she gave me considerable help in what I was trying to do. One great service she has rendered has already been made clear: she wore the ring constantly, thus relieving me of the anxiety of caring for it. I was mighty cautious not to have it in my possession more than a few minutes at a time.

My first move was to set down, in ordinary fashion, the list of the gem's attributes. I grouped together the fluctuating nature of its pale-blue color, its power of reproducing those who had gone into the Blind Spot, its combination of perfect solidity with extreme lightness; its quality of coldness to the touch of a male, and warmth to that of a female; and finally its ability to induct—I think this is the right term—to induct sounds out of the unknown. This last quality might be called spasmodic or accidental, whereas the others were permanent and constant.

Now, to this list I presently was able to add that the gem possessed no radioactive properties that I could detect with the usual means. It was only when I began dabbling in chemistry that I learned things.

By placing the gem inside a glass bell, and exhausting as much air as possible from around it, the way was cleared for introducing other forms of gases. Whereupon I discovered this:

The stone will absorb any given quantity of hydrogen gas.

In this respect it behaves analogously to that curious place on the door-frame. Only, it absorbs gas, no liquid; and not any gas, either—none but hydrogen.

Now, obviously this gem cannot truly absorb so much material, in the sense of retaining it as well. The simple test of weighing it afterward proves this; for its weight remains the same under any circumstances.

Moreover, unlike the liquids which I poured into the wood and saw afterward in the basement, the gas does not afterward escape back into the air. I kept it under a bell long enough to be sure of that. No; that hydrogen is, manifestly, translated into the Blind Spot.

Learning nothing further about the gem at that time, I proceeded to investigate the trim of the door. I began by trying to find out the precise thickness of that liquid-absorbing layer.

To do this, I scraped off the "skin" of the air-darkened wood. This layer was .02 of an inch thick. And—that was the total amount of the active material!

I put these scrapings through a long list of experiments. They told me nothing valuable. I learned only one detail worth mentioning; if a fragment of the scrapings be brought near to the Holcomb gem —say, to within two inches—the scrapings will burst into flame. It is merely a bright, pinkish flare, like that made by smokeless rifle-powder. No ashes remain. After that we took care not to bring the ring near to the remaining material on the board.

All this occurred on the first day after Ariadne was stricken. Jerome phoned to say that he had engaged the services of a dozen private detectives, and expected to get wind of the Rhamda any hour. Both Dr. Hansen and Dr. Higgins called twice, without being able to detect any change for the better or otherwise in their patient.

That evening Charlotte and I concluded that we could not hold out any longer. We must give in to the Rhamda. I phoned for a messenger, and sent an advertisement to the newspaper which Avec had indicated.

The thing was done. We had capitulated.

The next development would be another and triumphant call from the Rhamda, and this time we would have to give up the gem to him if we were to save Ariadne.

The game was up.

But instead of taking the matter philosophically, I worried about it all night. I told myself again and again that I was foolish to think about something that couldn't be helped. Why not forget it, and go to sleep?

But somehow I couldn't. I lay wide awake till long past midnight, finding myself growing more and more nervous. At last, such was the tension of it all, I got up and dressed. It was then about one-thirty, and I stepped out on the street for a walk.

Half an hour later I returned, my lungs full of fresh air, hoping that I could now sleep. It was only a hope. Never have I felt wider awake than I did then.

Once more—about three—I took another stroll outside. I seemed absolutely tireless.

Each time that I turned back home I seemed to feel stronger than ever, more wakeful. Finally I dropped the idea altogether, went to the house, and left a note for Charlotte, then walked down to the waterfront and watched some ships taking advantage of the tide. Anything to pass the time.

And thus it happened that, about eight o'clock—breakfast time at 288 Chatterton—I returned to the house, and sat down at the table with Charlotte. First, however, I opened the morning paper, to read our little ad.

It was not there. It had not been printed.

CHAPTER XXV

AT THE ELEVENTH HOUR

I DROPPED the paper in dismay. Charlotte looked up, startled, gave me a single look, and turned pale.

"What—what's the matter?" she stammered fearfully.

I showed her. Then I ran to the phone. In a few seconds I was talking to the very man who had taken the note from the messenger the day before.

"Yes, I handed it in along with the rest of the dope," he replied to my excited query. Then—"Wait a minute," said he; and a moment later added: "Say, by jinks, Mr. Fenton, I've made a mistake! Here's the darned ad on the counter; it must have slipped under the blotter."

I went back and told Charlotte. We stared at one another blankly. Why in the name of all that was baffling had our ad "slipped" under that blotter? And what were we to do?

This was the second day!

Well, we did what we could. We inserted the same notice in each of the three afternoon papers. There was still time for the Rhamda to act, if he saw it.

The hours dragged by. Never did time pass more slowly; and yet, I begrudged every one. So much for being absolutely helpless.

About ten o'clock that morning—that is to say, today; I am writing this the same evening—the front door bell rang. Charlotte answered and in a moment came back with a card. It read:

SIR HENRY HODGES

I nearly upset the table in my excitement. I ran into the parlor like a boy going to a fire. Who wouldn't? Sir Henry Hodges! The English scientist about whom the whole world was talking! The most gifted investigator of the day; the most widely informed; of all men on the face of the globe, the best equipped, mentally, to explore the unknown! Without the slightest formality I grabbed his hand and shook it until he smiled at my enthusiasm.

"My dear Sir Henry," I told him, "I'm immensely glad to see you! The truth is, I've been hoping you'd be interested in our case; but I didn't have the nerve to bother you with it!"

"And I," he admitted in his quiet way, "have been longing to take a hand in it, ever since I first heard of Professor Holcomb's disappearance. Didn't like to offer myself; understood that the matter had been hushed up, and—"

"For the very simple reason," I explained, "that there was nothing to be gained by publicity. If we had given the public the facts, we would have been swamped with volunteers to help us. I didn't know whom to confide in, Sir Henry; couldn't make up my mind. I only knew that one such man as yourself was just what I needed."

He overlooked the compliment, and pulled the newspaper from his pocket. "Bought this from a boy in the Mission a few minutes ago. Saw your ad, and jumped to the conclusion that matters had reached an acute stage. Let me have the whole story, my boy, as briefly as you can."

He already knew the published details. Also, he seemed to be acquainted—in some manner which puzzled me—with much that had not been printed. I sketched the affair as quickly as I could, making it clear that we were face to face with a crisis. When I wound up saying that it was Dr. Higgins who gave Ariadne two days, ending about midnight, in which she might recover if we could secure Rhamda Avec, Sir Henry gave me such a sharp glance as the doctor had given me; only, the Englishman reached out and squeezed one of my hands in silence. Then he said kindly:

"I'm afraid you made a mistake, my boy, in not seeking some help. The game has reached a point where you cannot have too many brains on your side. Time, in short for reenforcements!"

He heartily approved of my course in enlisting the aid of Miss Clarke and her colleagues. "That is the sort of thing you need! People with mentalities; plenty of intellectual force!" And he went on to make suggestions.

As a result, within an hour and a half our house was sheltering five more persons, to whom I should have to devote several chapters if I did full justice to their achievements. But I have space here only for a mention.

Miss Clarke has already been introduced. She was easily one of the ten most advanced practitioners in her line. And she had the advantage of a curiosity that was interested in everything odd, even though she labeled it "nonexistent." She said it helped her faith in the real truths to be conversant with the unreal.

Dr. Malloy was from the university, an out-and-out materialist, a psychologist who made life interesting for those who agreed with James. His investigations of abnormal psychology are world-acknowledged.

Mme. Le Fabre, we afterward learned, had come from Versailles especially to investigate the matter that was bothering us. Which is all that needs to be said of this internationally famous inquirer into mysteries. She possessed no mediumistic properties of her own, but was a stanch proponent of spiritism, believing firmly in immortality and the omnipotence of "translated" souls.

Professor Herold is most widely known as the inventor of certain apparata connected with wireless. But it goes without saying that, from Berlin to Brazil, Herold is considered the West's most advanced student of electrical and radioactive subjects.

I was enormously glad to have this man's expert, high-tension knowledge right on tap.

The remaining member of the quintette which Sir Henry advised me to summon requires a little explanation. Also, I am obliged to give him a name not his own; for it is not often that brigadier-generals of the United States army can openly lend their names to anything so far removed, apparently, from militarism as the searching of the occult.

Yet we knew that this man possessed a power that few scientists have developed; the power of coordination, of handling and balancing great facts and forces, and of deciding promptly how best to meet any given situation. Not that we looked for anything militaristic out of the Blind Spot; far from it. We merely knew not what to expect, which was exactly why we wanted to have him with us; his type of mind is, perhaps, the most solidly comforting sort that any mystery-bound person can have at his side.

BY THE time these five had gathered, Jerome had neither returned nor telephoned. There was not the slightest trace of Rhamda Avec; no guessing as to whether he had seen the ad. It was then one o'clock in the afternoon. Only six hours ago! It doesn't seem possible.

So there were eight of us—three women and five men—who went upstairs and quietly inspected the all but lifeless form of Ariadne and afterward gathered in the library below.

All were thoroughly familiar with the situation. Miss Clarke calmly commented to the effect that the entire Blind Spot affair was due wholly and simply to the cumulative effects of so many, many mistaken beliefs on such subjects; the result, in other words, of error.

Dr. Malloy was equally outspoken in his announcement that he proposed to deal with the matter from the standpoint of psychic aberration. He mentioned dissociated personalities, group hypnosis, and so on. But he declared that he was open to conviction, and anxious to get any and all facts.

Sir Henry had a good deal of difficulty in getting Mme. Le Fabre to commit herself. Probably she felt that, since Sir Henry had gone on record as being doubtful of the spiritistic explanation of psychic phenomena, she might start a controversy with him. But in the end she stated that she expected to find our little mystery simply a novel variation upon what was so familiar to her.

As might be supposed, General Hume had no opinion. He merely expressed himself as being prepared to accept any sound theory, or portions of such theories as might be advanced, and arrive at a workable conclusion therefrom. Which was exactly what we wanted of him. "I know it"—calmly.

Of them all, Professor Herold showed the most enthusiasm. Perhaps this was because, despite his attainments, he is still young. At any rate, he made it clear that he was fully prepared to learn something entirely new in science. And he was almost eager to adjust his previous notions and facts to the new discoveries.

When all these various viewpoints had been cleared up, and we felt that we understood each other, it was inevitable that we should look to Sir Henry to state his position. This one man combined a large amount of the various, specialized abilities for which the others were noted, and they all knew and respected him accordingly. Had he stood and theorized half the afternoon, they would willingly have sat and listened. But instead he glanced at his watch, and observed:

"To me, the most important development of all was hearing the sound of a dog's bark coming from the ring. As I recall the details, the sound was emitted just after the gem had been submitted to considerable handling, from Miss Fenton's fingers to her brother's and back again. In other words, it was subjected to a mixture of opposing animal magnetisms. Suppose we experiment further with it now."

Charlotte slipped the gem from her finger and passed it around. Each of us held it for a second or two; after which Charlotte clasped the ring tightly in her palm, while we all joined hands.

It was, as I have said, broad daylight; the hour, shortly after one. Scarcely had our hands completed the circuit than something happened.

From out of Charlotte's closed hand there issued an entirely new sound. At first it was so faint and fragmentary that only two of us heard it. Then it became stronger and more continuous, and presently we were all gazing at each other in wonderment.

For the sound was that of footsteps.

CHAPTER XXVI

DIRECT FROM PARADISE

THE sound was not like that of the walking of a human. Nor was it such as an animal would make. It was neither a thud nor a pattering, but more like a scratching shuffle, such as reminded me of nothing that I had ever heard before.

Next moment, however, there came another sort of sound, plainly audible above the footsteps. This was a thin, musical chuckle which ended in a deep, but faint, organlike throb. It happened only once.

Immediately it was followed by a steady clicking, such as might be made by gently striking a stick against the pavement; only sharper. This lasted a minute, during which the other sounds ceased.

Once more the footsteps. They were not very loud, but in the stillness of that room they all but resounded.

Presently Charlotte could stand it no longer. She placed the ring on the table, where it continued to emit those unplaceable sounds.

"Well! Do—do you people," stammered Dr. Malloy, "do you people all hear that?"

Miss Clarke's face was rather pale. But her mouth was firm. "It is nothing," said she, with theosophical positiveness. "You must not believe it—it is not the truth of—"

"Pardon me," interrupted Sir Henry, "but this isn't something to argue about! It is a reality; and the sooner we all admit it, the better. There is a living creature of some kind making that sound!"

"It is the spirit of some two-footed creature," asserted the *madame,* plainly at her ease. She was on familiar ground now. "If we only had a medium!"

Abruptly the sounds left the vicinity of the ring. At first we could not locate their new position. Then Herold declared that they came from under the table; and presently we were all gathered on the floor around the place, listening to those odd little sounds; while the ring remained thirty inches above, on the top of the table!

It may be that the thing, whatever it was, did not care for such a crowd. For shortly the shuffling ceased. And for a while we stared and listened, scarcely breathing, trying to locate the new position.

Finally we went back to our chairs. We had heard nothing further. Nevertheless, we continued to keep silence, with our ears alert for anything more.

"Hush!" whispered Charlotte all of a sudden. "Did you hear that?" And she looked up toward the ceiling.

In a moment I caught the sound. It was exceedingly faint, like the distant thrumming of a zither. Only it was a single note, which did not rise and fall, although there seemed a continual variation in its volume.

Unexpectedly the other sounds came again, down under the table. This time we remained in our seats and simply listened. And presently Sir Henry, referring to the ring, made this suggestion:

"Suppose we seal it up, and see whether it inducts the sound then as well as when exposed."

This appealed to Herold very strongly; the others were agreeable; so I ran upstairs to my room and secured a small screw-top metal canister, which I knew to be air-tight. It was necessary to remove the stone from the ring, in order to get it into the opening in the can. Presently this was done; and while our invisible visitor continued its scratchy little walking as before, I screwed the top of the can down as tightly as I could.

Instantly the footsteps halted.

I unscrewed the top a trifle. As instantly the stepping was resumed.

"Ah!" cried Herold. "It's a question of radio-activity, then! Remember Le Bon's experiments, Sir Henry?"

"Right-o," returned the Englishman coolly.

But Miss Clarke was sorely mystified by this simple matter, and herself repeated the experiments. Equally puzzled was Mme. Le Fabre. According to her theory, a spirit wouldn't mind a little thing like a metal box. Of them all, Dr. Malloy was the least disturbed; so decidedly so that General Hume eyed him quizzically.

"Fine bunch of hallucinations, doctor."

"Almost commonplace," retorted Malloy.

Presently I mentioned that the Rhamda had come from the basement on the night that Ariadne had materialized; and I showed that the only possible route into the cellar was through the locked door in the breakfast room, since the windows were all too small, and there was no other door. Query: How had the Rhamda got there? Immediately they all became alert. As Herold said:

"One thing or the other is true; either there is something downstairs which has escaped you, Fenton, or else Avec is able to materialize any place he chooses. Let's look!"

WE ALL went down except Charlotte, who went upstairs to stay with Ariadne. By turns, each of us held the ring. And as we unlocked the basement door we noted that the invisible, walking creature had reached there before us.

Down the steps went those unseen little feet, jumping from one step to the next just ahead of us all the way. When within three or four steps of the bottom, the creature made one leap do for them all.

I had previously run an extension cord down into the basement, and both compartments could now be lighted by powerful incandescents. We gave the place a quick examination.

"What's all this newly turned earth mean?" inquired Sir Henry, pointing to the result of Jerome's effort a few months before. And I explained how he and Harry, on the chance that the basement might contain some clue as to the localization of the Blind Spot, had dug without result in the bluish clay.

Sir Henry picked up the spade, which had never been moved from where Jerome had dropped it. And while I went on to tell about the pool of liquids, which for some unknown reason had not seeped into the soil since forming there, the Englishman proceeded to dig vigorously into the heap I had mentioned.

The rest of us watched him thoughtfully. We remembered that Jerome's digging had been done after Queen's disappearance. And the dog had vanished in the rear room, the one in which Chick and Dr. Holcomb had last been seen. Now, when Jerome had dug the clay from the basement under this, the dining-room, he had thrown it through the once concealed opening in the partition; had thrown the clay, that is, in a small heap under the library. And—after Jerome had done this, the phenomena had occurred in the library, not in the dining-room.

"By Jove!" ejaculated General Hume, as I pointed this out. "This may be something more, you know, than mere coincidence!"

Sir Henry said nothing, but continued his spading. He paid attention to nothing save the heap that Jerome had formed. And with each spadeful he bent over and examined the clay very carefully.

Miss Clarke and the *madame* both remained very calm about it all. Each from her own viewpoint regarded the work as more or less a waste of time. But I noticed that they did not take their eyes from the spade.

Sir Henry stopped to rest. "Let me," offered Herold; and went on as the Englishman had done, holding up each spadeful for inspection. And it was thus that we made a strange discovery.

We all saw it at the same time. Imbedded in the bluish earth was a small, egg-shaped piece of light-colored stone. And protruding from its upper surface was a tiny, blood-red pebble, no bigger than a good-sized shot.

Herold thrust the point of his spade under the stone, to lift it up. Whereupon he gave a queer exclamation. He bent, and thrust his spade under the thing. And he put forth a real effort.

"Well, that's funny!" holding the stone up in front of us. "That little thing's as heavy as—as—it's *heavier* than lead!"

Sir Henry picked the stone off the spade. Immediately the material crumbled in his hands, as though rotting, so that it left only the small, red pebble intact. Sir Henry weighed this thoughtfully in his palm, then without a word handed it around.

We all wondered at the pebble. It was most astonishingly heavy. As I say, it was no bigger than a fair-sized shot, yet it was vastly heavier.

Afterward we weighed it, upstairs, and found that the trifle weighed over half a pound. Considering its very small bulk, this worked out to a specific gravity of 192.6 or almost ten times as heavy as the same bulk of pure gold. And gold is heavy.

Inevitably we saw that there must be some connection between this unprecedentedly heavy speck of material and that lighter-than-air gem of mystery. For the time being we were careful to keep the two apart. As for the unexplained footsteps, they were still slightly audible, as the invisible creature moved around the cellar.

At last we turned to go. I let the others lead the way. Thus I was the last to approach the steps; and it was at that moment that I felt something brush against my foot.

I stooped down. My hands collided with the thing that had touched me. And I found myself clutching—

Something invisible—something which, in that brilliant light, showed absolutely nothing to my eyes. But my hands told me I was grasping a very real thing, as real as my fingers themselves.

I made some sort of incoherent exclamation. The others turned and peered at me.

"What is it?" came Herold's excited voice.

"I don't know!" I gasped. "Come here."

But Sir Henry was the first to reach me. Next instant he, too, was fingering the tiny, unseen object. And such was his iron nerve and superior self-control, he identified it almost at once.

"By the Lord!"—softly. "Why, it's a small bird! Come here, folks, and—"

Another second and they were all there. I was glad enough of it; for, like a flash, with an unexpectedness that startles me even now as I think of it—

The thing became visible. Right in my grasp, a little, fluttering bird came to life.

CHAPTER XXVII

SOLVED!

IT WAS a tiny thing, and most amazingly beautiful. It could not have stood as high as a canary; and had its feathers been made of gleaming silver they could not have been lovelier. And its black-plumed head, and long, blossomlike tail, were such as no man on earth ever set eyes upon.

Like a flash it was gone. Not more than half a second was this enchanting apparition visible to us. Before we could discern any more than I have mentioned, it not only vanished, but it ceased to make any sounds whatever. And each of us drew a long breath, as one might after being given a glimpse of an angel.

Right now, five or six hours after the events I have just described, it is very easy for me to smile at my emotions of the time. How startled and mystified I was! And—why not confess it?—just a trifle afraid. Why? Because I didn't understand! Merely that.

At this moment I sit in my laboratory upstairs in that house, rejoiceful in having reached the end of the mystery. For the enigma of the Blind Spot is no more. I have solved it!

Now twenty feet away, in another room, lies Ariadne. Already there is a faint trace of color in her cheeks, and her heart is beating more strongly. Another hour, says Dr. Higgins, and she will be restored to us!

The time is seven P.M. I did not sleep at all last night; I haven't slept since. For the past five hours we have been working steadily on the mystery, ever since our finding that little, red pebble in the basement. The last three hours of the time I have been treating Ariadne, using means which our discoveries indicated. And in order to keep awake I have been dictating this account to a stenographer.

This young lady, a Miss Dibble, is downstairs, where her typewriter will not bother. Yes, put that down, too, Miss Dibble; I want folks to know everything! She has a telephone clamped to her ears, and I am talking into a mouthpiece which is fixed to a stand on my desk.

On that desk are four switches. All are of the four-way, two-pole type; and from them run several wires, some going to one end of the room, where they are attached to the Holcomb gem. Others, running to the opposite end, making contact with the tiny, heavy stone we found in the basement. Other wires run from the switches to lead bands around my wrists. Also, between switches are several connections—one circuit containing an amplifying apparatus. By throwing these switches in various combinations, I can secure any given alteration of forces, and direct them where I choose.

For there are two other wires. These run from my own lead bracelets to another pair, in another room; a pair clamped around the dainty wrists of the *only* girl—so far as I am concerned.

For I, Hobart Fenton, am now a living, human transforming station. I am converting the power of the Infinite into the Energy of Life. And I am transmitting that power directly out of the ether, as conduced through these two marvelous stones, back into the nervous system of the girl I love. Another hour, and she will Exist!

It is all so very simple, now that I understand it. And yet—well, an absolutely new thing is always hard to put into words. Listen closely, Miss Dibble, and don't hesitate to interrupt and show me where I'm off. We've got a duty to the public here.

To begin with, I must acknowledge the enormous help which I have had from my friends: Miss Clarke, Mme. Le Fabre, General Hume, Dr. Malloy, and Herold. These folks are still in the house with me; I think they are eating supper. I've already had mine. Really, I can't take much credit to myself for what I have found out. The others supplied most of the facts. I merely happened to fit them together; and, because of my relationship to the problem, am now doing the heroic end of the work. Queer! I once begged Dr. Hansen to perform a blood transfusion. And now I am sending new life direct into Ariadne's veins; the Life Principle itself, out of the void! I call it a sacred privilege.

AS FOR Harry—he and Dr. Holcomb, Chick Watson and even the dog —I shall have them out of the Blind Spot inside of twelve hours. All I need is a little rest. I'll go straight to bed as soon as I finish reviving Ariadne; and when I wake up, we'll see who's who, friend Rhamda!

I'm too exuberant to hold myself down to the job of telling what I've discovered. But it's got to be done. Put in a fresh piece of paper, Miss Dibble; here goes!

I practically took my life in my hands when I first made connection. However, I observed the precaution of rigging up a primary connection direct from the ring to the pebble, running the wire along the floor some distance away from where I sat. No ill effects when I ventured into the line of force; so I began to experiment with the switches.

That precautionary circuit was Herold's idea. His, also, the amplifying apparatus. The mental attitude was Miss Clarke's, modified by Dr. Malloy. The lead bracelets were the *madame's* suggestion; they work fine. Sir Henry was the one who pointed out the advantage of the telephone I am using. If my hands become paralyzed I can easily call for help to my side.

Well, the first connection I tried resulted in nothing. Perfectly blank. Then I tried another, and another, meanwhile continually adjusting the coils of the amplifier; and as a result I am now able, at will, to do either or all of the following:

(1) I can induct sounds from the Blind Spot; (2) I can induct light, or visibility; or (3) any given object or person, *in toto*.

And now to tell how. One moment, Miss Dibble; I wish you'd ask my sister to make another pot of chocolate, if Hansen approves. Yes, put that down, too. It's only fair to the public, to know just how the thing affects me. No, no hurry, Miss Dibble. When she gets through eating. No, I'm just sleepy, not weak. Yes, that, too!

Let's see; where was I? Oh, yes; those connections. They've got to be done just right, with the proper tension in the coils, and the correct mental attitude, to harmonize. Oh, shucks; I wish I wasn't so tired.

One moment! No, no; I'm all right. I was just altering that *Beta* coil a bit; it was getting too hot. I— Queer! By Jove, that's going some! Say, Miss Dibble; a funny thing just now! I must have got an inducted current from another wire, mixed with these! And—I got a glimpse into the Blind Spot!

A GREAT— No; it's a— What a terrific crowd! Wonder what they're all— By Jove, it's— Good Lord, it is he! And Chick! No, I'm not wandering, Miss Dibble! I'm having the experience of my life! Don't interrupt!

Now—*that's* the boy! Don't let 'em bluff you! Good! Good! Tell 'em where to head in! Just another minute, Miss Dibble! I'll explain when— That's the boy! Rub it in! I don't know what you're up to, but I'm with you!

Er—there's a big crowd of ugly looking chaps there, Miss Dibble; and I can't make it out— Just a moment—a moment, Miss— What does it mean, anyway? Just—I—

Danger, by Heaven! *That's* what it means!

Miss Dibble! No; I'm all right. The—thing came to an end, abruptly. That's all; everything normal again; the room just the same as it was a moment ago. Hello! I seem to have started something! The wire down on the floor has commenced to hum! Oh, I've got my eye on it, and if anything—

Miss Dibble! Tell Herold to come! On the run! Quick! Did you? Good! Don't stop writing! I—

There's Chick! *Chick!* How did you get here? What? *You can't see me!* Why—

Chick! Listen! Listen, man! I've gone into the Blind Spot! Write this down! The connection—

That's Herold! Herold, this is Chick Watson! Listen, now, you two! The—the —I can hardly—it's from No. 4 to—to—to the ring—then—coil—

Both switches, Chick! Ah! I've—

NOTE BY MISS L. DIBBLE.—Just as Mr. Fenton made the concluding remark as above, there came a loud crash through the telephone, followed by the voice of Mr. Herold. Then, there came a very loud clang from a bell; just one stroke. After which I caught Mr. Fenton's voice:

"Herold—Chick can tell you what *it* wants us to—"

And with that, his voice trailed off into nothing, and died away. As for Mr. Fenton himself, I am informed that he has utterly disappeared; and in his stead there now exists a man who is known to Dr. Hansen as Chick Watson.

CHAPTER XXVIII

THE MAN FROM SPACE

BEFORE starting the conclusion of the Blind Spot mystery it may be just as well for the two publicists who are bringing it to the press to follow Hobart Fenton's example and go into a bit of explanation.

The two men who wrote the first two parts were participants, and necessarily writing almost in the present tense. While they could give an accurate and vivid account of their feelings and experiences, they could only guess at what lay in the future, at the events that would unravel it all. Under such circumstances it is remarkable that they could give such a good narrative.

That their accounts are proportioned and in sequence is probably due to the balance that is inherent in the Spot itself. It is so with all things of Nature. What the Creator has destined is always wrought in proportion; only the work of man is askew. And thus, while the thing may seem a bit marvelous, when explained it becomes very simple.

Surely it is a fortunate chance that the man who followed Harry Wendel was not a bit secretive. To an extent, however, he and the other were in antithesis. Perhaps Destiny chose the two for this very reason. At all events, we now are convinced that they were the hinges that were to swing wide the gate of revelation out of the Blind Spot.

But the present writers have the advantage of working, of seeing, of weighing in the retrospect. They know just where they are going.

In the light of what we now know, it is not the earth side of the Spot that is interesting. It is the other—the obverse side, or what we had only suspected. Up till now we have been puzzled by the sudden snapping and bursting of fortuitous phenomena. There was no one, not even Harry Wendel nor Hobart Fenton, who had measured it up to the standard of revelation. It was only Dr. Holcomb who had guessed, even remotely, at the truth: "Man is conceited. He is troubled with too much ego."

We know that the professor was right. Our conceit had led us away from the truth. It was necessary that we stop and look into the Spot itself.

The coming of Chick Watson brought new perspective. Hitherto we had been looking into the darkness. Whatever had been caught in the focus of the Spot had become lost to our five senses.

Yet, facts are facts. It was no mere trickery that had caught Dr. Holcomb in the beginning. One by one, men of the highest standards and character had been either victims or witness to its reality and power.

So the coming of Watson may well be set down as one of the deciding moments of history. He who had been the victim a year before was returning through the very Spot that had engulfed him. He was the herald of the great unknown, an ambassador of the infinite itself.

It will be remembered that, of all the distinguished inmates of the house, Dr. Hansen was the only one who had a personal acquaintance with Watson. One year before the doctor had seen him a shadow—wasted, worn, exhausted. He had talked with him on that memorable night in the café. Well he remembered the incident, and the subject of that strange conversation—the secret of life that had been discovered by the missing Dr. Holcomb. And Dr. Hansen had pondered it often since.

What was the force that was pulsing through the Blind Spot? It had reached out on the earth, and had plucked up youth as well as wisdom. *This* was the first time it had ever given up that which it had taken!

It was Watson, sure enough; but it was not the man he had known one year before. Except for the basic features Hansen would not have recognized him; the shadow was gone, the pallor, the touch of death. He was hale and radiant; his skin had the pink glow of alert fitness; except for being dazed, he appeared perfectly natural. In the tense moment of his arrival the little group waited in silence. There was no question of the man. He was an athlete, perfect, healthy—come out of the void. What had he to tell them?

But he did not see them at first. He groped about blindly, moving slowly and holding his hands before him. His face was calm and settled; its lines told decision. There was not a question in any mind present but that the man had come for a purpose.

Why could he not see? Perhaps the light was too dim. Some one thought to turn on the extra lights.

It brought the first word from Watson. He threw up both arms before his face; like one shutting out the lightning.

"Don't!" he begged. "Don't! Shut off the lights; you will blind me! Please; please! Darken the room!"

Sir Henry sprang to the switch. Instantly the place went to shadow; there was just enough light from the moon to distinguish the several forms grouped in the middle of the room. Dr. Hansen proffered a chair.

"Thank you! Ah! Dr. Hansen! You are here—I had thought— This is much better! I can see fairly well now. You came very near blinding me permanently! You did not know. It is the transition." Then: "And yet—of course! It's the moon! *The moon!*"

He stopped. There was a strange wistfulness in the last word. And suddenly he rose to his feet. He turned in gladness, as though to drink in the mellow flow of the radiance.

"The moon! Gentlemen—doctor—who are these people? This is the house of the Blind Spot! And it is the moon—the good old earth! And San Francisco!"

He stopped again. There was a bit of indecision and of wonder mixed with his gladness. The stillness was only broken by the scarcely audible voice of Mme. Le Fabre.

"Now we *know!* It is proven. The skeptics have always asked why the spirits work only in the half light. We know now."

WATSON looked to Dr. Hansen. "Who is this lady speaking? Who are these others?"

"Can you see them?"

"Perfectly. It is the lady in the corner; she thinks—"

"That you are a spirit!"

Watson laughed. "A spirit!" Then he repeated: "I a spirit? Let me see!"

"Certainly," asserted the *madame.* "You are out of the Blind Spot. I know; it will prove everything!"

"Ah, yes; the Spot." Watson hesitated. Again the indecision. There was something lying latent that he could not recall; though conscious, part of his mind was still in the apparent fog that lingers back into slumber.

"I don't understand," he spoke. "Who are you?"

It was Sir Henry this time. "Mr. Watson, we are a sort of committee. This is the house at 288 Chatterton Place. We are after the great secret that was discovered by Dr. Holcomb. We were summoned by Hobart Fenton."

Consciousness is an enigma. Hitherto Watson had been almost inert; his actions and manner of speech had been mechanical. That it was the natural result of the strange force that had thrown him out, no one doubted. The mention of Hobart Fenton jerked him into the full vigor of wide awake thinking; he straightened.

"Hobart! Hobart Fenton! Where is he?"

"That we do not know," answered Sir Henry. "He was here a moment ago. It is almost too impossible for belief. Perhaps you can tell us."

"You mean—"

"Exactly. Into the Blind Spot. One and the other; your coming was coincident with his going!"

Chick raised up. Even in that faint light they could appreciate the full vigor of his splendid form. He was even more of an athlete that in his college days, before the Blind Spot took him. And when he realized what Sir Henry had said he held up one magnificent arm, almost in the manner of benediction:

"Hobart has gone through? Thank Heaven for that!"

It was a puzzle. True, in that little group there was represented the accumulated wisdom of human effort. With the possible exception of the general, there was not a skeptic among them. They were ready to explain almost anything—but this.

In the natural weakness of futility they had come to associate the manner of death or terror with the Blind Spot. Yet, here was Watson! Watson, alive and strong; he was the reverse of what they had subconsciously expected. Already with each succeeding instant they could sense the vibrancy of his presence. It was like a current, living, splendid, magnetic.

"What is this Blind Spot?" inquired Sir Henry evenly. "And what do you mean by giving thanks that Fenton has gone into it?"

"Not now. Not one word of explanation until— What time is it?" Watson broke off to demand.

They told him. He began to talk rapidly, with amazing force and decision, and in a manner whose sincerity left no chance for doubt.

"Then we have five hours! Not one second to lose. Do what I say, and answer my questions!" Then: "We must not fail; one slip, and the whole world will be engulfed—in the unknown! Turn on the lights."

There was that in the personality and the vehemence of the man that precluded the opposition. Out of the Blind Spot had come a dynamic quality, along with the man; a quickening influence that made Watson swift, sure, and positive. His manner caught into their marrow. Somehow they knew that it was a moment of Destiny.

Watson went on:

"First, did Hobart Fenton open the Spot? Or was it a period? By 'period' I mean, did it open by chance, as it did when it caught Harry and me? Just what did Hobart do? Tell me!"

It was a singular question. How could they answer it? However, Dr. Malloy related as much as he knew of what Hobart had done; his wires and apparatus were now merely a tangled mass of fused metals. Nothing remained intact but the blue gem and the red pebble.

"I see. And this pebble: you found it by digging in the cellar, I suppose."

How did he know that? Dr. Hansen brought that curiously heavy little stone and laid it in Watson's hand. The newcomer touched it with his finger, and for a very brief moment he studied it. Then he looked up.

"It's the small one," he stated. "And you found it in the cellar. It was very fortunate; the opening of the Spot was perhaps a little more than half chance. But it was wonderfully lucky. It let me out.

"And with the help of God and our own courage we may open it again, long enough to rescue Hobart, Harry, and Dr. Holcomb. Then—we must break the chain—we must destroy the revelation; we must close the Spot forever!"

Small wonder that they could not understand what he meant. Dr. Hansen thought to cut in with a practical question:

"My dear Chick, what's inside that Spot? We want to know!"

But it was not Watson who answered. It was Mme. Le Fabre.

"Spirits, of course."

Watson gave a sudden laugh. This time he answered.

"My dear lady, if you know what I know, and what Dr. Holcomb has discovered, you would ask *yourself* a question or so. Possibly you yourself are a spirit!"

"What!" she gasped. "I—a spirit!"

"Exactly. But there is no time for questions. Afterward—not now. Five hours, and we must—"

Some one came to the door. It was Jerome. At the sight of Watson he stopped, clutching the stub of his cigar between his teeth. His gray eyes took in the other's form from head to shoe leather.

"Back?" he wanted to know. "What did you find out, Watson? They must have fed you well over yonder!"

And Jerome pointed toward the ceiling with his thumb. It wasn't in his stubby nature to give way to enthusiasm; this was merely his manner of welcome. Watson smiled.

"The eats were all right, Jerome, but not all the company. You're just the man I want. We have little time; none to spare for talk. Are you in touch with Bertha Holcomb?"

The detective nodded.

WATSON took the chair that Fenton had so strangely vacated and reached for paper and pencil. Once or twice he stopped to draw a line, but mostly he was calculating. He referred constantly to a paper which he took from his pocket. When he was through he spread his palm over what he had written.

"Jerome!"

"Yes."

"You are no longer connected with headquarters, I presume; but—can you get men?"

"If need be."

"You will need them!" Just then Watson noticed the uniform of General Hume. "Jerome, can you give this officer a bodyguard?"

It was both unusual and lightning-sudden. Nevertheless, there was something in Watson's manner that called for no challenge; something that would have brooked no refusal. And the general, although a skeptic, was acting solely from force of habit when he objected:

"It seems to me, Watson, that you—"

Those who were present are not likely to forget it. Some men are born, some rise, to the occasion; but Watson was both. He was clear-cut, dominant, inexorable. He leveled his pencil at the general.

"It *seems* to you! General, let me ask you: If your country's safety were at stake, would you hesitate to throw reenforcements into the breach?"

"Hardly."

"All right. It's settled. Take care of your red tape *afterward.*"

He wheeled to the detective. "Jerome, this is a sketch of the compartments of Dr. Holcomb's safe. Not the large one in his house, but the small one in his laboratory. Go straight to Dwight Way. Give this note," indicating another paper, "to Bertha Holcomb. Tell her that her father is safe, and that I am out of the Blind Spot. Tell her that you have come to open the laboratory safe.

"I've written down the combination. If it doesn't work use explosives; there is nothing inside which force can harm.

"In the compartment marked 'X' you will find a small particle about the size of a pea, wrapped in tin-foil, and locked in a small metal box. You will have to break the box. As for the contents, once you see the stone you can't mistake it; it will weigh about six pounds. Get it, and guard it with your life!"

"All right."

General Hume stepped forward. "You can leave that detail to me, Watson. We'll forego the red tape. I don't know what it's all about, but—I know *men!*"

He stood aside. Jerome placed Watson's instructions into his bill-fold, at the same time glancing about the room.

"Where is Fenton?" he asked.

It was Watson who answered. He gave us the first news that had ever come from the Blind Spot. He spoke with firm deliberation, as though in full realization of the sensation:

"Hobart Fenton has gone through the Blind Spot. Just now he is right here in this room."

Sir Henry jumped.

"In this room! Is that what you said, Watson?"

The other ignored him.

"Jerome, you haven't a minute to lose! You and the general; bring that stone back to this house at *any* cost! Hurry!"

In another moment Jerome and Hume were gone. And few people, that day, suspected the purport of that body of silent men who crossed over the Bay of San Francisco. They were grim, and trusted, and under secret orders. They had a mission, did they but know it, as important as any in history. But they knew only that they were to guard Jerome and the general at all hazards. One peculiarly heavy stone, "the size of a pea"! How are we ever to calculate its value?

As for the group remaining with Watson, not one of them ever dreamed that any danger might come out of the Blind Spot. Its manifestations had been local, and mostly negative. No; the main incentive of their interest had been simply curiosity.

But apparently Watson was above them all. He paid no further attention to them for a while; he bent at Fenton's desk and worked swiftly. At length he thrust the papers aside.

"I want to see that cellar," he announced. "That is, the point where you found that red pebble!"

Down in the basement, Sir Henry gave the details. When he came to mention the various liquids which Fenton had poured into the woodwork upstairs Watson examined the pool intently.

"Quite so. They would come out here—naturally."

"Naturally!"

Sir Henry could not understand; he frowned as he made the ejaculation. His perplexity was reflected in the faces of Herold, the two physicians, Dr. Malloy, Miss Clarke, and the *madame*—and Charlotte spoke for them all:

"Can't you explain, Mr. Watson? The woodwork had nothing whatever to do with the cellar. There was the floor between, just as you see it now. Hobart poured all manner of things into that trim, and it all just disappeared. Afterward he found it here."

"Naturally," Watson repeated. "It could be no place else! It was on its way to the other side, but it could go only half-way. Simply a matter of focus, you know. I beg pardon; you must hold your curiosity a little longer."

He began measuring. First he located the line across the floor-joists overhead, where rested the partition separating the dining-room from the parlor. Finding the middle of this line, he dropped an improvised plumb-line to the ground; and from this spot as center, using a string about ten feet long, he described a circle on the earth. Then, referring to his calculations, he proceeded to locate several points around the circle, marking these points with small stakes pressed into the soil. Then he checked them off and nodded.

"It's even better than the professor thought. His theory is all but proven. If Jerome and Hume can deliver the other stone without accident, we can save those now inside the Spot." Then, very solemnly: "But we face a heavy task. It will be another Thermopylæ. We must hold the gate against an occult Xerxes, together with all his horde."

"The hosts of the dead!" exclaimed Mme. Le Fabre.

"No; the living! Just give me time, *madame*, and you will see something hitherto undreamed of. As for your theory — tomorrow you may d o u b t whether you are living or dead!

"In other words, friends, Dr. Holcomb has certainly proven the occult by material means. He has done it with a vengeance. In so doing he has left us in doubt as to our own selves; and unless he discovers the missing factor within the next few hours we are going to be in the anomalous position of knowing plenty about the next world, but nothing about ourselves."

He paused. He must have known that their curiosity could not hold out much longer. He said:

"Now, just one thing more, friends, and I can tell you everything. I can answer every question, while we are waiting for Jerome and the general to return. But first I must see the one who preceded me out of the Spot."

"Ariadne!" from Charlotte, in wonder.

"Ariadne!" exclaimed Watson. He was both puzzled and amazed. "Did you call her—Ariadne?"

"She is upstairs," cut in Dr. Higgins. "I must see her!"

A MINUTE or two later they stood in the room where the girl lay. The apartment was full of flowers, which Charlotte with a woman's heart had arranged; but the fairest flower of them all was the sleeping occupant herself. The coverlet was thrown back somewhat, revealing the bare left arm and shoulder, and the delicately beautiful face upon the pillow. Her golden hair was spread out in riotous profusion. Red lips slightly parted, gave a glimpse of the tips of white pearls. The other hand was just protruding from the coverlet, and displayed a faint red mark, showing where Hobart's bracelet had been fastened at the moment he disappeared.

Charlotte stepped over and laid her hand against the maiden's cheek. "Isn't she wonderful!" she murmured.

But Dr. Higgins looked to Watson.

"Do you know her?"

The other nodded. He stooped over and listened to her breathing. His manner was that of reverence and admiration. He touched her hand.

"I see how it must have happened. Precisely what I experienced, only—" Then: "You call her Ariadne?"

"We had to call her something," replied Charlotte. "And the name—it just came, I suppose."

"Perhaps. Anyhow, it was a remarkably good guess. Her true name is *the* Aradna."

"*The* Aradna? Who—what is she?"

"Just that: the Aradna. She is one of the factors that may save us. And on earth we would call her—queen." Then, without waiting for the inevitable question, Watson said:

"Your professional judgment will not come to the supreme test, Dr. Higgins. She is simply numbed and dazed, from coming through the Spot." Charlotte had already told him of the girl's arrival. "The mystery is that she was permitted an hour of rationality before this came upon her. I wonder if Hobart's vitality had anything to do with it?"—half to himself. "As for the Rhamda"—he smiled —"he is merely interested in the Spot; that is all. He would never harm the Aradna; he had nothing whatever to do with her condition. We were mistaken about the man. Anyway, it is the Spot of Life that interests us now."

"The Spot of Life," repeated Sir Henry. "Is that—"

"Yes; the Blind Spot, as it is known from the other side. It overtops all your sciences, embraces every cult, and lies at the base of all truth. It is—it is everything."

"Explain!"

Watson turned to the dainty head upon the pillow. He ventured to touch the cheek, with a bit of tenderness in his action and of wistfulness near to reverence. It was not love; it was rather as one might touch a fairy, so slight was the maiden, and so dainty. In both spirit and substance she was truly of another world. Watson gave a soft sigh and looked up at the Englishman.

"Yes, I can explain. Now that I know she is well, I shall tell you all that I know from the beginning. It's certainly your turn to ask questions. I may now be able to tell you all that you want to know; but at least I know more than any other person this side of the Spot. Let us go down to the library."

He glanced at a clock. "We have nearly five hours remaining. Our test will come when we open the Spot. We must not only open it, but we must close it at all costs."

They had reached the lower hall. At the front door Watson paused and turned to the others.

"Just a moment. We may fail tonight. In case we do, I would like to have one last look at my own world—at San Francisco."

He opened the door. The rest hung back; though they could not understand, they could sense, vaguely, the emotion of this strange young man of brave adventure. The scene, the setting, the beauty, were all akin to the moment. Watson stood bareheaded, looking down at the blinking lights of the city of the Argonauts. The moon in a starlit sky was drifting through a ragged lace of cloud. And over it all was a momentary hush, as though the man's emotion had called for it.

No one spoke. At last Watson closed the door. And there was just the trace of tears in his eyes as he spoke:

"Now, my friends—" And led the way into the parlor.

CHAPTER XXIX

THE OCCULT WORLD

"IN TELLING what I know," began Watson, "I shall use a bit of a preface. It's necessary, in a way, if you are to understand me; besides, it will give you the advantage of looking into the Blind Spot with the clear eyes of reason. I intend to tell all, to omit nothing. My purpose in doing this is, that in case we should fail tonight, you will be able to give my account to the world."

It was a strange introduction. His listeners exchanged thoughtful glances. But they all affirmed, and Sir Henry hitched his chair almost impatiently.

"All right, Mr. Watson. Please proceed."

"To begin with," said Watson, "I assume that you all know of Dr. Holcomb's announcement concerning the Blind Spot. You remember that he promised to solve the occult; how he foretold that he would prove it not by immaterial but by very material means; that he would produce the fact and the substance.

"Now, the professor had promised to deliver something far greater than he had thought it to be. At the same time, what he knew of the Blind Spot was part conjecture and part fact. Like his forebears and contemporaries, he looked upon man as the real being.

"But it's a question, now, as to which is reality and which is not. There is not a branch of philosophy that looks upon the question in that light. Bishop Berkeley came near, and he has been followed by others; but they have all been deceived by their own sophistry. However, except for the grossest materialists, all thinkers take cognizance of a hereafter.

"No one dreamed of a Blind Spot and what it may lead to, what it might contain. We are five-sensed; we interpret the universe by the measure of five yardsticks. Yet, the Blind Spot takes even those away; the more we know, it seems, the less certain we are of ourselves. As I spoke to the *madame*, it is a difficult question to determine, after all, just who are the ghosts. At any rate, I *know*"— and he paused for effect—"I know that there are uncounted millions who look upon us and our workings as entirely supernatural!

"Remember that what I have to tell you is just as real as your own lives have been since babyhood.

"It was slightly over a year ago"— settling himself more comfortably in his chair, an example which the others followed—"slightly over a year ago that my last night on the earth arrived.

"I had gone out for the evening, in the forlorn hope of meeting a friend, of having some slight taste of pleasure before the end came.

"For several days I had been laboring under a sort of premonition, knowing that my life was slowly seeping away and that my vitality was slipping, bit by bit, to what I thought must be death. Had I then known what I now know, I could have saved myself. But if I had done it, if I had saved myself, we would never have found Dr. Holcomb.

"Perhaps it was the same fate that led me to Harry, that night. I do not know. Nevertheless, if there is any truth in what I have learned on the other side of the Blind Spot, it would seem that there is something higher than mere fate. I had never believed in luck; but when everything works out to a fraction of a breath, one ceases to be skeptic on the question of destiny and chance. *I* say, everything that happened that night was *forced* from the other side. In short, my giving that ring to Harry was simply a link in the chain of circumstances. It just had to be; the *prophecy* would not have had it otherwise."

Without stopping to explain what he meant by the word "prophecy," Watson went on:

"That's what makes it puzzling. I have never been able to understand how every bit has dovetailed with such exactness. We—you and I—are certainly not supernatural; and yet, on the other side of the Spot, the proof is overwhelmingly convincing.

"I was very weak that night. So weak that it is difficult for me to remember. It was only by overdoses of brandy that I could hold vigor enough to impart my story to my two friends, and to induce Harry Wendel to take that ring. I recall only the higher spots of the evening and our coming back to this house.

"The last I remember was my going to the back of the house; to the kitchen, I think. I had a light in my hands. The boys were in the front room, waiting. One of them had opened a door some yards away from where I stood.

"Coming as it did, on the instant, it is difficult to describe. But I knew it instinctively for what it was: the dot of blue on the ceiling, and the string of light. Then, a sensation of falling, like dropping into space itself. It is hard to describe the horrifying terror of plunging head on from an immense height to a plain at a vastly lower level.

"And that's all that I remember—from this side."*

WATSON opened his eyes.

The first thing was light and a sense of great pain. There was a pressure at the back of the eyeballs, a poignant sensation not unlike a knife-thrust; that, and a sudden fear of madness, of driveling helplessness.

The abrupt return of consciousness in such a position is not easy to imagine. After all he had gone through, this strange sequel must have been terribly puzzling to him. He was a man of good education, well versed in psychology; in the first rush of consciousness he tried, as best he could, to weigh himself up in the balance of aberration. And it was this very fact that gave him his reassurance; for it told him that he could think, could reason, could count on a mind in full function.

But he could not see. The pain in his eyeballs was blinding. There was nothing he could distinguish; everything was woven together, a mere blaze of wonderful, iridescent, blazing coloration.

But if he could not see, he could feel. The pain was excruciating. He closed his eyes and fell to thinking, curiously enough, that the experience was similar to what he had gone through when, upon learning to swim, he had first opened his eyes under the water. It had been under a blazing sun. The pain and the color—it was much the same, only intensified.

Then he knew that he was very tired. The mere effort of that one thought had cost him vitality. He dropped back into unconsciousness, such as was more of insensibility than slumber. He had strange dreams, of people walking, of women, and of many voices. It was blurred and indistinct, yet somehow not unreal. Then, after an unguessable length of time—he awoke.

He was much stronger. The lapse may have been very long; he could not know. But the pain in his eyes was gone; and he ventured to open the lids again in the face of the light that had been so baffling. This time he could see; not distinctly, but still enough to assure him of reality. By closing his eyes at intervals he was able to rest them and to accustom them gradually to the new degree of light. And after a bit he could see plainly.

He was on a cot, and in a room almost totally different from any that he had ever seen before. The color of the walls, even, was dissimilar; likewise the ceiling. It was white, in a way, and yet unlike it; neither did it resemble any of the various tints; to give it a name that he afterward learned—alna—implies but little. It was utterly new to him.†

*NOTE—In justice to Mr. Watson, the present writers have thought it best to transpose the story from the first to the third person. Any narrative, unless it is negative in its material, is hard to give in the first person; for where the narrator has played an active, positive part, he must either curb himself or fall under the slur of braggadocio. Yet, the world wants the details exactly as they happened; hence the transposition.
—EDITORS.

†NOTE—In explanation of this phenomenon of an unidentifiable color scheme, Professor Herold advances the following hypothesis: That the etheric vibrations which are responsible for the sensation of color may follow a different system as we know here are formed by consecutive undulations, thus: . . . . . But perhaps the lights on the other side of the Spot are formed by *rhythmic* undulations, like this: . . . . , or perhaps: . . . . Or any given combination that would repeat indefinitely, yet would not *synchronize*—would not register—with the "color alphabet" Mr. Watson had known.

Apparently he was alone. The room was not large; about the size of an ordinary bedroom. And after the first novelty of the unplaceable color had worn off he began to take stock of his own person.

First, he was covered by the finest of bed clothing, thick but exceedingly light. There was no counterpane, but two comforters and two sheets; and none of them corresponded to any color or material he had ever known. He only knew that their tints were light rather than dark.

Next, he moved his hands out from under, and held them up before his eyes. He was immensely puzzled. He naturally expected to see the worn, emaciated hands which had been his on that dramatic night; but the ones before him were plump, normal, of a healthy pink. The wrists likewise were in perfect condition, also his arms. He could not account for this sudden return of health, of the vigor he had known before he began to wear the ring. He lay back, pondering.

Presently he fell to examining his clothes. These were two garments made of a madras-like textile, rather heavy as to weight, but exceedingly soft as to touch. They were slightly darker than the bed clothing. In a way they were much like pajamas, except that both were designed to be merely slipped into place, without buttons or draw-strings. That is, they were tailored to fit snugly over the shoulders and around the waist, while loose enough elsewhere.

Then he noticed the walls of the room. They were after a simple, symmetrical style; coved—to use an architectural expression—or curved, where the corner would come with a radius much larger than common, amounting to four or five feet; so that a person of ordinary height could not stand close to the wall without stooping. Where the coved portion flowed into the perpendicular of the wall there was a broad molding, like a plate rail, which acted as a support for the hanging of pictures.

WATSON counted four of these pictures. Instinctively he felt that they might give him a valuable clue as to his whereabouts. For, while his mind had cleared enough for him to feel sure that he had truly come through the Spot, he knew nothing more. Where was he? What would the pictures tell?

The first was directly before his eyes. In size perhaps two by three feet, with its greater length horizontal, it was more of a landscape than a portrait. And Watson's eagerness for the subject itself made him forget to note whether the work was mechanically or manually executed.

For it revealed a young girl—about ten or twelve—very lightly draped, enjoying a wild romp with a most extraordinary creature. It was this animal that made the picture amazing; there was no subtle significance in the scene—there was nothing remarkable about the technique. The whole interest, for Watson, was in the animal.

It was a deer; perfect and beautiful, but cast in a Lilliputian mold. It stood barely a foot high, the most delicate thing he had ever looked upon. Mature in every detail of its proportion, the dainty hoofs, the fragile legs, smooth-coated body, and small, wide-antlered head—a miniature eight-pointer—made such a vision as might come to the dreams of a hunter.

Chick rose up in bed, in order to examine it more closely. Immediately he fell back again, slightly dizzy. He closed his eyes.

Shortly he began examining the other pictures. Two of these were simple flower studies. Watson scarcely knew which puzzled him most; the blossoms or their containers. For the vases were like large-sized loving cups, broad as to body, and provided with a handle on either side. Their colors were unfamiliar. As for the blossoms—in one study the blooms were a half-dozen in number, and more like Shasta daisies than anything else. But their color was totally unlike, while they possessed wide, striped stamens that gave the flowers an identity all their own. In the other vase were several varieties, and every one absolutely unrecognizable.

On the opposite side of the room was something fairly familiar. At first glance it seemed a simple basket of kittens, done in black and white—something like crayon, and yet resembling sepia. Alongside the basket, however, was a spoon, one end resting on the edge of a saucer. And it was the size of the spoon that commanded Chick's attention; rather the size of the kittens, any one of which could have curled up comfortably in the bowl of the spoon! Judging relatively, if it were an ordinary tablespoon, then the kittens were smaller than the smallest of mice.

Chick gave it up. Presently he began speculating about the time. He decided that, whatever the hour might be, it was still daylight. In one wall of the room was a large, oval window, of a material which may as well be called glass, frosted, so as to permit no view of what might lie outside. But it allowed plenty of light to enter.

Cut in the opposite wall was a doorway, hung with a curtain instead of a door. This curtain was a gauzy material, but its maroonlike shade completely hid all view of whatever lay beyond.

Chick waited and listened. Hitherto he had not heard a sound. There was not even that subtle, mixed hum from the distance that we are accustomed to associate with silence. He felt certain that he was inside the Blind Spot; but as to just where that locality might lie, he knew as little as before. He knew only that he was in a building of some sort. Where, and what, was that building?

Just then he noticed a cord dangling from the ceiling. It came down to within six inches of his head. He gave it a pull.

Whereupon he heard a faint, musical jangling in the distance. He tried to analyze the sound. It was not bell-like; perhaps the word "tinkling" would serve better. It reminded Chick of a set of those dainty Japanese porch-chimes, only louder, and very much smoother in tone. Provisionally, Chick placed the key at middle D.

A moment later he heard steps outside the curtain. They were very soft and light and deliberate; and almost at the same instant a delicate white hand moved the curtain aside.

It was a woman. Chick lay back and wondered. Although not artistically beautiful she was very good to look at, with large blue eyes of a deep tenderness and sympathy; even features; and a wonderful fold of rich brown hair, tastefully done, and held in place by a satiny net.

She started when she saw Chick's wide-opened eyes; then smiled, a motherly smile and compassionate. She was dressed in a manner at once becoming and odd, to one unaccustomed, in a gown that draped the entire figure, yet left the right arm and shoulder bare. Chick noticed that arm especially; it was white as marble, molded full, and laced with fine blue veins. He had never seen an arm like that. Nor such a woman. She might have been forty.

She came over to the bed, and placed a hand on Chick's forehead. Again she smiled, and nodded.

"How do you feel?" she asked.

Now, this is a strange thing; Watson could not account for it. For, although she did not speak English, yet he could understand her quite well. At the moment it seemed perfectly obvious; afterward, the fact became amazing.

He answered in the same way, his thoughts directing his lips. And he found that as long as he made no conscious attempt to select the words for his thought, he could speak unhesitatingly.

"Where am I?"

She smiled indulgently, but did not answer.

"Is this the—Blind Spot, ma'am?"

"The Blind Spot! I do not understand."

"Who are you?"

"Your nurse. Perhaps," soothingly, "you would like to talk to the Rhamda."

"The Rhamda!"

"Yes. The Rhamda *Geos.*"

CHAPTER XXX

THE PLUNGE

THE woman left him. For a while Chick reflected upon what she had said. In the full rush of returning vigor his mind was working clearly and with analytical exactness.

For the first time he noted a heaviness in the air, overladen, pregnant. He became aware of a strange under-current of life; of an exceedingly faint, insistent, crescending sound, pulselike and rhythmical, like the breathing undertones of multitudes. He was a city man, and accustomed to the murmuring throbs of a metropolitan heart. But this was very different.

Presently, amid the strangeness, he could distinguish the tinkle of elfin bells, almost imperceptible, but musical. The whole air was laden with a subdued music, lined, as it were, with a golden vibrancy of tintinnabulary cadence—distant, subdued, hardly more than a whisper; yet part of the air itself.

It gave him the feeling that he was in a dream. In the realms of the subconscious he had heard just such sounds—exotic and unearthly—fleeting and evanescent.

The notion of dreams threw his mind into sudden alertness. In an instant he was thinking systematically, and in the definite realization of his plight.

The woman had spoken of "the Rhamda." True, she had added a qualifying "Geos," but that did not matter. Whether Geos or Avec, it was still the Rhamda. By this time Watson was convinced that the word indicated some sort of title—whether doctor, or sir, or professor, was not important. What interested Chick was identity. If he could solve that he could get at the crux of the Blind Spot.

He thought quickly. Apparently, it was Rhamda Avec who had trapped Dr. Holcomb. Why? What had been the man's motive? Watson could not say. He only knew that the ethics of the deed was shaded with the subtleness of super-villainy. That back of it all was a purpose, a directing force and intelligence that was inexorable and irresistible.

One other thing he knew; the Rhamda Avec had come out of the region in which he, Watson, now found himself. Rather, he could have come from nowhere else. And Watson could feel certain that somewhere, somehow, he would find Dr. Holcomb.

In that moment Watson determined upon his future course of action. He decided to state nothing, intimate nothing, either by word or deed, that might in any manner incriminate or endanger the professor. It was for him to learn everything possible and to do all he could to gain his points, without giving a particle of information in return. He must play a lone hand and a cautious one—until he found Dr. Holcomb.

The fact of his position did not appal him. Somehow, it had just the opposite effect. Perhaps it was because his strength had come back, and had brought with it the buoyancy that is natural to health. Certainly he was thrice the man who had staggered across the café to Harry Wendel and Hobart Fenton. He could feel the old vigor of youth, the pulse of life and energy, the optimism and the old love of adventure. He could sense the vitality that surrounded him, poised, potential, waiting only the proper attitude on his part to become an active force. Something tremendous had happened to him, to make him feel like that. He was ready for anything.

Five minutes passed. Watson was alert and ready when the woman returned, together with a companion. She smiled kindly, and announced:

"The Rhamda Geos."

At first Chick was startled. There was a resemblance to Rhamda Avec that ran almost to counterpart. The same refinement and elegance, the fleeting suggestion of youth, the evident age mingled with the same athletic ease and grace of carriage. Only he was somewhat shorter. The eyes were almost identical, with the peculiar quality of the iris and pupil that suggested, somehow, a culture inherited out of the centuries. He was dressed in a black robe, such as would befit a scholar.

He smiled, and held out a hand. Watson noted the firm clasp, and the cold thrill of magnetism.

"You wish to speak with me?"

The voice was soft and modulated, resonant, of a tone as rich as bronze.

"Yes. Where am I—sir?"

"You do not know?"

It seemed to Watson that there was real astonishment in the man's eyes. As yet it had not come to Chick that he himself might be just as much a mystery as the other. The only question in his mind at the moment was locality.

"Is this the Blind Spot?"

"The Blind Spot!"—with the same lack of comprehension that the woman had shown. "I do not understand you."

"Well, how did I get here?"

"Oh, as to that, you were found in the Temple of the Leaf. You were lying unconscious on the floor."

"A temple! How did I get there, sir? Do you know?"

"We only know that a moment before there was nothing; next instant—you."

Watson thought. There was a subconscious sound that still lingered in his memory; a sound full-toned, flooding, enveloping. Was there any connection—

"'The Temple of the Leaf,' you call it, sir. I seem to remember having heard a bell. Is there such a thing in that temple?"

The Rhamda Geos smiled, his eyes brightening. "It is sometimes called the Temple of the Bell."

"Ah!" A pause, and Watson asked, "Where is this temple? And is this room a part of the building?"

"No. You are in the Sar-Amenive Hospital, an institution of the Rhamdas."

The Rhamdas! So there were several of them. A sort of society, perhaps.

"In San Francisco?"

"No. San Francisco! Again I fail to understand. This locality is known as the Mahovisal."

"THE Mahovisal!" Watson thought in silence for a moment. He noted the extremely keen interest of the Rhamda, the superintelligent flicker of the eyes, the light of query and critical analysis. "You call this the Mahovisal, sir? What is it: town, world, or institution?"

The other smiled again. The lines about his sensitive mouth were admissive of various interpretations: emotion, or condescension, or the satisfying feeling that comes from the simple vindication of some inner conviction. His whole manner was that of interest and respectful wonder.

"You have never heard of the Mahovisal? Never?"

"Not until this minute," answered Watson.

"You have no knowledge of anything before? Do you know *who you are?*"

"I—" Watson hesitated, wondering whether he had best withhold this information. He decided to chance the truth. "My name is Chick Watson. I am—an American."

"An American?"

The Rhamda pronounced the word with a roll of the "r" that sounded more like the Chinese "Mellican" than anything else. It was evident that the sounds were totally unfamiliar to him. And his manner was a bit indefinite, doubtful, yet weighted with care, as he slowly repeated the question:

"An American? Once more I don't understand. I have never heard the word, my dear sir. You are neither D'Hartian nor Kospian; although there are some—materialists for the most part—who contend that you are just as any one else. That is—a man."

"Perhaps I am," returned Watson, utterly confounded.

He did not know what to say. He had never heard of a Kospian or a D'Hartian, nor of the Mahovisal. It made things difficult; he couldn't get started. Most of all, he wanted information; and, instead, he was being questioned. The best he could do was to equivocate.

As for the Rhamda, he frowned. Apparently his eager interest had been dashed with disappointment. But only slightly, as Watson could see; the man was of such culture and intellect as to have perfect control over his emotions. In his balance and poise he was very like Avec, and he had the same pleasing manner.

"My dear sir," he began, "if you are really a man, then you can tell me something of great importance."

"I," Chick shot back, "can tell you nothing until you first let me know just where I stand!"

Certainly there was a lack of common ground. Until one of them supplied it, there could be no headway. Watson realized that his whole future might revolve about the axis of his next words.

The Rhamda thought a moment, dubiously, like one who has had a pet theory damaged, though not shattered. Suddenly he spoke to the woman.

"Open the portal," said he.

She stepped to the oval window, touched a latch, and swung the pane horizontally upon two pivots. Immediately the room was flooded with a strange effulgence, amberlike, soft, and of a sweetness as mellow as real sunshine filtered by the fairies.

But it was *not* real sunshine!

The window was set in the hither side of a portal in a rather thick wall, beyond which Watson could see a royal sapphiric sky, flecked with white and purple and amethyst-threaded clouds poised above a great amber sleeping sun.

It was the sun that challenged attention. It was so mild, and yet so utterly beyond what might be expected. In diameter it would have made six of the one Watson had known; in the blue distance, touching the rim of the horizon, it looked exactly like a huge golden plate set edgewise on the end of the earth.

And—he could look straight at it without blinking!

HIS thoughts ran back to the first account of the Rhamda. The man had looked straight at the sun and had been blinded. This accounted for it! The man had been accustomed to this huge, soft-glowing beauty. An amberous sun, pale-yellow, sleeping; could it be, after all, dreamland?

But there were other things: the myriad tintinnabulations of these microscopic bells, never ceasing, musically throbbing; and now, the exotic delight of the softest of perfumes, an air barely tinted with violet and rose, and the breath of wooded wild-flowers. He could not comprehend it. He looked at the purple clouds above the lotus sun, hardly believing, and deeply in doubt.

A great white bird dove suddenly out of the heavens and flew into the focus of his vision. In all the tales of his boyhood, of large and beautiful rocs and other birds, he had come across nothing like this. From the perspective it must have measured a full three hundred feet from tip to tip; it was shaped like a swan and flew like an eagle, with magnificent, lazy sweeps of the wings; while its plumage was as white as the snow, new fallen on the mountains. And right behind it, in pursuit, hurtled a huge black thing, fully as large and just as swift; a tremendous black crow, so black that its sides gave off a greenish shimmer.

Just then the woman closed the window. It was just as well; Watson was only human, and he could hide his curiosity just so long and no longer. He turned to the Rhamda.

The man nodded. "I thought so," spoke he with satisfaction, as one might, who has proved a pet and precious theory.

Watson tried from another angle. "Just who do you think I am, sir?'

The other smiled as before. "It is not what I may think," he replied, "but what I know. You are the proof that was promised us by the great Rhamda Avec. You are—*the Fact and the Substance!*"

He waited for Watson's answer. Stupefaction delayed it. After a moment the Rhamda continued:

"Is it not so? Am I not right? You are surely out of the occult, my dear sir. You are a spirit!"

It took Chick wholly by surprise. He had been ready to deal with anything—but this. It was unreal, weird, impossible. And yet, why not? The professor had set out to remove forever the screen that had hitherto shrouded the shadow: but what had he revealed? What had the Spot disclosed? Unreality or *reality*? Which was which?

In the inspiration of the moment, Chick saw that he had reached the crossroads of the occult. There was no time to think; there was time only for a plunge. And, like all strong men, Watson chose the deeper water.

He turned to the Rhamda Geos.

"Yes," said he quietly. "I—am a spirit."

CHAPTER XXXI

UP FOR BREATH

RHAMDA GEOS, instead of showing the concern and uneasiness that most men would show in the presence of an avowed ghost, evinced nothing but a deep and reverent happiness. He took Watson's hand almost shyly. And while his manner was not effusive, it had the warmth that comes from the heart of a scholar.

"As a Rhamda," he declared, "I must commend myself for being the first to speak to you. And I must congratulate you, my dear sir, on having fallen, not into the hands of Bar Senestro, but into those of my own kind. It is a proof of the prophecy, and a vindication of the wisdom of the Ten Thousand.

"I bid you welcome to the Thomahlia, and I offer you my services, as guide and sponsor."

Chick did not reply at once. The chance he had taken was one of those rare decisions that come to genius; the whole balance of his fate might swing upon his sudden impulse. Not that he had any compunction; but he felt that it tied him down. It restricted him. Certainly almost any rôle would be easier than that of a spirit.

He didn't feel like a ghost. He wondered just how a ghost would act, anyhow. What was more, he could not understand such a queer assumption on the Rhamda's part. Why had he seemed to *want* Chick a ghost? Watson was natural, human, embodied, just like the Rhamda. This was scarcely his idea of a fantom's life. Most certainly, the two of them were men, nothing else; if one was a wraith, so was the other. But—how to account for it?

Again he thought of Rhamda Avec. The words of Geos, "The Fact and the Substance," had been exactly synonymous with what had been said of Avec by Dr. Holcomb, "The proof of the occult."

Was it indeed possible that these two great ones, from opposite poles, had actually torn away the veil of the shadow? And was this the place where he, Watson, must pose as a spirit, if he were to be accepted as genuine?

The thought was a shock. He must play the same part here that the Rhamda had played on the other side of the Spot; but he would have to do it without the guiding wisdom of Avec. Besides, there was something sinister in the unknown force that had engulfed so strong a mind as the professor's; for while Watson's fate had been of his own seeking, that of the doctor smacked too much of treachery.

He must rescue Bertha's father. If he could pose in this world as a spirit it would give him a certain amount of prestige; and, if he could keep away from the miraculous, it would allow him a certain leeway for investigation. In a way, Watson was a skeptical mystic of a sort; he wanted to know just what was what, and why, and the wherefore generally. Finally he wanted to prove to his own satisfaction that the thing was not, after all, merely a masterpiece of knavery.

He turned to the Rhamda Geos with a new question:

"This Rhamda Avec—was he a man like yourself?"

The other brightened again, and asked in return:

"Then you have seen him!"

"I—I do not know," answered Watson, caught off his guard. "But the name is familiar. I don't remember well. My mind is vague and confused. I recall a world, a wonderful world it was from which I came, and a great many people. But I can't place myself; I hardly—let me see—"

The other nodded sympathetic approval.

"I understand. Don't exert yourself. It is hardly to be expected that one forced out of the occult could come among us with his faculties unimpaired. We have had many communications with your world, and have always been frustrated by this one gulf which may not be crossed. When real thought gets across the border, it is often indefinite, sometimes mere drivel. Such answers as come from the void are usually disappointing, no matter how expert our mediums may be in communicating with the dead."

"The dead!" startled. "Did you say—the dead?"

"Certainly; the dead. Are you not of the dead?"

Watson shook his head emphatically. "Absolutely not! Not where I came from. We are all very much alive!"

The other watched him curiously, his great eyes glowing with enthusiasm; the enthusiasm of the born seeker of the truth.

"You don't mean," he asked, "that you have the same passions that we have here in life?"

"I mean," said Watson, "that we hate, love, swear; we are good and we are evil; and we play ball and go fishing."

Geos rubbed his hands in a dignified sort of glee. What had been said coincided, apparently, with another of his pet theories.

"It is splendid," he exulted; "splendid! And just in line with my thesis. You shall tell it before the Council of the Rhamdas. It will be the greatest day since the speaking of the Jarados!"

WATSON wondered just who this Jarados might be; but for the moment he went back to the previous question.

"This Rhamda Avec: you were about to tell me about him. Let me have as much as I can understand, sir."

"Ah, yes! The great Rhamda Avec. Perhaps you may recall him when your mind clears a little more. My dear sir, he is, or was, the chief of the Rhamdas of all Thomahlia."

"What is the 'Thomahlia'?"

"The Thomahlia! Why, it is called the world; our name for the world. It comprises, physically, land, water, and air; politically, it embraces D'Hartia, Kospia, and a few minor nations."

"I see. The world of the Blind Spot!"

But the other had already said he did not understand the term.

"That's all right," said Watson. "I do. Go on. Who are the Rhamdas?"

"They are the head of—of the Thomahlia; not the nominal or political or religious heads—they are neither judicial, executive or legislative; but the real heads, still above. They might be called the supreme college of wisdom, of science and of research. Also, they are the keepers of the bell and its temple, and the interpreters of the Prophecy of the Jarados."

"I see. You are a sort of priesthood."

"No. The priesthood is below us. The priests take what orders we choose to give, and are purely—"

"Superstitious?"

The Rhamda's eyes snapped, just a trifle.

"Not at all, my dear sir! They are good, sincere men. Only, not being intellectually adept enough to be admitted to the real secrets, the real knowledge, they give to all things a provisional explanation based upon a settled policy. Not being Rhamdas, they are simply not aware that everything has an exact and absolute explanation."

"In other words," put in Watson, "they are scientists; they have not lifted themselves up to the plane of inquisitive doubt."

Still the Rhamda shook his head.

"Not quite that, either, my dear sir. Those below us are not ignorant; they are merely nearer to the level of the masses than we are. In fact, they are the people's rulers; these priests and other similar classes. But we, the Rhamdas, are the rulers of the rulers. We differ from them in that we have no material ends to subserve. Being at the top, with no motive save justice and advancement, our judgments are never questioned, and for the same reason, seldom passed.

"But we are far above the plane of doubt that you speak of; we passed out of it long ago. That is the first stage of true science; afterwards comes the higher levels where all things have a reason; ethics, inspiration, thought, emotion—"

"And—the judgment of the Jarados?"

Watson could not have told why he said it. It was impulse, and the impromptu suggestion of a half-thought. He had no notion whatever of the Jarados outside Geos' statement that he had something to do with a prophecy, and was, presumably, thus linked up with some sort of belief or superstition.

But the effect of his words upon the Rhamda and the nurse told him that, inadvertently, he had struck a keynote. Both started, especially the woman. Watson took note of this in particular, because of the ingrained acceptance of the feminine in matters of belief.

"What do you know?" was her eager interruption. "You have seen the Jarados?"

As for the Rhamda, he looked at Watson with shrewd, calculating eyes. But they were still filled with wonder.

"Can you tell us?" he asked. "Try and think!"

CHICK knew that he had gained a point. He had been dealt a trump card; but he was too clever to play it at once. He was on his own responsibility, and was carrying a load that required the finest equilibrium. Still, it was a good thing to know that he held something that might help him keep his balance in the stress of extremity, something of weight. Though the word was on the tip of his tongue, he decided it wise to forego any further question as to the Jarados. Better, thought he, to assume the wisdom of the silent owl than the skill of the chattering parrot.

"I really do not know," he said. "I—I must have time to think. Coming across the border that way you must give me time. You were telling me about the Rhamdas in general; now tell me about Avec in particular."

Geos nodded as though he could understand the fog that beclouded Watson's mind.

"The Rhamda Avec is, or was, the wisest of them all; the head and the chief, and by far the most able. Few beside his own fellows knew it, however; another than he was the nominal head, and officiated for him whenever necessary. Avec had little social intercourse; he was a prodigious student.*

"We are a body of learned men, you understand, and we stand at the peak of all that has been discovered through hundreds upon hundreds of centuries, so that at the present day we are the culmination of the combined effort and thought of man since the beginning of time. Each generation of Rhamdas must be greater than the one preceding. When I die and pass on to your world I must leave something new and worth-while to my successor; some thought, wisdom, or deed that may be of use to mankind. I cannot be a Rhamda else. We are a set of supreme priests, who serve man at the shrine of intelligence, not of dogma.

"Of course, we are not to be judged too highly. All research, when it steps forward must go haltingly; there are many paths into the unknown that look like the real one. Hence, we have among us various schools of thought, each following a different trail.

"I myself am a spiritist. I believe that we can, and often have, communicated with your world at various times. There are others who do not grant it; there are Rhamdas who are inclined to lean more to the materialistic side of things, who rely entirely, when it comes to questions of this kind, upon their faith in the teachings of the Jarados. There are some, too, who believe in the value of speculation, and who contend that only through contemplation can man lift himself to

*NOTE—This would seem to explain why Avec and Ariadne failed to recognize one another.

the full fruits of realization. At the head of us all—the Rhamda Avec!"

"What was his belief?"

"Let us say he believed all. He was eclectic. He held that we were all of us a bit right, and each of us a whole lot wrong. It was his contention, however, that there was not one thing that could not be proven; that the secret of life, while undoubtedly a secret in every sense of the word, is still a very concrete, tangible thing; and being concrete, it could be proven!"

Watson nodded. He remembered hearing another man make just such a statement—Dr. Holcomb.

"For years he worked in private," went on Geos. "We never knew just what he was doing; until, one day, he called us together and delivered his lecture."

"His lecture?"

"Rather, his prophecy. For it was all that. Not that he spoke at great length; It was but a talk. He announced that he believed the time had come to prove the occult. That it could be done, and done only through concrete, material means; and that whatever existed, certainly could be demonstrated. He was going to pull aside the curtain that had hitherto cut off the shadow.

"'I am going to prove the occult,' he said. 'In three days I shall return with the fact and the substance. And then I propose to deliver my greatest lecture, my final thesis, in which my whole life shall come to a focus. I shall bring the proof for your eyes and ears, for your fingers to explore and be satisfied. You shall behold the living truth!

"'And the subject of my lecture'"—the Geos paused, just as the man of whom he spoke must have paused—"'the subject of my lecture will be The Spot of Life.'"

CHAPTER XXXII

THROUGH UNKNOWN WATERS

THE *Spot* of Life! And the subject of Dr. Holcomb's lecture, promised but never delivered, had been announced as —The Blind *Spot!*

To Watson it was fairly astounding to discover that the two—Holcomb and Avec—had reached simultaneously for the curtain of the shadow. The professor had said that it would be "the greatest day since Columbus." And so it had proven, did the world but know it.

"And—the Rhamda Avec never returned?" asked Chick.

"No."

"But he sent back something within three days?" Watson was thinking, of course, of the doctor who had disappeared on the day which, Jerome overheard the Rhamda to say, was the last of his stay.

But Geos did not reply. Why, Chick could not guess. He thought it best not to press the question; in good time, if he went at it carefully, he could gain his end with safety. Right now he must not arouse suspicion. He chose another query.

"Did Avec go alone?"

"No. The Nervina went with him. Rather, she followed within a few hours."

"Ah!"

It was out before Watson could think. The Rhamda looked up suddenly.

"Then you have seen the Nervina! You know her?"

Chick lied. It was not his intention, just at present, to tie himself down to anything that might prove compromising or restraining.

"The name is—familiar. Who is this Nervina?"

"She is one of the queens. I thought— My dear sir, she is one of the beauty-queens of Thomahlia, half Kospian, half D'Hartian; of the first royal line running through from the day of the Jarados."

Chick cogitated for a moment. Then, taking an entirely new tack:

"You say the Rhamda and this Nervina, independently, solved the mystery of the Spot of Life, I believe you call it. And that Spot leads, apparently, into the occult?"

"Apparently, if not positively. It was the wisdom of Avec, mostly. He had been in communication with your world by means of his own discovery and application. It was all in line with the prophecy.

"Since he and the Nervina left, the people of the world have been in a state of ferment. For it was foretold that in the last days we would get in communication with the other side; that some would come and some would go. For example, your own coming was foretold by the Jarados, almost to the hour and minute."

"Then it was fortuitous," spoke Watson. "It was *not* the wisdom and science of Avec, in my case."

"Quite so. However, it is proof that the Rhamdas have fulfilled their duty. We knew of the Spot of Life, all the while; it was to be closed until we, through the effort of our intellect and virtues, could lift ourselves up to the plane of the world beyond us—your world. It could not be opened by ourselves alone, however. The Rhamda Avec had first to get in touch with your side, before he could apply the laws he had discovered."

Somehow, Chick admired this Rhamda. Men of his type could form but one kind of priesthood: exalted, and devoted to the advance of intelligence. If Rhamda Avec were of the same sort, then he was a man to be looked up to, not to hate. As for the Jarados—Watson could not make out who he had been; a prophet or teacher, seemingly, looming out of the past and reverenced from antiquity.

The Blind Spot became a shade less sinister. Already Watson had the Temple of the Leaf, or Bell, the Rhamdas and their philosophy, the great amber sun, the huge birds, the musical cadence of the perfumed air, and the counter-announcement of Rhamda Avec to weigh against the work and words of Dr. Holcomb.

The world of the Blind Spot!

As if in reaction from the unaccustomed train of thought, Watson suddenly became conscious of extreme hunger. He gave an uneasy glance around, a glance which the Rhamda Geos smilingly interpreted. At a word the woman left the room and returned with a crimson garment, like a bath-robe. When Chick had donned it and a pair of silken slippers, Geos bade him follow.

THEY stepped out into the corridor. This was formed and colored much as the room they had quit; and it led to another compartment, much larger—about fifty feet across—colored a deep, cool green.* Its ceiling, coved like the others, seemed made of some self-radiating substance from which came both light and heat. Four or five tables, looking like ebony work, but as frail as Chippendale, were arranged along the side walls. When they were seated at one of these, the Rhamda placed his fingers on some round, alna-white buttons ranged along the edge of the table.

"In your world," he apologized, "our clumsy service would doubtless amuse you; but it is the best we have been able to devise so far."

He pressed the button. Instantly, without the slightest sound or anything else to betray just how the thing had been accomplished, the table was covered with golden dishes, heaped with food, and two flagon-like goblets, full to the brim with a dark, greenish liquid that gave off an aroma almost exhilarating; not alcoholic, but something just above that. The Rhamda, disregarding or not noticing Watson's gasp of wonder, lifted his goblet in the manner of the host in health and welcome.

*NOTE—The word green is used here in the absence of the correct term for this particular shade.

"You may drink it," he offered, "without fear. It is not liquor—if I may use a word which I believe to be current in your world. I may add that it is one of the best things that we shall be able to offer you while you are with us."

Indeed it wasn't liquor. Watson took a sip; and he made a mental note that if all the things in the Thomahlia were on a par with this, then he certainly was in a world far above his own. For the one sip was enough to send a thrill through his veins, a thrill not unlike the ecstasy of supreme music—a sparkling exuberance, leaving the mind clear and scintillating, glorified to the quick thinking of genius.

Later Watson experienced no reaction such as would have come from drinking alcohol or any other drug.

It was the strangest meal ever eaten by Watson. The food was very savory, and perfectly cooked and served. Only one dish reminded him of meat.

"You have meats?" he asked. "This looks like flesh."

Geos shook his head. "No. Do you have flesh to eat, on the other side? We make all our food."

Make food. Watson thought best to simply answer the question:

"As I remember it, Rhamda Geos, we had a sort of meat called beef—the flesh of certain animals."

The Rhamda was intensely interested. "Are they large? Some interpret the Jarados to that effect. Tell me, are they like this?" And he pulled a silver whistle from his pocket and, placing it to his lips, blew two short, shrill notes.

Immediately a peculiar patter sounded down the corridor; a *ka-tuck, ka-tuck, ka-tuck*, not unlike galloping hoof-beats. Before Watson could do any surmising a little bundle of shining black rounded the entrance to the room and ran up to them. Geos picked it up.

It was a horse. A horse, beautifully formed, perfect as an Arab, and not more than nine inches high!

Now, Chick had been in the Blind Spot, conscious, but a short while. He knew that he was in the precise position that Rhamda Avec had occupied that morning on the ferry-boat. Chick recalled the pictures of the Lilliputian deer and the miniature kittens; yet he was immensely surprised.

The little fellow began to neigh, a tiny, ridiculous little sound as compared with the blast of a normal-sized horse, and began to paw for the edge of the table.

"What does he want?"

"A drink. They will do anything for it." Geos pressed a button, and in a moment he had another goblet. This he held before the little stallion, who thrust his head in above his nostrils and drank just as greedily as a Percheron weighing a ton. Watson stroked his sides; the mane was like spun silk; he felt of the legs, symmetrical, perfectly shaped, and not as large above the fetlocks as an ordinary pencil.

"Are they all of this size?"

"Yes; all of them. Why do you ask?"

"Because"—seeing no harm in telling this—"as I remember them, a horse on the other side would make a thousand of this one. People ride them."

The Rhamda nodded.

"So it is told in the books of Jarados. We had such beasts, once, ourselves. We would have them still, but for the brutality and stupidity of our ancestors. It is the one great sin of the Thomahlia. Once we had animals, great and small, and all the blessings of Nature; we had horses, and, I think, what you call beef; a thousand other creatures that were food and help and companions to man. And for the good they had done our ancestors destroyed them!"

"Why?"

"It was neglect, unthinking and selfish. A time came when our civilization made it possible to live without other creatures. When machinery came into vogue we put aside the animals as useless; those we had no further use for we denied the right to reproduce. The game of the forests was hunted down with powerful weapons of destruction; all went, in a century or two; everything that could be killed. And with them went the age of our highest art, that age of domesticated animals.

"Our greatest paintings, our noblest sculpture, came from that age; all the priceless relics that we call classic. And in its stead we had the mechanical age. Man likewise became a mechanism, emotionless, with no taste for Nature. Meat was made synthetically, and so was milk."

"You don't mean to say they did not preserve cows for the sake of their milk?"

"No; that kind of milk became old-fashioned; men regarded it as unsanitary, fit only for calves. What they wanted was something chemically pure; they waged war on bacteria, microbes, and Nature in general; a cow was merely a relic whose product was always an uncertainty. With no reason for the meat and no use for the milk, our vegetarians and our purists gradually eliminated them altogether. It was a strange age; utilitarian, scientific, selfish; it was then headed straight for destruction."

And he went on to relate how man began to lose the power of emotion; there were no dependent beasts to leaven his nature with the salt of kindness; he thought only of his own aggrandizement. He became like his machine, a fine thing of perfectly correlated parts, but with no higher nature, no soul, no feeling; he was less than a brute. In those days they even had artists, so called, who maintained that they could paint the emotions by means of mechanical streaks and daubs and blocks of color.

THE animals disappeared one by one, passing through the channel of death, into the world beyond the Spot of Life, leaving behind only these tiny survivors, playing things, kept in existence longer than all others because of a mere fad.

"Does your spiritism include animals as well as men?"

"Naturally; everything that is endowed with life."

"I see. Let me ask you: why didn't the Rhamdas interfere and put a stop to this wanton sacrilege against Nature?"

The Rhamda smiled. "You forget," replied he, "that these events belong far in the past. At that time the Rhamdas were not. It was even before the coming of the Jarados."

Watson asked no more questions for a while. He wanted to think. How could this man Rhamda Geos, if indeed he were a man, accept him, Watson, as a spirit? Solid flesh was not exactly in line with his idea of the unearthly. How to explain it? He had to go back to Holcomb again. The doctor had accepted without question Avec's naturalness, his body, his appetite. Reasonably enough, Geos, with some smattering of his superior's wisdom, should accept Watson in the same way.

At any rate, if he were merely expected to go on and act his natural self, his rôle as spirit would be easy enough.

And then, the Jarados: at every moment his name had cropped up. Who was he? Until Chick found out, he could not balance himself in the Thomahlia. Perhaps it would be better to forego his curiosity as to locality until he had acquired this vital knowledge; it would enable him to bear up his part.

So far he had heard no word that might be construed as a clue. That he had fallen into a maze of spiritism was just in accord with what he had expected; for, paradoxical as it all might seem, everything gibed with the original purpose—the search for the occult. The great point, just now, was that the Rhamda Geos accepted him as a spirit, as the fact and substance promised by Avec. But—where was the doctor?

Chick ventured this question:

"My coming was foretold by the Rhamda Avec, I understand. Is this in accord with the words of the Jarados?"

The Rhamda looked up expectantly and spoke with evident anxiety.

"Can you tell me anything about the Jarados?"

"Let us forego that," side-stepped Watson. "Possibly I can tell you much that you would like to know. What I want to know is, just how well prepared are you to receive me?"

"Then you come from the Jarados."

"Perhaps."

"What do you know about him?"

"This: some one should have preceded me! The fact and the substance—you were to have it inside three days! It has been several hundred times the space allotted! Is it not so?"

The Rhamda's eyes were pin-pointed with eagerness.

"Then it is true! You are from the Jarados! You know the great Rhamda Avec—you have seen him!"

"I have," declared Watson.

"In the other world? You can remember?"

"Yes," again committing himself. "I have seen Avec—in another world. But tell me, before we go on I would have an answer to my question: did any one precede me?"

"No."

Watson was nonplused, but he concealed the fact.

"Are you sure?"

"Quite, my dear sir. The Spot of Life was watched continually from the moment the Rhamda left us."

"You mean, he and the Nervina?"

"Quite so; she followed him after an interval of a few hours."

"I know. But you say that no one came out ahead of me. Who was it that guarded this—this Spot of Life? The Rhamdas?"

"They, and the Bars."

"Ah! And who are the Bars?"

"The military priesthood. They are the garrison of the Mahovisal, and of the Temple of the Bell. They are led by the great Bar Senestro."

"And there were times when these Bars, led by this Senestro, held guard over the Spot of Life?" To this Geos nodded; and Watson went on: "And who is this great Senestro?"

"He is the chief of the Bars, and a prince of D'Hartia. He is the fiancé of the two queens, the Aradna and the Nervina."

"The *two* of them?"

Whereupon Watson learned something rather peculiar. It seemed that the princes of D'Hartia had always married the beauty-queens. This Senestro had had a brother, but he died. And in such an event it was the iron custom that the surviving brother marry both queens. It had happened only once before in all history; but the precedent was unbreakable.

"Then, there is nothing against it?"

"Nothing; except, perhaps the prophecy of the Jarados. We now know—the whole world knows—that we are fast approaching the Day of Life."

"Of course; the Day of Life." Watson decided upon another chance shot. "It has something to do with the marriage of the two queens!"

"You *do* know!" cried the Rhamda joyously. "Tell me!"

"No; it is I who am asking the questions."

Watson's mind was working like lightning. Whether it was the influence of the strange drink, or the equally strange influence of ordinary inspiration, he was never more self-assured in his life. It seemed a day for taking long chances.

"Tell me," he inquired, "what has the Day of Life to do with the two queens and their betrothal?"

The Rhamda throttled his eagerness. "It is one of the obscure points of the prophecy. There are some scholars who hold that such a problem as this presages the coming of the end and the advent of the chosen. But others oppose this interpretation, for reasons purely material: for if the Bar Senestro should marry both queens it would make him the sole ruler of the Thomahlia. Only once before have we had a single ruler; for centuries upon centuries we have had two queens; one of the D'Hartians, and the other of the Kospians, sitting here in the Mahovisal."

Watson would have liked to learn far more. But the time seemed one for action on his part; bold action, and positive.

"Rhamda Geos—I do not know what is your version of the prophecy. But are you positive that no one has preceded me out of the Spot?"

"I am. Why do you insist?"

"Because"—speaking slowly and with the greatest care—"because there was a greater than I, who came before me!"

The Rhamda rose excitedly to his feet, and then sank back into his chair again. In his eyes was nothing save eagerness, wonder, and respect. He leaned forward.

"Who was it? Who was he?"

Watson's voice was steady as stone.

"The great Jarados himself!"

CHAPTER XXXIII

A LONG WAY FROM SHORE

ONCE more Watson had taken the kind of chance he preferred—a slim one. He knew practically nothing of where he was, what was in the wind; he knew just a trifle about the prophecy, and less than a trifle about the Jarados himself.

But he had studied ethics under Holcomb; he took the chance that these people, however occult and advanced they might be, were still human enough to build their prophecy out of an old foundation. If he were right, then the person of the Jarados would be inviolable. If the professor were prisoner, held somewhere in secret detinue, and it got noised about that he was the true phophet returned—it would not only give Holcomb immense prestige, but at the same time render the position of his captors untenable.

Chick needed no great discernment to see that he had touched a vital spot. The philosophy of the Rhamdas was firmly bound up with spiritism; they had gone far in science, and had passed out of mere belief into the deeper, finer understanding that went back of the shadow for proof. Certainly Watson was inwardly rejoiceful to see Rhamda Geos incredulous, his keen face whitening like that of one who has just heard sacrilege uttered—to see Geos rise in his place, grip the table tightly, and hear him exclaim:

"The Jarados! Did you say—the Jarados? He has come amongst us, and we have not known? You are perfectly sure of this?"

"I am," stated Watson, and met the other's keen scrutiny without flinching.

Would the game work? At least it promised action; and now that he had the old feel of himself he was anxious to get under way. Any feeling of fear was gone now. He calmly nodded his head.

"Yes, it is so. But sit down. I have still a bit more to tell you."

The Rhamda resumed his seat. Clearly, his reverence had been greatly augmented in the past few seconds. From that time on there was a marked difference in his manner; and his speech, when he addressed Chick, contained the expression "my lord"—an expression that Watson found it easy enough to become accustomed to.

"Did you doubt, Rhamda Geos, that I came from the Jarados?"

"We did not doubt. We were certain."

"I see. You were not expecting the Jarados."

"Not yet, my lord. The coming of the Jarados shall be close to the Day of the Judgment. But it could not be so soon; there were to be signs and portents. We were to solve the problem first; we were to know the reason of the shadow and the why of the spirit. The wisdom of the Rhamda Avec told that the day approaches; he had opened the Spot of Life and gone through it; but he had *not* sent the fact and the substance."

Watson smiled. There was just enough superstition, it seemed, beneath all the Rhamda's wisdom to make him tractable. However, Chick asked:

"Tell me: as a learned man, as a Rhamda, do you believe in the prophecy implicitly?"

"Yes, my lord. I am a spiritist; and if spiritism is truth, then the Jarados was genuine, and his prophecy is true. After all, my lord, it is not a case of legend, but of history. The Jarados came at a time of high civilization, when men could see and understand him; he gave us his teaching in records, and imposed his laws upon the Thomahlia. Then he departed—through the Spot of Life."

And the Rhamda Geos went on to say that the teachings of the Jarados had been moral as well as intellectual. Moreover, after he had formulated his laws, he wrote out his judgment.

"What was that?"

"An exhortation, my lord, that we were to give proof of our appreciation of intelligence. We were to use it, and to prove ourselves worthy of it by lifting ourselves up to the level of the Spot of Life. In other words, the spot would be opened when, and only when, we had learned the secrets of the occult, and—had opened the Spot ourselves!"

WATSON thought he understood partly. He asked:

"And that is why you doubt me?"

"You, my lord? Not so! You were found in the Temple of the Bell and Leaf; not on the Spot itself, to be sure, but on the floor of the temple. You were, both in your person and in your dress, of another world; you had been promised by the Rhamda Avec; and, in a sense, you were a part of the prophecy. We accepted you!"

"But I speak your language. Account for that, Geos."

"It need not be accounted for, my lord. We accept it as a fact. The affinity of spirit would not be bound by the limitation of artificial speech. That you should talk the Thomahlian language is no more strange than that Rhamda Avec, when he passed into your world, should speak your tongue."

"We call our language English," supplied Watson. "It is the tongue of the Jarados and of myself."

"Tell me of the Jarados, my lord!" with renewed eagerness. "In the other world—what is he?"

It was Chick's opportunity. By telling the simple truth about Dr. Holcomb he could enhance himself in the eyes of Rhamda Geos.

"In the other world—we call it America—the Jarados is a Rhamda much like yourself, the head and chief of a great many Rhamdas sitting in a supreme institution devoted to intelligence. It is called the University of California."

"And this California; what is it, my lord?"

"A name," returned Chick. "Immediately on the other side of the Spot is a region called California."

"The promised land, my lord!"

"Quite so," said Chick, who was typical of the State. "The promised land, indeed. There are some who call it paradise, even there." And for good measure he proceeded to tell much of his own land, of the woods, the rivers, the cities, animals, mountains, the sky, the moon, and the sun. When he came to the sun he explained that no man dared to look at it continuously with the bared eye. Its great heat and splendor astounded Geos.

In short the plain facts of ordinary life became miraculous; again and again the Rhamda interrupted, to ask for more explicit information about what Chick considered trifles. He answered everything, holding back only such facts as he surmised might be inferior to their counterparts in Thomahlia.

Concerning himself he nonchalantly stated that he was the fiancé of Holcomb's daughter; that is, son-in-law-to-be of the prophet Jarados; that he was sort of Junior Rhamda. He declared that he had come from the occult Rhamdas, through the other side of the Spot, in search of the Jarados who had gone before. As to his blankness up to now, and his perplexity—he was but a Junior; and the Spot had naturally benumbed his senses. Even now, he apologized, it was difficult to know and to recall everything clearly.

Through it all the Rhamda Geos listened in something like awe. He was hearing of wonders never before guessed in the Thomahlia. As the prospective son-in-law of the Jarados, Watson automatically lifted himself to a supreme height, a height so great that, could he only hold himself up to it, he would have a prestige second only to that of the prophet himself.

It was a great adventure for Chick Watson. From an obscure man in a large city he had risen suddenly to the height of a half-god in the world of the occult. For so he must regard himself.

All of a sudden he thought of a question. It gripped him with dread, the dread of the unknown. The question was one of *time*.

"How long have I been here, Rhamda Geos?"

"Over eleven months, by our system of reckoning. You were found on the floor of the temple three hundred and fifty-seven days ago; you were in a life-less condition; you must have been there some hours, my lord, before we discovered you."

"Eleven months!" It had seemed but that many minutes. "And I was uncon-scious—"

"All the time, my lord. Had we caught you immediately upon your coming, we could have brought you around within three days, but under the circumstances it was impossible to restore you before we did. You have been under the care of the greatest specialists in all Thomahlia."

Geos himself had been one of these. "The Council of the Rhamdas went into special session, my lord, immediately after your materialization, and has been sitting almost continually since. And now that you are revived, they are wait-ing in person for you to show yourself.

"They accept you. They do not know who you are, my lord; none of us have guessed even a part of the truth. The entire council awaits!"

But Chick wanted more. Besides, he looked at his clothing.

"I would have my own garments, Geos; also, whatever else was found on my person."

For Watson was thinking of a small but powerful pistol, an automatic re-peater, that he had carried on the night when he fell through the Blind Spot. This question of materiality was still a puzzle; if he himself had survived there was a chance that the firearm had done the same. It might and it might not pre-clude the occult. Anyway, he treasured the thought of that automatic; with it in his possession he would not be bare-handed in case of emergency.

THEY returned to the room in which Chick had awakened. The Rhamda left him. A few moments later he came back with a squad of men. Chick noted their discipline, movement, and uni-forms, and classed them as soldiers. Two men were stationed outside the door—one, a stout, dark individual in a blue uniform; and the other a lithe, athletic chap, blond and blue-eyed, wearing a bright crimson dress not unlike the garb of a Highlander. Chick instinctively pre-ferred both man and garb in crimson; there was a touch of honor, of lightness and strength that just suited him. The other was dark, heavy and sinister.

Both wore sandals, and upon their heads curious shakos, made of the finest down, not fur. Both displayed a heavy silken braid looped from one shoulder. Each carried a spearlike weapon, of some shining black material, straight-tapered to a needle point; but no other .rms.

Watson pointed to the two uniforms. "What is the significance, Geos?"

"One is from the queen, my lord; the other from Bar Senestro. The blue is the cloth of the Bars; the red, that of the queens. The Bar and the queen send this body-guard with their respective compli-ments."

Chick took the bundle that Geos had brought, and proceeded to don his own clothes, finding deep satisfaction in the fact that they had survived as intact as he. He felt, carefully, in his hip pocket; the automatic was still there, likewise the extra magazine of cartridges that he had carried about with him on that night.

In his other pockets he found two packets of cigarettes, a sack of tobacco, and some papers, a few coins and a little paper money—all very well in California, whatever they might be worth where he now was—and two photographs, one of Bertha and the other of her father. Not a thing had been disturbed.

He announced himself ready.

The Rhamda conducted him down the corridor, which he found to be lined with guards: red on the one side, blue on the other. These men fell in behind in two-man formation: two parallel files, one of the one color and one of the other.

It was a building of great size. The corridors were long and high, all with the wide-coved ceiling, and of colors that melted from one shade to another as they turned, not corners, but curves. Apparently each color had its own sug-gestive reason. Such rooms as Chick could look into were uniformly large, beautiful, and distinctly lighted.

The guard moved in silent rhythm; the chief sound was that made by Wat-son's leather-heeled shoes, drowning out, for once, the everlasting tinkling undertone of those unseen fairy-bells; that runeing cadence, never ceasing, silver, liquid, like the soul of sound.

THOUGH Watson walked with head erect, he had eyes for every little thing he passed. He noted the material of the structure and tried to name it; neither plaster nor stone, the walls were highly polished, and, somehow or other, capable of emitting perfume—light and wholesome, not heavy and oppressive. And in dark passages the walls glowed.

The corridor widened, and with a graceful curve opened upon a wide stairway that descended, or rather sank, to use Watson's own word for the feeling —sank into the depths of the building. To the right of one landing was a large window reaching to the floor; its panes were clear and not frosted as had been the others.

Chick got his first glimpse here of what might lay outside—an iridescent landscape, at first view astonishingly like an ocean of opals; for it was of many hues, red and purple and milky white, splashed violantin blue and fluorescence—a maze and shimmer of dancing, joyful colors, whirring in an uncertainty of polychromatic harmony. Such was his first fleeting impression.

At the next landing he looked closer. It was not unlike a monster bowl of bubbles; the same illusion of movement, the same delicacy and witchery of color, only here the sensation was not that of decomposition but of life; of flowers, delicate as the rainbow, tenuous, sinuous, breathing—weaving in a serpentine maze of dædalian hues; labyrinthine and inextricable; long tendrils of orchidian beauty, lifting, weaving, drooping—a vast sea of equatorial bloom; but—no trees.

"This is our landscape," spoke the Rhamda. "According to the Jarados, it is not like that of the next world— your world, my lord. After you meet the Rhamdas, I shall take you into the Mahovisal for a closer view of it all."

They reached the bottom of the stairway. Chick noted the architecture in the entrance-way at this point; the seeming solidity of structure, as if the whole had been chiseled, not built. The vestibule was really a hall, domed and high, large enough to shelter a hundred. Like the corridor outside Chick's room, it was lined with a row each of red and blue uniformed guards.

Invariably the one belonged to the blond, lithe, quick feeling type, the others averaging heavy, sturdy, formidable. The extremities of the two lines converged from an oval-topped doorway, very large,

having above it a design conventionalized from the three-leafed clover. One leaf was scarlet, one navy, the other green.

The door opened. The guards halted. Geos stepped aside with a bow, and Watson strode forward into the presence of the Council of the Rhamdas.

CHAPTER XXXIV

THE BAR SENESTRO

IT WAS a critical moment for Chick. Out of the impulse of his inner nature he had chosen the odds that he must now uphold against the combined wisdom of these intellectuals. He was alone, with no one to guide him save Geos, who undoubtedly was his friend, but who as undoubtedly would desert him upon the slightest inkling of imposture.

He found himself in a great, round room, or rather an oval one, domed at the top but tinted in a far more beautiful coloring—lazuli blue. The walls were cut by long, narrow windows reaching far up into the sweep where the side melted into the ceiling. The material of the windows was of the same translucent substance already noted, but slightly tinged with green, so that they shed a soft light, cool and quiet, over the whole assembly.

On the wall opposite the doorway was a large replica of the clover-leaf design outside, even more gem-like in brilliance; its three colors weaved into a trinity almost of flame. Whether the light was artificial or intrinsic, Chick could not say.

The floor of the place accommodated some three hundred tables, of the library type, and the same number of men bearing the distinguished stamp of the Rhamda. All were smooth-shaven, comparatively tall, and possessing the same esthetic manner which impressed one with the notion of inherited, inherent culture. The entire hall had the atmosphere of learning, justice, and the supreme tribunal.

For a moment Watson felt weak and uncertain. He could hold up against Geos and Avec, but in the face of such an array he wasn't so sure. There was but one thing to encourage him; the faces into which he looked. All were full of wonder and reverence. His mind went back to that original lecture by Holcomb; and he realized that, had the doctor delivered the proof which he had promised, he— Watson—would have doubtless felt and thought just as those now before him. Why fear the Rhamdas?

Then he looked about him more carefully. He had come out upon a wide platform, or rostrum. He now noticed that he was flanked on either side by thrones—two of them; they seemed made of golden amber. The one on the right was occupied by a man, the other by a woman. In the pause that was vouchsafed him Chick took note of these two, and wondered.

In the first place, the man was not a Rhamda. The jeweled semi-armor that he wore was more magnificent than the dignified garb of the Intellectuals; at the same time, his accouterments cheapened him, by contrast. He was executive, princely, with the bearing that comes of worldly ambitions and attainments; a man strangely handsome, vital, athletic; tall, well proportioned, with reddish, curling hair, dark, quick eyes and even features; except only for the mouth he might have been taken as a model of the Greek Alexander.

The clothes he wore were classic, as was everything else about him even to his sandals, his bare arms and his jeweled breastplate.

Watson had studied history. He had a quick impression of a composite—of genius, cruelty and sensuality. Here was one with three strong natures, a sort of Nero, Caligula and Alexander combined: the sensuality of the first, the cruelty of the second, and the instinctive fire and greatness of the immortal Macedonian. The man was smiling; not an amused smile, but one of interested, humorous tolerance.

When their eyes met, Chick caught the magnetic current of personality, the same sense of illusiveness that he and Harry Wendel had noted in the Nervina; only here it was negative, resisting instead of aiding. A number of the blue guard surrounded the throne, their faces dark, strong, and of unconquerable resolution, though slow to think.

On the other throne was a girl. Chick had heard enough from the Geos to guess her identity: one of the queens, the Aradna; frail, delicate, a blue-eyed maiden, with a waving mass of straw-gold hair hanging loosely about her shoulders. She too was classically attired, although there were touches of modernity here and there in the arrangement of ribbons; the garment matched her guards' crimson, and was draped about her shoulders so as to leave one bare, together with that arm. Across her forehead was a band of dark-blue gems, and she wore no other jewels.

She was not more than seventeen or eighteen, frail as a fairy, with eyes like blue-bells, lips as red as poppies, features that danced with delight and laughter and all the innocence that one would associate with elfin royalty. Instinctively Chick compared her with the Nervina.

THE senior queen had the subtle magnetism, the unaccountable fascination, the poise and decision that held and dictated all things to her superfeminine fancy. Like Harry, Chick had always held her "out of the moonbeams."

Not so the Aradna. Hers was the strength of simplicity, the frank, open delight of the maiden, and at the same time all the charm and suggestion of coming womanhood. When she caught Watson's eye she smiled; a smile free and unrestrained, out of an open, happy heart. She made a remark to one of her guards, who nodded a reply after the manner of a friend, rather than a courtier.

Watson turned to the Geos, who stood somewhat to one side, and a little to the rear.

"The Aradna?"

"Yes. The beauty-queen of D'Hartia. The man on the other side is the Bar Senestro."

Whatever feeling Chick entertained for the one was offset by what he felt for the other. He was between two forces; his instinct warned him of the Bar, skeptic, powerful, ruthless, a man to be reckoned with; but his better nature went out to the little queen.

At a motion from Geos, the whole assembly of Rhamdas stood up. The action was both dignified and reverent. Though Chick were, in their eyes, a miracle, there was no unseemly staring, nor jarring of curiosity; all was quietness, ease, poise; the only sound, that of the constant subtle music of those invisible bells.

Rhamda Geos began speaking. At the same time he placed a friendly hand on Watson's shoulder, a signal for every other Rhamda to resume his seat.

"The Fact and the Substance, my brothers."

Geos paused as he made use of the ultra-significant phrase. And then, in a few rapid sentences he ran over the synopsis of the affair, beginning with some philosophy and other details that Watson could not half understand, making frequent allusions to the Jarados and other writers of prophecy; then, he made some mention of his own particular brand of spiritism and its stand on materialization. This he followed with an account of the finding of Watson in the temple, his long sleep and ultimate reviving. At greater length he repeated the gist of their conversation.

Not until then was there a stir among the Rhamdas. Chick glanced over at the Aradna. She was listening eagerly, her chin cupped in her hand, her blue eyes full of interest and wonder, and natural, unfeigned, child-like delight.

Then the Bar caught Chick's glance; the newcomer felt the cold chill of calculation, the cynical weight of the skeptic, and a queer foreboding of the future; no light glance, but one like fire and ice and iron. He wondered at the man's beauty and genius, and at his emotional preponderance manifest even here before the Rhamdas.

The Geos went on. His words, now, were simple and direct. Watson felt himself almost deified by that reverent manner. The Rhamdas listened with visibly growing interest; the Aradna leaned slightly forward; even the Bar dropped his interest in Watson to pay closer attention to the speaker. For Geos had come to the Jarados; he was an orator as well as a mystic, and he was advancing Chick's words with all the skill of a master of language: ascending effect—climax—the Jarados had come among them, and— They had missed him!

For a moment there was silence, then a rustle of general comment. Chick watched the Rhamdas, leaning over to whisper to each other. Could he stand up against them?

But none of them spoke. After the first murmur of comment they lapsed into silence again. It was the Bar Senestro who broke the tension.

"May I ask, Rhamda Geos, why you make such an assertion? What proof have you, to begin with, that this man," indicating Watson with a nod, "is not merely one of ourselves: a D'Hartian or a Kospian?"

The Geos replied instantly: "You know the manner of his discovery, Bar Senestro. Have you not eyes?" Geos seemed to think that he had said the last word.

"Surely," rejoined the Bar good-humoredly. "I have very good eyes, Rhamda Geos. Likewise I have a mind to reason with; but my imagination, I fear, is defective. What I behold is just such a creature as myself; not otherwise. How hold you that this one is proof out of the occult?"

"You are skeptical," returned the Rhamda, evenly. "Even as you behold him, you are full of doubt. But do you not recall the words of the great Avec? Do you not know the Prophecy of the Jarados?"

"Truly, Geos; I remember them both. Especially the writing on the wall of the temple. Does not the prophet himself say: 'And behold, in the last days there shall come among ye—the false ones. Them ye shall slay'?"

"All very true, Bar Senestro. But you well know—we all know—that the true prophecy was to be fulfilled when the Spot was opened. Did not the fulfillment begin when the Avec and the Nervina passed through to the other side?"

"The fulfillment, Geos? Perhaps it was the sign of the coming of impostors! The end may not be until *all* the conditions are complied with!"

But at this moment the Aradna saw fit to speak. There was nothing save girlish sweetness in her tones, every note musical, mellow, full of good-will.

"Senestro, would you condemn this one without allowing him a word in his own defense? Is it fair? Besides, he does not look like an impostor to me. I like his face. Perhaps he is one of the chosen!"

At the last word the Bar frowned. His glance shifted suddenly to Watson, a swift look of ice-cold calculation.

"Very, very true, O Aradna. I, too, would have him speak in his own behalf. Let him amuse us with his tongue. What would your majesty care to hear, O Aradna, from this fantom?"

The words were of biting satire. Chick wheeled upon the Bar. Their eyes clashed; an encounter not altogether to Watson's credit. He was a bit unsteady, a trifle uncertain of his power. He had calculated on the superstition of the Rhamdas to hold him up until he caught his footing, and this unexpected skepticism was disconcerting. However, he was no coward; the feeling passed away almost at once. He strode straight up to the throne of the Bar; and once more he spoke from sheer impulse:

"The Aradna has spoken true, O Senestro, or sinister, or whatever you may be called. I demand fair hearing! It is my due; for I have come from another world. I follow—the Jarados!"

IF WATSON had supposed that he had taken the Bar's measure, he was mistaken. The prince's eyes suddenly glinted with a fierce pleasure. Like a flash his antagonism shifted to something astonishingly like admiration.

"Well spoken! Incidentally, you are well made and sound looking, stranger."

"Passably," returned the Californian athlete. "I do not care to discuss my appearance, however. I am certainly no more ill-favored than some others."

"And impertinent," continued the other, quite without malice. "Do you know anything about the Bar, to whom you speak so saucily?"

"I know that you have intimated that I may be an impostor. You have done this, after hearing what the learned Rhamda Geos has said. You know the facts; you know that I have come from the Jarados. I—"

But it wasn't Watson's words that held the Bar's attention. Chick's straight, well knit form, his quick, trained actions, over-balanced the question of the prophet in the mind of the man on the throne. His delight was self-evident.

"Truly you are soundly built, stranger; you are made of iron and whipcord, finely formed, quick and alert." He threw a word to one of his heavy-faced attendants, then suddenly stood up and descended from his throne. He came up and stood beside Watson.

Chick straightened. The prince was an inch the taller, his bare arms long-muscled, lithe, powerful; under the pink skin Chick could see the delicate, cat-like play of strength and vitality, and in the skin itself a velvety luster of youth and vigor. He sensed the strength of the man, his quick. eager, instinctive glance, his panther-like step and certainty of graceful movement—a voltaic, dynamic personality.

"Stranger," spoke the Bar, "indeed you *are* an athlete! What is your nationality—Kospian?"

"Neither Kospian nor D'Hartian; I am an American. True, there are some who have said that I am built like a man; I pride myself that I can conduct myself like one."

"And speak impertinently." Still in the best of humor, the prince coolly reached out and felt of Watson's biceps. His eyes became still brighter. If not an admirer of decorum, he could appreciate firm flesh. "Sirra! You *are* strong! Answer me —do you know anything about games of violence?"

"Several. Anything you choose."

But the prince shook his head. "Not so. I claim no unfair advantage; you are well met, and opportune. Let it be a contest of your own choosing. The greater honor to myself, the victor!"

But the little queen saw fit to interfere.

"Senestro, this is the code of a Bar? Is not your proposal unseemly to so great a guest? Restrain your eagerness for strength and for muscle! You have preferred charges against this man; now you would hurl your body as well. Remember, I am the queen; I can command it of you."

The Senestro bowed.

"Your wishes are my law, O Aradna." Then, turning to Watson: "I am over-

eager, stranger. You are the best-built man I have seen for many a circle.* But I shall best you." He paced to his throne and resumed his seat. "Let him tell his tale. I repeat, Geos, that for all his beauty this one is an impostor. When he has spoken I shall confute him. I ask only that in the end he be turned over to me."

IT WAS plain that the Thomahlia was blest with odd rulers. If the Bar Senestro were a priest, he was clearly still more of a soldier. The fiery challenge of the man struck an answering chord in Watson; he knew the time must come when he should weigh himself up against this Alexander, and it was anything but displeasing to him.

"What must I say and do?" he asked the Rhamda Geos. "What do they want me to tell them?"

"Just what you have told me: tell them of the Nervina, and of Rhamda Avec. The prince is a man of the world, but from the Rhamdas you shall have justice."

Whereat Chick addressed the Intellectuals. They seemed accustomed to the outbursts of the handsome Bar, and were now waiting complacently. In a few words Watson described the Nervina and Avec; their appearance, manners—everything. Fortunately he did not have to dissemble. When he had finished there was a faint murmur of approval.

"It is proven," declared the girl queen. "It is truly my cousin, the Nervina. I knew not the Rhamda, but from your faces it must have been he. Senestro, what say you to this?"

But the Bar was totally unconvinced.

"All this is childish. Did I not say that he is of our world—D'Hartian, or Kospian, or some other? Does not all Thomahlia know of the Nervina? Few have seen the Rhamda Avec, but what of it? Some have. What this stranger says proves nothing at all. I say, give him a test."

"The test?" from Geos, in a hushed tone.

"Just that. There is none who knows the likeness of the Jarados; none but the absent Avec. None among us has ever seen his image. It is a secret to all save the High Rhamda. Yet, in cases like this, well may the Leaf be opened."

Watson, wondering what was meant, listened closely to the prince as he continued: "It is written that there are times when all may see. Surely this is such a time.

*NOTE—Circle: a year.

98

"Now let this stranger describe the Jarados. He says that he has seen him; that he is the Prophet's prospective son-in-law. Good! Let him show us that he knows! Let him describe the Jarados to us!

"Then open the Leaf! If he speaks true, we shall know him to be from the Jarados. If he fail, then I shall claim him for purposes of my own."

Whatever the motives of the Senestro, he surely had the judgment of an Alexander, the genius of quick decision. Watson knew that the moment had come to test his luck to the uttermost. There was but one thing to do; he did it. He said to the Rhamda Geos, in a tone of the utmost indifference:

"I am willing."

Geos was distinctly relieved. "It is good, my lord. Tell us in simple words. Describe the Jarados just as you have seen him, just as you would have us see him.

"Afterwards we shall open the Leaf." And in a lower tone: "If you speak accurately I shall be vindicated, my lord. I doubt not that you are a better man than the prince; but place your reliance in the Truth; it will be one more proof of the occult, and of the Day approaching."

Which is all that Watson told. But first he breathed a prayer to One who is above all things occult or physical. He did not understand where he was nor how he had got there; he only knew that his fate was hanging on a toss of chance.

He faced the Rhamdas without flinching; and half closing his eyes and speaking very clearly, he searched his memory for what he recalled of the old professor. He tried to describe him just as he had appeared that day in Ethics 2b, when he made the great announcement; the trim, stubby figure of Professor Holcomb, the pink, healthy skin, the wise, gray, kindly eyes, and the close-cropped, pure white beard: all, just as Chick had known him. One chance in millions; he took it.

"That is the Jarados as I have seen him; a short, elderly, wise, *bearded* man."

There was not a breath or a murmur in comment. All hung upon his words; but there was not a sound in the room as he ceased speaking, only the throb of his own heart and the subtle pounding of caution in his veins. He had spoken. If only there might be a resemblance!

The Geos stepped forward a pace. "It is well said. If the truth has been spoken, there shall be room for no dispute. It shall be known throughout all Thom-

ahlia that the Chosen of the Jarados has spoken. Let the Leaf be opened!"

Chick never knew just what happened, much less how it was accomplished. He knew only that a black, opaque wave ran up the long windows, shutting off the light; so that instantly the darkness of night enveloped everything, blotting out all that maze of color; it was the blackness of the void.

Then came a tiny light, a mere dot of flame, over in the opposite wall; a pin point of light it was, seemingly coming out of a vast distance like an approaching star, growing gradually larger, spreading out into a screen of radiance that presently was flashing with intrinsic life. The corruscation grew brighter; little tufts of brilliance shot out with all the stabbing suddenness of shooting stars. To Chick it was exactly as though some god were pushing his way through and out of fire. In the end the flame burst asunder, diminished into a receding circle and sputtered out.

And in the place of the strange light there appeared the illuminated figure of a man. Leaning forward, Chick rubbed his eyes and looked again.

It was the bust of Professor Holcomb.

CHAPTER XXXV

THE PERFECT IMPOSTOR

CHICK gasped. Of all that assemblage —Rhamdas, guards, the occupants of the two thrones—he himself was the most astounded. Was the great professor in actual fact the true Jarados? If not, how explain this miracle? But if he were, how to explain the duality, the identity? Surely, it could not be sheer chance!

Fortunately for Chick, it was dark. All eyes were fixed on the trim figure which occupied the space of the clover-leaf on the rear wall. Except for Chick's strangled gasp, there was only the hushed silence of reverence, deep and impressive.

Then, another dot appeared. From its position, Watson took it to come from another leaf of the clover; another light approaching out of the void and cutting through the blackness exactly as the first had come. It grew and spread until it had filled the whole leaf; then, again the bursting of the flare, the diminishing of the light, and its disappearance in a thin rim at the edge. And this time there was revealed—

A handsome brown-haired *dog*.

Watson, of course, could not understand. The silence held; he could feel the Rhamda Geos at his side, and hear him murmur something which, in itself, was quite unintelligible:

"The four-footed one! The call to humility, sacrifice, and unselfishness! The four-footed one!"

That was all. It was a shaggy shepherd dog, with a pointed nose and one ear cocked up and the other down, very wisely inquisitive. Chick had seen similar dogs many times, but he could not account for this one; certainly not in such a place. What had it to do with the Jarados?

Still the darkness. It gave him a chance to think. He wondered, rapidly, how he could link up such a creature with his description of the Jarados. What could be the purpose of a canine in occult philosophy? Or, was the whole thing, after all, mere blundering chance?

That is what bothered Chick. He did not know how to adjust himself; life, place, sequence, were all out of order. Until he could gather exact data, he must trust to intuition as before.

The two pictures vanished simultaneously. Down came the black waves from the windows, gradually, and in a moment the room was once more flooded with that mellow radiance.

The Rhamda Geos stepped forward as a murmur of awed approval arose from the assembly. There was no applause. One does not applaud the miraculous. The Geos took his hand.

"It is proven!" he declared. Then, to the Rhamdas: "Is there any question, my brothers?"

But no word came from the floor. Seemingly superstition had triumphed over all else. The men of learning turned none but reverent faces toward Watson.

He forbore to glance at the Bar Senestro. Despite the triumph he was apprehensive of the prince's keen genius. An agnostic is seldom converted by what could be explained away as mere coincidence. Moreover, as it ultimately appeared, the Bar now had more than one reason for antagonizing the man who claimed to be the professor's prospective son-in-law.

"Is there any question?" repeated Rhamda Geos.

But to the surprise of Chick, it came from the little queen. She was standing before her throne now, in all her maidenly daintiness. Around her waist a girdle of satin revealed the tender frailty of her figure. She gave Watson a close scrutiny, and then addressed the Geos:

"I want to put one question, Rhamda. The stranger seems to be a goodly young man. He has come from the Jarados. Tell me, is he truly of the chosen?"

But a clear, derisive laugh from the opposite throne interrupted the answer. The Bar stood up, his black eyes dancing with mocking laughter.

"The chosen, O Aradna? The chosen? Do not allow yourself to be tricked by a little thing! I myself have been chosen by the inherited law of the Thomahlia!" Then to Chick: "I see, Sir Fantom, that our futures are to be intertwined with interest!"

"I don't know what you mean."

"No? Very good; if you are really come out of superstition, then I shall teach you the value of materiality. You are well made and handsome, likewise courageous. May the time soon come when you can put your mettle to the test in a fair conflict!"

"It is your own saying, O Senestro!" warned Geos. "You must abide by my lord's reply."

"True; and I shall abide. I know nothing of black magic, nor any other. But I care not. I know only that I cannot accept this stranger as a spirit. I have felt his muscles, and I know his strength; they are a man's, and a Thomahlian's."

"Then you do not abide?"

"Yes, I do. That is, I do not claim him. He has won his freedom. But as for endorsing him—no, not until he has given further proof. Let him come to the Spot of Life. Let him take the ordeal. Let him qualify on the Day of the Prophet."

"My lord, do you accept?"

Watson had no idea what the "ordeal" might be, nor what might be the significance of the "day." But he could not very well refuse. He spoke as lightly as he could.

"Of course. I accept anything." Then, addressing the prince: "One word, O Senestro."

"Speak up, Sir Fantom!"

Watson smiled despite himself. Surely the Bar was a real skeptic. Subconsciously Chick realized that, were their positions reversed, he would likely speak as had the prince. But he was where and what he was. And the question he had in mind did not permit of good humor; it had to be said in an aggressive spirit, if not in an aggressive voice.

"Bar Senestro—what have you done with the Jarados?"

An instant's stunned silence greeted this stab. It was broken by the prince.

"The Jarados!" His voice was unruffled. "What know I of the Jarados?"

"Take care! You have seen him—you know his power!"

"You have a courageous sort of impertinence!"

"I have determination and knowledge!

Bar Senestro, I have come for the Jarados!" Chick paused for effect. "Now what think you? Am I of the chosen?"

He had meant it as a deliberate taunt, and so it was taken. The Bar shot to his feet. Not that he was angered; his straight, handsome form was kingly, and for all his impulsiveness there was a certain real majesty about his every pose.

"You *are* of the chosen. It is well; you have given spice to the taunt! I would not have it otherwise. Forget not your courage on the Day of the Prophet!"

With that he stepped gracefully, superbly from the dais beneath his throne. He bowed to the Aradna, to Geos, to Chick and to the assembly—and was gone. The blue guard followed in silence.

THE rest of the ordeal was soon done. Nothing more was said about the Jarados, nor of what the Bar Senestro had brought up. There were a few questions about the world he had quit, questions which put no strain upon his imagination to answer. He was out of the deep water for the present.

When the assembly dissolved Chick was conducted back to the apartments upstairs. Not to his old room, however, but to an adjoining suite, a magnificent place that would have done honor to a prince.

But Chick scarcely noted the beauty of the place—its elaborate artistry of wall hangings, its enigmatic paintings and sculptures of diminutive creatures and of strong men in the nude, its amazingly fine artificial flowers, and the deep-napped carpet on the floor. His attention flew at once to something for which he longed—an immense globe, exactly like those used in schoolrooms as representations of the earth, only very much larger.

Chick spun it around eagerly upon its axis. The first thing that he looked for was San Francisco—or, rather, North America, so that he could locate the familiar indentation of the Golden Gate. If he was on the earth he wanted to know it! Surely the oceans and continents would not change*

But he was doomed to disappointment. There was not a familiar detail. Outside

of a network of curved lines indicating latitude and longitude, and the accustomed tilt of the polar axis, the globe was totally strange! So strange that Chick could not decide which was water and which was land.

After a bit of puzzling Chick ran across a yellow patch marked with some strange characters which, upon examination, were translated in some unknown manner within his subconscious mind, to "D'Hartia." Another was lettered "Kospia."

Assuming that these were land—and there were a few others, smaller ones, of the same shade—then the land area covered approximately three-fifths of the globe. Inferentially the green remainder, or two-fifths, was the water or ocean covered area. Such a proportion was nearly the precise reverse of that obtaining on the earth. Chick puzzled over other strange names—H'Alara, Mal Somnal, Bloudou San, and the like. Not one name or outline that he could place!

How could he make his discovery fit with the words of Dr. Holcomb, and with what philosophy he knew? Somehow there was too much life, too much reality, to fit in with any spiritistic hypothesis. He was surrounded by real matter, atomic, molecular, cellular. He was certain that if he were put to it he could prove right here every law from those put forth by Newton to the present.

It was still the material universe; that was certain. Therefore it was equally certain that the doctor had made a most prodigious discovery. But—what was it? What was the law that had fallen out of the Blind Spot?

He gave it up, and stepped to one of the suite's numerous windows. They were all provided with clear glass. Now was his opportunity for an uninterrupted, leisurely survey of the world about him.

As before, he noted the maze of splendid, dazzling opalescence, all the colors of the spectrum blending, weaving, vibrant, like a vast plain of smooth, Gargantuan jewels. As soon as the first blinding splendor had worn off he noted individualities in that chromatic sea, stationary billows, as it were.

Then he made out innumerable round domes, spread out in rows and in curves, without seeming order or system; *buildings,* every roof a perfect gleaming dome, its surface fairly alive with the reflected light of that amazing sun. Of such was the landscape made.

AS BEFORE, he could hear the incessant undertone of vague music, of rhythmical, shimmering and whispering

*NOTE—As to the possibility that Chick had in some manner become transferred to another planet, through the operation of some undiscovered law of affinity, General Hume offers this: A planet has often been vaguely observed in an orbit lying between that of Mercury and the sun. "Vulcan" is the name of this dubious member of our solar system. Now, granting that such a globe could exist and still be undetected, due to its proximity to the sun's brilliance, then the "Thomahlia" becomes explicable at once. The great size of the sun, as seen by Chick, also the curious nature of the atmosphere (which would have to be very dense, if it were to reflect the sun's rays enough to permit life), both fit in with this hypothesis.

sound. It was like the music that runs through dreams. And the whole air was laden with the hint of sweet scents; diapasmic, tinnient, and tinged with the perfume of attar and myrrh—of a most delicate ambrosia.

He opened the window.

For a moment he stood still, the air bathing his face, the unknown fragrance filling his nostrils. The whole world seemed thrumming with that hitherto faint quiver of sound. Now it was resonant and strong, though still only an undertone. He looked below him; as he did so, something dropped from the side of the window opening—a long, delicate tendril, sinuous and alive. It touched his face, and then— It drooped, drooped like a wounded thing. He reached out his hand and plucked it, wondering. And he found, at its tip, a floating crimson blossom as delicate as the frailest cobweb, so inconceivably dainty that it wilted and crumbled at the slightest touch.

Chick thrust his head out of the window. The whole building, from ground to dome, was covered—waving, moving, tenuous, a maze of incomprehensibly delicate color—orchids!

He had never dreamed of anything so beautiful, or so daintily splendid. He was acquainted with flowers, and knew many of the species; but none like these. Everywhere these orchids; to give them the name nearest to the unknown one. As far as he could see, living beauty!

And then, with his senses half-dulled with what they were experiencing, he noticed something stranger still.

From the petals and the foliage about him, little clouds of color wafted up, like mists of perfume, forever rising and intermittently settling. It was mysteriously harmonious, continuous—like life itself. Chick looked closer, and listened. And then he knew.

These mists were clouds—fogs—of tiny, multi-colored insects.

Watson was more than bewildered. It was all absolutely new. Everything that he had seen was exotic, wafted through sense to the degree of elysium. Nothing was as it should be.

He looked down farther, into the streets. They were teeming with life, with motion. He was in a city whose size made it a true metropolis. All the buildings were large, and, although of unfamiliar architecture, undeniably of a refined, advanced art. Without exception, their roofs were domed. Hence the effect of a sea of bubbles.

Directly below, straight down from his window, was a very broad street. From it at varying angles ran a number of intersecting avenues. The height of his window was great—he looked very closely, and made out two lines of color lining and outlining the street surrounding the apartments.

On the one side the line was blue, on the other crimson; they were guards. And where the various avenues intersected cables must have been stretched; for these streets were packed and jammed with a surging multitude, which the guards seemed engaged in holding back. As far up the avenues as Chick could see, the seething mass of fellow creatures extended, a gently pulsing, varicolored potential commotion. Chick wondered what it was all about.

As he looked, one of the packed streets broke into confusion. He could see the guards wheeling and running into formation; from behind, other platoons rushed up reenforcements. The great crowd was rolling forward, breaking on the edge of the spear-armed guards like the surf of a rolling sea.

Chick had a sudden thought. Were they not looking up at his window? He could glimpse arms uplifted and hands pointed. Even the guards, those held in reserve, looked up. Then—such was the distance—the rumble of the mob reached his ears; at the same time, spreading like a grass fire, the commotion broke out in another street, to another and another, until the air was filled with the new undertone of countless human tongues.

Chick was fascinated. The thing was over-strange. While he looked and listened the whole scene turned to conflict; the voice of the throng became ominous. The guards still held the cables, still beat back the populace. Could they hold out wondered Chick idly; and, what was it all about?

Something touched his shoulder. He wheeled. One of the tall, red-uniformed guards was standing beside him. Watson instinctively drew back, and as he did so the other stepped forward, touched the snap, and closed the window.

"What's the idea? I was just getting interested!"

The soldier nodded pleasantly, respectfully—reverently.

"Orders from below, my lord. Were you to remain at that window it would take all the guards in the Mahovisal to keep back the Thomahlians."

"Why?" Chick was astonished.

"There are a million pilgrims in the city, my lord, who have waited months for just one glimpse of you."

Watson considered. This was a new and a dazing aspect of the affair. Evidently the expression on his face told the soldier that some explanation would not be amiss.

"The pilgrims are almost innumerable, my lord. They are all of the one great faith. They are, my lord, the true believers, the believers in the Day."

The Day! Instantly Watson recalled Senestro's use of the expression. What did it mean? What was its bearing upon the enigma. of the Jarados, and what was its relation to Watson's own predicament?

He sensed a valuable clue. He caught and held the soldier's eye.

"Tell me," commanded Chick. "What is this Day of which you speak?"

CHAPTER XXXVI

AN ALLY, AND SOLID GROUND

THE soldier replied unhesitatingly: "It is the Day of Life, my lord. Others call it the 'first of the Sixteen Days.' Still others, simply the Day of the Prophet, or Jarados."

"When will it be?"

"Soon. It is but two days hence. And with the going down of the sun on that day the Fulfilment is to begin, and the Life is to come. Hence the crowd below, my lord; yet they are nothing compared with the crowds that today are pressing their way from all D'Hartia and Kospia toward the Mahovisal."

"All because of this Day?"

"And to see you, my lord."

"All believers in the Jarados?"

"All, truly; but they all do not believe in your lordship. There are many sects, including the Bars, that consider you an impostor; but the rest—perhaps the most—believe you the Herald of the Day. All want to see you, for whatever motive."

"These Bars: who are they?"

"The military priesthood, my lord. As priests they teach a literal interpretation of the prophecy; as soldiers they maintain their own aggrandizement. To be more specific, my lord, it is they who accuse you of being one of the false ones."

"Why?"

"Because it is written in the prophecy, my lord, that we may expect impostors, and that we are to slay them."

"Then this coming contest with the Senestro—" beginning to sense the drift of things.

"Yes, my lord; it will be a physical contest, in which the best man destroys the other!"

The guard was a tall, finely made and truly handsome chap of perhaps thirty-five. Watson liked the clear blue of his eyes and the openness of his manner. At the same time he felt that he was being weighed and balanced.

"My lord is not afraid?"

"Not at all! I was just thinking—when does this kill take place?"

"Two days hence, my lord; on the first of the Sixteen Sacred Days."

And thus Chick found a stanch friend. The soldier's name, he learned, was "the Jan Lucar." He was supreme in command of the royal guards; and Chick soon came to feel that the man would as cheerfully lay down his life for him, Watson, as for the little queen herself. All told, Chick was able to store away in his memory a few very important facts:

First, that the Aradna did not like the Senestro.

Second, that the Jan Lucar hated the great Bar because of the prince's ambition to wed the little queen and her cousin, the Nervina; also because of his selfish, autocratic ways.

Next, that were the Nervina on hand she would thwart the Senestro; for she was a very learned woman, as advanced as the Rhamda Avec himself. But that she was a queen first and a scholar afterwards; her motive in going through the Blind Spot was to take care of the political welfare of her people; her purposes were as high as the Rhamda Avec's, but partook of statesmanship rather than spirituality.*

Finally, that the Rhamdas were perfectly willing for the coming contest to take place, on the evening of the Day of the Prophet, in the Temple of the Bell and Leaf.

"Jan Lucar," Watson felt prompted to say, "you need have no fear as to the outcome of the ordeal, whatever it may be.

With your faith in me, I cannot fail. For the present, I need books, papers, scientific data. Moreover, I want to see the outside of this building."

The guardsman bowed. "The data is possible, my lord, but as to leaving the building—I must consult the queen and the Rhamda Geos first."

"But I said must," Watson dared to say. "I must go out into your world, see your cities, your lands, rivers, moun-

---

*NOTE—As far as Chick Watson was able to make out in the brief time at his disposal, the government of the Thomahlian world was like its philosophy—unified and it displayed a puzzling resemblance on the one side to the caste system of aristocracy, while on the other it was highly socialistic. How these two elements were reconciled, all under the constitutional form of an apparently free republic, remains for future investigations to reveal.

tains, before I do aught else. I must be sure!"

The other bowed again. He was visibly impressed.

"What you ask, my lord, is full of danger. You must not be seen in the streets—yet. There are followers of the Bar Senestro who, if they found you, would tear you to bits. Untold bloodshed would ensue inevitably. To half the Thomahlians you are sacred, and to the other half an impostor. I repeat, my lord, that I must see the Geos and the queen."

Another bow and the Jan disappeared.

CHICK stood back where, without being seen, he yet could watch through the window the spectacle below. The crowds had settled again into inertia, slowly surging and quiet, like a quiescent geyser that wanted only the tossing of one stone to send it into a boiling rage. What if they learned the truth about him?

In a few moments the Jan Lucar returned with the Geos.

"The Jan has told me, my lord, that you would go out."

"If possible. I want to see your world."

"I think it can be arranged. Is your lordship ready to go?"

"Presently." Watson laid a hand on the big globe he had already puzzled over. "This represents the Thomahlia?"

"Yes, my lord." And then, as Watson put no further question, the Geos eagerly asked: "Tell us, my lord, is the next world above our heads or under our feet? Or is it both? We have nothing but conjecture, and our curiosity is as great as it is natural. From the great mediums* we gained the impression, as a rule, that the occult world was an ethereal one, impossible to describe, floating in space and composed of drifting souls. But sometimes there were messages saying that it is a world much like our own, with rivers, mountains, life—reality. The great Avec held to that view, and worked on that basis; now, you have come, my lord, to confirm his theory. It is the wisdom of the Jarados!"

Watson thought best to keep away from that topic, and stick to the globe.

"How long is your day, Geos?"

"Twenty-four hours."

"I mean, how many revolutions in one circuit of the sun, in one year-circle?"

As he uttered the question Chick held

*NOTE—These mediums were individuals gathered from a certain savage tribe of near-aborigines, for some unaccountable reason unaltered by the Thomahlian civilization. "If they were Indians," comments Mme. Le Fabre, "then we have an explanation of what we call 'controls,' many of whom are known to our mediums as redmen."

his breath. It had suddenly struck him that he had touched an extremely definite point. The answer might *place* him!

"You mean, my lord, how long is a circle in terms of days?"

"Yes!"

"Three hundred and sixty-five and a fraction, my lord."

Watson was dumbfounded. Could there be, in all the universe, another world with precisely the same revolution period? But he could not afford to show his concern. He said:

"Tell me, have you a moon?"

"Yes; it has a cycle of about twenty-eight days."

Watson drew a deep breath. Inconceivable though it appeared, he was still on his own earth. For a moment he pondered, wondering if he had been caught up in a tangle of time-displacement.† Could it be that, instead of living in the present, he had somehow become entangled in the past or the future?

If so—and by now he was so accustomed to the unusual that he considered this staggering possibility with equanimity—if the time coefficient was at fault, then how to account for the picture of the professor, in that leaf? Had they both been the victims of a ghastly cosmic joke?

There was but one way to find out.

"Come! Lead the way, Geos; let us take a look at your world!"

CHAPTER XXXVII

LOOKING DOWN

PRESENTLY the three men were standing at the door of the vast room, one entire side of which was wide open to the outer air. It was filled by a number of queer, shining objects. At first glance Chick took them to be immense beetles.

The Jan Lucar spoke to the Geos:

"We had best take the June Bug of the Rhamda Avec."

Watson thought it best to say nothing, show nothing. The Jan ran up to one of the glistening affairs, and without the slightest noise he spun it gracefully around, running it out into the center of the mosaic floor.

"I presume," apologized the Geos, "that you have much finer aircraft in your world."

Aircraft! Watson was all eagerness. He saw that the June Bug was about ten feet high, with a bunchy, buglike body.

†NOTE—Referring to a theosophical theorem which, in the light of what followed, need not be mentioned here.

On closer scrutiny he could make out the outlines of wings folded tight against the sides. As for the material, it must have been metal, to use a term which does not explain very much, after all. In every respect the machine was a duplicate of some great insect, except that instead of legs it had well-braced rollers.

"How does it operate?" Watson wanted to know. "That is, what power do you use, and how do you apply it?"

The Jan Lucar threw back a plate. Watson looked inside, and saw a mass of fine, spider-web threads, softer than the tips of rabbit's hair, all radiating from a central gray object about the size of a pea. Chick reached out to touch this thing with his finger.

But the Geos, like a flash, caught him by the shoulder and pulled him back.

"Pardon me, my lord!" he exclaimed. "But you must not touch it! You—even you, would be annihilated!" Then to the Lucar: "Very well."

Whereupon the other did something in the front of the craft; touched a lever, perhaps. Instantly the gray, spidery hairs turned to a dull red.

"Now you may touch it," said the Geos.

But Chick's desire had vanished. Instead he ventured a question:

"All very interesting, but where is your machinery?"

The Rhamda was slightly amused. He smiled a little. "You must give us a little credit, my lord. We may seem backward to you, but we have passed beyond reliance upon simple machines. That little gray pellet is, of course, our motive force; it is a highly refined mineral,* which we mine in vast quantity. It has been in use for centuries. As for the hairlike web, that is our idea of a transmission."

Watson hoped that he did not look as uncomprehending as he felt. The other continued:

"In aerial locomotion we are content to imitate life as much as possible. We long ago discarded engines and propellers, and instead tried to duplicate the muscular and nervous systems of the birds and the insects. We fly exactly as they do; our motive force is intrinsic. In some respects, we have improved upon life."

"But it is still only a machine, Geos."

"To be sure, my lord; only a machine. Anything without the life principle must remain so."

The Jan Lucar pressed another catch, allowing another plate to lower and

*NOTE—Professor Herold is certain that radioactivity of some kind is indicated here.

thereby disclose a glazed door, which opened into a cozy apartment fitted with wicker chairs, and large enough for four persons. There was some sort of control gear, which the Jan Lucar explained was not connected directly with the flying and steering members, but indirectly through the membranes of the weblike system. It was uncannily similar to the nervous connections of the cerebellum with the various parts of the anatomy of an insect.

"Does it travel very fast?"

"We think so, my lord. This one, which is known as the June Bug, is the private machine of the Rhamda Avec. It is rather small, but the swiftest machine in the Thomahlia."

They entered the compartment. Watson took his seat beside the Geos, while the soldier sat forward next to the control elements. He laid his hands on certain levers; next instant, the machine was gliding noiselessly over the mosaic, on to a short incline and thence, with ever increasing speed, toward and through the open side of the room.

The slides had all been thrown back; the compartment was enclosed only in glass. Watson could get a clear view; and he was amazed at the speed of the craft. Before Chick could think they were out in mid air and ascending skyward with the speed of a rocket. Traveling on a steep slant, there was no vibration, no mechanical noise; scarcely the suggestion of artificial movement, except for the muffled swishing of the air which the craft shot through.

Were it not for the receding city below him, Chick could have imagined himself sitting still in a house while a windstorm tore by. He felt no change of temperature or any other ill effects; the cabin was fully enclosed, and heated by some invisible means. In short, ideal flight.

BUT they were still climbing, and getting hundreds of feet higher every instant. Looking down, Chick estimated that they were already a mile above the surface. It was the nearest he could conceive to traveling in a projectile. All in the utmost comfort.

For instance, the seats were swung on gimbals, so that no matter at what angle the craft might fly, the passengers would maintain level positions.

Below stretched the Mahovisal—a mighty city of domes and plazas, and, widely scattered, a few minarets. As before, it was hard to distinguish details in the flaming profusion of gemlike iridescence. At the southern end—or what

Chick's sense of direction placed as the southern end—there was a vast, square plaza, covering thousands of acres. Toward it, on two sides, converged scores of streets; they stretched away from it like the ribs of a giant fan.

On the remaining two sides of the plaza there was a tremendously large building with a V-shaped front, opening on the square. The play of opal light on its many-bubbled roof resembled the glimmer from a vast pearl.

In the air above the city an uncountable number of very small objects darted hither and thither like sparkling fire-flies. It was difficult to realize that they, as well as the June Bug, were aircraft.

To the west lay an immense expanse of silver, melting smoothly into the horizon. Watson took it to be the Thomahlian ocean. Then he looked up at the sky directly above him, and breathed a quick exclamation.

It was a single, small object, perfectly white, dropping out of the amethyst. It was coming down at a gentle angle from a height greater than the Himalayas. Tiny at first, almost instantly it assumed a proportion nearly colossal—a great bird, white as the breast of the snowdrift, swooping with the grace of the eagle and the speed of the wind. It was so very large that it seemed, to Chick, that if all the other birds he had ever known were gathered together into one they would still be as the swallow. Down, down it came in a tremendous spiral, until it gracefully alighted in a splash of molten color upon the bosom of the silver sea. For a moment it was lost in a shower of water jewels—and then lay still, a swan upon the ocean.

"What is it, Geos?"

"The Kospian Limited, my lord. One of our great airships—a fast one, we consider it."

"It must accommodate a good many people, Rhamda."

"About nine thousand."

"You say it comes from Kospia. How far away is that?"

"About six thousand miles. It is an eight-hour run, with one stop. Just now the service is every fifteen minutes. They are coming, of course, for the Day of the Prophet."

Watson continued to watch the great airship, noting the swarm of smaller craft that came out from the Mahovisal to greet it, until the Jan Lucar suddenly altered the course. They stopped climbing, and struck out on a horizontal level. It left the Mahovisal behind them, a shimmering spot of fire beside the gleaming sea. They were traveling east-ward. The landscape below was level and unvaried, of a greenish hue, and much like that of Chick's own earth in the early spring-time.

Being a Californian, Watson felt that they must soon encounter mountains. First there should be Diablo; then, on the other side of the San Joaquin Valley, the Sierra range. But neither materialized. There was only that vast expanse, level, and sometimes dotted with opalescent towns and cities. Ribbons of silver cut through the plain at intervals, crookedly lazy and winding, indicating a drainage from north to south, or *vice versa*. Looking back to the west, he could see the great, golden sun, poised as he had seen it that morning, a huge amber plate on the rim of the world. It was sunset.

Then he looked straight ahead. Far in the distance a great wall loomed skyward to a terrific height. So vast was it and so remote, at first it had escaped the eye altogether. An incredibly high range of mountains, glowing with a faint rose blush under the touch of the setting sun. Against the sky were many peaks, each of them tipped with curious, sparkling, diamond-like corruscations. As Chick continued to gaze the rose began to purple.

The Jan Lucar put the craft to another upward climb. So high were they now that the Thomahlia below was totally lost from view; it was but a maze of lurking shadows. The sun was only a gash of amber—it was twilight down on the ground. And Watson watched the black line of the Thomahlian shadow climb the purple heights before him until only the highest crests and the jeweled crags flashed in the sun's last rays. Then, one by one, they flickered out; and all was darkness.

Still they ascended. Watson became uneasy, sitting there in the night.

"Where are we going?"

"To the Carbon Regions, my lord. It is one of the sights of the Thomahlia."

"On top of those mountains?"

"Beyond, my lord."

Whereupon, to Chick's growing amazement, the Geos went on to state that carbon of all sorts was extremely common throughout their world. The same forces that had formed coal so generously upon the earth had thrown up, almost as lavishly, huge quantities of pure diamond. The material was of all colors, as diamonds run, and considered of small value; for everyday purposes they preferred substances of more somber hues. They used it, it seemed, to build houses with.

106

"But how do they cut it?"

"Very easily. The material which drives this craft—llodium—will cut it like butter."

Later, Watson understood.* He watched as the craft continued to climb; the Jan Lucar was steering without the aid of any outside lights whatever, there being only a small light illumining his instruments. Chick presently turned his gaze outside again; whereupon he got another jolt.

He saw—a *negative* sky!

AT FIRST he thought his eyes the victims of an illusion; then he looked closer. And he saw that it was true; instead of the familiar starry points of light against a velvet background, the arrangement was just the reverse. Every constellation was in its place, just as Chick remembered it from the earth; but instead of stars there were jet-black spots, set upon a faint, gray background.

The whole sky was one huge Milky Way, except for the black spots. And from it all there shone just about as much total light as from the heavens he had known.

Of all he experienced, this was the most disturbing. It seemed totally against all reason; for he knew the stars to be great incandescent globes in space. How explain that they were here represented in reverse, their brilliance scattered and diffused over the surrounding sky, leaving points of blackness instead? Afterward he learned that the peculiar chemical constituency of the atmosphere was solely responsible for the inversion of the usual order of things.

All of a sudden the Jan Lucar switched the craft to a level. He held up one hand and pointed.

"Look, my lord, and the Rhamda! Look!"

Both men rose from their seats, the better to stare past the soldier. Straight ahead, where had been one of the corruscating peaks, a streak of blue fire shot skyward, a column of light miles high, differing from the beams of a search-light in that the rays were *wavy*, serpentine, instead of straight. It was weirdly beautiful. Geos caught his breath; he leaned forward and touched the Jan Lucar.

"Wait," he said in an awed tone. "Wait a moment. It has never come before, but we can expect it now." And even as he

spoke, something wonderful happened.

From the base of the column two other streaks, one red and the other bright green, cut out through the blackness on either side. The three streams started from the same point; they made a sort of trident, red, green, and blue—twisting, alive—strangely impressive, suggestive of grandeur and omnipotence—holy!

Again the Rhamda spoke. "Wait!" said he. "Wait!"

They were barely moving now. Watson watched and wondered. The three streams of light ran up and up, as though they would pierce the heavens; the eye could not follow their ends. All in utter silence, nothing but those beams of glorified light, their reality a hint of power, of life and wisdom—of the certainty of things. Plainly it had a tremendous significance in the minds of the Geos and the Lucar; but their reverent interest was no greater than Watson's curiosity.

Then came the climax. Slowly, but somehow inexorably, like the laws of life itself, and somewhere at a prodigious height above the earth, the three outer ends of the red and the green and the blue spread out and flared back upon themselves and one another, until their combined brilliance bridged a great rainbow across the sky. Blending into all the colors of the prism, the bow became—for a moment—pregnant with an overpowering beauty, symbolical, portentous of something unusual and stupendous about to come out of the unknown to the Thomahlians. And next—

The bow began to move, to swirl, and to change in shape and color. The three great rivers of light billowed and expanded and rounded into a new form. Then they burst—into a vast, three-leafed clover—blue and red and green!

And Watson caught the startled words of the Geos:

"The Sign of the Jarados!"

CHAPTER XXXVIII

THE VOICE FROM THE VOID

EVEN while that inexplicable heavenly pageant still burned against the heavens, something else took place, a thing of much greater importance to Chick. And, it happened right before his eyes.

In the front of the car was a dial, slightly raised above the level of the various controlling instruments. And all of a sudden this dial, a small affair about six inches across, broke into light and life.

---

*NOTE—That there should be so many elements in the Thomahlia that are unknown here is parallel with the well-known fact that certain minerals, like mercury, are to be found only in a few spots on earth. Incidentally, both iron and copper are exceedingly rare on the other side of the Blind Spot.

First, there was a white blaze that covered the whole disk; then the whiteness abruptly gave way to a flood of color, which resolved itself into a perfect miniature of the tri-colored cloverleaf in the sky ahead. Chick saw, however that the positions of the red and green were just the obverse of what glowed in the distance; and then he heard the voice, strong and distinct, speaking with a slight metallic twang as from a microphone hidden in that little, blazing, colored leaf:

"Listen, ye who have ears to listen!"

It was said in the Thomahlian tongue. The Geos breathed:

"The voice of the Prophet Jarados!"

But next moment the unseen speaker began in another language—clear, silver, musical—in English, and in a voice that Chick recognized!

"Chick! You have done well, my boy. Your courage and your intuition may lead us out. Follow the prophecy to the letter, Chick; it *must* come to pass, exactly as it is written! Don't fail to read it, there on the walls of the Temple of the Bell, when you encounter the Bar Senestro on the Day of the Prophet!

"I have discovered many things, my boy, but I am not omnipotent. Your coming has made possible my last hope that I may return to my own kind, and take with me the secrets of life. You have done right to trust your instinct; have no fear, yet remember that if you—if we —make one false step we are lost.

"We must not let all that I have discovered go for nothing. The world, our world, must know what I now know.

"Finally, if you should succeed in your contest with the Senestro, I shall send for you; but if you fail, I know how to die.

"Return at once to the Mahovisal. Don't cross into the Region of Carbon. Take care how you go back; the Bars are waiting. But you can put full confidence in the Rhamdas."

Then the speaker dropped the language of the earth and used the Thomahlian tongue again: "It is I who speak —I, the Prophet; the Prophet Jarados!" All in the voice of Dr. Holcomb.

The blazing leaf faded into blackness, and the talking ceased. Chick was glad of the darkness; the whole thing was like magic, and too good to believe. The first actual words from the missing professor! Each syllable was frozen into Watson's memory.

The Geos was clutching his arm.

"Did you understand, my lord? We heard the voice of the prophet! What did he say?"

"Yes, I understood. He used his own language—my language. And he said"— taking the reins firmly into his hands— "he said that we must return at once. We must not go on; we must return to the Thomahlia. And we must beware of the Bars."

There was no thought of questioning him. Without waiting the Geos's command, the Jan Lucar began putting the craft about. Watson glanced at the sky; the great spectacle was gone; and he demanded of the soldier:

"How can we get back? How do we find our way?"

For there was no visible light save the strange, fitful glow from that uncanny sky, to guide them; no lights from the inky carpet of the Thomahlia, lights such as one would expect for the benefit of fliers. But the soldier touched a button, and instantly another and larger dial was illumined above the instruments.

It revealed a map or chart of a vast portion of the Thomahlia. On the farther edge there appeared an area colored to represent water, and adjoining this area was a square spot labeled "The Mahovisal." And about midway from this point to the near edge of the dial a red dot hung, moving slowly, over the chart.

"The red dot, my lord, indicates the position of the June Bug," explained the Jan. "In that manner we know at all times where we are located, and which way we are flying. We shall arrive in the Mahovisal shortly."

As he spoke the craft was gaining speed, and soon was traveling at an even greater rate than before. The red dot began to crawl at an astonishing speed. Of course, they had the benefit of the pull of gravity, now; apparently they would make the journey in a few minutes. But incredible though the speed might be, there was nothing but the red dot to show it.

The Geos felt like talking. "My lord, the sign is conclusive. It is a marvel, such as only the prophet could possibly have produced; with all our science we could not duplicate such splendor. Only once before has the Thomahlia seen it."

ALREADY they were near enough to the surface to make out the clustered, blinking lights of the towns on the plain below. Ahead of them queer streamers of pale rays thrust through the darkness. Watson recognized them as the beams of the far-distant searchlights; and then and there he gave thanks for one thing, at least, in which the Thomahlians had seemingly progressed no further than the people of the earth.

Coming a little nearer, Chick made out a number of bright, glittering, insect-like objects, revealed by these search-lights. The Jan Lucar said:

"The Bars, my lord. They are waiting; and they will head us off if they can."

"The work of Senestro, I suppose. I thought he claimed to some honor."

"It is not the prince's work, my lord," replied the soldier. "His D'Hartian and Kospian followers, some of them, have no scruples as to how they might slay the 'false one,' as they think you."

"Suppose," hazarded Watson, "suppose I *were* the false one?"

Both the Geos and the Jan smiled. But the Rhamda's voice was very sure as he replied:

"If you were false, my lord, I would slay you myself."

Watson was glad that, although ethics were against him in the abstract, yet the right was on his side. He didn't like it, but there was now no backing out. It was not only his own welfare; there was the Aradna, and the life of the professor at stake. Moreover there were the truths which the doctor had discovered: these must all be weighed against the mere fact that Chick was actually, in his own mind, a fraud. It became a little thing alongside the great fact that he must now play the part of the superman.

They were very near the Mahovisal. Below was the unmistakable opalescence, somehow produced by powerful illumination, as intense as sunlight itself. The red dot was almost above the black square on the lighted chart. And directly ahead, the air was becoming alive with the beam-revealed aircraft. How could they get by in safety?

But Chick did not know the Jan Lucar. The soldier said:

"My lord is not uneasy?"

"Of course not," with vast unconcern. "Why?"

"Because I propose something daring. I am free to admit, my lord, that were the Geos and I alone, I should not attempt it. But not even the Bars," with magnificent confidence, "can stand before us now! We have had the proof of the Jarados, and we know that no matter what the odds, he will carry us through."

"What are you going to do?"

"I propose to shoot it, my lord." And without explaining the Jan asked the Geos: "Are you agreeable? The June Bug will hold; the prophet will protect us."

"Surely," returned the Rhamda. "There is nothing to fear, now, for those who are in the company of the chosen."

Watson wonderingly watched the Jan as he tilted the nose of the June Bug and began to climb at an all but perpendicular angle straight into the heavens. And if their former ascent had been like that of a rocket, it was now almost as swift as thought. Mile after mile, in less than as many minutes, they hurtled toward the zenith, so that the lights of the city dimmed until only the searching shafts could be seen. Chick began to guess what they were going to do; that the Jan Lucar was nearly as reckless as he was handsome.

At last the soldier brought the craft to a level. They soared along horizontally for a while; the Jan kept his eye fixed on the red dot. And when it was directly above the black square he stated:

"It is considered a perilous feat, my lord. We are going to drop. If we make it from this height, not only will we break all records, but we will have proved the June Bug the superior in this respect as she is in speed. It is our only chance under any circumstances, but with the Jarados at our side, we need not fear that the craft will stand the strain. We shall go through them like a stone; before they know it we shall be in the drome—in less than a minute."

"From this height?" Chick concealed a shudder behind a fair show of skepticism. "A minute is not much time."

"Does my lord fear the drop?"

"Why should I? I have in mind the June Bug; she might be set afire through friction, in dropping so quickly through the air." Watson had a vivid picture of a blazing meteorite, containing the charred bodies of three men, dropping out of—

"My lord need not be concerned with that," the Jan assured him. "The shell of the car is provided with a number of tiny pores, through which a heat-resisting fluid will be pumped during the maneuver. The temperature may be raised a little, but no more.

"You see this plug," touching a hitherto unused knob among the instruments. "By pulling that out, the mechanism of the craft is automatically adjusted to care for every phase of the descent. Nothing else remains to be done, after removing that plug, save to watch the red dot and prepare to step out upon the floor of our starting-place."

"Has the thing ever been done before?" Watson was sparring for time while he gathered his nerve.

"I myself have seen it, my lord. The June Bug has been sent up many times, weighted with ballast; the plug was abstracted by clockwork; and in fifty-eight seconds she returned through the open end of the drome, without a hitch. It was beautiful. I have always envied her that plunge. And now I shall have the chance, with the hand of the Jarados as my guide and protector!"

Chick had just time to reflect that, if by any chance he got through with this, he ought to be able to pass any test conceivable. He ought to be able to get away with anything. He started to murmur a prayer; but before he could finish, the Jan Lucar leaned over the dial-map for the last time, saw that the red dot was now exactly central over the square that represented the city, and unhesitatingly jerked out the plug.

Of what happened next Watson remembered but little. The bottom seemed to have dropped out of the universe. He was conscious of a crushing blur of immensity, of a silent thundering within him—then, mental chaos, and a stunned oblivion.

CHAPTER XXXIX

WHO IS THE JARADOS?

IT WAS all over. Chick opened his eyes to see the Jan throwing open the plate on the side of the compartment. Neither the soldier nor the Rhamda seemed to have noted Chick's daze. As for the Jan, his blue eyes were dancing with daredeviltry.

"That's what I call living!" he grinned. "They can keep on looking for the June Bug all night! She's a great little boat!"

Chick looked out. They were inside the great room from which they had started; the trip was over; the plunge had been made in safety. Chick took a long breath, and held out a hand.

"A man after my own heart, Jan Lucar. I foresee that we may have great sport with the Senestro."

"Aye, my lord," cheerfully. "The presumptuous usurper! I only wish I could kill him, instead of you."

"You are not the only one," commented the Rhamda. "Half of the Rhamdas would cheerfully act as the chosen one's proxy."

And so ended the events of Chick Watson's first day beyond the Blind Spot, his first day on the Thomahlia; that is, disregarding his previous months of unconsciousness. He had good reason to pass a sleepless night, in legitimate worry for the outcome of it all; but instead he slept the sound sleep of exhaustion, awakening the next morning much refreshed.

He reminded himself, first of all, that today was the one immediately preceding that of his test—the Day of the Prophet. He had only a little more than twenty-four hours to prepare. What was the best and wisest proceeding?

He called for the Geos. He told him what data he wanted. The Rhamda said that he could find everything in a library in that building; and inside a half-hour he returned with a pile of manuscript, such as indicated that the library was run on a loose-leaf plan.

Left to himself, Chick found that he now had data relating to all the sciences, to religion, to education and political history and the law. The same array of exact information, if gleaned from the corresponding volumes found on the earth, would have required a truck-load of books.

The chronology of the Thomahlians, Chick found, dates back no less than fifteen thousand years.* An abiding civilization of that antiquity, it need not be said, presented somewhat different aspects from what is known on the earth.

It seemed that the Jarados had made his first appearance at an age corresponding with the twentieth century upon the earth. Conditions were about the same. There was absolutely no doubt that the man had come miraculously. That is, he had come out of the unknown, through a channel which he himself later termed the Spot of Life.

He had taught a religion of enlightenment, embracing intelligence, love, virtue, and the higher ethics such as are inherent to all great philosophies. But he did not call himself a religionist. That was the queer point. He said that he had come to teach an advanced philosophy of life; and he expressly stated that his teachings were absolute only to a limited extent.

"Man must seek and find," was one of his epigrams; "and if he find no more truths, then he will find lies." Which was merely a negative way of saying that some of his philosophy was only provisional.

But on some points he was adamant. He had arrived at a time when the unthinking, self-glorifying Thomahlians had all but exterminated the lower orders of creation. The Jarados sought to remove the handicap which the people had set upon themselves, and gave them, in the place of kindness which they had forgotten how to use, a burning desire for a

*NOTE—For the purposes of this account it will be unnecessary to relate any more of what Mr. Watson learned than has a bearing upon his adventures. Students are referred to such papers as Professor Herold, Sir Henry Hodges and Drs. Malloy and Higgins have given to the world in various periodicals.

positive knowledge, where before had been only blind faith. Also, he taught good-fellowship, as a means to this end, and thus indirectly helped to bring on the semi-socialistic era which economic conditions were working toward. He taught beauty, love, and laughter, the three great cleansers of humanity. And yet, through it all—

The Jarados was a mystic.

He studied life after a manner of his own. He was a stickler for getting down to the very heart of things, for prodding around among causes until he found the cause of the cause itself. And thus he learned the secret of the occult.

For so he taught. And presently the Jarados was recognized as an authority on what the Thomahlia called "the next world." Only, he showed that death, instead of being an ushering into a void, was merely a translation into another plane of life, a higher plane and a more glorious one. In short, a thing to be desired and attained to, not to be avoided.

THIS put the Spot of Life on an entirely different basis. No longer was it a fearsome thing. The Jarados elevated death to the plane of motherhood—something to glory in. And Chick gathered that his famous prophecy—which he had yet to read, where it hung on the wall of the temple—this prophecy gave every detail of the Jarados' profound convictions and teachings regarding the mystery of the next life.

And now comes a curious thing. As Chick read these details, he became more and more conscious of—what shall it be called?—the presence of someone or something beside him, above and all about him, watching his every movement. He could not get away from the feeling, although it was broad daylight, and he was seemingly quite alone in the room. Chick was not frightened; but he could have sworn that a very real personality was enveloping his own as he read.

Every word, somehow, reminded him of the miraculous sequence of facts as he knew them; the unerring accuracy with which he, quite unthinkingly and almost without volition, had solved problem after problem, although the chances were totally against him.

He became more and more convinced that he himself had practically no control over his affairs; that he was in the hands of an irresistible Fate; and that —he could not help it—his good angel was none other than the prophet who, almost ninety centuries ago, had lived and taught upon the Thomahlia, and in the end had returned to the unknown.

But how could such a thing be? Watson did not even know where he was! Small wonder that, again and again, he felt the need of assurance. He asked for the Jan Lucar.

"In the first place," began Chick without preamble, "you accept me, Jan Lucar, do you not?"

"Absolutely, my lord."

"You conceive me to be out of the spiritual world, and yet flesh and blood like yourself?"

"Of course," with flat conviction.

THAT settled it. Watson decided to find out something he had not had time to locate in the library.

"The Rhamda may have told you, Jan Lucar, that I am here to seek the Jarados. Now, I suspect the Senestro. Can you imagine what he has done to the prophet?"

"My lord," remonstrated the other, "daring as the Bar might be, he could do nothing to the Jarados. He would not dare."

"Then he is afraid to run counter to the prophecy?"

"Yes, my lord; that is, its literal interpretation. He is opposed only to the broader version as held by such liberals as the Rhamda Avec. The Bars are always warning the people against the false one."

"And the Senestro is at their head," mused Chick aloud. "This brother of his who died—usually there are two such princes and chiefs?"

"Yes, my lord."

"And Senestro plans to marry both queens, according to the custom!"

"My lord"—and the Jan suddenly snapped erect—"the Bar will do exceedingly well if he succeeds in marrying one of them! Certainly he shall never have the Aradna—not while I live and can fight!"

"Good! How about the Nervina?"

"He'll do well to find her first!"

"True enough. What would you say was his code of honor?"

"My lord, the Senestro actually has no code. He believes in nothing. He is so constituted, mentally and morally, that he cares for and trusts in none but himself. He is a skeptic pure and simple; he cares nothing for the Jarados and his teachings. He is an opportunist seeking for power, wicked, lustful, cruel—"

"But a good sportsman!"

"In what way, my lord?"

"Didn't he allow me the choice of combat?"

The Jan laughed, but his handsome face could not hide his contempt.

111

"It is ever so with a champion, my lord. He has never been defeated in a matter of physical prowess. It would be far more to his glory to overcome you in combat of your own selection. It will be spectacular—he knows the value of dramatic climax—and he would kill you in a supreme moment, before a million Thomahlians."

"It's a nice way to die," said Watson. "You must grant that much."

"I don't know of any nice way to die, my lord. But it is a good way of living— to kill the Bar Senestro. I would that I could have the honor."

"How does it come that the Rhamdas, superintellectual as they are, can consent to such a contest? Is it not degrading, to their way of thinking? It smacks of barbarism."

"They do not look upon it in that light, my lord. Our civilization has passed beyond snobbery. Of course there was a time, centuries ago when we were taught that any physical contest was brutal. But that was before we knew better."

"You don't believe it now?"

"By no means, my lord. The most wonderful physical thing in the Thomahlia is the human body. We do not hide it. We admire beauty, strength, prowess. The live body is above all art; it is the work of God himself; art is but an imitation. And there is nothing so splendid as a physical contest—the quick, lightning correlation of mind and body. It is a picture of life."

"Do the Rhamdas think this?"

"Most assuredly. A Rhamda is always first an athlete."

"Why?"

"Perfection, my lord. A perfect mind does not always dwell in a perfect body, but they strive for it as much as possible. The first test of a Rhamda is his body. After he passes that he must take the mental test."

"Mental?"

"Moral first. The most rigid, perhaps, of all; he must be a man above suspicion. The honor of a Rhamda must never be questioned. He must be upright and absolutely unselfish. He must be broad-minded, human, lovable, and a leader of men. After that, my lord, comes the intellectual test."

"He must be a learned man?"

"Not exactly, your lordship. There are many very learned men who could not be Rhamdas; and there are many who have had no learning at all who eventually were admitted. The qualifications are intellectual, not educational; the mind is put to a rigid test. It is examined for alertness, perception, memory, rea-son, emotion, and control. There is no greater honor in all the Thomahlia."

"And they are all athletes?"

"Every one, my lord. In all the world there is no finer body of men. I myself would hesitate before entering a match with even the old Rhamda Geos."

"How about the Rhamda Avec?"

"Nor he, either; in the gymnasium he was always the superior, just as he topped all others morally and mentally."

Did this explain the Avec's physical prowess, on the one hand, and the fact that he would not stoop to take that ring by force, on the other?

"Just one more thing, Jan Lucar. You have absolutely no fear that I may fail tomorrow?"

"Not the slightest, my lord. You cannot fail!"

"Why not?"

"I have already said—because you are from the Jarados."

And Chick, facing the greatest experience of his life, submerged in a sea wherein only a few islands of fact were visible, had to be content with this: his only friends were those who were firmly convinced of something which, he knew only too well, was a flat fraud! All his backing was based upon a misled faith.

No, not quite. Was there not that strange feeling that the Jarados himself was at his back? And had he not found that the prophet had been real? Did he not feel, as positively as he felt anything, that the Jarados was still a reality?

Chick went to bed that night with a light heart.

CHAPTER XL

THE TEMPLE OF THE BELL

IT WAS hard for Chick to remember all the details of that great day. Throughout all the morning and afternoon he remained in his apartments. Breakfast over, the Rhamdas told him his part in certain ceremonies, such as need not be detailed here. They were very solicitous as to his food and comfort, and as to his feelings and anticipations. His nonchalance pleased them greatly. Afterward he had a bath and rub-down.

A combat to the death, was it to be? Suits me, thought Watson. He was never in finer form.

The Jan Lucar was particularly interested. He pinched and stroked Chick's muscles with the caressing pride of a connoisseur. Watson stepped out of the fountain bath in all the vigor of health. He playfully reached out for the Lucar and tripped him up. He sought to learn

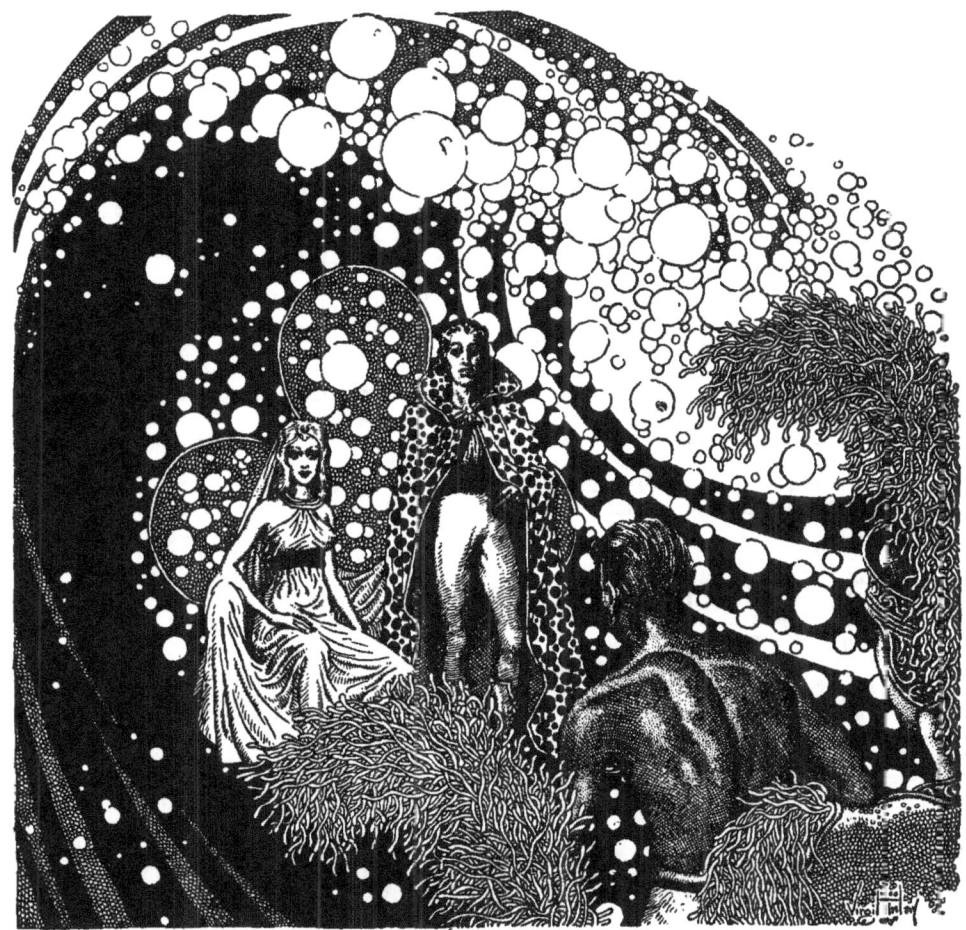

Enthroned on the crest of the black jade and silver wave were the Aradna and the Senestro. The Senestro stood up, and Chick could not but admire his adversary

just what the Thomahlians knew in the art of self-defense.

The brief struggle that ensued taught him that he need expect no easy conquest. The Jan was quick, active, and the possessor of a science peculiarly effective. The Thomahlians did not box in the manner of the Anglo-Saxons; their mode was peculiar. Chick foresaw that he would be compelled to combine the methods of three kinds of combat: boxing, jiu-jitsu, and the good old catch-as-catch-can wrestling. If the Senestro were superior to the Jan, he would have a time indeed. Though Watson conquered, he could not but concede that the Jan was not only clever but scientific to an oily, bewildering degree. The Lucar held up.

"Enough, my lord! You are a man indeed. Do not overdo; save yourself for the Senestro."

His eyes were smiling. His fingers twitched with eagerness and the delight of contest. He was a strong man, alert and nervy. The Californian athlete could not but admire this civilization that put a premium instead of disgrace upon the rivalry of clean, healthy manhood in this way.

Clothes were brought, and Chick taken back to his apartment. The time passed with Rhamdas constantly at his side. They were taking conscientious care with his very movement.

The Geos was not present, nor the little queen. Chick sought permission to sit by the window—permission that was granted after the guards had placed screens that would withhold any view from outside, yet permit Chick to look out.

As far as he could see, the avenues

were packed with people. Only, this time the centers of the streets were clear; on the curbs he could see the opposing lines of the blue and crimson, holding back the waiting thousands. In the distance he could hear chimes, faint but distinct, like silver bells tinkling over water.

Between the intervals strange choruses of weird, holy music. The full sweep of the city's domes and minarets were spread out before him. From eaves to basements the rolling luxuriance of orchidian beauty; banners, music, parade; a day of pageant, pomp, and fulfilment.

He could catch the pregnance of the air, the strange, laden undercurrent of spiritual salvation—something esoteric, undefinable, the ecstasy of a million souls pulsing to the throb of a supreme moment. He drew back. Someone had touched him.

"What is it?"

It was one of the Rhamdas. He had in his hand a small metal clover, of the design of the Jarados.

"What do I do?" asked Watson.

"This," said the Rhamda, "was sent to you by one of the Bars."

"By a Bar! What does it mean?"

The other shook his head. "It was sent to you by one who wished it to be known by us that he is your friend, even though a Bar."

JUST then Watson noted something sticking out of the edge of one of the clover leaves. He pulled it out. It was a piece of paper. On it were scrawled words *in English.*

The writing was penciled script, done in a poor hand and ill-spelled, but still English. Chick read:

> Arrah, me boy! Be of good cheer; there ain't a one in this world that can top a lad from Frisco. And it's Pat MacPherson that says it. Yer the finest laddie that ever got beyont the old witch of Endor. You and me, if we hold on, is just about goin' to play hell with the haythen. Hold on and fight like the divil! Remember that Pat is with ye!
> We're both spooks.
>
> Pat MacPherson.

Said Watson: Who gave you this? Did you see the man?"

"It was sent up, my lord. The man was a high Bar in the Senestro's guard."

Watson could not understand this. Was it possible that there were others in this mysterious region besides himself? At any rate, he wasn't exactly alone. He felt that he could count upon the Irish—or was the fellow Scotch? Anyhow, such a man would find the quick means of wit at a supreme moment.

Suddenly Watson noticed a queer feeling of emptiness. He looked out of the window. The music had ceased, and the incessant hum of the throngs had deadened to silence. It was suspended, awesome, threatening. At the same time, the Jan Lucar came to attention; at the opposite door stood the Rhamda Geos, black clad, surrounded by a group of his fellows.

"Come, my lord," he said.

The crimson guard fell in behind Watson, the black-gowned took their places ahead, and the Jan Lucar and the Geos walked on either side. They stepped out in the corridor. By the indicator of a vertical clock* Chick noted that it was nine. He did not know the day of the year other than from the Thomahlian calendar; but he knew that it was close to sunset. He did not ask where they were going; there was no need. The very solemnity of his companions told him more than would have done their answers. In a moment they were in the streets.

Watson had thought that they would be taken by aircraft, or that they would pass through the building. He did not know that it was a concession to the Bar Senestro; that the Senestro was but playing a bit of psychology that is often practised by lesser champions. If Watson's nerve was not broken it was simply because of the iron indifference of confident health. Chick had never been defeated. He had no fear. He was far more curious as to the scenes and events about him than he was of the outcome. He was hoping for some incident that would link itself up into explanation.

At the door a curious car of graceful lines was waiting, an odd affair that might be classed as a cross between a bird and a gondola, streaming with colors and of magnificent workmanship and design. On the deck of this the three men took their places; on the one side the Rhamda Geos, tall, somber, immaculate; on the other, the magnificent Jan Lucar in the gorgeous crimson uniform, gold-braided and studded with jewels; on his head he wore the shako of purple down; and by his side a peculiar black weapon which he wore much in the manner of a sword.

In the center, Watson—bareheaded, his torso bare and his arms naked. He had been given a pair of soft sandals, and a

---

*NOTE—These clocks resembled large thermometers in appearance. They were a sort of liquid hour-glass, so arranged that when the last hour of the day was reached, the apparatus automatically up-ended, so that the process began all over again.

short suit, whose one redeeming feature in his eyes was a pocket into which he had thrust the automatic that he valued so much. It was more like a picture of Rome than anything else. Whatever the civilization of the Thomahlians, their ritual in Watson's eyes smacked still of barbarism.

But he was intensely interested in all about him. The avenues were large. On either side the guards were drawn up eight deep, holding back the multitude that pressed and jostled with the insistent pandemonium of curiosity. He looked into the myriad of faces about him, splendid features, of intelligent men and women.

Not one face suggested the hideous; the women were especially beautiful, and from what he could see, finely formed and graceful. Even the older ones had a vigorous refinement that was wonderfully becoming. Many of them smiled; he could hear the curious buzz of conjecturing whispers. Some were indifferent, while others, from the expression of their faces, were openly hostile.

CHICK was in the middle of a procession, the Rhamdas marching before and the crimson guard bringing up the rear. A special guard; the inner one, Rhamdas, the outer one of crimson surrounding them all.

The car started. There was no trace of friction; it was noiseless, automatic. Chick could only conjecture as to its mechanism. The black column of Rhamdas moved ahead rhythmically, with the swing of solemn grandeur. For some minutes they marched through the streets of the Mahovisal. There was no cheering; it was a holy, awesome occasion. Chick could sense the undercurrent of the staring thousands, the reverence and the piety. It was the Day of the Prophet. They were staring at a miracle.

The column turned a corner. For the first time Watson was staggered by sheer immensity; for the first time he felt what it might be to see with the eyes of an insect. His heart went faint with insignificance. Had he been an ant looking up at the columns of Karnak, he would still have been out of proportion. It was immense, colossal, beyond man. It was of the omnipotent. It was the pillared portal of the Temple of the Bell.

Such a building a genius might dream of, in a moment of unhampered, inspired imagination. It was stupendous. The pillars were hexagonal in shape, and in diameter each of about the size of an ordinary house. Dropping from an immense height, it seemed as if they had originally been poured out in the form of molten metal from immense bell-like flares that fell from the vaulted architrave. Such was the design.

Chick got the impression that the top of the structure, somehow, was not supported by the foundation, but rather the reverse—the floor was suspended from the ceiling. It was the work of the Titans. So high and stupendous that at the first instant Watson felt numb with insignificance. What chance had he against men of such colossal conception?

How large the building was he could not see. The Gargantuan façade itself was enough to smother comprehension. It was laid out in the form of a triangle, one end of which was open toward the city; the two sections of the façade met under a huge, arched opening—the door itself. Watson recognized the structure as the one he had seen from the June Bug on the outskirts of the Mahovisal. The enormous plaza was packed with people, leaving only a narrow lane for the procession; and as far back as Chick could see the streets converged toward this vast space. Their numbers were incalculable. It was Benaric; it was prodigious.

The car stopped. The guards, both crimson and blue, formed a twentyfold cordon. Watson could feel the suspended breath of the waiting multitude. The three men stepped out—the Geos first, then the Jan Lucar, and Watson last. Chick caught the Lucar's eye; it was confident; the man was springing with vigor, jovial in spite of the moment.

"All waiting for you, my lord. The Senestro has chosen many witnesses to his folly. It will be a spectacle worthy of a place in history."

"Aye," supplemented the Geos. "Pride hath a fall."

But Watson was not so sure.

They passed between two of the huge pillars, and under the giant arch. To Chick it was much like walking between the supports of Atlas. The effect was so great that whenever he looked up he felt dizzy. For a few minutes they passed through what seemed, to Chick, a perfect maze of those titanic columns. And every foot of their way was marked by the lines of crimson and of blue, flanking either side.

Chick knew something of archeology and history. But it was the first time he had ever stepped out of his own epoch. Whether he was in the dim past or the far future he could not make out. A monster building, half temple and half auditorium, a Karnak coliseum: either it was a throw-back to Babylonian immensity or a conception of the future, a concept half god-like, half human, the work of the Titans and Cyclopean civilization.

An immense sea of people rose high into the forest of pillars as far as his eye could reach. He had never been in such a concourse of humanity. He had been in bowls, in athletic auditoriums that held one hundred thousand spectators; but they did not approach this. It was superlative, the last thing to be thought of—and a building.

THEY passed through an inner arch, a smaller and lower one, into what Chick guessed was the temple proper. And if Chick had thought the anteroom stupendous, he now saw that a new word, one which went beyond all previous experience, was needed to describe what he now saw.

It was almost too immense to be grasped in its entirety. Gone was the maze of columns; instead, far, far away to the right and to the left, stood single rows of herculean pillars. There were but seven on a side, separated by great distances; and between them stretched a space so immense, so incredibly vast, that a small city could have been housed within it. And over it all was not the open sky, but a ceiling of such terrific grandeur that Chick almost halted the procession while he gazed.

For that ceiling was the under-side of a cloud, a gray-black, forbidding thundercloud. And the fourteen pillars, seven on either side, were prodigious waterspouts, monster spirals of the hue of storm, with flaring sweeps at top and at bottom that welded roof and floor in one terrific whole. Sheer from side to side stretched that portentous level cloud; it was a span like the span of an epoch; and on either side it was rooted in those awful columns, seemingly alive, as though ready at any instant to suck up the earth into the infinite.

By downright will-force Watson tore his attention away and directed it upon the other features of that unprecedented interior. It was lighted, apparently, by great windows behind the fourteen pillars; windows too far away to be distinguishable. And the light revealed, directly ahead—

Something that Chick at first thought to be a cascade of black water. It leaped out of the rear wall of the temple, and at its crest it was bordered with walls of solid silver, cut across and designed with scrolls of gold and gem work; walls that swooped down and ended with two huge green columns at the base of that fantastic fall.

As they approached a swarm of tiny bronze objects, silver winged, fluttered out through the temple—tiny birds, smaller than swallows, beautiful and swift-winged, illusive. They were without number; in a moment the air of the temple was alive with flitting, darting spots of glinting color.

Then Chick saw that there were two people, mere marionettes in the distance, sitting high on the crest of that cascade. Wondering, Chick and the rest marched on through the silent crowd; all standing with bared heads and bated breaths, the worshiping Thomahlians filled every inch of that enormous place. Only a narrow lane permitted the procession to pass toward the base of that puzzling, silent, black waterfall.

They were almost at its base when Chick saw the vanguard of the Rhamdas unhesitatingly stride straight against the torrent, and then mount upon it. Up they marched; and Chick knew that the black water was black jade, and that the two people at its crest were seated upon a landing at the top of the grandest stairway he had ever seen.

Up went the Rhamdas deploying to right and left against the silver walls. The crimson and blue uniformed guards remained behind, lining the lane through the throng. At the foot of the steps Chick stopped and looked around, and again he felt numb at the sheer vastness of it all.

For he was looking now at the portal through which the procession had marched; a portal now closed; and above it, covering a great expanse of that wall and extending up almost into the brooding cloud above, was spread a mighty replica of the tri-colored Sign of the Jarados.

For the first time Chick felt the full significance of symbolism. Whereas before it had been but an incident of adventure, now it was the symbol of mystic revelation. It was not only the motif for all other decoration upon the walls and minor elements of the temple; it was the emblem of the trinity, deep, holy, significant of the mystery of the universe and the hereafter.

There was something deeper than mere fatalism; back of it all was the fact-rooted faith of a civilization. Watson had stepped into it all. The whole scene was enough to stagger him; he felt hazy, bewildered, unable to credit himself as a conscious unit in all this immensity.

But at that moment, as Chick paused with one foot on the bottom step of the flight, something happened that sent quivers of joy and confidence all through him. Someone was talking—talking in English!

Chick looked. The speaker was a man in the blue garb of the Senestro's guard. He was standing at the end of the line nearest the stair, and slightly in front of his fellows. Like the rest, he was holding his weapon, a black, needle-pointed sword, at salute. Chick gave him only a glance, then had presence of mind to look elsewhere as a man said, in a low, guarded voice:

"Ye air right, me lad; don't look at me. I know what ye're t'inkin'. But she ain't as bad as she looks! Keep yer heart clear; dinna fear. You an' me kin lick all Thomahlia! Go straight up on them stairs, an' stand that blagguard Senastro on his 'ead, jist like ye'd do in Frisco!"

"Who are you?" asked Watson, intent upon the great three-leafed clover. He used the same low, cautious tone the other had employed. "Who are you, friend?"

"Pat MacPherson, av coorse," was the answer. "An' Oi've said a plenty. Now, go aboot yer business."

Watson did not quibble. There was no time to learn more. He did not wish it to be noticed; yet he could not hide it from the Jan Lucar and the Rhamda Geos, who were still at his side. They had heard that tongue before. The looks they exchanged told, however, that they were gratified rather than displeased by the interruption. Certainly all feeling of depression left Chick, and he ascended the stairs with a glad heart and a resilient stride that could not but be noticed.

He was ready for the Senestro.

CHAPTER XLI

THE PROPHECY

REACHING the top of the jade steps, Chick found the landing to be a great dais, nearly a hundred feet across. On the right and left this dais was hedged in by the silver walls, on each of which was hung a huge, golden scroll-work. These scrolls bore legends, which for the moment Chick ignored. At the rear of the dais was a large object like a bronze bell.

The floor was of the usual mosaic, except in the center, where there was a plain, circular design. Chick took careful note of this, a circle about twenty feet across, as white and unbroken as a bed of frozen snow. Whether it was stone or not he could not determine. All around its edge was a gap that separated it from the dais, a gap several inches across. Chick turned to Geos:

"The Spot of Life?"

"Even so. It is the strangest thing in all the Thomahlia, my lord. Can you feel it?"

For Watson had reached out with his toe and touched the white surface. He drew it back suddenly.

"It has a feeling," he replied, "that I cannot describe. It is cold, and yet it is not. Perhaps it is my own magnetism."

"Ah! It is well, my lord!"

What the Rhamda meant by that Chick could not tell. He was interested in the odd white substance. It was as smooth as glass, although at intervals there were faint, almost imperceptible, dark lines, like the finest scratches in old ivory. Yet the whiteness was not dazzling. Again Watson touched it with his foot, and noted the inexplicable feeling of exhilaration. In the moment of absorption he quite forgot the concourse about him. He knew that he was now standing on the crux of the Blind Spot.

But in a minute he turned. The dais was a sort of a nave, with one end open to the stairway. Seated on his left was the frail Aradna, occupying a small, thronelike chair of some translucent green material. On the right sat the Bar Senestro, in a chair differing only in that its color was a bright blue. In the center of the dais stood a third chair—a crimson one—empty.

The Senestro stood up. He was royally clad, his breast gleaming with jewels. He was certainly handsome; he had the carriage of confident royalty. Chick noted the clearness of his eyes and the pink, healthy muscles of his arms. The smile on his lips was a bit disconcerting; there was no fear in this man, no uncertainty, no weakness. If confidence were a thing of strength, the Senestro was already the victor. Down in his heart Chick secretly admired him.

But just then the Aradna stood up. She made an indication to Watson. He stepped over to the queen. She sat down again.

"I want to give you my benediction, stranger lord. Are you sure of yourself? Can you overcome the Senestro?"

"I am certain," spoke Watson. "It is for the little queen, O Aradna. I know nothing of the prophecy; but I will fight for you!"

She blushed, and cast a furtive look in the direction of the Senestro.

"It is well," she spoke. "The outcome will have a double interpretation—the spiritual one of the prophecy, and the earthly, material one that concerns myself. If you conquer, my lord, I am freed. I would not marry the Senestro; I love him not. I would abide by the prophet, and await the chosen." She hesitated. "What do you know of the chosen, my lord?"

"Nothing, O Aradna."

"Has not the Rhamda Geos told you?"

"Partly, but not fully. There is something that he is withholding."

"Very likely. And now—will you kneel, my lord?"

Watson knelt. The little queen held out her hand. Behind him Chick could hear a deep murmur from the assembled multitudes. Just what was the significance of that sound he did not know; nor did he care. It was enough for him that he was to fight for this delicately beautiful maiden. He would let the prophecy take care of itself.

Besides these three on the dais there were only the Rhamda Geos and the Jan Lucar. These two remained on the edge nearest the body of the temple, the edge at the crest of the stair. The empty chair remained so.

Suddenly Chick remembered the warning of Dr. Holcomb: "Read the words of the Prophet." And he took advantage of the breathing-spell to peruse the legends on the great, golden scrolls:

THE PROPHECY OF THE JARADOS

Behold! When the day is at hand, prepare ye!

For, when that day cometh, ye shall have signs and portents from the world beyond. Wisdom cometh out of life, and life walketh out of wisdom. Yea, in the manner of life and of spirit ye shall have them, and of substance even like unto yourselves.

And it shall come to pass in the last days, that ye shall be on guard. By these signs ye shall know them; even by the truths I have taught thee. The way of life is an open door; wisdom and virtue are its keys. And when thy intelligence shall be lifted to the plane above—then shalt thou know!

Mark ye well the Spot of Life! He that openeth it, is the precursor of judgment. Mark him well!

And thus shall the last days come to pass. See that ye are worthy, O wise ones! For behold, in those last days there shall come among ye—

The chosen of a line of kings. First there shall be one, and then there shall be two; and the two shall stay but the one shall return.

The false ones. Them ye shall slay!

The four-footed: The call to humility, sacrifice and devotion, whom ye shall hold in reverence even as ye hold me, the Jarados.

And on the last day of all—I, the Jarados!

Beware ye of sacrilege! Lest I take from ye all that I have given ye, and the day be postponed—beware ye of sacrilege!

And if the false ones cometh not, ye shall know that I have held them. Know ye the day!

Sixteen days from the day of the prophet, shall come the day of the judgment; and the way shall be opened, on the last day, the sixteenth day of the Jarados.

Hearken to the words of the Jarados, the prophet and mouthpiece of the infinite intelligence, ruler of justice, peace, and love! So be it forever!

CHICK read it the second time. Like all prophecies, it was a bit Delphic; but he could get the general drift. In that golden script he was looking into the heart of all Thomahlia—into its greatness, its culture, its civilization itself. It was the soul of the Blind Spot, the reason and the whereof of all about him.

He heard some one step up behind him, and he turned. It was the Senestro, going over the words of the prophecy.

"Can you read it, Sir Fantom?" asked the handsome Bar. His black eyes were twinkling with sheer delight. "Have you read it all?"

He put a hand on Chick's shoulder. It was a careless act, almost friendly. Either he had the heart of a devil or the chivalry of a Norman. He pointed to a line:

"'The false ones. Them ye shall slay.'"

"And if I were the false one, you would slay me?" asked Watson.

"Aye, truly!" answered the splendid prince. "You are well made and good to look upon. I shall hold you in my arms; I shall hear your bones crack; it shall be sweeter music than that of the temple pheasants; who never sing but for the Jarados. I shall slay you upon the Spot, Sir Fantom!"

Watson turned on his heel. The ethics of the Senestro were not of his own code. He was not afraid; he stood beside the Jan Lucar and gazed out into the body of the temple. As far as he could see, under and past the fourteen great pillars and right up to the far wall, the floor was a vast carpet of humanity.

It was become dark. Presently a new kind of light began to glow far overhead, gradually increasing in strength until the whole place was suffused with a sunlike illumination. The Rhamda Geos began to speak.

"In the last day, in the Day of Life. We have the substance of ourselves, and the words of the prophet. The Jarados has written his prophecy in letters of gold, for all to see. 'The false ones. Them ye shall slay.' It is the will of the Rhamdas that the great Bar Senestro shall try the proof of the occult. On this, the first of the Sixteen Days, the test shall be—on the Spot of Life!"

He turned away. The Bar Senestro

stripped off his jewels, his semiarmor, and stood clad in the manner of Watson. They advanced and met in the center of the dais, two athletes, lithe, strong, handsome, their muscles aquiver with vitality and their skins silken with health. Champions of two worlds, to wrestle for truth!

A low murmur arose, crescending until it filled the whole coliseum. The silver-bronze pheasant flitted above the heads of all, flashing like bits of the spirit of light. And all of a sudden—

One of them fluttered down and lit on Watson's shoulder.

The murmur of the throng dropped to a dead silence. Next second a stranger thing happened. The little creature broke forth in full-throated song.

Watson instantly remembered the words of the Bar Senestro: "They sing but for the Jarados." He quietly reached up and caught the songster in his hand, and he held it up to the astonished crowd. Still the song continued. Chick held him an instant longer, and then gave him a toss high in air. He shot across the temple, a streak of melody, silver, dulcet, to the far corner of the giant Senestro.

But the thing did not jar the Senestro.

"Well done, Sir Fantom! Anyhow, 'tis your last play! I would not have it otherwise. Here's hoping you can die as prettily! Are you ready?"

"Ready? What for?" retorted Watson. "Why should I trouble myself with preparations?"

But the Rhamda Geos had now come to his side.

"Do your best, my lord. I regret only that it must be to the death. It is the first death contest in the Thomahlia for a thousand circles (years). But the Senestro has challenged the prophecy. Prove that you are not a false one! My heart is with you."

It was a good word at a needed moment. Watson stepped over onto the circular Spot of Life.

They were both barefooted. Evidently the Thomahlians fought in the old, classic manner. The stone under Watson's feet was cool and invigorating. He could sense anew that quiver of magnetism and strength. It sent a thrill through his whole body, like the subtle quickening of life. He felt snappy, joyous, confident.

The Senestro was smiling, his eyes flashing with anticipation. His muscled body was a network of soft movement. His step was catlike.

"What will it be?" inquired Watson. "Name your choice of destruction."

But the Bar shook his head.

"Not so, Sir Fantom. You shall choose the manner of your death, not I. Particular I am not, nor selfish."

"Make it wrestling, then," in his most off-hand manner. He was a good wrestler, and scientific.

"Good. Are you ready?"

"Quite."

"Very well, Sir Fantom. I shall walk to the edge of the Spot and turn around. I would take no unfair advantage. Now!"

CHICK turned at the same moment and strode to his edge. He turned, and it happened; just what, Chick never knew. He remembered seeing his opponent turn slowly about, and in the next split second he was spinning in the clutch of a tiger. Even before they struck the stone, Chick could feel the Senestro reaching for a death-hold.

And in that one second Watson knew that he was in the grip of his master.

His mind functioned like lightning. His legs and arms flashed for the counter-hold that would save him. They struck the Spot and rolled over and over; Chick caught his hold, but the Senestro broke it almost instantly. But it had saved him; for a minute they spun around like a pair of whirligigs. Watson kept on the defensive. He had not the speed and skill of the other. It was no mere test to touch the shoulders; it was a fight to the death; he was at a disadvantage. He worked desperately.

When a man fights for his life he becomes superhuman. Watson was put to something more than his skill; the sheer spirit of the Bar broke hold after hold; he was like lightning, pantherlike, subtle, vicious. Time after time he spun Chick out of his defense and bore him down into a hold of death. And each time Chick somehow wriggled out, and saved himself by a new hold. The struggle became a blur—muscle, legs, the lust for killing—and hatred. Twice Watson essayed the offensive; first he got a hammer-lock and then a half-Nelson. The Bar broke both holds immediately.

Whatever Chick knew of wrestling, the Senestro knew just a bit more. It was a whirring mass of legs and bodies in continuous convulsion, silent except for the terrible panting of the men, and the low, stifled exclamations of the onlookers.

And then—

Watson grew weak. He tried once more. They spun to their feet. But before he could act the Senestro had caught him in the same flying rush as in the beginning, and had whirled him off his feet. And when he came down the Bar had an unbreakable hold.

Chick struggled in vain. The Bar tightened his grip. A spasm of pain shot through Chick's torso; he could feel his bones giving way. His strength was gone; he could see death. Another moment would have been the end.

But something happened. The Senestro miraculously let go his hold. Chick felt something soft brush against his cheek. He heard a queer snapping, and shouts of wonder, and a dreadful choking sound from the Bar. He raised himself dizzily on one arm. His eyes cleared a bit.

The great Bar was on his back; and at his throat was a snarling thing—the creature that Chick had seen in the clover leaf of the Jarados.

It was a living dog.

CHAPTER XLII

PAT MACPHERSON'S STORY

TO WATSON it was all a blur. He was too weak and too broken to remember distinctly. He was conscious only of an uproar, of a torrent of multitudinous sound. And then—the deep, enveloping tone of a bell.

Some place, somewhere, Chick had heard that bell before. In his present condition his memory refused to serve him. He was covered with blood; he tried to rise, to crawl to this wriggling creature that was throttling the Senestro. But something seemed to snap within him, and all went black.

When he opened his eyes again all had changed. He was lying on a couch with a number of people about. It was a minute before he recognized the Jan Lucar, then the Geos, and lastly the nurse whom he had first seen when he awoke in the Blind Spot. Evidently he was in the hands of his friends, although there was one, a red-headed man, clad in the blue uniform of a high Bar.

He sat up. The nurse held a goblet of the green liquid to his lips. The Bar in blue turned.

"Aye," he said. "Give him some of the liquor; it will do him good. It will put the ould vim back in his bones."

The voice rang oddly familiar in Watson's ears. The words were Thomahlian; not until Chick had drained the glass did he comprehend their significance.

"Who are you?" he asked.

The Bar with the red head grinned.

"Whist, me lad," using Chick's own tongue. "Git rid of these Thomahlians. 'Tis a square game we're playin', but we're takin' no chances, belike. Git 'em

out of th' way so's we kin talk loike auld-timers. Oi've somethin' I got to tell ye."

Watson turned to the others. He made the request in his adopted tongue. They bowed, reverently, and withdrew.

"Who are you?" Chick asked again.

"Oi'm Pat MacPherson."

"How did you get here?"

The other sat upon the edge of the bed. "Faith, an' how kin Oi tell ye? 'Twas a drink, sor; a new kind av a high-ball, th' trichery av a frien' an' th' ould Witch av Endor put togither."

Obviously Watson did not understand. The stranger continued: "Faith, sor, an' no more do Oi. There's no one as does, 'cept th' ould doc hisself."

"The old doc! You mean Dr. Holcomb?"

Watson sat up in his bed. "Dr. Holcomb! Where is he?"

"In a safe place, me lad. Dinna fear f'r th' ould doctor. 'Twas him as saved ye—him an' your humble sarvent, Pat MacPherson, bedad."

"He—and you—saved me?"

"Aye—there on th' Spot o' Life. A bit of a thrick as th' ould doc dug oot o' his wisdom. Sure, she dinna work jist loike he said it, but 'twas a plenty t' oopset th' pretty Senestro, bad 'cess t' him!"

Watson asked, "What became of the Senestro?"

"Sure, they pulled him oot. Th' wee doggie jist aboot had him done for. Bedad, she's a good pup!"

"What kind of a dog?"

"A foine wan, sor. Sich as you an' me has seen in Australy, only wit' a bit stub av a tail. An' she's thot intilligent, she kin jist aboot talk Frinch. Th' Thomahlians all called her 'th' Four-footed,' an' if they kape on, they'll jist aboot make her th' Pope."

Watson was still thick-headed. "I don't understand!"

"Nor I, laddie. But th' ould doc does. He's got a foine head f'r figgers; an' he's thot scientific, he kin make iron oot o' rainbows."

"Iron out of—what?"

"Rainbows, sor. Faith, 'tis meself thot's seen it. Ah, 'tis th' dape thinker he is; an' he's been watchin' over ye iver since ye come. 'Twas hisself, lad, thot put it into your head t' call him th' Jarados."

"You don't mean to say that the professor put those impulses into my head!"

"Aye, laddie; you said it. He kin build up a mon's thoughts jist like you or me kin pile oop lumber. 'Tis thot deep he is wit' th' calc'lations!"

Watson tried to think. There was just one superlative question now. He put it.

"I dinna know if he's th' Jarados," was the reply. "But if so be not, then he's his twin brother, sure an' aisy."

"Is he a prisoner?"

"I would na say that, aither, 'though there's them as think so. But if it be annybody as is a-holdin' av him, 'tis the Senestro an' his gang o' guards."

WATSON looked at the other's uniform, at the purple shako on his head, the jeweled weapon at his side, and the Jaradic leaf upon his shoulder—insignia of a Bar of the highest rank.

"How does it come that you are a Bar, and a high one at that?"

The other grinned again. He took off his shako and ran his hand through his mop of red hair.

" 'Tis aither th' luck av th' Irish, me lad, or av th' Scotch. Oi don't ken which—Oi'm haff each—but mostly 'tis th' virtoo av me bonny red hair."

"Why?"

"Because, leastways in th' Thomahlia, there's always a dhrop av royalty in th' red-headed. Me bonnie top-knot has made me a fortune. Ye see 'tis th' mark av th' royal Bars thimselves; no ithers have it. What less could ye expec' from th' Irish, annyhow; besides, me Scotch ancestry was a wee bit canny."

Spoke Watson: "If you have come from Dr. Holcomb, then you must have a message from him to me."

"Ye've said it; you an' me, an' a few Rhamdas. an' mebbe th' wee queen is goin' t' take a flight in th' June Bug. We're goin' afther th' ould doc; an' ye kin bet there'll be as purty a scrap as ever ye looked upon. An' afther thot's all over, we're goin' t' take anither koind av a flight—into good old Frisco."

Chick instantly asked Pat if he knew where San Francisco might be.

"Faith, 'tis only th' ould doc knows, laddie. But whin we git there, 'tis Pat MacPherson that's a goin' for Toddy Maloney."

"I don't know that name."

"Bedad, I do. Him it was thot give me th' dhrink."

"What drink?"

"Th' dhrink thot done it. 'Twas a new kind av cocKthail. Ye see, I'd jist got back from Melbourne, an' I was takin' in th' lights that noight, aisy loike, whin I come t' Toddy's place. I orders a dhrink av whuskey.

" 'Whist, Pat,' says he, 'ye don't want whuskey; 'twill make ye dhrunk. Why don't ye take somethin' green, like th' Irish?' "

" 'Green,' says I. ' 'Tis a foine color—though Oi'm haff Scotch, an' canny. I

dinna fear annything thot comes fra' a bottle. Pass 'er oot!'

"An' thot he did. 'Twas 'creme de menthay' on th' bottle. 'An',' says he, ' 'twan't make ye dhrunk.' But he was a liar, beggin' yer pardin.

"For by an' by Oi see his head a growin' larger an' larger, until Oi couldn't see annything but a few loights on th' cailing, an' a few people on th' edges, loike. An' afther thot Oi wint oot, an' walked till Oi come to a hill. An' there was a moon, an' a ould hoose standin' still, which th' moon was not—th' same Oi thought quare. So Oi stood shtill to watch it, but bein' tired an' weary an' not havin' got rid o' me sea-legs, Oi sat me doon on th' steps av th' hoose for a bit av a rest, an' t' watch th' moon, thinkin' mebbe she'd shtand shtill by an' by.

"Well, sor, Oi hadn't been there more'n three 'r foor minits, whin th' door opened, an' oot shteps a little ould lady, aboot th' littlest an' ouldest Oi iver see in 'Frisco.

" 'Good avenin', Mother Machree,' says Oi, touchin' me hat.

" 'Mother Machree!' says she, an' gives me a sharp look. Also, she sniffs. 'Ye poor man,' says she. 'Ye'll catch yer death o' cold, out here. Ye better coom in an' lie on me sofy.'

"Now, sor, how was Oi to ken, bein' a sailor an' ignorant? She was only a ould lady, an' withered. How was Oi to ken thot she was th' ould Witch o' Endor?"

Watson's memory was at work on what he knew of the house at 288 Chatterton, especially regarding its occupants at the beginning of the Blind Spot mystery. The Bar's odd remark caught his attention.

"The Witch of Endor?"

"Aye; thot she were. Aither thot, or 'twas th' dhrink at Toddy Maloney's; which mebbe served me roight for takin' a shtrang dhrink whin I could 'a' had good whuskey. Anyway, bedad, I was bewitched!

"WHIN Oi woke up, there was nary a hoose at all, nor th' ould lady, nor Toddy Maloney's, nor 'Frisco. 'Twas a shtrange place I was, sor; a church loike St. Peter's, only bigger, th' same bein' harrd to belaive; only it was na' church at all, bein' thot there wasna crucifix nor image of th' Virgin—nothin' at all, at all, of th' true religion. An' th' columns looked loike waterspoots, an' th' sky above was fu' av clouds, the same bein' jest aboot ready to break into hell an' tempest. But ye've been there yerself, sor.

"Well, there was a mon beside me,

121

dressed in a kilt loike a Highlander, 'cept it wasn't a bit o' plaid but a plain blue color. An' he spakes a shtrange language, too, although Oi could undershtand; an' he says, says he:

" 'My lord,' was what he says.

" 'My lord!' spakes Oi. 'Oi dinna ken what ye mane at all, at all.'

" 'Are ye not a Bar?' says he.

" 'Thot Oi am not!' says Oi, spakin' good English, so's to be sure he'd undershtand. 'Oi'm Pat MacPherson, bedad.'

"But he couldna ken. Thin we left th' temple an' wint out into the shtrate, which same was in a big city an' kivered wit' flowers an' fu' av music. An' a great crowd av peoples come aroun' an' begun shoutin', as if they'd niver seen a mon at all, at all. By an' by we wint into anither buildin'. On th' table was a bottle fu' av th' green dhrink which Toddy Maloney had give me—leastways it looked th' same—but no whuskey. The Highlander—for such Oi thought him, not knowin' for sure who he might be—filled up some glasses, an' we took a dhrink. Ye see, I had a kind av a notion that anither av th' same would break th' shpell. But ye know, sor, what koind av liquor it was; it made me feel loike Oi were jest married.

" 'Ye're a Bar?' says he.

" 'Faith,' says I. 'Oi'm a MacPherson, an' proud av it!'

"And we got into a wee bit av a argiment. It dinna last long; not wit' a MacPherson. By an' by he cooled off, an' I ast some questions.

" 'For why sh'd iverybody look at me whin we crossed th' shtrate jest noo?'

" ' 'Tis y'r clothes,' says he.

"Now, Oi don't enjoy pooblicity, sor; wherefore th' wily Scotch in me told me what to do, an' th' Irish part av me did it. M'anin', I shtood him on his head, an' took his clothes off. An' afther Oi had dressed me oop in his clothes Oi wint oot into th' shtrates an' no one noticed. Thot is, until Oi took me hat off."

"You mean, that shako?"

"Yis; th' blamed heavy thing—'tis made o' blue feathers. Well, whin it got so hot it made me scalp sweat, Oi took it off; an' thin Oi knew what intilligent h'athen they be. For 'tis thot eddicated they are, sor, they ken th' value o' bonnie red hair. An' they called me—'My lord' an' 'your worship,' jest loike Oi were a king.

"Well, sor, 'twas a foine discivery. Whin I showed me bonnie red top I dinna have to pay for nothin'. Oi dinna have to work at all, at all; me hair was me purse.

" 'Pray God,' says Oi, 'that me head dinna git bald.'

"Well, sor, Oi had a toime thot was fit for th' Irish. Oi did iverything 'cept git dhrunk; there was nothin' to git dhrunk wit'. But afther a while th' wee bit av Highlander in me begun to give th' Irish in me some advice.

" 'Pat,' says th' Scotch half o' me. ' 'Tis a shtrange land we're in. Ken ye where we're at, Pat? What d'ye say to a few books an' a little l'arnin'?'

"An' the Scotchman in me was roight. For th' toime come very shortly whin we ran across anither, wit' jest as red hair as we had. He was a foine man, av coorse, an' all surrounded by blue guards. He took me into a room by hisself an' begin askin' questions.

"An' I lied, sor. Av coorse, 'twas lucky thot Oi had me Scotch l'arnin' an' caution to guide me; but whin Oi spoke, Oi wisely let th' Irishman do all th' talkin'. An' th' great Bar liked me.

" 'Verily,' says he, most solemncholy, 'thou art of th' royal Bars!'

"An' he made me a high officer, he did."

"Was he the Bar Senestro?" asked Watson.

"Nay; 'twas a mon far better—Senestro's brother, that died not long afther. Whin Oi saw th' Senestro, Oi had sinse enough to kape me mooth shut. An' now Oi'm a high Bar—next to th' Senestro hisself! What's more, sor, there's no one alive kens th' truth but yerself an' th' ould doctor."

IT WAS a queer story, but, in the light of all that had gone before, wonderfully convincing. Watson began to see light breaking through the darkness. "Now there are two," the old lady at 288 Chatterton Street had said to Jerome, when the detective came looking for the vanished professor. Had she referred to Holcomb and MacPherson? Two had gone through the Blind Spot, and two had come out—the Rhamda Avec and the Nervina. "Now there are two," she had said.

"Tell me a little more about Holcomb, Pat!"

" 'Tis a short story, lad. Oi can't tell ye much, owin' to orders from the old gent hisself. He came shortly afther th' death av th' first Bar, Senestro's brother. Seems there was some rumpus aboot th' old Rhamda Avec, which same Oi always kept away from—him as was goin' to prove th' spirits! Annyhow, we was guardin' th' temple, awaitin' th' spook as was promised. An' thot's how we got th' ould doc.

"But th' Rhamdas niver saw him. Th' Senestro doubled-crossed 'em, an' slipped th' doctor oop to th' Palace av Light."

"The Palace of—what?"

"Th' Palace av Light, sor. 'Tis th' home av th' Jarados. 'Twas held always holy by th' Thomahlians; no mon dared go within miles av it; since th' Jarados was here, t'ousands av years ago, no wan at all has been inside av it.

"But th' Senestro knew thot th' doctor was th' real Jarados, at least he t'ought so; an' he wasna afraid o' him. He's na coward, th' Senestro. He's afther th' little queen an' th' Nervina; he's got a plenty o' nerve, he has. He put th' doctor in th' Jarados' ould home! Only th' Prophecy worries him at all, at all."

At last Watson was touching firm ground. Things were beginning to link up—the Senestro, the professor, the Prophecy of the Jarados.

"Well, sor, we Bars have kept th' ould doctor prisoner there iver since he come, wit' none save me to give him a wee bit word av comfort. But it dinna hurt th' old gent. Whin he finds all them balls an' rainbows an' eddicated secrets, he forgets iver'thing else; he's contint wit' his diskivery. 'Tis th' wise head th' doctor has; an' Oi make no doobt he's th' real Jarados, so Oi do."

The red-haired man went on to say that the professor knew of Chick's coming from the beginning. He immediately called in MacPherson and gave him some orders, or rather directions, which the Irishman could not understand. He knew only that he was to go to the Temple of the Leaf and there touch certain objects in a certain way; also, he was to arrange to get near Chick, and give him a word of cheer.

"But it dinna work as he said it, sor; he had expected to ketch th' Senestro. Instead, 'twas th' dog got th' Bar. A foine pup, sor; she saved yer loife."

"Where's the dog now?"

"She's on th' Spot av Loife, sor. She willna leave it. 'Tis a shtrange thing to see how she clings to it. Th' Rhamdas only come near enough to feed her, bedad. Only, they niver call her a dog; she's th' 'Four-footed One,' to thim."

Thus Chick learned that, as soon as he got well, he and MacPherson were to seek the doctor, and help him to get away with the secrets he had found, the truths behind the mystery of the Spot.

"An' 'tis a glorious fight there'll be, lad. Th' Senestro's a game wan; he'll not give up, an' he'll not let go th' doctor 'til he has to."

This was not unwelcome news to Chick. A battle was to his liking. It reminded him of the automatic pistol which he still had in his pocket—the gun he had not thought to use in his desperate struggle with the Bar Senestro.

"Pat," said he, with a sudden inspiration, "when you came through, did you have a firearm?"

MacPherson reached into his pocket and silently produced a thirty-two caliber pistol, of another make than Chick's, but using the same ammunition. From another pocket he drew out a package carefully bound with silken thread. He unrolled the contents. It was an old clay pipe!

"Oi came through," he stated plaintively, "wit' two guns; an' nary a bit av powder for ayther!"

Chick smiled. He searched his own pockets. First he handed over his extra magazine full of cartridges, and then a full package of smoking tobacco.

"Wirra, wirra!" shouted MacPherson. "Faith, an' there's powder for both!" His hands shook as he hurried to cram the old pipe full of tobacco. The cartridges could wait. He struck a match, and gave a deep sigh of content as he began to puff.

"Bedad, sor," unsteadily, " 'tis only a shmoker as would ken th' true an' fu' joy av Pat MacPherson!"

CHAPTER XLIII

THE HOME OF THE JARADOS

CHICK had been grievously hurt in the contest with the Senestro, but thanks to the Rhamdas he came around rapidly. It was a matter of less than a week.

Things were coming to a climax; Chick needed no lynx's eye to see that the die had been cast between the Bars and the Rhamdas. Soon the Senestro must make a bold move, or else release the professor.

Chick had not long to wait. It came one evening. Once again he found himself in the June Bug, accompanied by the Geos, the Jan Lucar, and—the little Aradna herself. Their departure was swift and secret.

This time Watson was not worried over height, nor any other sensation of flight. The doctor's safety alone was of moment. He said to the Rhamda:

"Are we alone? Where is the Bar MacPherson?"

"He is somewhere near; we are not alone, my lord. Several other machines are flying near by also; they carry many of the Rhamdas and the crimson guard of the queen. The MacPherson will arrive first. We are going straight to the Palace of Light, my lord."

"Are we to storm the place?" thinking of the fight MacPherson had predicted.

"Yes, my lord. Many shall die; but it

123

cannot be helped. We must free the Jarados, although we commit sacrilege."

"But—the Senestro?"

"That depends, my lord. We know not just what may be done." He gave no explanation.

They had climbed to a tremendous height. The indicator showed that they were bearing east. The darkness was modified only by the faint glow from that stardusted sky. Looking down, Chick could see nothing whatever. His companions kept silence; only the Aradna, sitting forward by the side of Jan Lucar showed any perturbation. They climbed still higher and higher still, until it seemed that they must leave the Thomahlia altogether. Always the course was eastward. At last the Jan said to the Geos:

"We are now over the Region of Carbon, sir. Shall I risk the light? His lordship might like to see."

"Follow your own judgment."

"Oh," exclaimed the Aradna; "do it, by all means! There is nothing so wonderful as that!"

The Jan touched a small lever. Instantly a shaft of light cut down through the blackness. Far, far below it ended in a patch on the ground. Watson eagerly followed its movements as it searched from side to side, seeking he knew not what. And then—

There was a flash of inverted lightning, a flame of white fire, a blinding, stabbing scintillation of a million corruscations. Watson clapped a hand to his eyes, to cut off the sight. It was stunning.

"What is it?" he cried.

"Carbon," answered the Geos, calmly.

"Carbon! You mean—diamond?"

"Yes, my lord. So it interests you very much? I did not know. Later you shall see it under more favorable conditions." Then, to the Jan: "Enough."

Once again they were in darkness. For some minutes silence was again the rule. Watson watched the red dot moving across the indicator, noting its approach to a three-cornered figure on one edge. Suddenly there appeared another dot; then another, and another. Some came from below, others from above; presently there were a score moving in close formation.

"They are all here," said the Jan to the Geos.

The other nodded, and explained to Chick: "It is the Rhamdas and the Crimson guards. The MacPherson is just ahead. We shall arrive in three minutes."

And after a pause he stated that the ensuing combat would mark the first spilling of blood between the Bars and the Rhamdas. At a pinch the Senestro might even kill the Jarados, to gain his ends. "His wish is his only law, my lord."

The red dots began to descend toward the three-cornered figure. One minute passed, and another; then one more, and the June Bug landed.

With scarcely a sound the Lucar brought the craft to a full stop. In a moment he was assisting the Aradna to alight. As for the Geos, he took from the machine two objects, which he held out to the Aradna and to Chick.

"Put these on. The rest of us fight as we are."

They were cloaks, made of a soft, light, malleable glass, or something like it.* Watson asked what they were for.

"For a purpose known only to the Jarados, my lord. There are only two of these robes. With them he left directions which indicated plainly they are for your lordship and the Aradna."

WONDERING, Chick helped the Aradna don her garment and then slipped into his own. Nevertheless, he pinned more faith in the automatic in his pocket. He did not make use of the hood which was intended to cover his head.

"Pardon me," spoke the little queen. She reached over and extended the hood till it protected his skull. "Please wear it that way, for my sake. Nothing must happen to you now!"

Chick obeyed with only an inward demur. What puzzled him most was the isolation. Seemingly they were quite alone; there was nothing, no one, to oppose them.

But he had merely taken something for granted. He, being from the earth, had assumed that strife meant noise. It was only when the Aradna caught him by the arm, and whispered for him to listen, that he understood.

It was like a breeze, that sound. To be more precise, it was like the heavy passage of breath, almost uninterrupted, coming from all about them. And presently Chick caught a queer odor.

"What is it?" he breathed in the Aradna's ear.

"It is death," she answered. "Cannot you hear them—the deherers?"

She did not explain; but Watson knew that he was in the midst of a battle which was fought with noiseless and terribly efficient weapons—so efficient that there were no wounded to give voice to pain. Before he could ask a question a

*NOTE—It would seem that in this matter the Thomahlians have succeeded in retaining a scientific secret now lost on the earth.

familiar voice sounded out of the darkness at his side.

"Where is the Geos?"

"Here, Bar MacPherson," answered the Rhamda.

"Good! It is well you came, sir. We were discovered a few minutes ago; already we have lost many men. Just give us the lights, so that we can get at them! It is a waste of men, with the advantage all on the other side."

Then, lapsing into English for Chick's benefit: "'Tis welcome ye are, lad! Ivery mon helps, now. But—who be this?" He peered at the little queen.

"It is the Aradna!"

Off came the Irishman's hat. To Chick he said: "Lad—dinna ye ken this is na place for a lassie?"

"It is her right, Pat. She is the queen. Have you your automatic?"

"Aye; thot Oi have."

"What are these sounds? You say they are fighting?"

"'Tis th' deherers ye hear, lad. They foight wit' silent guns. Don't let 'em hit ye, or ye'll be a pink pool in th' twinklin' av yer eyelid. 'Tis na joke."

"Are they more powerful than firearms?"

"I dinna say, lad. But they're th' divil's own weapon for fightin'. Certain 'tis, though, where th' pink death cooms is na place for a lassie."

Chick did not answer—he had heard a low command from the Geos. Next instant the space before them was illuminated by clear, white light, in the form of a circle—bright as day. In the center shimmered an object like a mist of blue flame, a nimbus of dazzling, actinic lightning. There was no sign of man or life, no suggestion of sound—nothing but the nimbus, and the brilliant space about it. The whole phenomenon measured perhaps three hundred feet across.

They were in darkness. Chick took a step forward, but he was held back by MacPherson.

"Nay, lad; would ye be dyin' so soon? 'Tis fearful quick. See—"

He did not finish. A red line of soldiers had rushed straight out of the blackness into the circle of light. It seemed they were charging the nimbus. They were stooping low, discharging their queer weapons; about three hundred of them—an inspiring sight. They charged in determined silence.

Then—Watson blinked. The line disappeared; the thing was like a miracle. It took time for Chick to realize that he was looking upon the "pink death" MacPherson had warned him against—the work of the deherers, whatever the word

meant. For where had been a column of gallant guards there was now only a broad stream of pink liquid trickling over the ground. It was annihilation itself—too quick to be horrible—inexorable and instantaneous. Chick involuntarily placed himself in front of the Aradna.

"Th' blue thing in th' middle," observed the Irishman, coolly, "is th' Palace av Light; 'tis held by th' Senestro jest now. An' all we got to do is get th' ould doc out."

"But I see no building!"

"'Tis there jest the same. Ye'll see it whin th' docthor gits toime off his rainbows. 'Tis absent-minded he gits whin he's on a problim, which same is mostly always, sor. We shtay roight here 'til he gits ready to dhrop on th' Senestro."

WATSON waited. He knew enough now to cling to the shadow, there with MacPherson, the Geos, and the Aradna. In the center of the great light-circle the nimbus of blue stood out like a vibrating haze, while all about, in the darkness, could be heard the weird sound made by the passage of life.

"When will the Jarados act?" inquired the Geos of the Irishman. But he got no reply. MacPherson spoke to Watson:

"Get yer gun ready, lad; get yer gun ready! Look—'tis th' ould boy himself, now! I wonder what the Senestro t'inks av thot?"

For the nimbus had suddenly dissolved, and in its place there appeared one of the quaintest, yet most beautiful buildings that Watson had ever seen. It was a three-cornered structure, low-set, and of unspeakably dazzling magnificence; a building carved and chiseled from solid carbon. Chick momentarily forgot the doctor.

In front of it stood a line of Blue Guards, headed by the Senestro. Their confusion showed that something altogether unexpected had happened. They were ducking here and there, seemingly bewildered by the sudden vanishing of that protecting blue dazzle. The Senestro was trying to restore order; and in a moment he succeeded. He led the way toward a low, triangular platform, at the entrance—a single white door—to the palace.

Pat MacPherson's automatic flashed and barked. Next instant Watson was in action. The Bar next to the Senestro staggered, then collapsed against his chieftain. Another rolled against his feet, causing him to stumble; an act that probably saved his life, for the platform in a second was covered with writhing, bleeding, dying Bars.

The Senestro managed to reach the doorway. MacPherson cursed.

"Come on!" he yelled to Watson. "We'll git him aloive!"

Watson remembered little of that rush. There stood the great Bar at the doorway, surrounded by his dying and his panic-stricken men. The cloak given Chick by the Geos impeded his progress; with a quick movement he threw it off, and ran unprotected alongside the Irishman. He was eager, full of fire—certain. The Blue guards saw them coming; they leveled their weapons. But before they could discharge them they met the same fate as had the Reds. A tremor in the air, and they were gone, leaving only a pink pool on the ground.

Senestro alone remained untouched. He was about to open the white door; for a second he posed, defiant and handsome. MacPherson took steady aim and pulled the trigger; the weapon snapped —empty. With a shout he threw it full in the Senestro's face.

The great Bar ducked swiftly, and almost with the same motion dodged into the building. Chick and Pat were right after him.

Two to one, it looked easy to capture him.

Inside was darkness. Chick ran head on against the side wall; turning, he bumped into another. The sudden transition from brilliance to blackness was overwhelming. He stopped and felt about carefully—momentarily blind. What if the Senestro found him now?

He called MacPherson's name. There was no reply. He tried to feel his way along, finding the wall irregular, jagged, sharp cornered. But the way must lead somewhere. He reached a turn in the passage; it was still too dark for him to see anything. He proceeded more cautiously, wondering at those craggy walls. And then—

Chick clapped his hands to his eyes. It was as if he had been shot into the core of the sun—the obsidian darkness flashed into lightning—a light beyond all enduring. Chick staggered, and cried in pain.

And yet, reason told him just what it was, just what had happened. It was the carbon; he was in the heart of the diamond; the Senestro had led him on and on, and then—had flashed some intense light upon the vast jewel. Watson knew the terrible helplessness of the blind. His end had come!

And so it seemed. Next instant some one came up to him—some one he could hear if he could not see. It was the Senestro.

"Hail, Sir Fantom! Pardon my abrupt manner of welcome. I suppose you have come for the Jarados?" And he laughed, a laugh full of mockery and triumph. "Perhaps you think I intend to kill you?"

Watson said no word. He had been outwitted. He awaited the end. But the Senestro saw fit to say, with an irony that told how sure he was:

"However, I am opposed to killing in cold blood. Open your eyes, Sir Fantom! I will give you time—a fair chance. What do you say—shall we match weapon against weapon?"

Watson slowly opened his eyes. The blinding light had dimmed to a soft glow. They were in a sort of gallery whose length was uncertain; between him and the outlet, about ten feet away, stood the confident, ever-smiling Bar.

"You or I," said he, jauntily. "Are you ready to try it? I have given you a fair chance!"

He raised his dagger-like weapon, as though aiming it. At the same instant Chick pulled the trigger from the hip, snap aim.

The gun was empty.

Another second, and Watson would have been like those spots of color on the ground outside. He breathed a prayer to his Maker. The Senestro's weapon was in line with his throat.

But it was not to be. There came a flash and a stunning report; the deherer clattered against the wall, and the Senestro clutched a stinging hand. He was staring in surprise at something behind Chick—something that made him turn and dart out of sight.

Chick wheeled.

Right behind him stood the familiar form of the Jan Lucar; and a few feet beyond, a figure from which came a clear, cool, nonchalant voice:

"I would have killed that fellow, Chick, but he's too damned handsome. I'm going to save him for a specimen."

Watson peered closer. He gave a gasp, half of amazement, half of delight. For the words were in English, and the voice—

It was Harry Wendel.

CHAPTER XLIV

DR. HOLCOMB'S STORY

IF THERE was the least doubt in Chick's mind that this were really Harry, it was dispelled by the sight of the person who next moment stepped up to his side. It was none other than the Nervina.

"Harry Wendel!" gasped Watson. It was too good to be true!

"Surest thing you know, Chick. It's me, alive and kicking!" as they grabbed one another.

"How did you get here?"

"Search me! Ask the lady; I'm just a creature of circumstance. I merely act; she does all the thinking."

The Nervina smiled and nodded. Her eyes were just as wonderful as Chick remembered them, full of illusiveness, of the moonbeam's light, of witchery past understanding. She was every inch a queen.

"Yes," affirmed she. "You see, Mr. Watson, it is the will of the Prophet. Harry is of the Chosen. We have come for the great Dr. Holcomb—for the Jarados!"

And she led the way. Watson followed in silent wonder; behind him came the Geos and the rest, quiet and reverent. The soft glow still held, so that they seemed to be walking through walls of cold fire. At the end of the passage they came to a door.

The Nervina touched three unmarked spots on the walls. The door opened. The queen stood aside, and motioned for Chick and Harry to enter.

It was a long room, pear-shaped, and fitted up like the most elaborate sort of laboratory. And at the far end, seated in the midst of a strange array of crystals, retorts and unfamiliar apparatus, was a man whom the two instantly recognized.

It was the missing professor, looking just as they remembered him from the days when they sat in his class in Berkeley. There was the same trim figure, the same healthy cheeks, pleasant eyes and close-cropped white beard. Always there had been something unperturbable about the doctor—he had that poise and equanimity which is ever the balance of sound judgment. Neither Chick nor Harry expected any rush of emotion, and they were not disappointed.

Holcomb rose to his feet, revealing on the table before him a queer, dancing light which he had been studying. He touched something; the light vanished, and simultaneously there came an unnameable change in the appearance of certain of those puzzling crystals. The doctor stepped forward, hand extended, smiling; surely he did not look or act like a prisoner.

"Well, well," spoke he; "at last! Chick Watson and Harry Wendel! You are very welcome. Was it a long journey?"

His eyes twinkled in the old way. He did not wait for their replies. He went on:

"Have we solved the Blind Spot? It seems that my pupils never desert me. Let me ask: have you solved the Blind Spot?"

In just such a fashion would he have spoken from behind his desk in Ethics 2b. And in much the same manner he would have used in that same class, Harry made reply:

"We've solved nothing, professor. What we have come for is, first, yourself; and second, for the secrets you have found. It is for us to ask—what is the Blind Spot?"

The professor shook his head.

"You were always a poor guesser, Mr. Wendel. Perhaps Chick, now—"

"Put me down as unprepared," answered Chick. "I'm like Harry—I want to know!"

"Perhaps there are a lot of us in the same fix," laughing. "We, who know more than any men who ever lived, want to know still more! It may be, after all, that we know very little; that, even though we have solved the problem." His eyes twinkled again, aggravatingly.

"Tell us, then!" from Harry, on impulse, as always. "What is the Blind Spot?"

But Holcomb shook his head. "Not just now, Harry; we have company." The Geos and the Jan had entered. "Besides, I am not quite ready. There remain several tangles to be unraveled."

As he shook hands with the Geos, he spoke in the Thomahlian tongue. "You are more than welcome."

The Rhamda bent low in reverence and awe. His voice was hushed. He spoke:

"Art thou the Jarados, my lord?"

"Aye," stated the doctor. "I am he; I am the Jarados!"

IT WAS a staggerer for both young men. Neither could reconcile the great professor of his schooldays with this strange, philosophic prophet of the occult Thomahlians. What was the connection? What was the law—the sequence? What was the fate that was leading, urging, compelling it all?

For, to all that Chick already knew about the workings of the Prophecy, he must now add the opportune arrival of Harry Wendel. Mere coincidence could not account for them all; there must be a core to the mystery, some great occult force that would explain the sequence. But the doctor must tell it in his own way. Chick said only this:

"Professor, you will pardon our eagerness. Both Harry and I have had adventures, without understanding what it was all about. Can't you explain? Where are we? And—why?" And then:

"Your lecture on the Blind Spot! You promised it to us—can you deliver it now?"

The professor smiled his acknowledgment.

"Part of it," he said; "enough to answer your questions to some extent. Had I stayed in Berkeley I could have delivered it all, but"—and he laughed—"I know a whole lot more, now; and, paradoxically, I know far less!

"First let me speak to the Geos."

He learned that the struggle outside had terminated successfully for the Rhamda and his men. All was quiet. The Senestro had made his escape in safety back to the Mahovisal. The doctor ordered that he was not to be molested. Apparently the professor held everything at his own dictates.

The Geos and the others left the room, escorting the Aradna, who was too exhausted for further experiences. There remained with the doctor, Chick, Harry, and the Nervina.

"I will reduce that lecture to synopsis form," began the professor. "I shall tell you all that I know, up to this moment. First, however, let me show you something."

He indicated the table from which he had risen. Chief among the objects on its top were fragments of minerals, some familiar, some strange. Above and on all sides were the crystal globes—or, at least, what Chick named as such—erected upon as many tripods. One of these the professor moved toward the table.

Simultaneously a tiny dot appeared on a small metal plate in the center of the table. At first almost invisible, it grew in a moment to the size of a speck, and gradually, after a minute or so, to a definite bit of matter.

The professor moved the tripod away. Near by crystals, inside of which some dull lights had leaped into momentary being, subsided into quiesence. And the three observers looked again and again at the solid fragment of material that had grown before their eyes on that table.

Something had been made out of nothing!

The doctor picked it up and held it unconcernedly in his fingers.

"Can anybody tell me," asked he, "what this is?"

There was no answer. The professor tossed the thing back on the table. It gave forth a sharp, metallic sound.

"You are looking at ether," spoke he. "It is the ether itself—nothing else. You call it matter; others would call it iron; but those are merely names. I call it ether in motion—materialized force—coherent vibration.

"Like everything else in the universe it answers to a law. It has its reason—there is no such thing as chance. Do you follow? That fragment is simply a principle, allowed to manifest itself through a natural law!

"Try to follow me. All is out of the ether—all! Nothing exists except in terms of electrons, which is merely the substance of the ether. Variety in matter is simply a question of varying degrees of electronic activity,* depending upon a number of ratios. Life itself, as well as materiality and force, comes out of the all-pervading ether.

"This object here," touching the crystal, "is merely a conductor. It picks up the ether and sends it through a set degree of vibrational activity. Result? It makes iron!

"If you wish you may go back to the twentieth century for a parallel—by which I mean, electricity. It is gathered crudely; but the time will come when it will be picked up out of the air in precisely the same manner that men pick hydrocarbons out of petroleum, or as I sift the desired quality of ether through that globe.

"This, I am convinced, is one of the fundamental secrets of the Blind Spot. Is there any question?"

Wendel managed to put one.

"You said, 'back in the twentieth century.' Is it a question of time displacement, sir?"

"Suppose we forego that point at present. You will note, however, that the Thomahlian world is certainly far in advance of our own."

"Professor," asked Watson, "is it the occult?"

"Ah," brightening; "now we are getting back to the old point. However, what is the occult?" He paused; then—"Did it ever occur to you boys, that the occult might prove to be the real world, proving that life we have known to be merely a shadow?"

SILENCE greeted this. The professor went on:

"Let me ask you: Are you living in a real world now, or an unreal one?" There was no response. "It is, of course, a reality; just as truly as if you were in San

---

*NOTE—"Since the professor left the earth, science has found that even the electron can be subdivided. This most recent 'ultimate particle' of materiality is known by the name of the 'quantel.' It does not, of course, have any adverse effect upon the doctor's hypothesis; on the contrary, it vastly strengthens the probability that the Thomahlia can be explained solely in terms of etheric activity." Kindly supplied by Mr. Herold.—Editors. (1921)

Francisco. So," very distinctly, "perhaps it is merely a question of viewpoint, as to which is the occult!"

"Just what we want to know," from Harry.

"And that," tossing up his hands, "is exactly what I cannot tell you. You asked me what is the occult, and I reply by asking you which. I have found out many things, but I cannot be sure. I left certainty in Berkeley.

"Today I feel that there is some great fate, some unknown force that defies analysis, defies all attempts at resolution—a force that is driving me through the rôle of the Jarados. We are all a part of the Prophecy!

"We must wait for the last day for our answer. That Prophecy must and will be fulfilled. And on that day we shall have the key to the Blind Spot—we shall know the where of the occult."

He took a sip from a tumbler of the familiar green fluid.

"Now that I have told you this much, I am going back to the beginning. I, too, have had adventures.

"How did I come to discover the Blind Spot?

"It was about one year prior to my last lecture at the university. At the time I had been doing much psychic research work, all of which you know. And out of it I had adduced some peculiar theories. For example:

"Undoubtedly there is such a thing as a spirit world. If all the mediums but one were dishonest, and that one produced the results that couldn't be explained away by psychology, then we must admit the existence of another world.

"But reason tells us that there is nothing but reality; that even thought is a fact; so that if there were a spirit world it must be just as real, just as substantial as our own. Moreover—somewhere, somehow, there must be a definite point of contact!

"That was approximately my theory. Of course I had no idea how close I had come to a great truth. To some extent it was pure guesswork.

"Then, one day Judge Kennedy brought me the blue stone. He told me its history, and he maintained that it was lighter than air, which of course I disbelieved until I took it out of the ring and saw for myself.

"I went at once to the house at 288 Chatterton. There I found an old lady who had lived in the house for some time. I asked to see the cellar where the stone had been unearthed. Understand, I had no idea of the great discovery I was about to make; I merely wanted to see. And I found something almost as impossible as the blue stone itself—a green one, heavier than any known mineral, answering to no known classification but that of an entirely new element. It was no larger than a pea, but of incredible weight.

"That day was full of discovery.

"Coming up-stairs I found the old lady a bit perturbed. I had told her my name; she had recognized me as well.

"'Come with me,' said she. And then: 'Oh, dear! This is a strange place, sir.'

"With that she opened a door. She was very old and very uncertain; and it seemed to me almost in her dotage. Yet she was scarcely afraid.

"'In there,' she said, and pointed through the door.

"I entered an ordinary room, furnished as a parlor. There was a sofa, a table, a few chairs; little else.

"'Come, mother; what do you mean?' I asked.

"'The man!'

"'The man! What man?'

"'Oh!' she exclaimed, looking up at me through pitiful, colorless eyes: 'he came here one night when the moon was shining. He sat down on the step. He was a handsome young man, and I smelled liquor on his breath. He was just the kind of a lad that's in need of a mother.

"'So I asked him in to lie on the sofa. He was tired, you see, and—I once had a son of my own.'

"She stopped, and it was a moment before she continued. I could feel the pressure of her hand on my arm, pitiful, beseeching.

"'So I took him in there. In there; see? On that sofa. I saw it! They took him! Oh, sir; it was terrible!'

"She was weird, uncanny, strangely interesting. But her emotion stopped her; I had to use a bit of persuasion to get the rest of the tale.

"'He just lay down there. I was standing by the door when—they took him! I couldn't understand, sir. I saw the blue light; and the moon—it was gone. And then—' She looked up at me again and whispered: 'And then I heard a bell—a very beautiful bell—a church bell. Don't you like church bells, sir? But you know, don't you? You are the great Dr. Holcomb. That's why you went into the cellar, wasn't it? Because you know!'

"Her manner as much as her story, impressed me. I said:

"'Mother, I must give this room a careful examination. Would you be good enough to leave me to myself?'

"She closed the door after her. I had the green stone in my hand; it was very heavy, and I placed it on one of the chairs. The blue stone I still held. At the moment I hadn't the least notion of what was about to happen. I was not even guessing; it was all accident, from beginning to end.

"All of a sudden the room disappeared! That is, the side wall; I was not looking at the dingy old wall-paper, but out through and into an immense building, dim, vast, and immeasurable.

"Directly in front of me was a white substance like a stone of snow. Upon this substance was seated a man, about my own age, as nearly as I could make out. He looked up just as I noted him.

"Our recognition was mutual. Immediately he made a sign with one hand. And at once I took a step forward; I thought he had motioned. It was all so real and natural. Though his features were dim he could not have been more than ten feet distant. But, at that very instant, when I made that one step, the whole thing vanished.

"I was still in the room at 288 Chatterton!

"That's what started it all, boys. Had this occurred to any one else in the world I should have labeled it an unaccountable illusion. But I was myself. It had happened to me, not to another.

"I had my theory; between the spiritual and the material there must be a point of contact. And—I had found it! I had discovered the road to the Indies, to the Occult, to all that other men call unknowable. And I called it—

"The Blind Spot."

CHAPTER XLV

THE ARADNA

THUS had the professor got into actual touch with the occult—by sheer accident. Up to that time it had been only a hypothesis; now it was a fact. His next step was to open up direct communication.

"That was difficult. To begin with, I worked to repeat the phenomena I had seen, getting some haphazard results from the start. My purpose throughout was to exchange intelligent comment with the individual I had beheld on that snow-stone within the Spot; and in the end I succeeded.

"He gave me fairly explicit warning as to when the Blind Spot should open, not only to the eye, but in its entirety, as it had done for the young man of whom the old lady had told me. We agreed through signs that he would come

through first. Truly it was to be a great occasion—second only to the coming of Columbus.

"Understand, up to the instant of his actual arrival I did not know just what he was like. I had to be content with his sign-talk, by which he assured me that he was a real man, material, of life and the living.

"I made my announcement. You know most of what followed. The Rhamda came to Berkeley; together we returned to 288 Chatterton, for it was imperative that we hold the Spot open or at least maintain the phenomenon at such a point that we could reopen it at will. Both of us were guessing.

"Neither of us knew, at the time, just how long the Rhamda could endure our atmosphere. He had risked his life to come through; it was no more than fair that I should accede to his caution and insure him a safe return to his own world.

"But things went wrong. It was ignorance, as much as accident. At 288 Chatterton I was caught in the Blind Spot, and without a particle of preparation was tossed into the Thomahlia.

"When I came through, the Nervina went out. Thus I found myself in this strange place with no one to guide me. And unfortunately, or rather, fortunately, I fell into the hands of the Bar Senestro.

"Now, for all that he is a skeptic, the Senestro is a brave man; and like many another unbeliever, he has a sense of humor. My coming had been promised by Avec; so he knew that somehow I was a part of the Prophecy—the prophecy which, for reasons of his own, he did not want fulfilled.

"So he isolated me here in the house of the Jarados. A bold sort of humor, I call it—to defy the Prophecy in the very spot where it was written!

"But it was fortunate. I was in the house of the old prophet, with its stores of wisdom, secrets, raw elements and means for applying the laws of nature. All that I hitherto had only guessed at, I now had at my disposal: libraries, laboratories, everything. I was a recluse, with no interruptions, and perfect facility for study.

"First of all I went into their philosophy. Then into their science, and afterward into their history. Whereupon I made a rather startling discovery.

"Apparently *I am the Jarados.*

"For my coming had been foretold almost to the hour. As I went on with the research I found many other points that seemed familiar. Plainly there was something that had led me into the Spot; and most certainly it was not mere chance. I became convinced that not merely my own destiny, but a higher, a transcendental fate was at stake.

"In the course of time I became certain of this. Meanwhile I mastered most of the secrets of this palace—the wisdom of the ancient Jarados. Though a prisoner, I was the happiest of men—which I still remain. The Bars kept close watch over me, constantly changing their guard. And it was on one of those occasions that I found MacPherson."

The professor's account of what the Scotch-Irishman had told him tallied point for point with what Chick already knew.

Also, it confirmed the old lady's tale in Holcomb's mind.

"I might say that during all my experiments at 288 Chatterton she was never a witness, never knew just what I was doing. She was old and feeble; it was best.

"Well, after MacPherson's coming I was pretty much my own master. I induced the Senestro to allow MacPherson to remain as a constant bodyguard. But I never told Pat what was what, except that some day we should extricate ourselves.

"You may wonder why I did not open the Spot.

"There were several reasons: First, in the nature of the phenomena it must be opened only on the earth side, except on rare occasions when certain conditions are peculiarly favorable. That is why the Rhamda Avec could not do it alone; I know now that I should have imparted to him certain technicalities. I possessed two of the keys then; now, I know there are three.

"And I have learned that each of these is a sinister thing.

"The blue stone, for instance, is life, and it is male. Rather a sweeping and ambiguous statement; but you will comprehend it in the end. Were a man to wear that it would kill him, in time; but a woman can wear it with impunity.

"Perhaps you will appreciate that statement better if you note what I have just done through the medium of that crystal. The blue gem is an inductor of the ether; and in a sense, it is one of the anchors of the Spot of Life, or the Blind Spot—whatever we want to call it—the Spot of Contact.

"The other two particles—the red and the green one—are respectively the Soul and the Material. Or, let us say, the etheric embryos of these essentials.

"The three stones constitute an eternal trinity.

"AS FOR the substance of the Spot itself, that I cannot tell, just yet. But I do know that the whole truth will come out clear in the fulfilment of the Prophecy. I am convinced that it has translated Watson, and now Harry Wendel and the Nervina."

"Can you control it?" asked Chick.

"To a limited extent. I have been able to watch you ever since your coming. You did not know about Harry, but I saw him come—in the arms of the Nervina."

"That's the way I came, all right," spoke up Harry. "I was pretty nearly all in."

The Nervina nodded.

"It is so. I knew the Senestro. I was afraid that Harry would fall into his hands. I had previously endeavored to have him give the jewel to Charlotte Fenton. I did not trust the great Bar; Harry—"

She did not say any more, but her tone implied a great deal. Chick looked at his friend—he remembered Harry's first dance with the Nervina. Could it be that, after all, there was love between them?

But it was not until afterward, when the two young men were alone, that Chick bluntly put the question. Harry did not evade it.

"Chick, I know just why you ask it. It is because of Charlotte. It makes me a sort of a cad. But what am I to do? I can only tell you honestly that I love the Nervina; and I can tell you just as honestly that I love Charlotte. Only—and here is the point—there is a difference.

"The queen is spiritual, fascinating, beyond definition—out of the moonbeams. From the very first I knew her as part of myself. I realized that there was something luring me on, some destiny, something beyond my control. I cannot help but love the Nervina. As for Charlotte, she is of the earth, the playmate of my childhood, sweet and innocent. I have loved her all my life. Frankly, what ought I to do?"

Watson did not know. But he asked:

"Was the Nervina ever the open rival of Charlotte? Has she ever intimated that she loves you?"

"No, to both questions. You don't know the Nervina, Chick. There is not a hair of that sort in her beautiful head. She did everything to drive me to Charlotte—begged, coaxed. Only because of her distrust of the Senestro did she decide to come through the Blind Spot with me. She knew what to do. As soon as we got here, she bundled me off, privately nursed me back to health if not strength, and when the time came rushed me up here at the last second to be in at the finish."

Watson thought of the dog, Queen. She also had come through just in time to save his life. Did Harry know anything about her? When Wendel had related what he knew, Chick commented:

"It's almighty strange, Harry. Everything works out to fit in exactly with that confounded Prophecy. Perhaps that accounts for your affinity for the Nervina; it is something beyond your control, or hers. We'll have to wait and see."

There was not long to wait. They spent the interval in the Palace of Light, acquiring fresh data on the science, philosophy and political economy of the Thomahlia—most of all, facts regarding the great Prophecy. The palace was full of Rhamdas, summoned by Dr. Holcomb, who, as the Jarados himself, was now issuing orders concerning the great day, the last of the sixteen days, now very close at hand; the day which the Rhamdas constantly alluded to as "the Day of Judgment."

THE Senestro went unmolested. Returning to the Mahovisal, he had cleverly backtracked on his previous acts so as to side in with the facts of the day. After all, the Senestro was not an absolute skeptic—no man is, entirely—and like the versatile genius that he was, he worked now to further the truths of the Prophecy.

Still the millions continued to descend upon the Mahovisal. Coming from the furthermost parts of the Thomahlia, the pilgrims' aircraft kept the air above the city constantly alive. There were days such as no man had ever known. Even the Rhamdas, trained to composure, gave evidence of the strain. The atmosphere was tense, charged with expectancy and hope. A whole world was coming to what it conceived as its judgment, and its end. And—the Spot of Life was the Blind Spot!

At last the doctor summoned the two young men. It was night, and the June Bug was waiting. This time the Geos himself was at the controls.

"We are going to the Mahovisal," spoke the doctor—"to the Temple of the Bell and Leaf. There is still something I must know before the Judgment." He was speaking English. "If we can bring the Prophecy to pass just so far, and no farther, we shall be able to extricate ourselves nicely. Anyway, I think we shall not return to the Palace of Light."

He held a black leather case in his hand. He touched it with a finger.

"If this little case and its contents gets through the Blind Spot it will advance civilization — our civilization — about a thousand-fold. So remember: Whatever happens to me, be sure and remember this case! It must go through the Spot!"

He said no more, but took his seat beside the Geos. The young men took the rear seats. In a short time they had crossed the great range of mountains, and were hovering over the Mahovisal.

There was no sound. Though the city was packed with untold millions, the tension was such that scarcely a murmur came up out of the metropolis. The air was magnetic, charged, strained close to the breaking point; above all, the reverence for the Last Day, and the hope, rising, accumulating, to the final supreme moment.

For the Sixteenth Day was now only forty-eight hours removed.

Both Chick and Harry realized that their lives were at stake; the doctor had made that clear. In the last minute, in the final crisis, they must crowd their way through the Blind Spot. Only the professor knew how it was to be done.

At the temple they found the Nervina and the Aradna waiting. The Jan Lucar was with them. The Geos had secured entrance by a side door. From it they could look out, themselves unobserved, over the entire building and up on the Spot of Life. The place was packed— thousands upon thousands of people, standing in silent awe and worship, one and all gazing toward the all-important Spot. There was no sound save the whisper of multitudinous breathing.

Said Harry to Chick:

"I see Queen up there!"

The Geos noted where he pointed, and remarked:

"The Four-footed One, my lords. She came out of the Prophecy; and she has not left the Spot since she came. You do not remember seeing her when you came through," to Harry, "because you were unconscious."

Harry circled the group, and bounded up the great stairs. In a moment he was patting his dog's head. She looked up and wagged her tail to show her pleasure. But she was not effusive. Somehow she wasn't just like his old shepherd. She glanced at him, and then out at the concourse below, and lolled her tongue expectantly. Then she settled back into her place and resumed watch—exactly as any of her kind would have held guard over a band of sheep.

The dog was serious. Afterward, Wendel said he had a dim notion that she was no longer a dog at all, but a mere instrument held in the hand of Fate.

"What's the matter, old girl?" he asked. "Don't you like 'em?"

For answer she gave a low whine. She looked up again, and out into the throng; she repeated the whine, with a little whimper at the end. Down below the Rhamda Geos heard.

"Strange," he murmured. "Only once before has the Four-footed One given voice, since the moment of her coming through, and that was the day after his lordship"—meaning Harry—"arrived. On that day she was heard to greet the Nervina with a single word as of welcome." *

Harry returned to the others. Nothing was said of what he had done. At once the Geos led the group through a small, half-hidden door, beyond which was a narrow, winding stairway of chocolate-colored stone. The Geos halted.

"Dost wish the building emptied, O Jarados?"

"I do. When we come back from under the Spot of Life, we should have the place to ourselves."

Accompanied by the two queens the Rhamda returned to the main body of the temple. Dr. Holcomb, Harry, and Chick were left to themselves.

The professor took out a note-book. In it were traced a map, or chart, together with several notations.

"The three of us," said he, "are going to take a look at the under side of the Blind Spot. This stairway leads up into a secret chamber inside the foundations of the great stair; and according to this data I found in the palace, together with some calculations of my own, we ought to find some of the secrets of the Spot."

He led the way up the steps. At the top of the flight they came to a blank, blue wall. There was no sign of a door, but in the front of the wall stood a low platform, in the center of which was set a strange, red stone. The professor consulted his chart, then opened his black case. From it he took another stone, red like the other, but not so intense. This he touched to the first, and waited.

Inside a minute a light sprang up from the contact. Immediately Harry and Chick beheld something they had not seen on the wall—a knob, or button. The doctor pulled sharply on it. Instantly a door opened in the wall.

They passed into another room. It was not a large place—about thirty feet across, perhaps, stone-walled and with a

---

*NOTE—This apparently refers to the mysterious bark which Hobart Fenton and his sister, Charlotte, heard on the day after Wendel's disappearance as they sat on the front porch of the house at 288 Chatterton.—Editors.

low ceiling. From all sides a soft, intrinsic glow was given off. There were no furnishings.

But from the center of the ceiling, occupying almost all the space overhead, a snow-white substance hung as if suspended. Were it not for its color and its size, it might have been likened to an immense, horizontal grindstone, hung in mid air, with apparently nothing to hold it there. Around its side they could make out a narrow gap between it and the ceiling. And directly along its lower edge, running all the way around the circle, was a series of small, fiery jewels, inset, and of the order and color of the sign of the Jarados—red, blue, and green, alternating.

The professor produced an electric torch, and held it up to show that the gap between the stone and the ceiling was unbroken at any point. Then he counted the jewels on the lower edge. Chick made out twenty-four. Three were missing from their sockets—all told, then, there should have been twenty-seven.

THE doctor noted the positions of the three empty sockets and, drawing a tapeline from his pocket, proceeded to measure the distances from each of the three—they were widely separated around the circle—from each other. Then he turned to Chick and Harry.

"Do you know where we are?"

"Under the Spot of Life," it was easy to answer.

"You are in San Francisco!"

"Not in—in—" Chick hesitated.

"Yes. Exactly. This is 288 Chatterton—the house of the Blind Spot." He paused for them to digest this. Then, "Harry—did you not say that Hobart Fenton was with you on that last night?"

"Hobart and his sister, Charlotte. I remember their coming at the last minute. They were too late, sir."

The professor nodded.

"Well, Harry, the chances are that Hobart is not more than twenty feet away at the present moment. Charlotte may be sitting right there"—pointing to a spot at Harry's side—"this very instant. And there may be many others.

"No doubt they are working hard to solve the mystery. Unfortunately the best they can do is to guess. We hold the key. That is—I should correct that statement —we hold the knowledge, and they hold the keys."

"The keys?" Harry wanted to know more.

The professor pointed to the three empty sockets in the great white stone above their heads. "These three missing stones are the keys. Until they are reset, we cannot control the Spot. I had found two of them before I came through. I take it that both of you remember the blue one?"

"I think," agreed Harry, "that neither of us is ever likely to forget it! Eh, Chick?"

The professor smiled.

"However, Harry, it was very fortunate. Or perhaps I should say it *had to be*. In the nature of the case, your experience may be of immense benefit, indirectly, to our own world. You simply did not realize the potency of the gem. Had you been of the other sex, it would have added to your vitality instead of sapping it."

"Say—I had some such notion at the last minute!" said Harry. "That's why I gave it to Charlotte instead of to Hobart, to wear. But you say there are three. I never knew of but one."

The professor did not answer. He was holding the light up to the snow-stone, at a spot that would have been the point of intersection had lines been drawn from the three missing gems, and the resulting triangle centered. He held his hand up to the substance. It was slightly rough at that point, as though it had been frozen.

Then he ran his fingers across the surrounding surface. It was smooth.

"Ah!" he exclaimed. "I thought so! That helps considerably. Chick—put your hand up here. What do you feel?"

"Rough," said Chick, feeling of the intersection point. "Slightly so, but cold and—and magnetic."

"Now feel here."

"Cool and magnetic, doctor; but smooth. What does it prove?"

"Let's see; do you understand the term 'electrolysis'? Good. Well, there should be another clue—not similar, but supplementary, or rather, complimentary—on the earth side. Perhaps one of you found it while you lived in that house." The professor eyed both men anxiously. "Did either of you find a stain, or anything of that sort, on the walls, ceiling, or floor of any room there?"

Both shook their heads.

"Well, there ought to be," frowned the doctor. "I am positive that, should we return now, we could locate some such phenomenon. From this side it is very easy to account for; it's simply the disintegrating effect of the current, constantly impinging at the point of contact, or the intersection. Having acted on this side, it must have left some mark on the other."

WATSON was still running his hand over the snow-stone. Once before, when he had stood bare-footed in the contest with the Senestro, he had noted its cold magnetism.

"What is this substance, professor?"

"That, I have not been able to discover. I would call it a neutral element, for want of a more exact term; something that touches both aspects of the spectrum."

"Both aspects of the spectrum?"

"Yes; as nearly as the limitations of my vocabulary will permit. If you recall, I showed you a simple experiment the other day in the palace. By means of an inductor I drew out the iron principle from the ether, and built up the metal. Only it was not precisely iron, but its Thomahlian equivalent. Had you been on the earth side, you would have seen nothing at all, not even myself. I was on the wrong aspect of the spectrum.

"Also, you see here the Jaradic colors —the crimson, green and navy—the shades between, the iridescence and the shadows. Had you been on the other side you wouldn't have seen one of them; they are not precisely our own colors, but their equivalents on this side of the Spot.

"In the final analysis, as I said before, it gets down to ether, to speed and vibration—and still at last to the perceptive limitations of our own earthly five senses. Just stop and consider how limited we are! Only five senses—why, even insects have six. Then consider that all matter, when we get to the bottom of it, is differentiated and condensed ether, focused into various mathematical arrangements, as numberless as the particles of the universe. Out of all these our five senses pick out only a very small proportion, indeed.

"This is one way to account for the Blind Spot. It may be merely another phase of the spectrum—not simply the unexplored regions of the infra-red or the ultra-violet, but a region co-existent with what we normally apprehend, and making itself manifest through apertures in what we, with our extremely limited sense-grasp, think to be a continuous spectrum. I throw out the idea mainly as a suggestion. It is not necessarily the true explanation.

"Let us go a bit farther. Remember, we are still upon the earth. And that we are still in San Francisco, although all the while we are also in the Mahovisal. This is 288 Chatterton Place, and at the same time it is the Temple of the Bell. It might be a hundred or a thousand other places just as well, too, if my

134

hypothesis is correct; which we shall see.

"Now, what does this mean? Simply this, gentlemen, that we five-sensed people have failed to grasp the true meaning of the word 'Infinity.' We look out toward the stars, fancying that only in unlimited space can we find the infinite. We little suspect that we ourselves are infinity! It is only our five senses that make us finite.

"As soon as we grasp this the so-called spiritual realm becomes a very substantial fact. We begin to apprehend the occult. Our five-sensed world is merely a highly specialized phase of infinity. Material or spiritual—it is all the same. That is why we look upon the Thomahlians as occult, and that is why they consider us in the same light.

"It is strictly a question of sense perception and limitations, which can be covered by the one word, 'viewpoint.' Viewpoint—that is all it amounts to.

"There is no such thing as unreality; but there is most certainly such a thing as relativity, and all life is real.

"Of course I knew nothing of this until the discovery of the Blind Spot. It will, I think, prove to be one of the greatest events in history. It will silence the skeptics, and form a bulwark for all religion. And it will make us all appreciate our Creator the more."

The professor stopped. For some moments there was silence. Then Watson came out with a question:

"But this snow-stone, or Blind Spot stone—how did it get here? Does the Jarados say? But they say you are the Jarados; you say so yourself!"

The professor looked very thoughtful.

"That's a tremendous question, gentlemen. Apparently I am the Jarados himself. At least, I have fulfilled the Prophecy as only he himself could have done it—in the light of his own writings. It is all coming out according to the way he predicted.

"To understand it perhaps we should investigate the theory of reincarnation. It brings us back to the planes of what men call the spirit world. Perhaps I was the Jarados; perhaps I *did* put this stone in its place. But I don't remember it.

"Just now I have only one desire—to bring the Prophecy to pass, and to save ourselves by going out through the Spot of Life. It can be done by our efforts on the last day. Meanwhile we must work hard to get in touch with the three keys on the outside."

"What are we to do?" offered Harry.

But the professor chose not to answer. With his tape he began taking a fresh series of measurements, with reference to the empty sockets and one particularly brilliant red gem, which seemed to be "number one" in the circle. From time to time the doctor jotted down the results, and made short calculations. Presently he said:

"That ought to be enough. Now, suppose we—"

At that instant something happened. Harry Wendel caught him by the shoulder. He pointed to the suspended stone.

It was moving!

It was revolving, almost imperceptibly, like some vast wheel turning on its axis. So slowly did it rotate, the motion would have escaped attention were it not for the gems and their brilliance.

Suddenly it came to a stop, short and quick, as though it had dropped into a notch. And from above they heard the deep, solemn clang of the temple bell.

"What is that?" asked Harry, startled. "Who moved the stone?"

"Can it be," flashed Chick, "that Hobart Fenton has found the keys?"

"That remains to be seen!" from the doctor. "Come—we must find out what has happened!"

Within a minute they knew. As they came out of the private door on to the now emptied floor of the great temple, they saw the senior queen, the Nervina, coming down the great stairway from the Spot of Life.

"What is it?" called Harry, apprehensively.

"The Aradna!" she replied. Her voice was curiously strained. "Something happened, and—she has fallen through the Spot!"

CHAPTER XLVI

OUT OF THE OCCULT

"HOW did it happen?"

"I scarcely know. We went up to play with Queen. The dog was unwilling to leave the place, and Aradna teasingly tried to crowd her off on to the steps. She succeeded, but—well, it was all over that quick. The Aradna was gone!"

But the Spot had by this time lost a good deal of its terror. Knowing what was on the other side, and who, made a great difference. As the doctor said later in a private consultation with Chick and Harry:

"It's not so bad. That is, if Hobart Fenton is at work there. I think he is. Really, I only regret that we didn't know of this beforehand; we could have sent a message through to him."

And the professor went on to explain what he meant. At the time he spoke, it was twenty-four hours after the Aradna's going; another twenty-four hours would see the evening of the Last Day—the sixteenth of the sacred Days of Life—what the Rhamdas alluded to as "the Day of Judgment." And the Mahovisal was a seething mass of humanity, all bent upon seeing the fulfilment of their highest hopes.

"Bear in mind, young gentlemen, that if the Spot should not open at the last moment, you and I are done for. We will be self-condemned 'False Ones'; our lives will not last one minute after midnight to-morrow night if we fail to get through!

"That Prophecy means *everything* to the Thomahlians. There was a time when they accepted it on faith; now it is an intellectual conviction with every last one of them. And one and all look forward to a new and glorious life beyond the Spot—in the occult world—our world!

"Now, the ticklish part of the job will be to open the Spot just long enough to permit us to get through, yet prevent the whole Prophecy from coming to pass. We've got to get through, together with that black case of mine, and then shut the door in the face of all Thomahlia!"

Nothing more was said on the subject until late the following afternoon, as the doctor, Harry, and Chick sat down to a light meal. They ate much as if nothing whatever was in the wind. From where they sat, in one part of a wing of the temple, they could look out into the crowded streets, in which were packed untold numbers of pilgrims, all pressing toward the great square plaza in front of the temple. No guards were to be seen; the solemnity of the occasion was sufficient to keep order. But the terrific potentiality of that semi-fanatical host did not cause the doctor's voice to change one iota.

"There is no telling what may happen," he said. "For my own part I shall not venture near the Spot of Life until just at the end. I shall remain in the chamber underneath.

"But you two ought to show yourselves immediately after sun-down. Certain ancient writings indicate it. You, and the Nervina, will have to mount the stair to the Spot, and remain in sight until midnight—until the end.

"So we must be prepared for accidents." He took some papers from his pocket, and selected two, and gave one to each of his pupils. "Here are the details of what must be done. In case only one of us gets through, it will be enough."

"But—how can these be of any use, on such short notice?" Harry asked.

"Cudgel your brains a bit, gentlemen," good-humoredly. "You will soon see my drift." Later, Chick understood this clearly enough. "This is one of those occasions when the psychic elements involved are such that, without doubt, it were best if you reacted naturally to whatever may happen.

"Now, you will note that I have made a drawing of the Blind Spot region; also certain calculations which will explain themselves.

"Moreover, I have written out the combination to my laboratory safe in my house in Berkeley. The green stone is there. Bertha will help, as soon as she understands that it is my wish; no explanation will be needed.

"You may leave the rest to me, young gentlemen. Act as though you had no notion that I were down below the Spot. I shall be merely experimenting a bit with that circle of jewels, to see if the phenomena which affected the Aradna can't be repeated. I fancy it was not mere accident, but rather the working of a 'period.'"

He said no more about this, except to comment that he hoped to get into direct communication with Hobart Fenton before midnight should arrive. However, he did say, in an irrelevant sort of a manner:

"Oh, by the way—do either of you happen to recall which direction the house at 288 Chatterton faces?"

"North," replied Harry and Chick, almost in the same breath.

"Ah, yes. Well, the temple faces south. Can you remember that?"

They thought they could. The rest of the meal was eaten without any discussion. Just as they arose, however, the doctor observed:

"It may be that Hobart Fenton has got to come through. I wish I knew more about his mentality; it's largely a question of psychic influence—the combined, resultant force of the three material gems, and the three degrees of psychic vibration as put forth by him and you two. We shall see.

"SOMETHING happened to-day — the Geos told me about it, which may link up Hobart very definitely. It was about one o'clock when one of the temple pheasants began to behave very queerly up on the great stair. It had been walking around on the snow-stone, and flying a bit; then it started to hop down the steps.

"About sixteen steps down, Geos says, the pheasant stopped and began to flutter frantically, as though some unseen person were holding it. Suddenly it vanished, and as suddenly reappeared again. It flew off, unharmed. I can't quite account for it, but—well, we'll see!"

He spoke no more, but led the way out into the entrance to the wing. There they waited only a moment or two, before the Nervina and her retinue arrived. Without delay a start was made for the great black stairway.

The doctor alone remained behind.

There was a guard-lined lane through the crowd, allowing the Nervina and the rest easy access to the foot of the steps. Reaching that point she paused for a look around, and Chick and Harry made good use of their eyes.

The sun had just gone down; the artificial lights of the temple had not yet been turned on. Overhead, the great storm-cloud hung portentously, even more ominous than in the brighter light. The huge waterspout columns, the terrific size of the auditorium, were none the less impressive for the incalculable horde that filled every bit of floor space. At the front of the building the archway gave a glimpse of the vastly greater throng waiting outside.

But all was quiet, with the silence of reverence and supreme expectation. Chick turned his gaze back upon his more immediate surroundings.

The long flight of stairs was lined on either side, from bottom to top, with the Rhamdas. On the landing there stood only two of the three chairs that Chick had seen on the previous occasion. The green one had been brought down and placed in the center of an open spot just at the foot of the stairs.

In this chair sat the Bar Senestro. Deployed about him, at a respectful distance, was a semicircle of the Bars, many hundred in number. Behind the Bars, separating them from the crowds at their backs, were grouped the crimson and blue guardsmen. Among them, no doubt, were the Jan Lucar and the MacPherson, but Chick could locate neither.

The Nervina, taking Harry's arm, ascended the steps. Chick followed, with the Rhamda Geos at his side. At the top of the flight the Nervina was escorted to one of the chairs, while Chick placed the Geos in the other.

It left the two Californians on their feet, to move around to whatever extent seemed commensurate with dignity. Chick noted that Harry, with less than six hours of Thomahlian life remaining to him, was making good use of every moment. Half his time was spent in trying to catch the Nervina's eye; a process apparently much to her liking. Her cheeks were slightly suffused during the whole of the evening. Chick judged that a man in Harry's position needed the firm hand of a friend. He drew him aside.

"What do you suppose"—indicating the handsome, confident figure in the chair at the base of the stairs—"what do you suppose friend Senestro is thinking about, old man?"

Harry frowned. "You know him better than I do. You don't think he has reformed?"

"Not on your life; not the Bar. He's merely adjusted his plans to the new situation. He sees that the Prophecy is likely to be fulfilled; so, he counts on being the first to get through, after the Nervina. Then, whether the rest of the Thomahlia follows or not—he calls himself their divinely appointed leader now, I understand—he will get through, and marry the two queens anyhow!"

"You really think that's his code?"

"Such a man couldn't have any other."

PERHAPS it was because the crowd was so terrifically large. Or, there may have been something in the destiny of things, that would not permit the chief actors to feel nervous. Certain it is that neither of the two men experienced the least stage fright. Had they been on display before a crowd one-tenth the size, anywhere else, both would have been ill at ease. This was different—enormously so.

No longer was there any circulation in the crowd. People remained in their places now, just as they expected the end to find them. Chick and Harry marveled at their composure, strangely in contrast with the ceaseless activities of the temple pheasants, darting everywhere overhead.

Suddenly Harry remarked:

"I've got an idea, Chick! It's this: How does the professor expect to send a message to Hobart?" Chick could not guess. Harry pointed to Queen, crouching, as always, just on the edge of the stone. "By means of the dog!"

"By George!" ejaculated Chick. "Why not?"

But already Harry had taken his sheet of instructions from his pocket, and was rolling it into a compact pellet. Then he went to Queen, and with a ribbon borrowed from the Nervina, tied the message tightly to the dog's collar.

"Hobart will be certain to see it," said he. "I wonder if the doctor's figured it out yet?"

"He's playing with a tremendous force," observed Chick, thoughtfully. He reached out and touched the snow-stone with his foot, just as he had done before, and fancied that he could feel that queer electric thrill even through the leather of his shoes. "Still, it's worth any risk he may be taking down in that chamber. If only he could send Queen through! Hobart—"

He never finished the sentence. He staggered, thrown off his balance by reason of the fact that he had been resting the weight of one foot on the stone and—it moved!

Moved—shifted about its axis, just as it had done forty-eight hours previously, when the Aradna had dropped through.

And Chick had only a flash of a second for a glimpse of the startled faces of Harry, the Nervina and the Geos, the huge multitude below the stair, Queen on the other side, and the fateful Prophecy on the walls above him, before—

A figure came into existence at his side. It was that of a powerfully built man, on whose wrists were curious red circles. And Chick shouted in a great voice:

"Hobart!"

And then came blackness.

CHAPTER XLVII

THE LAST LEAF

WATSON'S story was now completed. During the entire recital his auditors had spoken scarcely a word. It had been marvelous—almost a revelation. With the possible exception of Sir Henry Hodges, not one had expected that it would measure up to this. For the whole thing backed up Holcomb's original proposition:

"The Occult is concrete."

Certainly, if what Watson had told them was true, then Infinity had been squared by itself. Not only was there an infinity that we might look up to through the stars, but there was another just as great, co-existent, here upon the earth. The occult became not only possible, but unlimited.

The next few minutes would prove whether or not he had told the truth.

It was now close to midnight.

Jerome and General Hume had returned from Berkeley. Their quest had been successful; Watson now had the missing green stone. A number of soldiers were stationed about the house. Watson noted these men when he had finished his account, and said:

"Good. We may need them, although I hope not. Fortunately the Spot is small, and a few of us can hold it against a good many. What we must do is to extricate our friends and close it. Afterward we may have time for more leisurely investigation. But we must remember, above all things, that black case of Professor Holcomb's! It holds the secrets.

"Now I must ask you all to step out of this room. This library, you know, is the Blind Spot."

He directed them to take positions along the balustrade of the stairway, out in the hall—through the wide archway, where they could have a clear view, yet be safe.

It was a curious test. With nothing but his mathematics and his drawing to go by, Watson was about to set the three stones in their invisible sockets. He spread the map out carefully, likewise his calculations; they gave him, on this floor, the precise positions that he had charted on the earth of the cellar. A glance toward the front of the house—north—then a little measuring, three chalk-marks on the carpet, and he was ready for the final move.

He took the fateful ring, and with a pen-knife pried up the prongs that held the stone. As it popped out he caught it with one hand. Then he looked at the row of wondering faces along the stair.

"I think it will work," he said. "But, remember—don't come near! I shall get out as best I can myself; don't try to save me."

With that he held the jewel on the first of the three chalk-marks on the circumference of the great circle. He held it tight against the carpet and then let go. Up it flashed about one foot—and disappeared.

There was no sound. Next Watson took the red stone. With it, the process was inverted. Instead of holding it to the floor he raised it as high as he could reach, directly above the second mark. Then he let it drop.

It did not reach the floor. It fell a little more than half-way, and vanished.

The third stone, the green one, was still remaining. Watson took it to the third and final mark on the circle, taking care to keep outside the circumference that marked the Spot. This mark was directly in front of the archway. He turned to them.

"Watch carefully," he spoke. "I do not know what has transpired in the temple during the past few hours. Be ready for *anything*. All of you!"

He dropped the stone.

With the same motion he dodged out into the hall.

Though there was no sound there was something that every one felt—a sibilant undertone and cold vibration—a tense flash of magnetism. Then the dot of blue—a string of incandescence; just as had been spoken.

The Blind Spot was opening.

Watson silently warned the others to remain where they were, and himself crowded back against the stair. As he did so, some one came noiselessly down the steps from the floor above, passed unnoticed behind the watchers, and thence across the hall.

It was a slender, frail figure in white—the Aradna, walking like one in a slumber—to be more exact, like one in the grip of a higher will. Before they could make a move she had stepped into the Blind Spot, under the dot of blue, and into the string of light. And then—she was gone.

It was as swift as a guess. It was inexorable and unseen; and being unseen, close akin to terror. The group watched and waited, scarcely breathing. What would happen next?

There came a sudden, jarring click—like the tapping of iron. And next instant—

The Spot opened to human sight.

THE library at 288 Chatterton Place was gone. Instead, the people on the steps were gazing down from back of the Spot of Life, straight into the tempest-born Temple of the Jarados.

It was as Chick had described it—immense, colossal — beyond conception. Thronged literally with millions, as far as the eye could see—through the great doors and out into the plaza beyond, and the converging streets back of that—was gathered all Thomahlia, reverent, like those waiting for the crack of doom.

Above the horde, high on the opposite wall, stood out the monster Clover Leaf of the Jarados; three-colored—blazing like liquid-fire; it was ominous with real life.

Running down from the dais were the black steps that looked, just as Watson had said, not so much a stairway as a cataract. Over all, the ceiling of storm, and on the sides the prodigious waterspouts; it was staggering.

At that moment the whole concourse rippled with commotion. Arms were uplifted; one and all pointed toward the dais. They, too, were looking through the Spot. Then the multitude began to move.

It heaved, and surged, and rolled toward the center. The guards were pressed in upon the Bars, the Bars upon the Rhamda-lined stair. There was no resisting that flood of humanity. On, and up it came, sweeping everything before it.

Directly in the foreground lay the snow-stone. On its center stood the dog Queen, crouching, waiting, bristling. By her side Harry Wendel crouched on one knee, as if awaiting the signal. Behind him, the Nervina, supporting the awakening Aradna. And in front of all, the powerful bulk of Hobart Fenton, standing squarely at the head of the stair, ready to grapple the first to reach the landing.

But most important of all, there stood the doctor himself. He was at the Nervina's side; in his hand, the case of priceless data. He was gazing through the Spot, and making a signal of some kind to Watson, whereupon the latter leaped to the edge of the unseen circle.

Something had gone wrong. The Spot was not fully open. Nothing but sight could get through.

Yet there was no time for anything. Up the stairs came the Bars, leading and being pressed forward by the horde. At their head dashed the Bar Senestro, handsome as Alexander. Hobart stepped forward to meet him, but the doctor stopped him with a word.

Only a few seconds elapsed between death and salvation. Again Dr. Holcomb signed to Watson; not a sound came through. Watson hesitated.

The dog Queen shot to her feet. The Senestro, outdistancing all the rest and dodging Hobart, had leaped upon the dais.

Upon the wall across the temple the great Leaf of the Jarados stood out like sinister fire. It pulsed and vibrated—alive. The top petal—the blue one—suddenly broke into a waving seethe of flame.

Still Watson held back. He could not understand what Holcomb meant.

Queen waited only until the Senestro set foot on the dais. She crouched, then leaped.

It was done.

With a lightning shift of his nimble feet, the high-tempered Bar kicked the shepherd in the side. Caught at full leap, she was knocked completely over, and fell upon the snow-stone.

It was the Sacrilege!

Even the Bars beyond the Senestro stopped in horror. The Four-Footed One—sacred to the Jarados—it was she who had been touched! Had the Senestro undone all on the Spot of Judgment? What would be the end?

Fenton acted. He caught the Senestro before he could get his balance, and with a mighty heave he hurled him over the side of the stair. A second, and it was over.

Another second was the last. For the

139

great Leaf of the Jarados had opened.

The green and red stood still; but out of the blue came a dazzling light, a powerful beam; so brilliant, it seemed solid. It shot across the whole sweep of the temple and touched the Prophecy. Over the golden scrolls it traced its marvelous color, until it came to the lines:

Beware ye of sacrilege! Lest I take from ye all that I have given ye, and the day be postponed—beware ye of sacrilege!

For a moment the strange light stood still, so that the checked millions might read. Then it turned upon the dais.

There it spread, and hovered over the group, until it seemed to work them together—the Nervina to Harry, the Aradna to Hobart. Not one of them knew what it was; they obeyed by impulse—it was their destiny; the Chosen, and the queens.

The light stopped at the foot of Dr. Holcomb. Then the strangest thing happened.

Out of the light—or rather, from where it bathed the snow-stone—came a man; a man much like Holcomb, bearded and short and kindly.

He was the real Jarados!

Unhesitatingly the professor stepped up beside him. Then followed Hobart and the Aradna, Harry and the Nervina, and lastly, from the crowd of Bars, MacPherson. The whole concourse in the temple stopped in awe and terror.

Only for a second. Then the Jarados and all at his side—were gone.

And upon the snow-stone there stood a sword of living flame.

It stood there for just a breath, exactly where the group had been.

And it was gone.

That was all.

No; not quite all. For when the Blind Spot closed that night at 288 Chatterton Place, there came once more the deep, solemn peal of the Bell of the Jarados.

CHAPTER XLVIII

THE UNACCOUNTABLE

WERE this account merely a work of fiction, it would be a simple matter to harmonize things so as to have no unaccountables in it. As it is, the present writers will have to make this quite clear:

It is not known why the Rhamda Avec failed to show himself at the crucial moment. Perhaps he could have changed everything. We can only surmise; he has not been seen or heard from since.

Which also is true of Mr. Chick Watson. He disappeared immediately after the closing of the Spot, saying that he was going to Bertha Holcomb's home. No trace has been found of either to date. Doubtless the reader has noted advertisements in the papers, appealing to the authorities to report any one of Watson's description applying for a marriage license.

As for his two friends, Wendel and Fenton, together with the Aradna and the Nervina, they and MacPherson and the doctor absolutely vanished from all knowledge, either of the Thomahlia or the earth. The Jarados alone can tell of them.

Mme. Le Fabre, however, feels that she can explain the matter satisfactorily. Abridged, her theory runs:

"There is but one way to explore the Occult. That way is to die.

"For all that we were so strongly impressed with the reality of Mr. Watson, I am firmly convinced that he was simply a spirit; that everything we saw was spirit manifestation.

"Dr. Holcomb and all the rest have simply gone on to another plane. We shall never see them again. They are dead; no other explanation will hold. I repeat, it is useless to look any further for Chick Watson, or to expect any further demonstration on the part of any other concerned. They are spirits."

Giving this version to the public strictly for what it is worth, the present writers feel it only right to submit the conclusions reached by Dr. Malloy and concurred in by Drs. Higgins and Hansen, also, with reservations, by Professor Herold and by Miss Clarke.

"To a certain extent, and up to a certain point, it is possible to account for the astonishing case of the Blind Spot by means of well-known psychological principles. Hallucinations will cover a great deal of ground.

"But we feel that our personal experiences, in witnessing the interior of the Thomahlia, cannot be thus explained away. Our accounts tally too exactly; and we are not subject to group hypnosis.

"To explain this we believe a new hypothesis is called for. We submit that what we saw was not unreal. Assuming that a thing is real or unreal, and can never be in a third state which is neither one nor the other, then we should have to insist that what we saw was *real*.

"We stand ready and prepared to accept any theory which will fit the facts—all the facts, not merely a portion."

Again refraining from any comment we pass on to the more exhaustive opinion of Sir Henry Hodges. Inasmuch as this seems to coincide very closely with the hypothesis of Professor Holcomb, and as the reputation of Sir Henry is a thing of weight, we are quoting him almost verbatim:

"There is a well-known experiment in chemistry, wherein equal quantities of water and alcohol are mixed. Let us say, a pint of each. Now, the resulting mixture ought to be a quart; but it is not. It is somewhat less than a quart.

"Strange, indeed, to the novice, but a commonplace to every student of the subject. It is strange only that, except for Dr. Holcomb and this man Avec, science has overlooked the stupendous significance and suggestion of this particular fact.

"Now, consider another well-known fact: No matter how you try you cannot prevent gravity from acting. It will pull every object down, regardless of how you try to screen it from the earth.

"Why? Because gravity penetrates all things. Again, why? Why should gravity penetrate all things?

"The answer is, because gravity is a function of the ether. And the ether is an imponderable substance, so impalpable that it passes right through all solids as though they were not there.

"These are two highly suggestive points. They show us, first, that two substances can exist within the space formerly thought to be completely filled by one. Second, they show that *all* substances are porous to the ether.

"Very well. Bear in mind that we know nothing whatever directly about the ether; our knowledge is all indirect. Therefore—

"It may be that there is more than one ether!

"Conceive what this means. If there were another ether, how could we become aware of it? Only through the medium of some such phenomenon as the Blind Spot; not through ordinary channels. For the ordinary channels are microscopes and test-tubes, every one of which, when traced to the ultimate, is simply a concrete expression of *the one ether we know!*

"In the nature of the case our five senses could never apprehend a second ether.

"Yet, knowing what we do about the structure of the atom, of electronic activity, of quantels, we must admit that there is a huge, unoccupied space—that is, we can't see that it is occupied—in and between the interstices of the atom.

"It is in the region, mingled and intertwined with the electrons which make up the world we know so well, that—in my opinion—the Thomahlian world exists. It is actually coexistent with our own. It is here, and so are we. At this very instant, at any given spot, there can be, and almost certainly is, more than one solid object—two systems of materiality, two systems of life, two systems of death. And if two, why, then, perhaps there are even more!

"Holcomb is right. We are Infinity. Only our five senses make us finite."

CHARLOTTE FENTON does not indulge in speculation. She seems to bear up wonderfully well in the face of Harry Wendel's affinity for the Nervina, and also in the face of her brother's disappearance. And she philosophically states:

"When Columbus returned from his search for the East Indies, he triumphantly announced that he had found what he sought.

"He was mistaken. He had found something else—America.

"It may be that we are all mistaken. It may be that something entirely different from what any one has suspected has been found. Time will tell. I am willing to wait."

To make it complete, it is felt that the following statement of General Hume is not only essential, but convincing to the last degree.

"My view regarding this mystery is simply this: I have eyes, and I have seen. I don't know whether the actors were living or dead. I am no scientist; I have no theory. I only know. And I will swear to what I saw.

"I am a soldier. The two men who are bringing this to press have shown me their copy.

"It is correct."

THE END

The sequel to this story, "The Spot of Life," written by Austin Hall after the death of Homer Eon Flint, will be printed in a future issue of this magazine.

Monsieur De Guise

By PERLEY POORE SHEEHAN

THAT any one should live in the center of Cedar Swamp was in itself so singular as to set all sorts of queer ideas to running through my head. A more sinister morass I had never seen. It was as beautiful and deadly as one of its own red moccasins, as treacherous and fascinating.

It was a tangle of cypress and cedar almost thirty miles square, most of it under water—a maze of jungle-covered islands and black bayous. There were alligators and panthers, bear and wild pig. There were groans and grunts and queer cries at night, and silence, dead silence by day.

That was Cedar Swamp as I knew it after a week of solitary hunting there. I no longer missed the sun. My eyes had become used to the perpetual twilight. My nerves no longer bothered me when I stepped into opaque water, or watched a section of gliding snake. But the silence was getting to be more than I could bear. It was too uncanny.

And now, just after I had noticed it, and wondered at it for the hundredth time, I heard a voice. It was low and clear—that of a woman who sings alto. There were four or five notes like the fragment of a strange song. And then, before I had recovered from the shock of it, there was silence again.

I was up to my knees in water at the time, wading a narrow branch between two islands. I must have stood there for a full minute waiting for the voice to resume, but the silence closed in on me deeper than ever. With a little shiver creeping over one part of my body after another, I stole ashore.

The island was one of the highest I had yet encountered. I had not taken a dozen steps up through the dank growth of its shelving shore before I found a deeply worn path. This, I could see, ran down to the water-front in one direction, where I caught a glimpse of a boat-house masked by trees. I turned and followed the path in the other direction up a gentle slope.

As I advanced, the jungle around me thinned out and became almost park-like. There were open stretches of meadow and clumps of trees, suggesting the landscape garden. But I was so intent on discovering the owner of the voice that the wonder of this did not at first impress me. I had, moreover, an eerie, uneasy sensation of being watched.

I walked slowly. I carried my gun with affected carelessness. I looked around me as though I were a mere tourist dropped in to see the sights.

I HAD thus covered, perhaps, a quarter of a mile, when the path turned into an avenue of cabbage-palmetto, at the further end of which I saw a house. It was large and white, with a pillared porch, such as they used to build before the war. It was shaded by a magnificent grove of live-oak trees. There were beds of geranium and roses in front, and clusters of crêpe-myrtle and flowering oleander on a well-clipped lawn.

It all gave an impression of infinite care, of painstaking upkeep, of neatness and wealth, yet, there was not a soul in sight. Not a servant was there. No dog barked. I saw no horses, no chickens, no pigeons, nor sheep; nor familiar animate emblem whatever of the prosperous farm.

I stood in the presence of this silent and lonely magnificence with a feeling that was not exactly fear, but rather stupefaction. For a moment I was persuaded that I had emerged from the great swamp into some unknown plantation of its littoral. But a moment was enough to convince me that this could not be. I was, without the slightest doubt, almost at the exact center of the morass. I was too familiar with its circumference and general contour to be wrong as to that. For a dozen miles at least, in every direction, Cedar Swamp surrounded this island of mystery with its own mysterious forests and bayous.

Once again I was acutely aware of being stared at. Almost at the same instant a man's voice addressed me from behind my back. "Monsieur," it asked, "why do you hesitate?"

I might as well confess it right away—I believe in ghosts. I have seen too many things in my life that were not to be explained by the commonly accepted laws of nature. I have lived too much among the half-civilized and learned too much of their odd wisdom to recognize any hard and fast definition of what is real and what is not.

From the moment I heard that bit of song in the swamp, I felt that I was passing from the commonplace into the weird. My succeeding impressions had confirmed this feeling. And now, when I heard the voice behind me: "Monsieur, why do you hesitate?"—I was not sure that it was the voice of a human being at all.

I turned slowly, my mind telling me that I should see no one.

It was with a distinct feeling of relief, therefore, that I saw a small, pale, well-dressed old man smiling at me as though he had read my secret thoughts. His face was cleanly shaven and bloodless. His head, partly covered by a black velvet skull-cap, was extremely large. His snow-white hair was silky and long. His eyes, which were deeply sunken, were large and dark. His appearance, as well as the question which he had just put to me, suggested the foreigner. He was not alone un-American; he appeared to be of another century, as well.

I said something about intruding. He made a brusk gesture, almost of impatience, and, telling me to follow him, started for the house.

It was as though I was an expected guest. Only the absence of servants maintained that feeling of the bizarre, which never left me. The interior of the house was in keeping with its outward appearance—sumptuous and immaculate. My host led me to the door of a vast chamber on the first floor, motioned me to enter, and, standing at the door, said:

"Monsieur, luncheon will be served when you reappear. Pray, make yourself at home."

Then he left me.

Two details of this room impressed me: the superlative richness of the toilet articles, all of which were engraved with a coat-of-arms, and the portrait of a woman, by Largillière. All women were beautiful to Largillière, but in the present instance he had surpassed himself. The gentle, aristocratic face, with its tender, lustrous eyes, was the most alluring thing I had ever seen. At the bottom of the massive frame was the inscription: *"Anne-Marie, Duchesse de Guise. Anno 1733."*

I was still marveling at the miracle

which had brought such an apparition to the heart of an American swamp when I heard a light step in the hallway, and I knew that my host was awaiting me.

The luncheon, which was served cold in a splendid dining-room, had been laid for two. I wondered at this, for still no servant appeared, and surely I could not have been expected. And my host added to my mystification rather than lessened it when he said: "Monsieur, I offer you the place which is usually reserved for my wife."

Apart from this simple statement, the meal was completed in silence. Now and then I thought I surprised him, nodding gravely, as though someone else were present. I suspected him several times of speaking in an undertone. But, my mind was so preoccupied with the inexplicable happenings of the preceding hour that I was not in a condition to attack fresh mysteries now.

He scarcely touched his food. Indeed, his presence there seemed to be more in the nature of an act of courtesy than for the purpose of taking nourishment. As soon as I had finished he at once arose and invited me to follow him.

ACROSS the hall was a music-room, with high French windows, opening on the porch. He paused at one of these windows now and plucked the flower from a potted heliotrope. The perfume of it seemed to stimulate him strangely. He at once became more animated. A slight trace of color mounted to his waxen cheeks. Turning to me, abruptly, he remarked:

"I mentioned just now my wife. Perhaps you noticed her portrait?"

As he spoke, a faint breath of the heliotrope came to me, and with it, by one of those odd associations of ideas, the portrait by Largillière. I saw again the gentle face and the lustrous eyes, but the date—1733. Surely, this was not the portrait he referred to.

But he had seen the perplexity in my face, and he broke out in French: *"Oui, oui; c'est moi, monsieur de Guise."* And then, in English. "It was the portrait of my wife you saw, *madame la duchesse par monsieur Largillière."*

"But then, *madame,* your wife," I stammered, "is dead."

He was still smelling the heliotrope. He looked up at me with his somber eyes for a moment as though he had failed to grasp my meaning. Then he said:

"No, no. There is no such thing as death—only life. For, what is life?—the smile, the perfume, the voice. Ah, the voice! Will you hear her sing?"

143

FOR a brief instant my head turned giddily. The world I had always known, the world of tragedies, of sorrows, of physical joys and pains, the world of life and death, in short, was whirling away from beneath my feet. And I began to recall certain old stories I had heard about the visible servants of the invisible, the earthly agents of the unearthly. Such things have been known to exist.

Monsieur de Guise was walking up and down the room murmuring to himself in French. I could catch an occasional word of endearment. Once I saw him distinctly press the heliotrope to his lips. He had forgotten my presence, apparently. He was in the company of some one whom he alone could see. And then he seated himself at the piano.

I had a presentiment of what was coming. I dropped into a chair and closed my eyes. Again the heliotrope perfumed the air around me. I saw the smooth brow, the sympathetic eyes, the magic smile of the Duchesse de Guise, and then a voice—that voice I had heard in the swamp—began to sing, so soft, so sweet, that a little spasm twitched at my throat and a chill crept down my back. It was a love-song, such as they sang centuries ago. I know little French, but it told of love in life and death—*"Moi, je t'ai, vive et morte, incessament aimée."*

And when I opened my eyes again, all that I saw was the shrivelled black figure of Monsieur de Guise, his silvered head thrown back with the air of one who has seen a vision.

Subconsciously I had heard something else while listening to the song. It was the swift, muffled throb of an approaching motorboat. Monsieur de Guise had heard it, too, for now he left the piano and approached the window. Presently I could see a dozen negroes approaching along the avenue of palms. They seemed strangely silent for their race.

"These are my people," said my host. "Once a week I send them to the village. They will carry you away."

The afternoon was far advanced when I bade Monsieur de Guise farewell. As I looked back for the last time the sunset was rapidly dissolving the great white house and its gardens in a golden haze. His figure on the porch was all that linked it to the world of man.

Late that night I was landed at a corner of Cedar Swamp, adjacent to my home. My black boatman, who had spoken never a word, immediately backed his barge away into the darkness, leaving me there alone. And, although I have since made several efforts to repeat my visit to Monsieur de Guise, I have never been successful. Once, indeed, I found again what I believed to be his island, but it was covered entirely with a dense, forbidding jungle. Which will doubtless discredit this story, as it has caused even me to reflect.

But grant that the story is true, and that Monsieur de Guise was merely mad. Why, then, in a certain event, which I need not mention, may God send me madness, too!